Jo:
Keep this one. He's
a nice guy.

signature
11-05-04

LOOKIN' IN THE MIRROR

by

A. M. HATTER

authorHOUSE

1663 LIBERTY DRIVE, SUITE 200
BLOOMINGTON, INDIANA 47403
(800) 839-8640
www.authorhouse.com

© 2004 by A. M. HATTER. All rights reserved.

No part of this book may be reproduced, stored in a retrieval system, or transmitted by any means, electronic, mechanical, photocopying, recording, or otherwise, without written permission from the author.

First published by AuthorHouse 04/02/04

ISBN: 1-4184-1174-4 (e)
ISBN: 1-4184-1175-2 (sc)

This book is printed on acid free paper.

A disclaimer wasn't the highest item on my list, as I assumed that people would have the good sense to know that this is a work of fiction. It is, after all, classified as fiction. However, due to comments that I've already received, I felt that I should be proactive and provide a disclaimer to any presumption that this may be real or based on reality. So here it is:

This entire work is fiction. Entities like the "NBA," "The Sonic Boom," or songs that have been quoted in the book have been used in fictional scenarios to lend credibility to my characters as real people that exist in our time. Neither I, nor my characters personally know the musical artists quoted in this book, or have any relation to the goings on of the NBA or any other "real life" people or organizations mentioned in this book, with exception to being fans. All people, names, places, events, and likenesses are purely born from my imagination or used in fictional situations.

So, if you ever find yourself thinking, "Wow, this seems real. I wonder if this is based on her life..." or, "That's not right. There's no building on that street," keep this in mind: I made it up.

ACKNOWLEDGEMENTS

Thank you:

To The Creator and The Inspiring Force that drove me to, and through, this project. Please stay with me; we have a lot more to accomplish.

To my parents for being real parents, and for still being married—happily.

To my little bro, the yin to my yang.

To Aunt B & Myrissa for helping me during my move.

To the rest of my fam for being fun people.

To all that helped me, including my co-workers and friends for not only tolerating my insanity and incessant fanaticism about this ridiculous book, but also for pretending to be interested: GC, Ronta, Chakela, Keith, Charles, Larry, Kay, Kem, A. Pittman, Lonzie, Tracy J, Diane, Noel, Reina Castillo, Lisa Ramos, Sharmine, Tina, Amos, Veronica, Q, Arthena, Eddie, Jermaine, Bishop, the security guards at work, Uncle James, Mr. Shelton, Torrance, C. Tucker, Kayla, Kysa, Taz, Worm, Wes in Cali, Jason, Aisha, Chop, Dawn, Denean, Devan, Drum Major Mike, Murph, and ScoobYE.

To my sorors of Sigma Gamma Rho Sorority, Inc., who supported during my absence from "the cause."

To Jackson State, my dear old college home.
LOVE THE BOOM!
To all others who I may have missed.
To all those who buy the book.
To those who love it.

DEDICATION

To my family.

To America.

To the one I shall love forever.

To Tasha, the deuce of our trio:

Holla atcha girls, man…where ya been?

PREFACE

When I first started writing this book, I had no intention of writing a preface. I've never seen the point. To me, the preface is just a section for the writer to ramble about some junk that never really mattered to me—the few times that I have read the preface. But I thought to myself, "Wouldn't it be a great way to answer the questions that folks I've met have been asking me?" So I changed my mind.

What is this book about? I'm not really sure. I could say that it's about a man that needs a change and a woman that refuses to settle down, but that would oversimplify their personalities. Perhaps it's a deeper look at how gender roles have changed; it's the lead female of the book that doesn't want to get married and the lead male who does. It's about living and being American. Maybe it's about bad choices, regret, and the internal struggles that we all face in love and life. I shrug. For me, the whole project (a sequel was planned almost from the beginning) was more about style and structure: using vernacular and writing styles to define my characters, using paragraph alignment and the mirrors as points of identification, and how many chapters it would take to sufficiently show what's going on or who someone truly is.

What made me want to write a book? Well, some would say it was inevitable. I actually started the two characters as two separate books when I was in college, but I was too involved in the college experience. So the stories ran cold not long after I molded my characters' personalities. Then, at the helm of 2002, I got to a point where I asked myself what I really want to achieve in life. So I took account of my natural talents and their possibilities, and decided to merge those two unfinished book ideas from college. I figured that I could write a book fast enough to have something to be proud of while I'm still twenty-something. And that sounds great, but really, I just don't wanna pander to anyone for a real job in writing. That would make it boring and I'm not staying in a nine-to-five for the rest of my life. I'm not that good with corporate boundaries.

So how is my book different from the jillions of others out on the market? Man, don't be silly. In the year two-thousand-anything, there is nothing new in writing. Just as there are eighty types of the same movie every year, there are eighty types of the same book. It's just a new writer and a new title. What a newsflash: you can write in active or passive voice, and first, second, or *third* person! Wow! Wanna get on plot points?

My focus wasn't to be different, per se. It was merely to write in a way that suited me. I didn't want to be excessively literary, devoting two pages to describing a wall or the way a dog lifted its leg to pee. But I wanted to make it kind of like a soap opera. I wanted to weave hints here and there, make every little nuance have a purpose. And just when you think you can skip over something because the character is rambling, you'll find later on that you missed a little detail and you have to go back. (But to where??)

So pay attention.

Well, I guess that's all I have to ramble about. I hope that you've gotten something out of all of this. If nothing else, I guess I've answered some of those stupid questions that they ask in lit classes, like why do you think the writer wrote this book?

(I had to pay my mortgage.)

2002

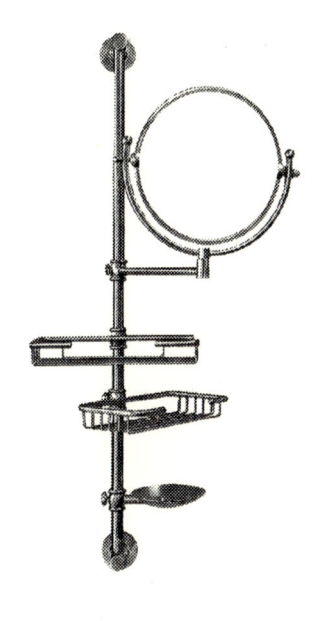

April 13

Saturday Morning

A. M. HATTER

Youuuu got me hum-pin' dayyy and niiiight, oh ba-by...

(((SMACK!!)))

I sat up and looked at the clock. It was seven a.m. The alarm went off thirty minutes ago.

Seven o'clock! Damn! I'm gonna be late for work!

I threw off the covers and jumped out the bed, then I paused for a moment of strategic planning:

Okay, I can jump in the shower for a five-minute wash down, then throw on my blue suit...

Shirt and tie...shirt and tie...

Oh yeah, that stuff I brought from the cleaners—downstairs hangin' in the laundry room.

What's next?

Socks?

Damn!

Where are my socks?

I lunged toward the dresser to see if I had any clean blue or black socks to wear with my suit. As I flew past the closet I happened to glance at the calendar.

It's Saturday. Whew...

I took a deep sigh of relief and laughed at myself for a moment. A dilemma arose: *do I go back to sleep or do I make use of the extra time I now have? If I stay up, what do I do?*

You need to mow the lawn, my conscience said. My body froze for a couple of seconds before it moved to achieve its true desire: go back to bed.

(((Ring, ring!)))

LOOKIN' IN THE MIRROR

Uuuuh. Meeting the lawn mower this morning must be fate.

"Hello?"

"Did I wake you up?"

"Naw. What's up?"

"Oh, I was just calling to talk. You haven't called. Anything new?"

"No. Just the same ol' stuff," I yawned and stretched. My breath was horrible. "...Hey mom, can I call you back?"

"*No*, you can't. You haven't called me in almost two week*s*. That's why I called to wake you up and bug you. If you can't call at a good time, then I'll call when I feel like it."

"Okay, mom," I sighed, "Alright. Sorry I haven't called. I've been workin' on this project at work. We're acquiring a lot of new companies so I've been traveling a lot...I'm thinkin' I *might* wanna transfer to the head position at one of them."

"Oh, that's good! Where is it? What will you be doing?"

"Well, the company does PR and marketing, but I'll be doin' the same stuff that I do now."

"Where is it?"

"D.C."

She paused. "Oh, I don't know about that, baby. That's far," she said.

"Mom, I can't dictate where my job'll take me. Besides, I'll be makin' more money."

"You make a lot of money now! Why do you need more? You don't have a fam-il-lee. You're just trying to run ayway bee-cawse of what happened with Denise. You can't do that, Gerald."

"No, that's not why. I *wanna* be in D.C. I think it's time to try somethin' new."

"But you'll be so far from us, Gerald."

"Terrence is far…hell, he's in the NBA!"

"*Watch* your mouth! …And I know he's in the NBA, that's why we want you and Tam-a-ra close."

"Mom, if I get this job, I'll have enough money and vacation time to make you *and* dad sick of seein' me."

"But why do you want to move so far from us? What about you and…what's her name? Kiana! I thought things were going well for you? Is *she* okay with you leaving her behind?"

"Mom, I haven't dated Kiana for almost two months."

"Really? What happened?"

"She was flaky."

"What do you mean?"

"Well…I mean, she *talked* all this game about how I'm great and junk, and I'm intelligent, and she never meets men like me…but she didn't know if she liked me."

"Huh? I think you're right about her."

"Yeah, so I'm not seein' her anymore."

She exhaled heavily. "Do you think she was see-*ING* someone else?" (Retired drama teacher…always tryin' to emphasize enunciation.)

"I don'know. It didn't really matter. We weren't serious, so that would've been cool. But to just *not know* if you even *like* somebody…"

LOOKIN' IN THE MIRROR

"That's trooo," she replied.

"Yeah, well, I guess that's what I get for datin' a twenty-two-year-old."

"Twenty-*two*?"

"Yeahhh. I don't know what it is…lately I've been attractin' all these young chicks…twenty-two, twenty-three—*NINETEEN!*"

"*NINE-TEEN*???" She laughed loudly. "You've been hanging out at the colleges haven't you? Go ahead, admit it. I won't tell your dad."

"Naw, man, I just meet these girls on the fly. It's funny. When I was their age, I couldn't pay 'em to give me the time of day. Now, that I'm almost ten years older than some of 'em, they're on me left and right."

"Well…girls are finicky like that."

"Hey, where's dad?" I asked.

"He's in the kitchen making a sandwich…oh, no, he's finished. Do you want to talk to him?"

"Yeah, let me holler at'm."

She put down the phone and he picked it up, smacking on his sandwich.

"Ay son! What's hap'nin'?"

"Ahh, nothin' much dad. I'm going to D.C. on business. I might move there if things go well."

"Oh rilly? You gahnna mehk some mo' munney?"

"Yeah. I think I'm in line to take a higher position."

"Well dat's awright, then! Getcha ass otta Texas!"

"Hey dad, you watchin' the football draft?"

"I don'know…when is it? Nex' week, right?"
"Yeah."
"Hmm…I might catch tha be-ginnin', but I don't think I'll watch tha whole thang. At some point you just gotta do somethin' witcha day, ya know? But I do wahnna see who da Saints take."

"*Oh*, yeah. I heard they got some good plans."

He lowered his voice to a scruffy whisper, like he was plannin' a conspiracy.

"Ay, I'm changin' tha subject nah…Didja mom get on ya rilly hawd about the merrij-kids subject? 'Cause she been tawkin' about folks' grankids that she sees at church and I meant to give ya a head's up on'nat."

"Oh, naww. She didn't really talk about that too much. I think 'cause I told her I wanna move to D.C. She was just try'na talk me outta movin'."

Returning to a normal tone, "Oh, yehh…she found out that Tam'ra's goin' for the WNBA draff nex' yeah—"

"Whaaaa???"

"Yehhh."

"Man, that's straight! Are any teams lookin' at 'er?"

"Yehh, a lotta teams—Sacramenno, New Yawk, Detroit, I think Washin'ton is lookin' atta, too. She might be up theah witchu."

"Ah, okay… But they're all *farrr*. Man, *that's* why she was soundin' all worried. You *know* momma ain't gon' tell me not to take more money…I *knew* somethin' was up."

LOOKIN' IN THE MIRROR

"Yehhh! An' I don'know why she ackin awl suhprised. Tam'ra *said* she was gon' do it two yeahs ago! The girl went'n'got an agent, but it's just a phase'n' it's gon' pass," he paused, "Well, maybe Houston'll tayka and ya mom'll calm the hell down. She been so tense lehtly. I haven't gotten any in a week."

"Awww, come on, man! I don't wanna hear all'at!"

He laughed really loud. He does that mess on purpose, tryin' to gross us out.

"I don't undahstand how yawl can be so adverse to ya parents havin' sex. We're the two people you *know* do it...*you're* the eh-vuh-dence!"

"Hey, I'm perfectly fine with the illusion that my siblings and I were conceived by asexual reproduction. Anything else is an abomination."

"Well I beg to diffa."

"And that's fine, but now I'm gonna get off the phone and cut the grass 'cause you won't stop talkin' 'bout wantin' to bone my momma."

* * *

Ahhhhhhh...It's good to be at home. My house only had me back for a week. First I went to a business seminar in Atlanta for four days, then I went to Memphis to meet people in this company we're about to buy, and then I went to Oklahoma to see my cousin in a rodeo. Now I gotta go to D.C. to start another buyout. It's bad when you have to go *home* for R&R.

I looked at the calendar again to see what I had on my plate.

```
11a: pick up Dante
2p:  guitar lesson
3p:  b-ball w/ the guys
```

Awww, yeah! Today's my day with Dante. I'll get him to mow my lawn, then I can just do the edging and spray for bugs! I thought. *Why didn't I think of this earlier?*

Dante is the kid that me and my boy Will mentor. Actually, Will is matched to him, but we were both still tryin' to settle down from our wilder days when they got hooked up so we silently partnered on the mentorship thing so that neither of us would drop the ball where the kid is concerned.

When we met him he was 8 and both of his parents were in and out of prison for drugs, robbery...pimpin' and panderin'...you name it, they did it. His grandmother, Millie, got custody, but she was fifty-nine and gettin' sick. She couldn't possibly raise a young man in today's world—not alone anyway. He wasn't doin' well in school, gettin' Ds and all—just gettin' by. He didn't really even have any hopes of prospering, but he wanted to be just like Darius Miles. So we sat him down and told him even though Darius Miles *looks* like a thug, he's a millionaire and has millionaire responsibilities. He's made it. Dante hasn't. And Dante *won't* unless he gets his act together. So now, he's thirteen years old and actually brags about his grades. I'm just glad he has grades he can brag about.

Sometimes I'll pick him up and spend a whole day with him...sometimes the whole weekend, if his

LOOKIN' IN THE MIRROR

grandma says it's cool. During the summers, we've even let him shadow us at work. We want him to see what it's like to be around real men with ambitions. Not guys like the shiftless knaves in his neighborhood. They just rap all the time and talk about how deep their lyrics are. That's just not productive.

He likes hangin' out with us, and really, I'm glad. Not to get mushy, but—you know, it feels good that I can provide a positive male influence. Especially since Black boys don't have a whole lot to look up to on the local level. And it's kinda like I'm gettin' my practice in for fatherhood, I guess. His grandma is funny 'cause she said it's okay to "whoop his tail" if need be. But I don't whoop him. That's not my job. I just have him read the *Wall Street Journal*. Then, sometimes, he needs to be "pledged," so I make him do push-ups or hold his arms out to the side "'til *I* get tired." But if he's *really* smellin' himself, I'll make him do yard work. The attitude usually takes a walk after a short while, especially if he's standin' in the corner, holdin' his arms out while I grab a snack and sit on the couch to watch a game. He wants to parlay on the couch too, but—OH! No sir—you gave your grandmother lip when she asked you to sweep the kitchen. Most times, offering to take him back home is its own punishment 'cause he wants to get out the house. However, it's usually best to go with positive reinforcement 'cause kids always wanna feel useful, like they're helping.

As I headed to the garage, I thought about how I'd break the news of relocation to Dante and Millie. Will already knows my plans, but I haven't even thought about how I'd tell them. *Do I tell her first? Do I tell him first? Maybe I'll just sit 'em both down and tell 'em at the same time.* Of course, I'd keep in touch with the boy, but it's no doubt that he'd have to make an adjustment to my absence. I'm sure Millie wouldn't be too happy about it, either. My only worry is that I'll be another absent male figure in his life. *I wonder if Nouri or Carlos could fill in when I'm gone. He's pretty comfortable around them. But which one? ...Oh, well. I'll think about it later.* I locked the house and jumped in the car. *It's too early to think about all this. I don't even know if I have the job yet.*

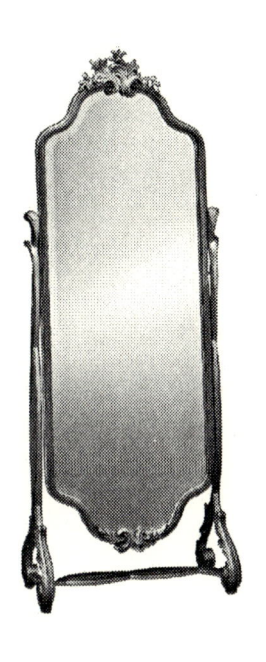

April 13

Saturday Evening

A. M. HATTER

> *(((smack-smack-smack)))*
> *Look at that girl!*
> *(((smack)))*
> *Damn! Damn, I'm sexy!*
> (pose)
> (pose)
> *You don't want none-uh dis!*
> (pose)
> *Mmmmm, fineness. Just sexy.*
> (hold pose)
> *Oooooh...now **that's** art.*
> *I wanna sculpt me. Mental note: get art supplies next weekend.*

It's the bomb to be as great as me: I'm sexy as all get-out, well dressed, outrageously funny, down-to-earth, *and* I watch sports!

The only problem is that I'm also educated, comfortably paid (well, it's enough to take care of me), and dauntingly independent. There's no man that knows how to get with me. I'm not sure if I should be proud of that or not…? But I suppose that's why I'm in my drawls, staring at my reflection, and smacking *myself* on the ass (as Prodigy's 'Smack My Bitch Up' blasts from my stereo—☺).

Catch the analogy:

Your average caveman approaches me. He grunts, "Mmm. Ahh. Brought steak for you."

I reply, "Oh wow! Thanks, that's great. But I'm not hungry right now."

Instead of appreciating that I was at least moved by his gesture, he focuses on the fact that it wasn't what I wanted at that time. Does he then make

LOOKIN' IN THE MIRROR

an effort to find out what I want? No. Instead, he becomes frustrated with the fact that I didn't want his steak and decides I'm too picky, thus, leaving me to fend for myself. When, really, I just wasn't hungry at the time and I'd have gladly eaten it later. Furthermore, he hasn't the capacity to understand that what I want might simply be for him to sit down and put his arm around me. So I, in turn, realize that he's a dumb ass for not knowing this and get rid of him. *You can't fire meee! 'Cause I QUIT!*

Hell, I just cut this guy from my roster a week or two ago. It was nothing serious; we'd just been hanging for a few months. Though, *he* thought we'd be perrrrrfect for each other—I mean, dude was *so* into me. But the problem was that 1) he just wasn't my type, and 2) I recently found out that the guy had been in a relationship for two years—and counting!

At first I was trippin' because, damn, did he think I'd never figure it out? Hell, I knew from the jump that there was some chick calling him just by the way he answered his cell phone. But I figured it might be a homegirl. If I had gone over to his house, though, I'd have figured it out sooner; but what business did I have going to his apartment during dating hours anyway? I wasn't trying to put myself in the position of having to escape from a man in heat. But I recently went to his place en route to a theater that's closer to him. And I got a chance to look around while he was still grabbing a few things from the closet, or here or there.

What I encountered was a spirit that was so innately feminine that I knew he was a cheater as soon

A. M. HATTER

as I walked in. From the homey-looking magnets on his refrigerator, to a few choice books set neatly between what looked like leftover college books (what man would actually read Dr. Phil, The Color Purple, *and* E. Lynn Harris???), to the spic-and-span appearance of everything being in its place, I knew that there was a woman in his life. Obviously, though, he hadn't paid attention to anything she'd done to mark her territory—and I'm sure he probably paid the same amount of attention to her in general. So, me being me, I pointed out a few of my observations:

"So, you read E. Lynn?" I said, grinning. "You must be really evolved."

"Huh???" he replied. Of course he had absolutely no idea what I was talking about.

After which, I began my full review of his household, from the front door all the way to the hallway, continuing as we left. We talked about it more in the car because I called him out for trying to run game; but the situation wasn't simply that. His deal was that he wasn't feeling comfortable in his relationship anymore and pegged me as his escape, pretty much. But it would seem to me that if he wanted out, he should just break up. But he didn't want to be alone, so he continued their relationship even though he was unhappy.

Consequently, I told him that he's full of shit and didn't know what he wanted. That shit just didn't make sense. He's a grown ass man. So *be* a man and pick a side of the fence. Quite obviously, I discontinued our friendship at the end of that encounter. He didn't want to stop seeing me, but I wasn't going to be a party to some pansy ass attempt to call it quits, first off. Secondly, I refuse to be "rebound girl"; and third, I'm just not with anything that'll make me look like a co-conspirator.

Laying it on the line, I told him it's as simple as this: if you don't want her, break up; if you do, leave me the hell alone, you're wasting my time. And he had the nerve to say I'm mean. That fool had the gall to pull me into another chick's territory and had the *nerve* to say I'm mean for telling it like it is?? What if she had just happened to come over? I don't know if she's crazy or not! She might've waltzed in wielding a knife for all I know! Besides, he knew when he met me that I'd give him my mind when I deemed necessary. To me, if you've subjected yourself to being close to me (or attempting that, anyway), then we're going to be open, too. I'm not the one to wonder, "Where is our relationship going?" "Does he like me?" "Is he trying to be serious or is he going to fool around on me?" I just ask—or tell you. Anything less is just plain stupid.

It's one thing to be silly…I'll admit I have my times when I'm youthfully natured (immature). I have this thing about not wanting to accept growing up; but when I make time for you in my life, you better bring the funk. I don't like to waste my time. Stupid people need not apply. I can't stand stupid people. They just irk me in a way that I can't possibly understand. They say things like, "That's *your* opinion." Like they're making a fucking point. Of course it's my friggin' opinion! I'm the one that's saying it. Duhhh!

Sometimes, I've wondered if my bluntness would create problems with any guy that I attempt to

A. M. HATTER

build something with. But then, why would I want to get…m-m-married? That's too weird. Actually devoting time to someone other than myself…my name eventually becoming something other than Victoria J. Phillips. *And why do I have to change my name? I like my name! Why can't he change his?*

I suppose it's inevitable, though. You know, you're born, you go to school, you get a job, get married, have kids…blah, blah, blah. It's a necessary evil. Besides, someone as great as I can't very well stay single forever. Sometimes I wonder who actually will catch my attention long enough to dupe me into the Disney ending…*hmm, something to ponder.*

Okay, the real point: Do I realize that I'm totally self-absorbed? Yes. Why don't I work on it? Because it doesn't get in the way of my friendships, for starters. Even though I am completely egotistical, people still love me, and they love that about me. (Don't ask me why—I think they're lunatics.) Further, I have so much more to offer; I display great logic and loyalty, friendship and advice, frankness, dedication, and I actually do work to make myself better. Hence, the reason why I am so self-centered. Do you know anyone else as great as I?

It's possible, but probably not. ☺

Amid my self-appreciation, I'd been on the phone, talking about nonsense with my homeboy, Turk.

"Man! It would be so cool to be like that old chick on 'Studio54'! She was all eighty and shit, gettin' her party on!"

LOOKIN' IN THE MIRROR

"But wasn't she on drugs??" he pointed out.
((Beeeep!))
"Hey, hold on Turk, okay?"
"Yeah."
I clicked over.
"Hello?"
"Hey, you goin' over to the apartment tonight?"
"Yeah."
"When you leavin'?"
"Um...in about twenty, I guess. No, probably thirty or so. I gotta put on some clothes and I'll probably lolligag a bit. I'm talkin' to Big Turk on the other line. Where are you?"
"I just turned on their street."
"Oh, okay. Well, I'll go ahead'n'get dressed."
"A'ight."
"Bye."
"Bye."
((Click-Click.))

Shawn always calls to make sure that I'll actually join the rest of the gang for girls night. It's part of her strategy to keep me on the ball. Apparently, if she doesn't check up on me, I'll end up getting lost or something. I *guess*...

Anyhow...the dresser beckoned and I chose to drape my body in a small T-shirt that had capris sleeves and a pixelated picture of a middle finger on the front, low-rise cargo pants, and my favorite beat-up tennishoes. *Oh yeahhh...I'm chick sport to the max.*

"You know," I said, resuming my conversation with Turk, "I wish I had a mannequin-man... kinda like that dude on that old Nickelodeon show 'Today's Special', where the mannequin-man would take off the hat and be a man, then put it on and be a mannequin."

"Why?" he asked.

"'Cause then I could bring Guy-A to life, then put him up when I get tired of him and go play with Guy-C. Guy-A wouldn't know I'm playin' with another mannequin. He's in plastic state."

"You lousy female chauvinist," he said, laughing.

I laughed proudly.

"You're so bad. You're about as bad as I am."

He almost sounded pleased to say that.

"I just like new people...they give me more to talk about. And you know that's essential for a windbag like me."

He laughed, appreciating my self-deprecating attitude. "You know what? You really are the bomb."

I smiled. "I knoooowww."

"That's my dawwg!"

Then we giggled back and forth for about thirty seconds.

"Well, I need to go now. I'm goin' over Candace and Kenya's."

I got off the phone, grabbing my dread cap, cell phone, keys and purse on the way out. Then I set the alarm and locked the door. I looked up the street and saw a bunch of cars taking up nearly all of the paved space. *Can someone please tell Puffy and the family to go home??* I thought to myself. When I got the car revved up, I was on my way. I bobbed and weaved through the street like someone taking a parking lot road test with the orange cones, as I switched out my Black As Jet CD to put in MC Divinity. (Yes, I just shamelessly shouted out to the hometown artists. It's all about that ATL, shawty. We support like that!)

* * *

About thirty minutes and five feet later, I walked through the door.

"Girl, you crazy! You know Michael Jackson ain't been Black for two decades!" Kenya yelled out.

"Hey! Don't you talk about Michael Jackson," I hollered. "And that goes for Prince, too!" I continued, "And 'The Last Dragon'! Those are classics and they're never to be debated!"

They stared at me blankly…until they collectively burst into laughter.

"Man, Vicki gets all emotional and shit. She don't play about her entertainers," Candace said with one of those accept-her-as-she-is looks on her face.

It was girls' night, which gave us poetic license to be freewheeling asses. These are the nights we use to catch up on each other's weekly happenings and talk about anything, ranging from birthplaces to philosophy. Usually, we'll get together at a local sports bar and check out "the talent," but sometimes we'll watch a movie. This time, a 3-to-1 vote pulled out 'Love Jones' for some good old-fashioned reminiscing. Naturally, I—being the box office connoisseur—was the one who dissented, but of course, not without some castigation.

"It's about *love*, Vic. We shoulda known yo' cold-hearted ass wouldn't understand," Kenya snapped.

"Nooo. *Bull*shit is what it's about," I snapped back. "Some immature dumb asses is what it's about," I continued, "It's not that it's a bad *movie*, 'cause it had a pretty good pace and all—and I liked the tension with the married dude…but the main characters were just…*stupid*!"

"Well tell us what's stupid about 'em, then," Candace asked. Someone always wants me to put up some proof. *As if* they can ever dispute my superior logic.

"Well, for one: if you go and have sex with some dude and claim that y'all ain't special, then don't go gettin' jealous or try to feel hurt when you see him with someone else. Especially when you took your hot ass back to your ex-boyfriend—which, y'all know, was stupid in the first place. Secondly, since they obviously had these feelings for each other, *somebody* should've said somethin'. Hell, were they adults or in high school???"

"But that's the way people act in real life. That's the way love is," Kenya asserted.

"Yeah, in *high* school! But once you're so old, you need to just grow up. You can't go around thinkin' like a fifteen-year-old when you're damn-near thirty! And if you make a choice, you need to deal with it; or if not, just walk away and don't think about it again. But they were gettin' all twisted about some bullshit, actin' like they couldn't tell the other person had feelings for 'em. But, noooooo! They didn't wanna sit down like two rational adults and talk about it! That makes too much sense!"

Candace gave up, "A'right, a'right, a'right!"

"That was just stupid."

Kenya retorted, "But you think all movies about love are stupid."

"No, that's not true. I adored 'Love & Basketball'…"

"But—" Kenya started. I'm sure, to make the point that I was about to address.

"Yeah, ol' dude acted stupid in that, too, but that was because one, they really were in high school and two, he found out his dad—his lifetime role model—was a busta. That man *lied* to his *face*. *Nobody* would act right after that!" I pointed at the 'Love Jones' DVD cover. "*These* folks are just stupid!"

Then, there's Shawn. She's like our parliamentarian. We'll go off on tangents, lose our focus—completely forget what we wanted to do, but she puts it all back on point. If anything, I just have to commend her for being able to tolerate *my* unruly ass.

"Well I don't care," Shawn asserted, "We voted yo' ass out, so let's just watch the damn movie and get home so I can get some from my husband. Unlike y'all, I don't need a movie. I got the real shit at home!"

The married woman always wants to brag about getting some from her husband. Any other time she'd be complaining about his ass. Go figure.

As you can tell, these three are my girl posse. We do all that corny stuff that the chick flicks show— well, except for dancing around tables and shit—but mostly, we'll just get together and gripe or admire

A. M. HATTER

"talent." *Mmmmmm...Scantily clad meeeeen. Rrrrrrrrrrrr.* Oops, sorry. Had a 'Simpsons' moment there. *Where was I? Oh yeah, the girl posse.*

Shawn and I have known each other since the tenth grade. We're, by far, the tightest of the group (no doubt, because we've known each other the longest). She knows my family, and I know hers...blah, blah, blah...this is my dawg beyond all doubt. Of course, Kenya and Candace aren't chopped liver, but Shawn and I think more alike. When it comes down to it, she's the only one of the three whose advice I accept, almost without debate.

Kenya and Candace moved here after college. Kenya is from... ...Mississippi, and Candace is from Virginia. They were assigned as roommates during their sophomore year in college and have been friends ever since. Well, I think they're sorority sisters, too. Yeah, they are. They have this obsessive need to decorate in blue and-or gold (they usually go with this celestial print), and buy anything that has or references poodles. (They own one, too. His name is Ro.) They're kinda retarded in that aspect. Anyway, after they moved up here, Candace got a job working for a marketing firm, like, straight out of college. She's one of those really prepared people that always has things go the right way—naturally, from all that preparation and stuff. Kenya on the other hand, somewhat flies by the wind. She'll have a pretty good idea of how to prepare, but doesn't finish the job; though, somehow (by the grace of God) things still work out for her in the long run.

LOOKIN' IN THE MIRROR

For instance, she worked for BET (before VIACOM) when she first moved up here because she created a good relationship while interning. But not long after she got hired, she decided it was too ghetto and quit. She said she "will not contribute to the corruption of the Black community." Most people spend some time unemployed after making that kind of move, but she got hired at a local TV station. It doesn't end there…Kenya became the morning show assistant producer after only being there for, like, six months. Who knows how this stuff happens? It's almost as nonsensical as African-American romantic comedies.

Anyway, we all met through Candace and Shawn. Shawn works in human resources at the firm where Candace works. So what, at first, was seeing each other in the hall every now and then became hanging out every weekend by way of Prince coming to town. Shawn had gotten tickets for me, her, my roommate, and one of my roomie's friends. But when a cheap trip to Italy plopped in their laps, we had to find new concert partners. So a day before the concert, Shawn happened to see Candace in the elevator and expressed her despair about having extra tickets that she didn't know what to do with in such short notice; which became the day's uplift for Candace because she and Kenya wanted to go, but were too late because the tickets were sold out. The rest, as they say, is history.

So Shawn left after the movie to get some ass. Kenya was kind of jealous because she doesn't have a beau, but Candace and I just wanted to check some talent on the tube and started flipping channels.

Candace shouted all ghettofied, "I don't need all the drama of being married just to get some. Gimme a picture of Lenny Kravitz and I'll get my self-lovin' on!"

I cracked a grin and rolled my eyes, shaking my head in disbelief. You just have to let those moments of TMI slide.

"Hey! Turn it back a sec!" I yelled.

"What??" Kenya gave me a shocked look. "Did I miss somethin'? What are you lookin' for?"

"Tiger Woods, man!" I said with complete authority as if dictating a new trend and added slowly, "IIII waaannnna *lick* hiiiim." I licked my lips.

"Tiger Woods???"

"Hell yeah!" I said.

"He's not cute."

I bucked my eyes at her. "Man, you crazy! Tiger Woods is sexy!" I continued, "See, you gotta understand the phases! Me??? I *love* to watch guys start growin' up…they get to that 19-through-21 phase and they start sprouting the extra muscle, a little extra fuzz on the chin. They wook wike gwown up wittle boyyys. It's so cuuute," I paused as I stared at Tiger walking, "Daaamn, he got nice thighs."

Kenya couldn't understand, "He's wearin' baggy slacks. What're you talkin' about?"

"That's 'cause y'all can't see the talent. You need to have *refined* eyes. But me…*I know* how to pick up meat." I scooted closer to the TV to demonstrate. "See, he's in that phase that starts at 25 or 26, when guys start picking up more weight in their face-neck-shoulder-chest areas. That's *man weight*."

LOOKIN' IN THE MIRROR

I slid my finger up and down the screen to highlight the shoulder/waistline contrast. "But see, he's still young, so he's still holdin' that upper body inverted triangle," I explained, shaking my head, "Mmm, mmm, mmm…sexy. We'll see if he keeps it into the 30-weight phase."

I looked at them briefly, nodding my finger at them, "Mmmmm…those thighs…you know, Eminem has nice thighs, too. I saw him in the back of one of Turk's mags once. NICE." I nodded dramatically and looked back at the TV. "I could pull Tiger Woods. He don't wanna meet me. I'd *have* him…for *lunch*."

They burst into laughter. And I could understand their amusement. I wouldn't take me seriously either. But they know not the talent of the *last* dragon. Shit, I'm greatness…*personified…TIMES* ten! They don't understand.

Candace lamented, "Girl, you need to be on TV or somethin'. Yo' ass is retarded." We laughed some more. "Now get outta the way so I can change the channel."

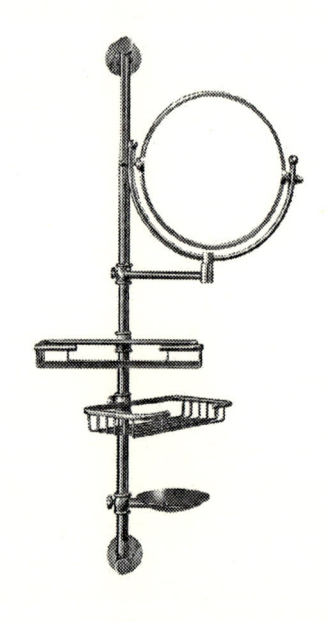

April 14

Sunday, Early Evening

LOOKIN' IN THE MIRROR

I sat on my couch staring at the ceiling. Some triflin' movie about being a playa—or somethin' to that effect—just went off. This crap they're callin' "Black entertainment"...yeah right. That's funny, it doesn't seem to entertain any of the Blacks I know.

The phone rang.

My brother, Terrence, called to vent about his wife, who I call Wanda 'cause she's ghetto like the character on 'In Living Color'. Apparently she bought some very expensive jewelry and went over to her friend's house to show off. But her friend stays in the hood—not the projects, the hood. (*You know* the areas: ashy, dilapidated houses with NO grass *at all*—just dirt'n'trees, though they have the nerve to have a current-year luxury car with rims, and the classic car sittin' on blocks with a "for sale" sign in the window. People hangin' out at the gas station—*all day*. The otherwise-normally-dressed person in front of the grocery store with snow boots on at the peak of a summer day. The twelve-year-olds ridin' tricked-out bikes at, like, midnight—little kids are *never* in bed any more, and the strange look of homelessness that *everyone* has, even though they're gettin' on the bus dressed in work clothes. Yeah...the hood.) Anyway, somebody came up to rob her and she pulled out—get this—a bag of nickels and started fightin' back. While, I'll give her props for defending herself, I have to wonder why she'd wear somethin' like that in the hood in the first damn place. And, who *just has* a bag of nickels?!

He lost SO many cool points for marryin' her. And he knows it, too. About three weeks after they got

A. M. HATTER

married, he called me whinin', "Man, I don't wanna be married no mo'... I didn't know it would be like this... She's too ghetto... I didn't know she was that ghetto, man," woopty, woopty, woo. But she got pregnant a week later...so he's still with her. (It still amazes me that he doesn't have any other kids—that we know of.)

We got off the phone after about thirty minutes. I went upstairs for an afternoon nap. I sighed and fell onto the bed. I had this weird dream that I was in line at this store, this huge factory-type place. It was real bland lookin', gray all over, with steam comin' from every direction. There were all these huge pipes, wall to wall, ceiling to floor. When I walked up, I looked around and only guys were in line. At first I felt like leavin' 'cause I wasn't tryin' to be around a bunch of hard-legs, but I wondered why all those men were in line instead of workin'. And then they'd leave, grinnin' ear-to-ear, with these strange-lookin' women on their arms. The women were attractive, but they looked...like humanoid wax figures. When I got to the front, I saw it was a factory that made women. So then I figured I'd stay around for a while.

I walked up, the customer service robot asked to see my list and I handed it to him. I don't know where I got the list. It was just there. Then the robot fed it into this machine, but then the machine spit it out. The DOS-system screen read, "Syntax error," and started flashin'. All the other guys started grumblin' about the hold up.

One of the tech workers came from the back to set the robot and machine back to normal.

LOOKIN' IN THE MIRROR

I was like, "What's wrong with the machine? Will I get my woman?"

He removed the list from the machine and said, "We can't make this."

I said, "Why not?"

He replied, "Because your requirements are too vague."

I didn't understand so he took the next guy's list. It had five wishes on it:
Measurements: 36-26-40
Height: 5 feet, 7 inches
Race: Hispanic
Hair: 15 inches
Age: 25

The tech guy fed it into the computer and eight minutes later, a Hispanic woman popped out, fittin' that description to a T. In fact, she kinda looked like Maria Conchita Alonso.

He explained that what I want is abstract, sometimes too specific, and not quantifiable by a machine. Then he goes, "Not only that, it's just too friggin' long."

I looked down at my list and I felt like *Damn, I just can't get what I want*. My needs went unmet, yet again. My list had four times what the other guy's list had and nothing was physical.

College degree, higher education certification, military training, or if none, a really, really good job.

Free of psychosis, mental imbalances, and diseases.

No tattoos. (How would she look, seventy years old, with grand children and tattoos? That's disgusting.)

No gold teeth. (Do I even need to explain?)

No smoking or excessive drinking.

No ghetto hair or ridiculous nails.

She should care about her appearance, without going overboard.

Financially prudent. (She's not spending me into the poor house.)

She has to appreciate my efforts.

Rational, trusting, sensible, strong, classy, street, intellectual, silly, sensitive, soft, and freaky; knows when to be what.

Doesn't trip out over sissy shit.

Doesn't freak out over a couple of cuss words.

She has her own life, habits, activities, etc. (She doesn't need to be under me every damn minute of the day.)

Keeps in-house business in the house.

She has to like 'The Simpsons', at least one sport, and have good taste in movies. (Like 'Dogma', for example.)

Communicates on an adult level.

Strong spiritual grounding and awareness.

Healthy family ties.

Independent, but without the attitude.

Real. (I don't wanna meet the "representative.")

I didn't think it was out of the ordinary. The way I figure, no woman wants some scrubby man. We're no different. But contrary to my opinion, my list was apparently too specific. Adding insult to injury, a guy behind me snatched the crumpled list from my hand and proceeded to chastise me for being so descriptive and scrutinizing. All the guys pointed fingers and laughed, sayin' I'm like a woman and that I need to "Man up; ask for Halle Berry and get the fuck on!"

(((Riiiiiiing!!)))

"Hello?" I answered sluggishly.

"What's up?"

LOOKIN' IN THE MIRROR

"Hey Mia. What's goin' on?"

She sighed, "Nothin' much… I'm tired, but I don't wanna go to sleep. But, I don't have anything to do. Did I wake you up?"

"Well, yeah, but it's cool. I didn't particularly like the dream I was havin'."

"Oh really? What was it about?"

I yawned and sat up, wiping my hand over my face. "I was in some line at a factory where they made women. But the computer wouldn't make my woman 'cause my list was too specific."

She laughed, "That's your unconscious tellin' you that you're too picky."

"Whatever."

"I'm jo-king," she said, "Besides, I admire you for havin' standards. Any woman who has some sense would appreciate that about you. Don't worry, you'll find that special lady."

"Yeah, okay, Mia. Damn…you're about like my mom. Just ready to marry me off to somebody."

"She just wants some grandchildren."

"Yeah, yeah. Okay. Next subject."

She giggled. "So when are you going to D.C.?"

"Tonight. I hope I finish by Thursday so I can have some time to kick it—oh, guess who I saw at the grocery store?" I added.

"Who?"

"Denise."

"Umph. Did you speak to her?" she replied with an attitude. I could almost *hear* her neck rollin'.

"Didn't want to, but she saw me before I could duck into the next aisle."

"What'd you do? Were you mean to her?"

"Naw. I just answered her questions—'How ya doin'? Whatcha been up to?' and all that—I was tryin' to hint that I didn't really wanna talk. I don't even know why she spoke. If I did what she did, I wouldn't speak to me. I'd be too afraid of gettin' knocked out."

She replied, "Yeah, well, you know bitches got nerve. Besides I'm pretty sure she knows you won't do anything."

"Whatchu try'na say, man?"

"Nothin'. Just that it's not like you'll *actually* knock the girl out."

"Uh-huh. Movin' on, uh, did you see Antoine's magazine article?" I asked.

Confused, she replied, "Antoine's article? What article?"

"My mom was readin' the latest issue of Black & Proud, right? She sees an article by Antoine, so naturally, she reads it. Homeboy, hometown—you know, supportin'."

"Right…"

"The article was about what happened with Denise."

It took her a second to clue in, at first. "Nooo. You're lyin'."

"Nope."

"He had the *nerve* to write about *that*???" she asked, totally shocked.

"Apparently so."

"Did you even know he was gonna write about it?"

"Nope."

"*Day-um*! He could've at least warned you before he put you on blast!"

"Hell, that's how I felt."

"Your name wasn't in it, though, right?"

"Naw, nothin' like that. Well, he had our same initials. But my name is Gary and her name is Dana or somethin'. It was kinda weird 'cause he had *all* the details. Even down to what I was wearin'. The way I clenched my fist and stuff," I sighed, "Writers."

"That ain't cool... Oh! Hey," she interjected, "I gotta go. I forgot I gotta run to the store. You're leavin' tonight, right?"

"Yeah."

"Well have a nice trip and good luck with the meetings," she said.

"Oh, thanks. Talk to ya later."

"Bye-bye."

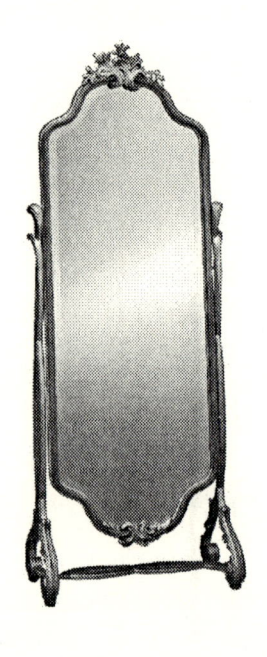

April 16

Tuesday

LOOKIN' IN THE MIRROR

Homeless people these days are so amusing. I was sitting at the bar in this silver-themed coffee shop, trying not to laugh at the vagrants outside the window making gestures, dancing, and-or having conversations with themselves. Normally, I sit there and watch them like a TV show, but the wait staff always rides me about it when they realize what I'm laughing at, so I turn my head away. In doing so, I overheard this woman sitting next to me at the counter telling her colleague about some twenty-something college guy dating her sixteen-year-old cousin and how the girl's parents wanted to press charges for statutory rape.

It's funny how when guys get arrested for stuff like that, people act like the girls were ignorant prey, untainted and oblivious to the guy's whole perverted game. While I won't deny that the guy was stupid, even sinister, for getting with her in spite of obvious laws, I'm not going to write her participation off so quickly. Women are just as freaky, cold, and calculating as men are. We just don't admit to it all the time. Besides, she was probably just using him for status.

There's a weird state of mind when you're in high school. For instance, what's being "grown up" in high school should actually be shameful. And what is not accepted as cool is, in truth, being truly mature—a lot of the time, that is. You know, it's funny, girls need all these "qualifications" to ensure their maturity, stature, loveability (if that's even a word), not to mention their ability *to* love. In hindsight (life's best, but post-necessary teacher), you can pinpoint when and where things go wrong. But then, when you're in

A. M. HATTER

high school, it doesn't really matter. You just giggle in total naïveté, thinking you're on top of the world. On the other hand, you don't think about how old or young you are… you're just you.

*What the hell am I **talking** about???* I hate when my mind wanders into total oblivion. I toss around rhetoric and aimless thoughts, not even paying attention to what I'm doing physically. But I knew the first thing on my agenda was to finish my coffee and get the hell out of the place so I could avoid this guy who I'd been ignorantly staring at during my space-time. *Hmmmm, ironic that I would space out in a space-like coffee bar.*

I really must pay more attention to what I'm doing. But when I try to remind myself to wake up, my brain forces me back into whatever I was thinking about. As I walked down to work and I found myself thinking about that whole high school thing again. Where, on one hand, you think it's cool that you can pick up an older man when you're, like, 16. But on the other side of the coin, he looks really pathetic from a college girl's point of view because he's grown, getting with some high schooler. Then, from a parent's point of view, he's just some pervert preying on their untainted high school angel that doesn't know any better. But why was he dating a 16-year-old anyway? Were adults not working out for him? Maybe he's one of those losers that gets them young so he can train them to do whatever he says, giving it up whenever he wants.

All these thoughts took me back to the summer before the ninth grade. My friend, April, got with this

LOOKIN' IN THE MIRROR

guy up the street from her. He was going into his junior year in high school. Not a jock, but popular and very well-liked by most chicks at school. Well, eventually, they got really close. He used to go over to her house and eat dinner with her family. One afternoon, when her family went out, she claimed she had cramps and stayed home. But in fact, it was her scheme to finally have sex with the almighty Michael Denworth. Needless to say, they got that much closer. Then school started. She used to write little notes to him and leave them in his locker at school. They were supposed to be the world's tightest couple. But outside of the dream world, he was sexin' half of the new girls in school, some of the upperclasswomen, and spreading rumors that he had sex with April and her sister at the same time.

According to him, he totally turned April out and she'll serve you up as long as you're an upperclassman with a car that'll take her out to dinner. Adding insult to injury, he read this really deep note that she wrote to him out loud in the middle of the cafeteria during lunchtime. All this spurred her four new rules:

>Stay off your back, you think best on your feet.
>Don't believe the hype. It's all game.
>Observation shows you who you're dealing with.
>(most important) Never *ever* put it in writing.

After he pulled that number on her rep, she went totally underground. She started taking nerd classes, loading up with a lot of extra-curriculars. Some people that she used to hang with didn't even realize that she was still in school there. And I don't think she's ever been the same. For one thing, everyone used to like her. I mean, *everyone*. And the people who hated her, still liked her and hated that they liked her. She was like a freaking boy band.

But afterward, her reviews got so polar. People either loved her to death, or they couldn't stand her for all she was worth because "she's such a bitch now." The only good thing that came out of the whole sitch is that she didn't get pregnant. And that was probably a matter of chance because five of the other girls Michael was with got pregnant. (Fertile bastard, ain't he?)

She eventually found happiness, though. When she left for college, she found this sexy piece hanging about the campus and they hooked up later in their matriculation. They're perfectly suited for each other. She still won't ease up on that kismet word. She called on my way to work. My cell phone ring is this delightful little tune. You might know it: the theme to 'Howdy Doody'. Old people always trip out when they hear it because they swear up and down that I'm too young to know about that show. I know I about gave my co-worker and "potnuh," Big Turk, a stroke when he first heard it. Really, I think it may have sent him into a state of regression for a quick minute.

At any rate, I ended my latest conversation with April as I walked into my office building. They're getting married next summer—June or July, she thinks—and of course, I have to be the maid of honor. She's all pumped and optimistic. I hate when she gets like that. She almost gets me to believing in that chick-

LOOKIN' IN THE MIRROR

flick happiness. And she's forever interrogating me about when I'm going to fall in love or settle down...like I need that kind of stress! Why settle down when I can have my picks of the litter at any point in time? I'm young. I'm intelligent. And guys want me. What more could a girl ask for?? ☺

"Sup, Big Turk!" I waved light years away from him, as I passed the security desk.

He waved me over, "Hey! Come here! I got somethin' to tell you!"

"Call me later today! I'm in a rush!" I answered, backing onto the elevator.

I got to my cubicle and finally got a chance to read this magazine that I had been neglecting for the last two weeks. There was an article this guy wrote about a friend whose girl totally left him high and dry. It was so depressing. Apparently, the two had a really good relationship—from what the writer could see. Though, he did note that his friend disappeared from existence while they were together. But the girl just left suddenly and took everything: the pictures off the wall, the dishes, the pots and pans...the welcome mat. Yes, the "WELCOME" mat.

Daaamn, I thought. *I hope all that shit was hers. 'Cause that's fucked up!*

I felt sorry for him. Don't even know the guy. I continued reading as the writer's depiction played out in my mind:

> All laughter ceased when we entered the barren room. Gary trailed in seconds later with the mail, still laughing about this young cat from work that said if Roy Jones bulked up, he could take Tyson—in his heyday. Yeah, you read that right. And

A. M. HATTER

hard as he was laughing, Gary froze as well when he saw the room.

We just stood there with our jaws hanging.

We first thought he might've been robbed. But all of his electronics, his DVDs, the gargantuan record collection: untouched. Only her stuff was gone. She even took the "WELCOME" mat.

It only took seconds for the fellas to clear out, mumbling about running errands and of chores that needed to be done.

Gary dropped on the couch and stared at the ceiling.

I leaned against the wall, knocked for six rounds at once. I knew he was hurting, but there's an unspoken male code to suffer in silence. It's times like this that you almost wish you were a woman.

Women have no problem crying, or simply talking things out.

All he did was ask me to leave.

"Hey Vic. Wow, you're really into that mag. What is that? Black & Proud?" It was my co-worker, fiddling with my portfolio, thinking that I'd tell her what's in it if she fiddled long enough.

"Now Sherry, you know I'm always in my own world. And what are you lookin' for, girl? You're always fiddlin' with somethin'."

"Nothin' girl…you know me. I'm just bored."

"Well, you got to leave woman. Go'n, scoot. I gotta finish my piece for the next issue…just like YOU! *There's* something you can do!" I laughed as I nervously tried to get rid of her.

I hate it when she comes around. She's been known to steal people's ideas before. *She'll never do it to me!* I don't know why she hasn't been fired yet. She only got hired because she was fucking the staff manager, and they broke up almost a year ago. She has no editorial experience, news background, or knowledge of writing in general. (Well, she can kind of write…if you consider catalog item descriptions as a form of journalism.) But then, I'm sure if they fired her, then she could bring up some shit about sexual harassment. The unspoken "no sex, no job" rank intimidation. I often wonder if while they might be nervous about that possible lawsuit, she may not even be thinking that far. Hell, she probably has a goon on the side ready to pick her up.

    I tried to refocus so I could get some work done, but just as I figured I was getting anywhere, the phone rang. It's so frustrating when you're distracted and you can't get *un*distracted. It was my other good friend, Theresa, calling with another life problem. I honestly don't know why I bother because she always calls with some problem that I give her advice about— and very good advice, too! But she never uses it. Then it always turns out that I was right to begin with, and she'll call again with the initial problem plus whatever has developed from the point that she didn't take my advice.

    I thought to myself, *Oh, it's time to get rid of Derek, now, eh?* She always wants to know how to get rid of her current boyfriend who has come to bore her because she's found this other guy who is the cat's meow. Every new guy is the cat's meow to her. It's always the same routine: there's some new find who is "the one," then she gets bored with him after, like, two weeks. Then she finds another and wants to know how to discard the other one. It's quite tiresome. In the 13

A. M. HATTER

or so years I've known her, there have only been a few times when her problem was conflicting enough for me to actually pay attention. And, like always, I give her advice because I have game for days...oh yeah, and that's what friends do (I'm rolling my eyes). Still, she never takes it.

"Theresa, I can't talk to you right now. I'm trying to finish my story. You know, the one I told you I need to write for tomorrow's issue? The one that my boss wants to see *yesterday*?"

"Yeah, but gimme just a little time. It'll only take a few minutes. I'm really confused right now."

"Theresa. I gotta go! Besides, you never take my advice anyway."

"But Vic! I really need your help right now!"

"Why? You wanna know how to get rid of Derek so you can date—*who* this time?"

She sighed, "No."

"Then what? 'Cause I really have to work. I've wasted enough time as it is."

"I'm pregnant."

You know how in TV shows there's that little record scratch that they do when there's something *really* unexpected? That's exactly what I imagined. (I wish I could have sound effects on-hand like that. It would be so cool.) But, Theresa. Pregnant. Those are two words I didn't expect to hear together for years to come. I didn't know what to say. But then, I really didn't even know what the problem was. I mean, she's pregnant. Okay, it happens. Deal with it. But then, the real question would be, *is she thinking about abortion*?

"Soooo, when did you find out? How far along are you?"

"Well, I've suspected it for a while now 'cause, you know, I told you I was late two weeks ago."

"Yeah."

"So I finally took a test this morning, but I don't know exactly how far I am."

"Okay… So… Does Derek know? What are you going to do?"

"No, he doesn't know yet. I don't know if I'm goin' to tell him… …I'm thinkin' about getting an abortion."

"WHAT???!!!" I was embarrassed at how loud I said that. I hoped no one was looking.

"Theresa. I KNOW you aren't talkin' about killin' that boy's baby before he knows it even exists!"

"But Vic, it's my body."

She didn't even sound like she could convince herself to believe that line.

"If you really believe that, then you're dumber than both of us could be. Hell, I'm completely thrown that you'd even say that, considering how you tripped out about your mom not tellin' you that you have an older brother that she put up for adoption! That's the most selfish bullshit I've heard you say in my life. Regardless of what I think about Derek, he still deserves to know that he's conceived a child."

"But—"

"And I know you don't want it! Duhhhh!! *I* don't want you to be pregnant, either, 'cause I know your retarded ass wouldn't know what to do with a kid.

A. M. HATTER

But hell, you're not even gonna tell him??? What the hell are you thinkin'???"

"Vic, that's not fair! You're talkin' all high and mighty about what I should do and *I'm* the one who has to deal with this, not you! *I'm* the one who has to get fat for nine months! *I'm* the one who'll have to deal with Derek from now until eternity! *I'm* the one who'll have to stop having fun because I have a child! How can you tell me what's wrong or right?? *You* don't have any *kids*. You don't even have a *man*!"

I laughed at the ridiculous comment she'd just made because what I was about to say would quickly put her in her place. (Especially when you use that serious whisper tone.)

"Okay…well if *I'm* such an inconsiderate person and *I* don't have to deal with all this, then why'd you even call me for advice? *You're* the one who went off and danced with the naked-head bandit! I told you don't mess with Derek. You remember *that*? And I told you to slow down with the fuckin'. But NOOOOO, you didn't listen to me. Now you're pregnant. And you wanna act all surprised even though you're almost twenty-eight fuckin' years old. Shit, you knew when you crawled into that bed that there's a chance you could get pregnant. And if you didn't want to deal with Derek from now until eternity, you shouldn't have *fucked* him. *Especially* without a condom. Hell, according to you, you didn't even tell him to *pull out*. So don't get mad at me 'cause you did *everything* wrong. And I'm not even gonna honor the 'you don't have a man' statement 'cause, at least, *I'm not pregnant*."

LOOKIN' IN THE MIRROR

We were silent for a long time. Which was a welcomed pause because I actually got on a good roll with my article. But after a while, my ear started getting sweaty from being pressed against the phone. And my neck was hurting from leaning over.

"Look, Theresa, just go take a nap. You need to calm down and let things come into perspective. I'll talk to you when I get off work."

Okay. I took a breath so *I* could bring things into perspective and get organized. *Damn, Theresa's pregnant, I need to get this work done, I need to vent— big time, and where'd my notes go?? I hate when that happens!* The phone rang again. My boss. He wanted my piece and a transcribed interview for another story that he was working on. I'm actually kind of glad that she called and made me mad. I got enough down to cover my ass for now.

I emailed him my opinion for tomorrow, responses for my column next week and the quotes from the interview. But a more pressing issue was a side gig that I've been working on with this young chick Anita that I met in the cafeteria one day. She mentioned that she wanted to start her own thing and that she even has some big-timer cousin with investment capital, but she didn't have a real idea on what she wanted to do. So I asked her what she did in her spare time, or what she has a passion for that she feels is unrealistic. She said, "Fashion." So we bounced a few ideas off of each other and eventually came upon a name: DEFI. We went in on trade marking the name and logo.

A. M. HATTER

For about three months, we'd been working—hard—on season lines and a specific look that we want to achieve. Something trendy, but kind of weird. *My main goal was just to fill that annoying little gap the industry has yet to fill with underwear for women with rounder hindquarters.* (I *hate* that! You can't get the support you need unless you wear some big, grandma panties. You may as well wear two pairs of pants!) Still, the only thing is I don't really want to take this fashion thing all the way because I'd have to switch careers and I'm just fine where I am. But I wanted to help her get to the top, while I eventually become a [mostly] silent partner, with exception to retaining co-founder credits, royalties or maybe a board seat, or something. And she's cool like that. She was so accommodating with writing out details of our partnership. She even signed and dated the whole deal. I was like, *Awww, isn't that cuuuute. A makeshift contract.* ☺

She told me last week that she found out some important people would be in town and that they agreed to meet with us. But we're kind of sneaking around the rules. She checked the schedule for the conference room on her floor and found out that it was empty for a couple of hours so she set the meeting for that time. Hopefully, nobody will find out about us using the conference room for outside business.

So I rushed down the hall with a stack of papers and my portfolio in hand, trying to make it to the conference room. Then I dropped it all, like a klutz. This was about the eightieth thing that happened to

LOOKIN' IN THE MIRROR

make my day "doomed for ruin." Then *he* walked in from the elevator...

He was magnificence...deliciousness in flesh, wearing a navy blue pinstriped suit, with cuffs at the ankles. His jacket was slightly opened, revealing his suspenders. *I loooooove suspenders*. I don't know why they do what they do to me. Suspenders and those beards that perfectly square the mouth (like Boris Kodjoe's) just drive me crazy.

He stood there in the doorway and looked at his watch on the chain hanging out of his pocket. I was staring so hard that I was about to drool. I couldn't believe that there would ever be a man in my presence so perfect: his collar, his sleeves, his cufflinks, his creases, the cuffs at the bottom of his pants—so incredibly detailed and precise. And he wasn't movie star fine...he's that fine that you see on the street. The kind of guy that stays around the corner from you, but you don't know his name or if he has a girlfriend.

I was about to write him off in my mind as just another pretty face, but he glanced at me and cut over to help me pick up my papers.

"Aw, I didn't see you down hur. Lemme help you with that," he said.

His voice beat out Barry White's 100 times over. It was smooth and deep like a midnight slow jam deejay. I just knew that he thought I was weird or something. I felt like I couldn't keep my eyes off of him. I did my best to keep my eyes traveling, but I couldn't stop looking. His skin was so even-toned and smooth, like someone just finished mixing it in a bowl. Not a pimple or a scratch or a hair bump in sight.

A. M. HATTER

And his beard was just as precise as his suit. His goatee perfectly squared his soft, round lips. I hadn't heard a single word he said. He might as well have been talking like the teacher on 'Charlie Brown'. I hoped he didn't think I was retarded. But he just had these *lips*...they were *made*...not to be kissed, but to be cast in stone for women across the world to show to their husbands as instructions on how to achieve perfection.

When all my papers were straight, he stood to a full length 6'3 and his body had that I'm-30-but-I-work-out thickness. He reached out his hand to help me up. He had a MAN'S hands: strong and thick, with long fingers. *I loooooove huge hands...with long fingers.* Then he grinned, exposing his straight, perfectly spaced teeth. This man was an icon of extra-human perfection. I had never seen anyone like him. I wanted to cast his figure in stone. When I finally came to, I managed to thank him and finish my journey to the conference room.

Suddenly, I felt...lighter.

Wait, wait...this is corny. I can't go around with music in my head like some Fred Astaire movie. I'm Victoria J. Phillips! I can't just go around acting giddy. It's gonna ruin my rep! Besides, I have a job to do. If I go in there all starry-eyed, these people will think I'm crazy. I need a distraction...something to sober me up. Think, Vic, THINK. What's something that'll get me in the right frame of mind?

Sherry, who always seems to be on Prozac, suddenly found her way into my path. "Heyyy, Vic! Do you know where Howard is?"

LOOKIN' IN THE MIRROR

"Nope...haven't seen him all day," I replied, inching away. Sherry was just what I needed to sober up. This time I was very glad to see her...though, not for long.

"Oh. So you haven't seen him?"

Trick, didn't I say I haven't seen him??? "Nah."

"You think he might have walked through here?" she asked, yet again.

I could've sworn I said I haven't seen him. Am I talkin' to myself??? "I have no idea, Sherry," I replied calmly even though she was starting to piss me off.

"Isn't he normally upstairs about this time?"

I don't know! Man, let me check my back pocket to see if he's there, muthafucka! "Man, Howard goes to so many meetings... I have no idea. I haven't seen him all day."

"So he hasn't walked through here yet?"

DAMMIT! Didn't I say I haven't seen him??? Oooo, I can't stand her dumb ass. "Sherry, I haven't seen him. I gotta go."

"You goin' home? Workin' on somethin' big?" she asked, noticing my portfolio.

"No, someone's meeting me downstairs."

"Oh, you gotta give that to someone?" She gave me a big nod and winked. "You need any help?"

"No, I got it, but thanks."

Ugh... I can't stand her. She's so freakin' nosey!

I glided into the conference room, looking as calm and cool as Billy D. The room felt really casual

A. M. HATTER

and friendly, as one of the hot shots was sitting on the table and the other was standing about two inches from Anita's face.

"And this is my partner Victoria," Anita said, snagging the opportunity to step back. Everyone did the smile-and-shake-hands routine. "I was just tellin' these two clowns how great an artist you are." We all laughed. She continued, "This is Rick and Terry. They're the buyers for Clark and Spielman."

"Wow. You're the two that were just hired—what? Two-three years ago, right?"

They looked at each other. Rick replied, "Has it been that long? Gee wiz, we need to find another job!" and they bowled over into a fit of laughter.

"You guys have truly turned those stores around, though! I mean, you can literally mark the point where your being hired there really changed things. The clothing is so top-rate now," I added.

"Which is why we're here to see you," Terry remarked, "We looked at the pictures Anita emailed us and you two are really going somewhere. It's reminiscent of the fifties Van Hoffman company, but with this…new spark. I really admire your work."

Anita's eyes shot open and she smiled confidently. "Well, thank you."

Said Terry, "I just don't understand how you do it. It's like you've got it down to a formula."

"Well, yeah…but if I told you what it was—"

"You'd have to kill me?" Terry interrupted.

"No, we wouldn't get the job," I chuckled dryly at my deadpan delivery, "Well, let me show you what we've got. This year, we wanted to break away from the adopted truths of fall colors: they're all dull or match trees…"

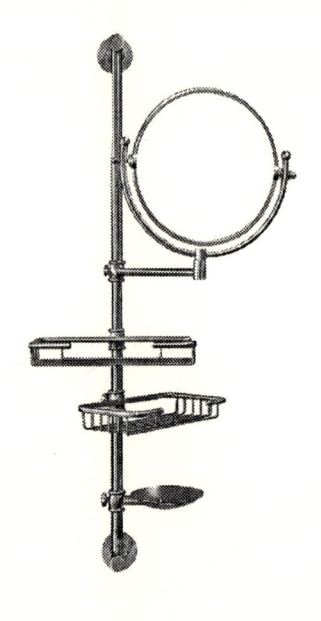

Tuesday, close to noon

LOOKIN' IN THE MIRROR

I hate being in different time zones. Time doesn't move the same. Your sleep schedule is off, and it seems like the day is shorter when you go east. It's weird. I hate it. I called myself wakin' up early but it's almost lunch.

My boy, Carlos, called me on my cell tellin' me about some guy he was hangin' with Saturday night. He said, "You know, the one that was in the blue shorts with those weird colored shoes."

"Ohhh, yeah. Ol' dude with the rubber bands in his beard, right?"

"Yeah, *him*."

"Okay, so what about'm?" I asked.

"We went out to this strip club last night. I forget the name—some new club. But anyway, man, I ain't never goin' out with him again. He's gonna fuck around and get locked up."

"Why you say that?"

"Man, we're sittin' against the wall, right? I went to the stage to tip the stripper or whatever. And man, you shoulda seen 'er."

"She was straight?"

"Yeah, man. She had a *FAT ASS*. Kinda like Angie Walker."

"Oh, a'ight!"

We got sidetracked from the story, laughin' and talkin' about broads we knew from high school and college that were fine. Gettin' dressed diverted my attention from the fact that we'd been rambling and Carlos never really finished his story. But it didn't *really* matter, 'cause I wasn't *really* listenin'. He always seems to make his way back to what he was originally talkin' about anyway.

"Man, how did we get on high school?" he said. "I know I didn't call you to talk about that."

I let him mull over it for a sec and trace his thoughts back.

"Oh yeah, dude from the rec center! So anyway, when I figured I gave her enough money, I turned around and he was hollerin' at one of the waitresses. So I stayed back until she left. And when she left he waved for me to come over. He's tellin' me how he bought ol' girl a drink or whatever and invited her to sit with'm. I'm like, 'That's cool.' She looked run over, but I told him she was fine so he could feel good." He paused for my laugh and continued, "So we're sittin' there and all…she came back, and they're talkin', havin' a ball or whatever, right?"

I replied, "Yeah."

"Then he said somethin' to distract her—I don't know what he said, but she looked the other way and he put somethin' in her drink!"

"*What*??? Aww hell naw! That's messed up!" I replied.

You hear about stuff like that on the news, but you never think you'll *know* anyone like that.

"I was stuck, man!" he exclaimed.

"Damn, that ain't even cool."

"I know! And I'm sittin' there like 'Damn, what am I gonna do?' I mean, all blockin' aside, that's just bogus, man."

"So what'd you do?" I asked.

LOOKIN' IN THE MIRROR

"Well, she drank the drink and got up...she waited on some other tables, but she would come back and talk to 'im. After a while, she started actin' weird. He was tryin' to talk her into goin' somewhere wit'm. But I went and told one of the bouncers that one of the waitresses was lookin' kinda sick and I described her. So he told a manager and I *guess* she got home okay. I don'know."

"Oh. Did ol' dude see you?"

"Naw, he just thought they got mad that she was sittin' down a lot," he said.

"Man, that's messed up. All these women out here that'll just *give* it to you... You *hardly* even *need* game anymore...and he put somethin' in her drink. That's some punk ass shit."

"Yeah... Well, what're you doin' today, man?"

"Actually, I'm in D.C. right now. I won't be back home 'til this weekend."

"Oh, a'right."

"Man, there's this place down the street from the hotel I'm in...I went there last night to get somethin' to eat. It's like Hooters in space or somethin'."

He laughed at the prospect. I laughed from actually seein' it.

"Man, that don't even make sense. But then...it kinda sounds cool," he laughed.

"It's a'ight. They got these chicks with big tits, wearin' tight silver clothes. 'Cause, you know, *everything* in space is silver!"

We always laugh at clichéd marketing techniques.

A. M. HATTER

"But let me get off this phone, man. I'm 'bout to eat," I said.

"Going back to space Hooters, huh?"

"Hell yeah," I chuckled.

On my way back to "Hooters: The Space Voyage," I saw this guy who looked just like a guy I hung out with in college. That was the coolest white guy I'd ever known. We got into some *shit* in college. The tales I could tell...man, I remember one time he wanted to loot the kitchen at this pub 'cause one of his old teammates worked in there and showed him how to jimmy the lock in the back so they could get in at night. We never went hungry again. But after that night, I let him do all the lootin'. You know...a brutha just doesn't need any trouble.

But this can't be Kev, I thought. *It's gotta be some lookalike*. But the closer I got, the more he looked like him. I didn't wanna say hi, then find out that it's not him; I could only see the side of his face. Then I got about ten feet from him and he turned.

"Gerald?" he said.

"Awww, Kev! What's uuup!!"

"What're you doin' here man? You look great!"

"Thanks. I'm here on business," I answered.

"Wow. That's great! Y'know, I just moved up here a couple weeks ago," he told me.

"Straight? I'm thinkin' about movin' here, myself."

He replied, "Hey, that's cool! It could be like old times!"

LOOKIN' IN THE MIRROR

"Woah, man...I don't know if I can get into your brand of trouble anymore."

"Come on, G! You should know me better than that! I've moved on! I'm doin' bigger, better things!" he said. "My company transferred me and gave me a raise. I can't get in trouble anymore."

"That's tight, man. Congratulations."

"Thanks. So whatcha doin'? Lemme buy you lunch, man. Let's catch up!"

"Well, actually, I was just gonna grab a snack and run...can we get together another day? I'll be here through the week," I said.

"Yeah, that's cool."

We traded information and headed in separate directions. *Man, I thought to myself, I can't believe I ran into Kevin Schaefer. This is gonna be a good day. I always had good days when I saw him.*

Anyway, I walked up to the coffee shop and dropped some change to this homeless guy that asked me for some money. (He said he wanted to get drunk, so as long as he was being honest...) But I tried to get inside before any others moved to take advantage of my humanitarianism. I walked in and looked for a seat. The space bar isn't one of those places that seats their guests, so I took a spot in the back. As I looked through the menu, I remembered that they only have coffee and appetizers like cheese sticks and personal sized pizzas. I could get a hamburger *meal* for the same price as some of their coffees.

I looked around and somethin' caught my eye: apparently I had a new fan. There was some chick starin' at me from the bar. Starin' *hard*. I might've tried to holla but it was clear she didn't even see me. She was straight-up kickin' it with the the little white rabbit. So I figured I'd have a little fun with her and stare back. I guess she woke up 'cause she kinda snapped back and turned the other way. Then she got up and left.

Hmmmmmm...Cute.

Nice walk...cute lil frame...

Woahhh. Wussup dookie? Allll-ry-tee-then...How YOU durin?

After out-staring the weird chick, I looked around the café for somethin' else to grab my attention. I remembered that I hadn't checked my email in a couple of days. Occasionally, I do the 'net-dating thing...it passes the time. I used to think that 'net-daters were crazy, just like everyone else did. But my boy, Antoine, made a good point: he said the women I wanna meet aren't chillin' at the clubs or in the mall 'cause they have better things to do. But, they do have computers and email 'cause they're also COOs or lawyers, or build websites. He made a lot of sense, so I've been 'net-dating for about three months now.

I plugged my laptop into one of their jacks and got on the Internet. I love this whole wireless thing. As soon as I logged into my email, *some*thin' *told* me not to check the messages and *definitely* not to respond. But wha'd I do?

The first letter was from MsPhatBooty:

> I liked your page. Maybe we could hook up some time and get to know eachother better. Check out my

LOOKIN' IN THE MIRROR

page and let me know when you gonna take me out.

The second was from 2thik4U:

> Yo, what's up? I'm 5'3, 190. Let me know if you can handle this.

The third, ClassyLady410:

> Greetings. I don't usually approach men on the 'net because, I don't feel that a woman should approach a man. But I saw your page and felt that you met my standards. Most men can't support my taste in the finer things, but I think that you can. Let's get together for lattés.

Number four was junk mail

Last—and certainly the least, ImDaFinest:

> Waddup nigga, u fine as hell. I like ya home page. Sound like one a doze educated niggas. I can dig dat. Muhfuckas like you realy know how to treat a bitch rite. U seem so considerit. Make sho u get back wit me, wit yo fine ass.

The last one took the cake. *I sound like one of those educated niggas??? I really know how to "treat a bitch rite"??? Ohhh, my God! THIS is the state of women today? I think I'll just jack off for the rest of my life.*

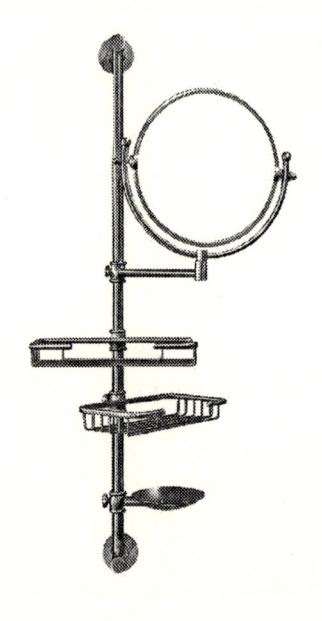

That Evening

LOOKIN' IN THE MIRROR

RHOyalHighness: you know what I hated most about you being with Denise?

Bou-G: what?

RHOyalHighness: when she told u she was jealous of u talkin/hangin w/ me. And u *actually* put me on pause!

Bou-G: tru. I never should've cut u off. We've been friends 2 long 4 that.

RHOyalHighness: u gave up 2 much of urself 2 please her. That's unrealistic and unfair.

Bou-G: tru

Bou-G: I'm glad I'm not w/ her anymore. She held my spirit down.

RHOyalHighness: u ain't neva lied! I've *never* seen u that whipped b4 in my life! U've always been so independent N the past.

Bou-G: Hey! Guess who I saw today?

RHOyalHighness: Who?

Bou-G: Kevin Schaefer!

RHOyalHighness: Hell 2da naw! 4 real?

Bou-G: yeah! I was going down the street 2 this coffee shop & saw him. he said his co. moved him up here & gave him a $ raise.

RHOyalHighness: that's really good!

Bou-G: and I talked 2 my folks the other day...dad said Tam is getting drafted by the WNBA. She might b up here 2, if DC gets her. But he said a lot of other teams are looking @ her 2

RHOyalHighness: that's the bomb! I'm really proud of her. and now y'all got 2 playin pro ball...& twins @ that! That's cool. Tamara getting drafted... ^5!

RHOyalHighness: woah... how'd your mom respond to this news?? Does she know you wanna move to DC yet?

Bou-G: yeah, I told her that day. She was trying 2 talk me outta moving. Then I talked to my dad and he told me about Tamara. that's when I realized why my mom was being like that

RHOyalHighness: what's your time table for moving?

RHOyalHighness: if you don't get the position, are you gonna stay here or go ahead and move?

RHOyalHighness: hello?

RHOyalHighness: GERALD!!!!!!!!!!!!!!!!!!!!!

RHOyalHighness: what's taking u so long to respond? I know ur a** can type fast!

Bou-G: oh, my bad. I'm chattin with this chick that's up here. I'm trying 2 get a date before I leave. She's pretty cute. I'm sending u her page link in email.

RHOyalHighness: tryin 2 get a date b4 u leave??? Killin time, huh?

Bou-G: I just wanna go on 1 date b4 I leave. The way I figure, I'll kick it w/ Kev a couple nights, & @ least 1 date = well-rounded experience.

RHOyalHighness: I got the pic. She's str8. She still ain't cute as me, tho.

RHOyalHighness: I'm surprised u're even n u're room...why aren't u out?

Bou-G: I was writing notes 2 remember 4 the meeting. I'm not looking fwd 2 it. This is gonna take all week!

RHOyalHighness: well, I'll leave U 2 ur mackin. Hubby's home & I'm gonna get some.

Bou-G: LOL! Go get yours... Gotta tell U about these bogus ass emails I got next time.

LOOKIN' IN THE MIRROR

RHOyalHighness: see u when u get back!
Bou-G: Peace.
RHOyalHighness: bye-bye.

Mia is the only female that knows me as well as my mom. She was our lone ranger, the girl in our bunch. Everyone in the neighborhood knew: mess with her and you gotta answer to the crew. My sister & brother had a crew just like that, but they were much younger than we were. Kids in the neighborhood called them "Part 2", as a continuation of our "Crew."

In the other I-M, I was doin' pretty well w/ Ms. Cutie. We were tryin' to decide where we wanted to go on our date. I was about to leave this chat room that I'd been idling in, then Will showed up and we just started shootin' the breeze about pretty much, nothin', but I was also amused by what was goin' on with the other people in the room. Folks on the internet be trippin'.

Im_Will_I_Wont: yo, G!, you in here?
MissCelie: Hey, Deezl, CALuv is really a man
Bou-G: yeah, what's up?
MissCelie: and he doesn't even live in Cali
Dolla-dolla-bill: Hey Will!
Im_Will_I_Wont: saturday still on?
VinDeezL100: how do you know?
Bou-G: well, I don't know...I might be out til Sun.
MissCelie: cuz my cousin knows him. they work at the same store
Bou-G: I'll let u know
Dolla-dolla-bill: Hey Will!

A. M. HATTER

    Lik-M-low: iiiiiiiiiiiittttttttt sssssssuuuuuucccccckkkkkkksssss   iiiiinnnnn hhhheeeeerrrrrreeeee

Im_Will_I_Wont: oh, cool

VinDeezL100: how'd you find out?

Dolla-dolla-bill: what WON'T u do?

MissCelie: I told her about our last convo b/c it was funny

Im_Will_I_Wont: hey, uhhh, have u seen Antoine's latest piece?

MissCelie: and when I mentioned the handle, she recognized it from some of their convos

Bou-G: I already know about it, Will

Dolla-dolla-bill: WON'T u lick my balls?

Im_Will_I_Wont: oh…

MagicDic214: All the fine b**ches need to IM me

VinDeezL100: that's f*d up, Celie

Bou-G: I'm cool w/ it, man. I ain't trippin

MissCelie: I kno. But I just wanted u 2 kno cuz I know u guys r IMing

Im_Will_I_Wont: a'ight…long as u ain't trippin

VinDeezL100: Hey, I'm gonna email u the pic he sent me.

Lik-M-low: @@@@@@@@@@@@@@@@@@@@@@@@@

Bou-G: lol…I'm talking to this chick in IM

VinDeezL100: lemme know when u get it

Bou-G: she wanna go 2 a New Orleans *style* restaurant, lol

MissCelie: ok

Lik-M-low: >>

LOOKIN' IN THE MIRROR

Im_Will_I_Wont: LOL, folks just don't know
MissCelie: I got it, DeezL
VinDeezL100: ok
Lik-M-low:
<<<<<<<<<<<<<<<<<<<<<<<<<<<<<<<<<<<<<<<<<<

Bou-G: I hope she ain't a holy roller...
Lik-M-low:
<<<<<<<<<<<<<<<<<<<<<<<<<<<<<<<<<<<<<<<
Dolla-dolla-bill: WILL u toss my salad?
Bou-G: she asked me if I believe in God just b/c I don't like gospel
MENLuvMe: Hey everybody!
keepgrinding24-7: has anyone seen BigBooty4U?
Im_Will_I_Wont: oh yeah? lol, u might wanna keep her then
MagicDic214: hey menluvme
Lik-M-low: no
VinDeezL100: no
MagicDic214: no
MissCelie: no
Im_Will_I_Wont: I just had a holy roller 'bout 3 wks ago - she gave it up *real* quick
MissCelie: HEY! That's my cousin! He sent u a pic of my cousin!
Bou-G: of course.
VinDeezL100: what/??????? r u serious??
MagicDic214: I tried to call u the other night
Im_Will_I_Wont: she workd that brain too, man...
MissCelie: YES! Omg! I have
MENLuvMe: oh really? Why didn't u leave a message?
Bou-G: << shaking head. u somethin else...

A. M. HATTER

    MagicDic214: I don't like talking to voicemail, man
    MissCelie: to tell her!
    VinDeezL100: LOL! No offense, but your cuz is pretty cute
    Im_Will_I_Wont: I talked to Ant the other day
    MENLuvMe: well…that's why I haven't called back.
    CALuv: WHO'S THE B8TCH IN HERE, TELLIN FOLKS I'M A MAN????
    MagicDic214: CHILL WITH THE CAPS, CALuv!!!!!!!!!!!!!!!!!!!!
    Bou-G: really. What's up w/ him?
    Lik-M-low: <<<listening to snoop dogg
    keepgrinding24-7: get off the caps, a**hole!
    Im_Will_I_Wont: he's gettin his hair locked up
    CALuv: F8CK YOU! I'LL KICK YOUR QSS!
    keepgrinding24-7: u ain't kickin my *zz, faggot!
    Bou-G: it's about time. he's been talkin about doin that for a few years now
    Dolla-dolla-bill: Yo, he doesn't wanna kick your *ss, he wants to lick it!
    CALuv: F8CK U, M8THA F8CKA! I'LL WOOP BOTH OF Y'ALL SSSES, STR8 CALI STYLE, B8TCH! U DON'T WONT NONE!
    Im_Will_I_Wont: lol, that's what I said
    Lik-M-low: Guess who's back in the mutha f*ckin houuse
    MagicDic214: Hey MenLuv, that's shady that u haven't called. I thought we were cool?
    Bou-G: guess who I saw today?
    Lik-M-low: wit a fat d*ck for yo' mutha f*ckin mouuuth

LOOKIN' IN THE MIRROR

MENLuvMe: I put an alert on CALuv, everybody
Im_Will_I_Wont: who
Lik-M-low: Ur right! I do luv u! can I hit that?
Dolla-dolla-bill: too late, I already did
Bou-G: Schaefer
VinDeezL100: ^5
Im_Will_I_Wont: whaaaaaat??? how's he doin?
MENLuvMe: Magic, we are cool, but I can't call u 12x a day. I have to work
keepgrinding24-7: I luv u!
Bou-G: he's doin alright, livin up here now
MagicDic214: so basically u're sayin u don't wanna mess w/ me no more
Dolla-dolla-bill: WILL!!!
Bou-G: man, lemme tell u about these emails I got
MENLuvMe: it's not that, I just can't call u all the time
VinDeezL100: so, Celie, how's it goin w/ ur BF?
MagicDic214: but u can come over whenever you want and f8ck me all night…
Im_Will_I_Wont: what happened?
MENLuvMe: Magic, that's not cool.
keepgrinding24-7: why u gotta put a n**ga on blast, yo?
Bou-G: maaaaan…I'm startin to wonder why I even listened to Ant…
keepgrinding24-7: yo, Menluv! Drop the zero, I'll treat u like a queen
MagicDic214: u know, it's shady that u don't wanna holla at ya boy until u got time to fit me in

A. M. HATTER

Im_Will_I_Wont: oh, talking bout datin on the net?
MENLuvMe: this is not the time to discuss this
MissCelie: LOL! that sounds like a line from a porn movie, DeezL
Dolla-dolla-bill: WILL! I bet I know what u WILL do!
Bou-G: yeah, man
MENLuvMe: you have my number. u can call right now and we can talk about it
MagicDic214: ZERO? who's name were u yelling the other night, who's sheets were u biting?
Bou-G: this one chick talkin bout she 5'3, 190
Dolla-dolla-bill: u WILL SUCK it!!!
MENLuvMe: I don't have to deal with this. I'm leaving.
Lik-M-low: YOOZ A HOOOOOOO
Im_Will_I_Wont: aww, man.
Im_Will_I_Wont: <<<laughin @ G
VinDeezL100: pow, chika-pow, chika-pow-wowwwww
Lik-M-low: YOOZ A HOOOOOOOO
VinDeezL100: well, I'm signing off now. c u 2morrow, Celie
Im_Will_I_Wont: that's u all the way, dawg!
Dolla-dolla-bill: u WILL lik my sack!
MissCelie: bye DeezL
Bou-G: Yeah & this other 1 talkin bout she doesn't feel a woman should approach a man
Dolla-dolla-bill: it sucks in here
Bou-G: But she thinks I can "support" her taste in "the finer things"
Dolla-dolla-bill: u guys suck!
Miss Celie: then leave, Dolla

LOOKIN' IN THE MIRROR

Im_Will_I_Wont: hell naw... hi-cappin ass
Dolla-dolla-bill: u can't tell me what to do!
Bou-G: I know, man... but I just gotta FWD u the other one... it was just too triflin
Lik-M-low:
&(^*/&%&^${$_(&@)@^!*&$#*@_](#+)(#*@^#^%@!(#
Lik-M-low:
##
####

Dolla-dolla-bill: I know what you WILL do!
Im_Will_I_Wont: lol, damn
MissCelie: LikM! r u that bored???
Dolla-dolla-bill: u WILL bow down and hummmmmmm on my balls!
MissCelie: don't u have anything to talk about?
Bou-G: well, I'm gonna start surfin now. I probably won't respond anymore...
Dolla-dolla-bill: I know what u WILL do!
Im_Will_I_Wont: a'ight...peace.
MissCelie: go IM somebody...u're wack
Dolla-dolla-bill: HEY WILL! SEE THIS>>>>> (_I_)
Dolla-dolla-bill: KISS IT!!!!

A new IM box popped up.

2Kute: Hey there.
Bou-G: Hey, who's this?
2Kute: just a chick who's bored.
Bou-G: so you decided to IM me, huh?
2Kute: lol, it's not like that.
Bou-G: so what made you IM me?
2Kute: your profile said you're black and that you like rock and techno and other music.
Bou-G: you like that kind of music?
2Kute: actually, yeah. I grew up in a mixed neighborhood, so I have varied tastes.
Bou-G: Oh really? Where'd you grow up?
2Kute: Oklahoma
Bou-G: Oh, cool. I got folks in Oklahoma. What part are you from?
2Kute: Tulsa
Bou-G: That's where my people are from.
2Kute: oh really?
Bou-G: Yeah, you know Donovan Hollis?
2Kute: That's my brother!
Bou-G: Anita??
2Kute: Who is this?
Bou-G: this is Gerald!
2Kute: maaaan! that's a trip!
Bou-G: I thought your SN was Ghettobooty or something?
2Kute: It was, but I don't use it anymore. That's so middle school.
Bou-G: yeah...that was kinda wack.
2Kute: so whats up with your SN?
Bou-G: awww, this broad on here said I'm bougie cuz I don't like chicks w/ tats
2Kute: lol...I guess. So what r u doin' on here?

LOOKIN' IN THE MIRROR

Bou-G: just killin time... I'm in DC on biz

Bou-G: what r u up to?

2Kute: You haven't talked to Donovan in a while, have you?

Bou-G: Actually, I just came from one of his rodeos last weekend. Why?

2Kute: cause I've been living in DC for 6 months now.

Bou-G: What??? Nobody even told me!

Bou-G: You get a job up here or something?

2Kute: Yeah. It was hard at first b/c nobody was hiring, but a friend of mine let me stay with her for a while until I got a job. I've been slowly paying her back since I got hired.

Bou-G: wow. You keep that friend. Not many will trust you to do that.

2Kute: lol, you ain't lyin'. u know us. We don't help our mommas.

Bou-G: So what do u do?

2Kute: I'm in the tech support department for one of those sidewalk journals.

Bou-G: Oh, so you're using your degree! Congrats!

2Kute: lol

Bou-G: So what's it called?

2Kute: Sidewalk Journal

Bou-G: ha! hell naw... I guess I'll have to snag a copy while I'm here, then. See what y'all r about.

2Kute: Yeah, do that! There's this chick in there, that's my girl... she has a column called "Rants, by Jay Phillips", and man! She *keeps* me rollin'!

2Kute: And there's this other writer, I don't know him, but he's from some little town outside New Orleans and at the top of his column, they always

A. M. HATTER

have his pic and a short profile: "Arthur Hightower: Lifetime Saints fan and pounder of uteri!!!!

Bou-G: hell naw! That dude is *sick*! ROFL

Bou-G: Man, you are soo lucky. You don't know how many people pay loads of money for college and end up working in completely different fields. When I started, I was teaching to pay off my student loans. (one of those Clinton bills) but my degree was in business.

2Kute: Really? I didn't know you taught...

Bou-G: Well, not really... I was just trying to emphasize my point.

2Kute: LOL! You dork!

2Kute: even so, at least teaching is professional. This girl I know is still at home working at the mall. Her degree is in psychology. She can't do nothin' until she gets her masters.

Bou-G: yeah, psychology is a tenure field. It's funny, I'd think that if you have to have a masters to be able to really work in that field, then the bachelor wouldn't be an option...

Bou-G: or it would have a 5-6 year minimum for completion. It doesn't make sense to get a 4-year degree that you can't use.

2Kute: tru...but at least I got out of that wack-ass town!

2Kute: Woooo-hoooo!

2Kute: <<<doing happy dance

Bou-G: Tulsa isn't all that bad...it's no Houston, but it's not that bad.

2Kute: whatever. I'm just glad to be out of that hellhole. You couldn't pay me to go back.

Bou-G: Then DC is treating you well?

2Kute: Yeah, it's cool. The men up here are great! there's so much to do

LOOKIN' IN THE MIRROR

2Kute: and not just club stuff. I go to these performance venues where they have jazz some nights, poetry...sometimes improv.

Bou-G: that's cool. I'm glad you're liking it.

Bou-G: well, I'm gonna lay it down now. Get some shut-eye. Call me tomorrow so we can hook up while I'm here: 212-158-0064, room 325.

2Kute: Okay. See ya.

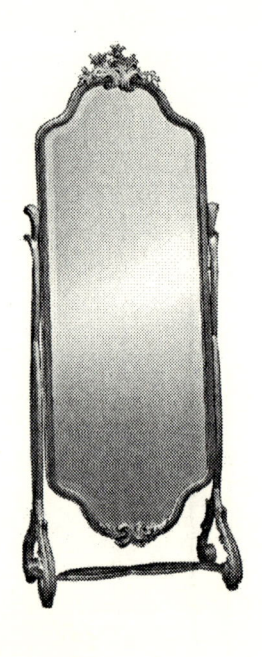

Wednesday Evening

LOOKIN' IN THE MIRROR

DeFi was a big success. Rick and Terry offered to sneak some of our pieces into an upcoming fashion show a few months ahead to test reactions. My college professors always told me that I had a knack for schmoozing and bullshitting. Somehow I picked up the BS talent in high school. It's an aptitude that has proven useful in all walks of life, then and now (unlike algebra).

I'd been floating on a zephyr ever since Monday. Just couldn't stop mentally fluffing my ego. I laid back on my couch to think. All I needed to do was find my roommate so that we could go dancing. I decided that I needed a gay bar. They have great music and the fem guys can accessorize like nobody's business. I like to get ideas from them. I also realized that I needed some male entertainment, and gay bars are cool for that because a lot of the guys look really good, but I don't have to worry about them trying to pick me up. They don't want me; they're gay. I love it. Then I can just sit back and fulfill my calling, which is to peep talent. Who needs a boyfriend? There are men all around, ripe for my viewing. I don't have to meet you...hell, I don't care to know you. I just want to chill and peruse your body.

Except for Mr. Man in the suit from the other day. *Who was he?* I wondered, *What is his name? What was he doing there? Will I ever see him again? Oh, of course I will,* I answered myself, *I'll see him once or twice every week as he comes in to have lunch with his wife, I'm sure. That must've been why he was there.* Alanis Morissette must've been thinking about me when she sang the part about meeting the man of

A. M. HATTER

your dreams and then meeting his beautiful wife. But with my luck, it won't even be that… I'll probably meet his beautiful husband.

((((*Click, click-click.*))))

The door bopped open. "Hey! What's on for tonight, Vic?"

My roommate was just the person to interrupt my parade of cynicism. She wasn't trying to hear drama or anything—at least until tomorrow, after she's had a great dance with a Latin hottie. She's been hollering about some guy at the salsa club that looked like John Secada for two weeks now.

"Man, I wanna go to the club… Let's go to the salsa club," she said, looking all bright-eyed.

"Girl, I'm *right* behind you!"

Hanging her coat, "I hope I see my little hottie tonight," she said then roamed to the kitchen.

"GIRL, YOU'RE STILL TALKIN' ABOUT HIM??" I yelled to her, as she dug something out of the refrigerator to chomp on.

She walked back into the front room with a stick of mozzarella string cheese and bucked her eyes at me, "GIRL! I'm telling you! He was SO SEXY!" She exhaled. "I mean… I couldn't even talk. He just took my hand, asked me to dance, and I followed. He was," she paused, "magically delicious." I laughed at her as she looked to the ceiling all mesmerized. "Besides, you *know* if you saw some guy that looked just like *your* man, Enrrrrrrique, you'd probably keel over and die, too."

I laughed. "True. You do have a point there. But, I'd keel over and die if I saw a number of guys at

LOOKIN' IN THE MIRROR

the club…Vin Diesel, Keith Hamilton Cobb, Oded Fehr, Steve Harris, Lennox Lewis, Antonio Sabato, Jr., Russel Wong… ooh! Lenny Kravitz! Duhhhlllllllllllllllllll…."

"Okay, wipe the drool, honey. That's not attractive and you can't go to the club with me looking like a butt-hole." (laughter)

"You know what? I was thinking the other day that maybe I should try to look like some kind of wacko. Then I won't attract the guys with piercings anymore."

She giggled. "Ohhh-kayyyy??"

"Man! I don't know what it is with me. I went to the clubs at home and only the guys with gold teeth would holla. When I stopped going, people acted like they didn't understand why. Suddenly, I'm anti-Black—and *I'M* BLACK! But when I go to the 'white clubs', it's the rave guys with piercings. And at the salsa clubs, it's the short guys with a million tattoos! I don't *get* it!"

"At least you don't attract gay women."

I laughed hard at that one. She did have one up on me.

"That's true!" I exclaimed. "Still, I wonder why those guys think that I'd be interested in them. I mean, I look as plain as they come. Here they are with gold teeth or tattoos or piercings out the wazzoo and they think that *I'd* like that? Do I *look* like someone who'd be attracted to that??"

"Oh, but you know the funniest time was when we went to—what? Was it Chicago? …. NO! It was Georgia! That time when I went home with you for

Thanksgiving and that homeless man tried to talk to you when we got off the train!!!" She erupted into laughter.

"Man, that wasn't funny."

"You were SO devastated! You just kept talkin' about how your stock had dropped!" She continued laughing. "Ohhhhhh! That was *SO* funny!"

"That wasn't funny," I said, staring at her blankly with the slightest hint of I'm-gonna-kick-your-ass-in-a-second-if-you-keep-messing-with-me.

"You're just mad 'cause it happened to *you*! 'Cause if it was me, you'd never let me live it down."

"Whatever, man. Look, are we goin' to the club or what? I gotta blow off some steam."

"Dag, what's got yo' drawls in a knot?"

"Man," I shook my head, "you wouldn't believe what happened the other day."

She looked at me as I paused, intrigued and confused at the same time. She knows I'll tell a good story, even when it's bad news. "Something tells me I should get ready for a story."

"Hell yeah! Man, I went in, already in a rush 'cause I had to do this story, right?"

She listened intently as I recanted Monday's events, with all its peaks and valleys. In the meantime, we readied ourselves for a night on the town. I decided to wear light-colored jean bellbottoms, tight in the butt and very wide at the bottom with a wide belt in *very* deep purple, and a fitted lavender top with choir-robe sleeves. My shoes were cool because they were authentic 70s stack-heeled sandals. I got them from a consignment shop. I love them to death because the fronts look like g-strings for your feet and they have a psychedelic pattern with purple, gray and lavender. They're ultra cool. My roommate put on some tight brown pants and a brown, khaki, and ivory striped sleeveless vest-like top with long tails. I love that thing. She accented with an ivory choker that had a gold fob dangling.

It's funny when we go out because we never cease to run into these movie-like scenarios. This particular night, we ran into this chick sitting on the steps outside our place, sobbing like a teenager who was just dumped. My roommie, being the do-gooder that she is, asked her what was wrong.

The girl replied with her face in the pit of her elbow, "I (gasp) just (gasp) caught my (gasp) boyfriend cheating on (gasp) me."

*Oh my gosh. She **is** a teenager who's just been dumped*, I thought. *How old is this chick? Is she **for real**?? Crying **outside**, on the **steps** about her boyfriend???* Don't get me wrong: catching your boyfriend cheating is certainly a heartbreaker. And to cry is not an unusual reaction. But, *outside on the steps*??? Sheesh, have some dignity!

They continued to talk and I grew antsy. Roomie wanted to play consoler and I wanted to dance. There was only one thing to do, if only to get things moving again.

"Hey, you wanna go out with us? It's girls night out!" I said with the most dignified voice I could think of and flashed a grin.

"I don't have any money."

"We'll cover you," my roommate replied.

A. M. HATTER

That wasn't, in the slightest way, part of my plan. It was so convenient it almost seemed like a scam. But I didn't want to stand there until I got bored enough that I start being mean, so I went along with it for roomie's sake. And with that, the three of us were off to see the wizard, like a formulaic feel-good movie full of self-discovery and tumultuous friendships. It was real life, but I smelled so much corn in the air that I could've sworn it was Thanksgiving. But I have to admit: it *is* more fun in a chick trio, running down that Triangle like Tex Winter.

(Sam Barry, you got *nothin'* on *this*! Whatchu want?! Whatchu want??? Shiiiiiiiiiiiiiit, boyyyyyyyyyyyy! Whaaaaaaaaaaaaaat????)

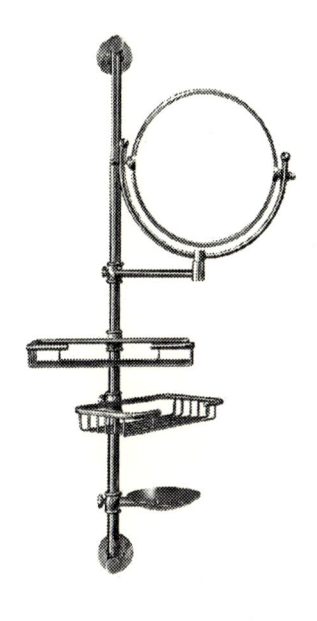

Wednesday, 1p.m.

A. M. HATTER

"I'd like to bring your attention to page 15, regarding the employee benefits expenses."

I spotted an error that would've completely thrown off accounting and possibly gotten someone fired. I was about to get some big cool points.

"I don't—ohhh, I see it. Wow. You have a good eye, Gerald."

Bob Logan was one of those young cats, maybe mid-to-late thirties, that started his own business in his twenties and jumped on the trend of sellin' out to retire early. He was real cool...*real* cool. Any time we weren't in a meeting, he toted me along on these constitutionals, and went on and on about how he just wanted to "leave the corporate world and just travel, or maybe teach, or...well I'll figure it out when I cross that road." It was cool to me 'cause we'd dip out, go catch a game or whatever... Come back, handle business and call it a day. He had free tickets to some of everything. I wanna be like Bob when I grow up. He's my role model.

"Thanks," I replied.

I'm the man! I'm the man! (Doing old school dances: Cabbage patch, Reebok, BizMarkie, MC Hammer—Uh-oh! Uh-oh! Hold the leg!)

"I'm sure it'll show in the notes. We'll correct that and have the new pages for you tomorrow when you come in."

I nodded. "That's fine, but fax them to Texas as soon as you have them. If anyone spots the error, I want them to know that it's already handled."

"I'll handle that as soon as the meeting is over, Mr. Boudreaux."

LOOKIN' IN THE MIRROR

The chick almost scared the shit outta me. I really hadn't noticed that she—one of his many assistants that always responded, "I'll handle that as soon as…"—was sittin' in the corner the whole time. They're like those fembots from 'Austin Powers'. Well, without the machine gun tits anyway. I think they're cyborgs.

I smiled just slightly and nodded to give approval. We continued crunchin' numbers and goin' over contracts until everything looked clear.

"Well, this was very productive! You wanna grab a bite to eat?" Bob asked.

"Hey, I'm game," I replied. I knew he had something up his sleeve to make it a business lunch so he could use the company credit card.

"Good! I want you to meet a couple of our local celebrity accounts. We'll make it a working lunch. I took the liberty of scheduling it right after the meeting. I figured you'd be hungry," he let out fat chuckle, "I hope you don't mind."

"No, not at all. Who am I going to meet?"

He gave me a sly grin, "You'll see when we get there."

I don't think he really knew. He probably just called a few people and waited to see who'd show up. We took the train to this posh restaurant attached to a ritzy hotel. We saw one of the accounts on the way to the hostess desk.

"Hey! John! I'm glad you could make it!" They gripped hands and Bob swung his other hand in my direction. "John, this is Gerald Boudreaux. He's here for the Blitson purchase."

85

"Oh, okay. Nice to meet you Gerald." We gripped hands. "Boo-droh…is that French?"

"Yeah, yeah…my dad is from Louisiana," I replied.

"Oh, okay," he nodded, "I bet that's a cool accent to have in the family."

"Well, you can call it that. I call it barely comprehensible!" I laughed. "I used to hate goin' to my grandparents' house because they'd always smack me for disobeying them…*I* just didn't know what the hell they were sayin'!"

They laughed as I adlibbed. I had 'em rollin'.

Comin' out of the laughter, Bob broke news to John: "Gerald will hopefully be the head honcho when the deal is done."

"Oh, wow. So, you'll be movin' here?" John asked.

"Well, yeah… I mean, if I'm chosen for the position," I grinned, "then I guess I'll start house-huntin' in the fall or winter."

"Really, what area?"

"Not sure…maybe Bethesda or Chevy Chase, I don't know, possibly Alexandria—or right inside Silver Spring. I hear that's really comin' up."

"Oh, yeah. I just bought over there. I'll tell ya about some good houses after lunch."

The waitress informed us that our table was ready. I observed all the patrons as we waded through the packed restaurant. They were all kindsa weird: they had this pseudo-New Yorker-Californian-southern business-style to 'em. There was just no gauge to who they were. Some had the crisp-cuffed look, and some

LOOKIN' IN THE MIRROR

were all Hollywood-ish, like this woman wearing this extra tight mini-skirt posed up next to the bar...she had her leg propped out to the side. What's that about? Then, others had the Michael J. Fox: white shirt with a tie and jeans. *What kind of place is this?* I wondered, *Is it upscale or not?* Our table was just inside from the sun deck. The other guy was already seated.

"Barry! Are we late?" Bob asked as he looked at his watch.

"No, no. You guys aren't late. I was really, really early." He stood up and shook our hands. "I just came from getting my hair cut down the street so I just decided to walk on over. I've only been here about ten, fifteen minutes."

"Oh, all right... Well, let me introduce you to Gerald Boudreaux. He's the liaison for the Blitson purchase."

"Oh really!" Barry said. His voice had a hearty, gruff quality. *(HA! Hearty & Gruff...sounds like a new kind of spaghetti sauce.)* "Got any idea who might be takin' Bob's place?" he asked while sittin' down.

"No, not yet. As far as I know, they haven't even really started lookin' at candidates," I replied.

We must've stayed there for about two hours, just talkin' and eatin'. Barry is quite the character. Actually, they both are. Barry is one of those rough, comical guys like a loud uncle at a family barbeque. John was funny too, but with pointed analytical humor and he used a lot of analogies. Apparently the two appear on a local show that reviews movies and critiques both local and syndicated movie critics. The two originally produced the show from their own pockets and solicited Logan Marketing to handle all of their PR. The partnership has since recruited sponsors and thickened their fan base, but the partnership would only continue based on their impression of me.

"Okay," Barry said finishing off his chew, "you tell me your top ten and we'll tell you if we're stayin' with Logan."

Woah, heart beating...do they always make their decisions that way? I thought.

"Top ten guy movies, or top ten comprehensive?" I asked, so I could get an idea of what they wanted to hear.

"Just...your top ten. We wanna know what you like," Barry replied vaguely.

Dammit. No clues. He's good.

"You know, I might have to cop out on that one, man. I'm a well-versed guy when it comes to movies. I mean, I could *say* Godfather-one, Fight Club, and Dogma...Star Wars—the franchise, ummm...Caveman, Spiderman...Misery, umm, the Matrix franchise...and... Terminator-two, but then I'd be leavin' out classics like Krull, The Usual Suspects, Maltese Falcon, A Christmas Story, Comin' To America, Austin Powers, Thomas Crown Affair, American Beauty, Good Will Hunting, The Color Purple, Clash of the Titans, Five Heartbeats, Galaxy Quest, The Shadow, Batman-one... Come on, you gotta break it down into genres for me," I finished with a smile.

They both looked shocked.

LOOKIN' IN THE MIRROR

"That's a pretty comprehensive list," John said, nodding slowly, "You're the first person I've met to say Krull in the same breath as The Usual Suspects."

"*Cave-man*???" Barry questioned, lookin' like he halfway knew what I was talkin' about, but couldn't believe it. "Are you talkin' about the movie with Ringo Starr and Dennis Quaid from, like, 1980?"

"Yeah. Caveman," I replied with a straight look, "'Macha! Macha!'"

Barry pounded his fist on the table. "Are you *kidding* me???" His eyes blew up to the size of grapefruit. Bob looked tense. But I knew that anyone who'd seen the movie couldn't hate me for thinkin' it's tight.

A huge smile spread across this face. "That's one of my favorite movies! I have that in my stash that I keep to the side!" He looked at John, "You know my stash of non-serious movies that nobody can talk about?"

"Oh, yeah. [Whispering] This guy is serious about his stash! If you say anything close to not loving those movies, he'll kick your ass."

Everyone laughed.

"I'm not joking!" John assured us.

Bob looked a hundred times more relaxed, like the cartoon character that drinks some water after eatin' a red chili pepper.

Barry continued with his amazement, "I can't believe you know that movie, man! I *never* run into people who have seen that! Dude, you're cool with me."

A. M. HATTER

And so it stood: I was cool with Barry. Logan—soon, Blitson Marketing—kept the account.

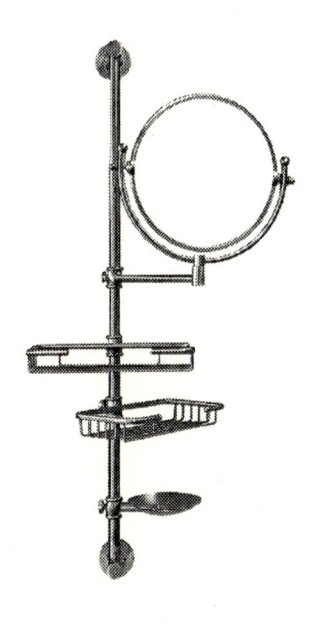

Thursday Night

(The Date)

A. M. HATTER

I checked out of my hotel and moved in with my cousin Anita for the remaining days of the trip. Before I left, I blocked out the whole week for the trip, and like I originally hoped, finished early. I later found out from Bob that John and Barry know a lot of people in the business arena, including some of Logan's other accounts. So he's *extra* happy that I went over well with them 'cause now that they're backin' me, the firm should sail smoothly. When I talked to my assistant earlier, she told me that "Mr. Logan, and some guys named John and Barry faxed in recommendations for you to become head of that division." So, you know a brutha's in a good mood, kinda dustin' off my shoulders and all.

I had few suits to choose from, it didn't take me long to get ready. Every blue moon, I can be a bit of a pretty boy. Tonight would've been one of those nights if I had my whole wardrobe. It was hard to decide which suit I wanted to wear.

For the past two nights I tried as much as possible not to talk to Donna, other than finalizing arrangements to meet—which we handled through email, to decrease any chances of canceling dinner. I figured that if we got a chance to talk at length, she might say somethin' kinda stupid and I wanted to go on at least one date before leavin' D.C. Since she was cute in the pic she sent me, I figured *why not?* But Anita obviously refused to quit buggin' me about it.

"What if she's ugly, man?" she asked.

"I'll have to suck it up and deal with it. Besides, I'll get cool points 'cause people will think I like her personality," I laughed.

LOOKIN' IN THE MIRROR

"Why do you *have* to go out with her? She might be crazy. What if she tries to kill you?"

"And? She *can't* kick my ass! Fight-or-flight'll switch on, then I'll just push her down, throw her weapon and run."

"What I don't get is…if you think she has the possibility to irk you if you talk to her, then why do you wanna go out with her anyway?"

"A lot of women irk me if we talk at length. I'm just try'na give her a chance."

"Man, you could take *me* out! At least you know I'm already cute. And I'm not crazy, either."

"Anita, if you're bored, call one of your men and go out with them. You're not suckering me into financin' your meal."

She started whinin', "Jairrr-uuuuld!"

My look told her it wasn't workin'.

"Man, you suck," she said and left. I finished gettin' ready.

* * *

I found out that Donna stays far from Anita's place so she decided that we'd both take the train and meet at the station. I thought it might be kinda hard to find her in the train station considering we'd never seen each other, but she gave me specific directions about where she'd be standin' and what she'd be wearin'. I guess that's enough.

So I got off the train and exited the station to the street where she said she'd be. I scanned the area to

A. M. HATTER

see if she was standin' outside, but I didn't see her. Though I did notice some country lookin' woman in this bright red dress. *HA!!* I almost laughed in her face. It looked like she was wearin' her momma's Easter dress from 1982. All she needed was the mutha fuckin' *hat*!

...Wait...red dress. Naw... Well, she's about 5'7. Thick legs... ...NO. That can't be her, I thought. (I hoped. I wished.) I looked around quickly for some other woman that might be wearin' red. *Blue, no. Maybe her...no, that's orange. Damn. Yellow...she's wearing pants. Mmmm-hmmm! Come to daddy! ...Okay, that's not her.*

I knew the country chick in the corner was Donna when I saw her. She looked exactly like the picture—well, her face did, anyway. (In the picture, she was wearin' this cute jean outfit with a hat. Damn! I'm supposed to be careful of the hats.) But I stood around, thinkin' that maybe—just maybe—my luck would be better.

It wasn't. She walked right up to me with this grin on her face.

Her mouth smacked as she started to talk, "You Jerrld?"

NOOOOOOOOOOOOOOOOOOOOOOOOOO OOOOOOO!

I wanted to hail a cab and move to Maine. All that time I'd been dodgin' her, thinkin' that she might be a "hallelujah person" and it turned out she's ghetto. If I had just called her, I'd have known this from jump. But no, I had to go out on a date before I left D.C. Hell, I could've gone out with Anita and been in a

LOOKIN' IN THE MIRROR

woman's company. She's my cousin, but who cares. Nobody else would know. Besides, I know I'd have fun with her. She probably knows all the cool clubs, too. But I'm out with...*Wanda*. I mean, Ophelia Shante'.

"Uh—yeah. Donna?"

[Smack] "Yeeeeah!"

NOOOOOOOOOOOOOOOOOOOOOOOOOOOOOOOOOOO[breath]OOOOOOOOOOOOOOOOOOOOOOOOOOOOOOOOOOOOOOOOOO!!!!!!

She smacked her mouth again, "So whatchu think?"

"Oh! Uh...Wow! I don't even know what to say!" I replied.

Smackin' her mouth, yet again, "You so sweeeeet."

"So...you ready to have dinner?" I asked her.

If she smacks her mouth again, I'll throw her across the street, I thought.

She nodded, grinnin' ear-to-ear.

"O-kayyy," I replied reluctantly.

We decided to walk to the club; she said it wasn't far. But she talked the *whole damn time*—she just wouldn't shut up—about *everything* pointless. And she kept smackin' her damn mouth! You'd think she was chewin' some gum or somethin'. (Why do people do that? You don't have to suck the roof of your mouth to talk. Just talk.) And of course she used ALL the ghetto lines: "See, wha' ha' happen wuh..." and— actually, the only thing she kept sayin' was "had" in places that she didn't need a helping verb. Like, "Then, my daddy *had* died." You don't need "had." The man died. That's it. "We *had **went*** to da sto'." Why do *I* get the dumb ones?? I got this dumb chick magnet or somethin'.

But anyway, the walk wasn't long—for me, anyway, but it was a little longer than I figured she'd wanna do, 'cause she was wearin' heels. But when we got there...man, I wanted to laugh. That place was straight-up in the alley. You look at it and you think, *hoodlum headquarters*, not some reputable jazz/dinner club. But it wasn't *totally* dilapidated...just...dirty lookin'. It looked like one of those places that would be on the soap operas as the shady liquor dive on the bad side of town where the down-and-out guy goes to wallow in his misery.

So we walked up to the line and there wasn't much of a wait. (But it didn't matter 'cause, hell, every minute felt like a millennium. I just kept waitin' for it all to end.) Don't you know that as soon as we walked up, people started snickering? That's how badly she was dressed, man. It wasn't that she was ugly. She just didn't know how to dress. (She only looked cute in that picture she emailed me 'cause her cousin bought the whole outfit for her birthday. She explained that on the way. Among other things.) It was one of those times where you're so humiliated you wanna laugh. Even this older dude in a *mustard-gold* suit was laughin'! I just kept thinkin' to myself, *how the hell did this happen?*

And it didn't end there! When she realized that they were all laughin' at her, she started shoutin' bible scriptures! I was like, *Oh my God! When's it gonna end!* It was like she was at Sunday school. You know how little kids do the Easter scriptures, where it's like [scripture], then the bible verse? Well that's how she did it, but really loud and ghetto. Some of the guys in line started to cheer her on and stuff. They're in line talkin' 'bout, "Preach it sista!" Everybody else looked like, "Why won't she shut up?" Then some dude walked up and told "us" that "we" had to be quiet or leave. So she wanted to leave. (Gerald: gettin' happy like a holiness church.) We went up the street to a café, had a couple of sandwiches and I called it a night. I need to sue her for emotional distress. Pain and suffering. I want punitive damages.

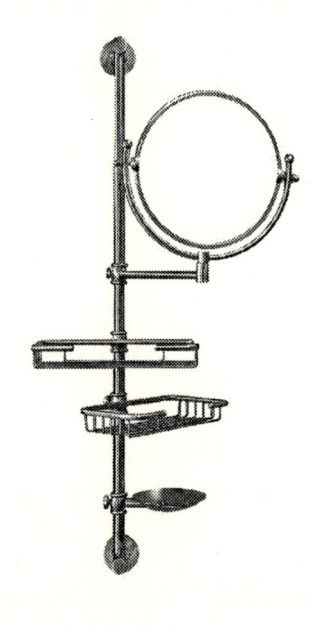

Friday, April 19

Eeeeearly Morning

LOOKIN' IN THE MIRROR

Anita made extensive use of her right to laugh at me when I told her about last night on the way to the airport. She went on and on sayin', "I told you so," and "See, that's what you get," laughin' to the point of tears between comments.

"What'd you get into last night?" I asked, tryin' to take attention off of me.

She sighed, "Well, at first this one guy I know called...I don't know why he's still callin' me, 'cause I never call him back."

I laughed. "What's wrong with'm?"

Her expression turned sour. "He's huuff, man...he's always tellin' these wack ass jokes, try'na get me to laugh."

I just chuckled. "So you went out with him?"

"Naw, I hooked up with this other guy I know."

"Oh. How long have y'all been datin'?" I asked while tryin' to get comfortable.

"Umm... I guess about three months, but it's not serious. We just get together every now and then to have dinner or hang out," she replied.

"Oh, that's cool... Man, I'm tired. I hope I have a row to myself. I'm gonna sleep like a baby," I let my seat back, "Wake me up when we get there."

"Hey man! Naw, you ain't goin' to sleep in here!"

"Why not?"

"Because *you're* the one who wanted to leave two days early, at the butt-crack-uh-dawn! I don't even have to be up right now! Hell, *I* should make *you* drive! ...Uh-uh, ain't *nobody* sleepin' in here unless I'm sleepin', too."

A. M. HATTER

I sat up, "Man, damn."

She started tellin' me about some chick she knows who's bad with her money and spends her time being flat broke, frequently borrowing money from her parents and friends or moochin' off of guys she dates. But I fell asleep somewhere during her speech about how people who have the fortune of being from families like her friend's or ours don't have the right to mess up or be broke. I don't know if she was being nice to me by lettin' me sleep, or if she just didn't know, but I was glad to be snoozin'—until I started one of those dreams where you slip and fall.

I jerked awake and gasped.

"Aaaah goody. That's whatchu get for fallin' asleep while I was talkin'," she said as she pulled up to the curb. "Anyway, we're here."

Since I didn't have to check any oversized luggage, I went straight to the gate. The downside is that I still had an hour and a half wait for my plane. I knew that if I sat down, I'd fall asleep, so I tried my best to keep movin'.

First I went to the bathroom to take care of some business.

As I walked in, the scent of disinfectant burned my nostrils. I settled at the urinal on the far end. Just when streamin' went live, this guy walked in and apparently forgot bathroom etiquette. *What the hell?? He couldn't go to the urinal at THE OTHER end??* I was trapped. I'm standin' there midstream and dude wants to be at the urinal *right next* to me! And *then*...he wanna talk. He was tryin' to peek—I know he was. You don't talk to a man as he's handlin' his

LOOKIN' IN THE MIRROR

biz-ness! I didn't wanna hear about how early he had to wake up. Hell, he saw I was there. Did he think I was bright and shining? And I didn't wanna hear about how he wanted to go home and see his wife, either. I shoulda peed on his ass!

Nevertheless, I just hurried up and got the hell out. I walked around...walked around...looked in some of the stores, read a few magazines...next thing I new, I found myself in an *airport bar* (I usually clown people who hang in airport bars) talkin' to the bartender.

"Haud night?" he asked, with one of those TV versions of a New York/Italian accent.

"No, not really. I'm just ready to go home," I replied.

He was a young guy—maybe about my age or a little older, with a thick upper body, a slight belly (no doubt, from being in his thirties), and a 2-day shadow.

"You look like you could use a drink," he said.

"Oh, noooo. It's too early for that."

"I hear ya," he replied, "Well, can I get anything else for ya?"

"No, but thanks man. I'm just tryin' to stay up."

"Here on bizness?" he asked.

"Yeah...I *was*."

"What's wit' that tone? Sounds like a story," he cracked a grin, waitin' on one.

I exhaled, "You know, man, if I wasn't as tired I might give you the story, but I just don't feel like talkin' about it," I said, shakin' my head in self-pity.

A. M. HATTER

"Man, you look rough… Here, have a juice on the house. What's your taste? Tomato? Orange, cranberry…?"

"Orange juice," I answered, as he did his bartender stuff and slid the glass up to me. I stuffed some singles in his tip jar, "Thanks man, thanks a lot."

"Ahh, no prob'm," he replied leanin' over the bar, "So, you travel a lot?"

"Well, yeah, but a lot more than usual in the last year…I've been workin' with the Blitson buyouts."

"Ohhhhh! Yeah, I heard about that. So you're a big wig, huh?"

"Well…let's just say I still got a long way to go," I replied.

Nodding, "Okay! I see a guy's modest and stuff… You're all right wit' me."

A voice came in over the intercom sayin' that my flight check-in would start.

"Well, that's me. I'm gonna go check in," I said, pickin' up my jacket and bag.

"Alright, guy. It was good talkin' to ya. Have a nice flight."

"Thanks. Have a good one."

Of course I still had to wait another month until I actually boarded the damn plane. The problem was, just as I thought I'd be able to get some rest, there I was again stuck with some asshole who just *wouldn't* shut the hell up. I'm on the plane at an ungodly hour of a Friday mornin' and the *only* jackass that's hooked on speed is next to me. Not only that, but he sat his fat ass

LOOKIN' IN THE MIRROR

in the chair next to me, when there were other seats open! Come on, now.

I started feelin' regretful for leavin'; all I could think was, *I should've stayed...kicked it with Anita and Kev.* I wish I could've kicked it with Kev, man. He wanted me to go with him to this drum'n'bass club. Well, we were stuck between that and college night at this other place, lol. But we'd pretty much decided on the drum'n'bass. It prob'ly woulda been tight as hell, too. Hangin' with Kev, you'll find yourself in some pretty funny situations.

I remember one time we caught one of those rock fest deals in Tulsa right after college. They're pretty cool venues. They'll bring some popular acts and a bunch of indie groups tryin' to be discovered. They pass out indie CDs and sell a lot of rave paraphernalia. But I stopped goin' to those 'cause, well, frankly I thought I was too old to go anymore. I could see if it was an actual concert, but these fests usually harbor a bunch of young cats. Sure, there's always the old guys with the bellies and long hair, but I'm not tryin' to be one of 'em.

So I was standin' around at the rock fest, and a random mosh pit sprung up. Somehow I made eye contact with a drunk guy (I don't know how it happened, but I just looked around and there he was). Then I thought to myself, *Back up or you're gonna get your ass stomped in the pit*. But the drunk guy looked at me and said, "Duuuude, you should get in therrre! Yerrrrr big enough!" Then he started laughin', spewing liquor-laden fumes and I'm tryin' like hell to just be nice and not puke all over his ass. A little while later

A. M. HATTER

this small-framed dude walked up, lookin' like he just busted out of some Woodstock footage, holdin' two beers. A dilemma arose: beer or mosh pit?? You could see it on his face. But his folding lawn chairs came into play, which I hadn't even noticed. (And I'm not talkin' about those 70s tri-fold lawn chairs with the fishing twine seat and the plastic armrests; I'm talkin' 'bout the new Teflon joints with the titanium alloy frames that collapse down to a simple tube.) He asked me to hold his beers while he and his inebriated friend started foldin' up the chairs and contemplating what to do with 'em. Kev returned from the Port-o-Potty as they weighed their options:

Beer Guy looked at me.
I looked at him.
Drunk Guy looked at Beer Guy
They looked at Kev.
Kev looked at me, then back at Beer Guy.

I handed the beers back and Beer Guy yelled, "Duuude! You guys got yerselves a couple-uh chairs!!" Then he high-fived me, and they downed the beers as they charged into the mosh pit, yellin', "Wooooooooooo-hoooooooooooooo!"

I looked at Kev, "...Did they just give us their chairs??"

Already stuffin' the chair tubes into his bag, "I think so!" he laughed.

When the band finished their set he said, "Let's go before they realize what they've done."

Man, that was comedy! It would've been fun to kick it with Kev again. But, after that date, I just gotta

LOOKIN' IN THE MIRROR

go back home. Me and Kevin can kick it some other time. I'm thinkin' I'll be movin' up there soon anyway.

* * *

I got home about ten years later...walked in the door, sat my stuff down and plopped on the couch. My brain started havin' bouts with itself:
Go to sleep. There's nothing to do.
I slept on the plane. Don't waste the day.
I can't go to sleep, I gotta tell Mia about what happened. It'll be comedy.
Call Dante.
I don't have enough energy for Dante today.
Go to sleep. You didn't get enough on the plane. Damn... fat... guy.

Zzzzzzzzzzzzzzzzzzzzzzzzzzzzzzzzzzzzzzzzzz zzzzzzzzzzzzzzzzzzzzzzzzzzzzzzzzzzzzzzzzzzzzzzz zzzzzzzzzzzzzzzzzzzzzzzzzzzzzzzzzzzzzzzzzzzzzzz zzzzzzzzzzzzzzzzzzzzzzzzzzzzzzzzzzzzzzzzzzzzzzz zzzzzzzzzzzzz.

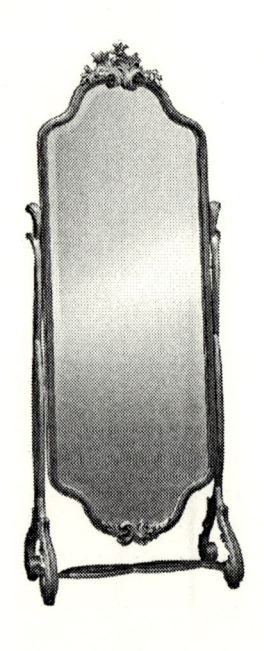

April 18

LOOKIN' IN THE MIRROR

Nothing is more annoying than being with one guy and trying to check out another guy, but not quite being able to see that other guy. Especially when you have to stick your neck out to see the other person; but you can't because you're with a guy already and you don't want to get called out.

I met this dude on the internet about two months ago. He saw my list of requirements and didn't seem to have a problem with it, so I assumed he met all the qualifications: no kids, non-smoker, stable job, light/no drinking, no tattoos, etc. He told me his height and weight when he sent me his picture: all approved. So we talked for about a month and he seemed like the kind of guy I could hang out with, so we agreed to go out for dinner.

Anyway, we were getting into the rail station and I caught a glimpse of a guy that looked exactly like Mr. Man in the suit. I just knew it was him, but I couldn't confirm. And the train took off before I could get a really good look. (Damn!)

"So do you go out with a lot of guys from the 'net?" date guy (Lamar) asked.

"Uuummm, yes and no. See, all the guys I date are usually from the 'net, but I don't just date a *whole lot* of guys. Does that make any sense?"

"Yeah. I know what you mean," he said. "So, you said in your email that you have a day off coming up. Any idea what you're gonna do?"

"Nah. I'll probably just sleep in."

"What? That's terrible. You really should find something to do, instead of sleeping all day."

"Like what? Mr. Smarty pants."

"Well, you could go to the park."

"Go to the *park*?? What would I do at the *park*?"

He shrugged. "Walk around...read."

"Walk around or read??? If I wanted to do that in the first place, I would've planned it. But seeing how that's not a premier activity in *my* world, that's why it got left off the list. Besides, I can walk around in my neighborhood or on the treadmill at my gym. If I wanted to read, I can read in my bed. What sense does it make to waste a Metro ride—not to mention the time—*just* so I can walk or read at the park? That's stupid! Furthermore, if I wake up at noon, rather than 8:30, there's still a lot that I can accomplish. Stores don't even open 'til 10. You're actin' like the mornin' is the most active part of the day." I paused and murmured, "Go to the park...*this* guy."

I shook my head in annoyance and laughed at his silly arrogance. He thought he had it all figured out. I'm sooo lazy and he just makes the most of his day, every day.

"Okay, okay. I just thought your time would be better spent doing something other than sleeping."

"But what's wrong with sleepin'?"

"It's lazy."

"But if I work like a dog every other day of the week, then haven't I earned the right to catch up on sleep that I've lost?"

He shrugged, "Yeah, I guess so."

"Well, then stop assuming that sleeping is automatically lazy, 'cause you never know what

LOOKIN' IN THE MIRROR

people's schedules are like. Besides, if it bothers you so much, then mind your own business."

He squinted and grinned at me, with that *Man, she's interesting* look on his face. "Have you ever considered law?"

"No, 'cause I don't wanna read all those documents. I'd get bored too quickly and I'm too argumentative to successfully argue any case. I'd go to jail for contempt every day. And when I get really heated, I start cussing…a lot," I admitted.

"The judge wouldn't like that too much," he laughed.

"Exactly."

We had dinner at a small jazz club in Georgetown. They serve New Orleans-style food. I really thought he'd be too dry for that type of thing, but to his credit, he's into Roy Ayers! If I didn't like Roy Ayers so much, I'd have been bored. Really, I wanted to go salsa dancing. I really don't know how to do any salsa; I usually just go and shake my hips a little. They just look so cool and the music is so peppy. Some people will dress up, but it's not about being spiffed up, they go for a workout. I like those active-dancing atmospheres like salsa—and the Chicago stepping clubs. They're cool, too.

Anyway, we're at the jazz joint, right? We walked up and the line was fairly short, but growing. Lamar and I kept a pretty good rate of conversation going, so I wasn't really paying attention to other stuff, although I generally glance around every now and then.

A. M. HATTER

We stood there, clowning our people (because you know we don't know how to dress) and their various levels of "overdressedness." This woman ahead had on a long gold sequined gown and big hair. Everything about her was overdone, from her make up—and earrings only Atlas could support—to her bright ass metallic gold heels. *That woman was sharp, sista! *snap* (wink-wink, nudge-nudge)*

Her date was just as bad: he had on just about every shade of yellow you could think of—with matching gators of course! I'm sure his intent was to match her excessive gold, but it just wasn't working. Not to mention the ponytail; he just reeked of the name Earl (but his homies call him Snake!). *Go 'head playa!*

For a long time these two were our only entertainment...then *they* turtled toward the line...

The guy was okay. Had on a nice casual suit...no prob there. But his date! OH MAN!! These two MUST have been on a blind date because the guy looked totally caught off-guard by his company. She must've been some kind of holy-roller because she had on a church dress. I mean, it's one thing to go semi-formal...cosmopolitan...even formal. But this chick had on some *80s ass* CHURCH DRESS!

It was this button-down springtime-red dress that fell mid-calf, with white collars, and the puffy Cinderella shoulders had a white button on each armband. The dress was lined in white cord and had these hideous, country ass flowers on her pumps—PUMPS, man! At the *club*! As soon as I saw them walk up, I immediately turned back to Lamar. You could hear the line snickering. And her hair was so

LOOKIN' IN THE MIRROR

fresh, it *looked* like you could smell the grease—and she had roller crimps. ☹

The poor guy looked so queasy. He had to know his date looked like an ass. As they stood there, more people took notice and it became painfully obvious that they were the main attraction. One guy ahead of Lamar and I laughed so loud you could probably hear him inside the club. Even Mr. Mustard Suit laughed!!

If that wasn't bad enough, church lady had the balls to start preaching when she realized everyone was laughing at her.

"This shall they have for their *pride*, because they have reproached and magnified themselves against the people of the LORD of hosts! Zephaniah 2, 10!"

Her date looked at her with a mixed expression of alarming confusion and disbelief as she continued wielding bible scriptures at us pride-stricken evildoers.

"Let not the foot of *pride* come against me, and let not the hand of the wicked remove me! Puh-salms 36, 11! In the mouth of the foolish is a rod of *pride*: but the lips of the wise shall preserve them! Proverbs 14, 3!"

Two guys in line started shouting back, "Preach it, sista!" and so forth.

What the hell? This ain't church! I'm trying to see Roy Ayers!

"The fear of the LORD is to hate evil: *pride*, and arrogancy, and the evil way, and the froward mouth, do I hate! Proverbs 8, 13!"

A. M. HATTER

She was causing such a commotion that it began to annoy the door people—not to mention, me. Someone of authority came outside to rectify the situation. He wasn't big like a bouncer, but he walked with importance and he had on one of those suits like he owns the club. The man marched up to Reverend Woman and shared a few words with her. By the way he moved his hands, one could only assume that he gave her the choice to shut up or leave. But they left, and that was clearly the memorable experience of the night. After that, everything was pretty tame. We waded through the line and eventually entered the tavern.

And man, was it was packed! Worse than sardines! There was pretty much standing room only—not that it was a big place anyway. But I can credit them with having a good ventilation system because if there were people smoking, I didn't really smell it.

It's funny how expressive the management was about wanting you to shut up. But I can understand. If you go to listen, then listen and quit running your mouth. Seems easy, but it was hard to be quiet after what happened in line. ☺

* * *

Evaluation: He kinda ticked me off, calling me lazy but he did all right with the little New Orleans and Roy Ayers. And he can dress! That's a big plus. Besides, he didn't say anything else stupid all night

LOOKIN' IN THE MIRROR

and he's really cute. And he didn't try to put his arm around me or hold my hand or kiss me. Good shot.

Verdict: A warm...no, cool maybe. I'll keep him around for further testing; he better have good taste in movies. He better like Italian food...and Michael Jackson.

And Prince.

And Incubus.

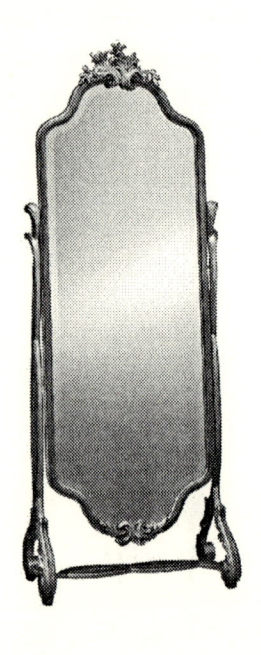

Friday Night

LOOKIN' IN THE MIRROR

"Man this show better be the bomb, chargin' me twenty-five damn dollars," Candace complained.

"Look, trust me on this. It's greatness," I assured her. "A few booger wolves creep in every now and then, but the standard is, *the* epitome! They bring in Black guys, White guys…a couple of Latin dudes—*all* fine. And they let you touch, too!"

Shawn couldn't join us for the "art" show. She and her hubby needed personal time so she stayed home and said she'd catch up with us next weekend.

The only thing I hate about these shows is that they take so damn long to get the men to the stage. I'm like, *I don't wanna see the emcee or play any freakin' games with a bunch of women; I don't care if the dancers are on hard or not. I just want them to come out, take off their clothes—hell, they can come out buck-naked already, it'd save some time—and then dance around a little. Then I can giv'm a five for effort and smack'm on the ass…NEXT*! Still, they're wayyyyy better than the male reviews at home. For that to be the strip capitol, they sure leave a lot to be desired—on the women's end, naturally, because the guys get all they want and then some.

Overall, the best "art show", as I call them, that I've been to was in Chicago. It was this cabaret style private show and the guys got *buck*-ass-naked! It sure woke me up. And it was my first show, too?! They wrapped body parts around the audience members and went tumbling around. I was like, *Daaaaaaaaaamn!* This one woman even put one guy's penis in her mouth. I was like, *Man, you don't know him! He could have a disease! Wake up the next morning with gonorrhea of the throat! Nasty ass.*

So we're sitting there, when finally, the emcee announced the first dancer. (I never remember their names.)

Candace jerked back in her seat. "Oh shit! I wasn't ready for this!" she declared.

"I told you!" I replied, nodding like I had the inside track or something.

The dancer cracked his whip and the audience screamed. The Egyptian-style music vaguely reminded me of something from a soundtrack... *'Prince of Egypt' or maybe 'The Mummy'?*

Kenya sat there making catcalls as the dancer passed by our table, kissing and licking her lips at him. "He is *fine*!" She giggled. "He got a big ol' booty!"

I just sat there with my head tilted to the side and this supreme look of contentment on my face. There was no need to make catcalls...no need for wild cheering or sultry faces. I just sat there, visually entertained (at last), chewing my gum slowly, like a hick chewing a straw of hay on his makeshift porch as the sun goes down. *Look at me: I'm Don Juanita, the Godmother.*

Three more dancers passed through, each better than the one preceding them. Well...the first two were tight as hell, but the third and fourth would make one super tight dude if you mix and match a few parts. Especially #3... He had a thrust that would shatter your whole bloodline. But the fifth came out and put it on us! Just his entrance alone was worth the cover.

LOOKIN' IN THE MIRROR

Somehow this cat got music from 'Silence of the Lambs' and came in on this dressed-up dolly. He was costumed like an escaped horror movie figure, covered head-to-toe in black leather with a black leather mask, like the people use for S&M. Hell, he deserved another $30. Given the costume, he could've punked out and gone with the Jason music, but I gave him cool points for going with a more leery, suspenseful sound...one that's only subconsciously recognized by the average person. I like him already.

He gets to the stage and the helpers, obviously acting according to instruction, fearfully reached to untie the cord as the dancer guy growled and jerked back and forth, trying to release himself from the cord and dolly that imprisoned him. The helpers reached once, and yanked their hands back...again, when they thought the "monster" wasn't looking and yanked back again. On the third time they reached for the cord, they were successful and got the hell out of dodge, as they released the cannibal to attack the unsuspecting audience; which, by the way, was totally entranced. It was pretty much the only time that you could clearly hear the music.

The six-feet-plus monster jumped off the dolly and landed in a squatting position with a loud boom. He growled and stretched his body upward like a raptor from 'Jurassic Park', then the music changed to 'Centipede' *(WOW! He knows Rebe Jackson!!! Points! Points! Points!)*, and he turned around and grabbed this woman from her seat and put her over his shoulder. He pounced around the room and lifted her above his head...paused and spun her to the floor. She opened her eyes to find she was okay and lying on her stomach. Then he jumped onto his arms and landed in a push-up position, but he rolled his back into a grind on her buttocks and proceeded into a full body caress. Her eyes blew up and the audience went wild. Then he tucked his arms under hers and rolled over onto his back. With some strange and quick maneuver, he got them both to a standing position. I can't really describe it, but it looked cool as hell. Even *I* started to show some reaction.

    Then ol' dude started to work the rest of the room and finally take off his clothes, revealing his exquisite form. I was overwhelmed with appreciation of the art set before me: his chest, thighs, stomach, those arms…his back. They were all in amazing congruence with one another, not overly muscled but just meaty enough to give you what you want. It was all…*just right*. Then, there was the, um… Yeah, that was just right, too.

    He got to our table and stopped. He stood there rolling his pelvis around. Kenya and Candace stuffed money in his thigh strap and Kenya lightly smacked him on the butt as he walked around her toward me. He looked back and grinned. He didn't have his mask off, but I could tell because I saw the shape of his head contort under the mask; which could only have been cheeks expanding, since people's heads don't just go around contorting.

    The sexy beast approached me and pulled out my chair so I could stand up. I put on my front, like he wasn't phasing me the slightest bit. He danced with me, moving his hips from side to side and running his hands down the sides of my hips. I looked him up and down, just molesting his ass with my eyes. Then he pulled back and turned me around. He stretched my arms up and wrapped them around his neck, all the while bumping and grinding on my backside. He wrapped his arm around my waist.

"Hold on," he whispered through the mask.

Huh? What stripper actually talks? They just dance.

In one fell swoop, he lifted me slightly and cartwheeled us through the room on one arm. I just closed my eyes and glued every loose body part to something on him. My arms clenched to his neck for dear life and my legs twined around his. He knew I'd be dizzy when we stopped—and I was—then he let me fall just slightly so he could catch me all romantically and shit. *This guy. Coming to the freakin' rescue, he is.*

He released me from his "torture" and I stuck a twenty in his g-string, making sure to cop a feel as I did it. He grinned through the mask and moved on to the next woman like a superhero off to save another innocent. The whole audience chanted, "Take the mask off! Take the mask off!" But he danced around until his time ended. Meanwhile, the helpers started collecting his money and discarded clothing. As the music (by then, some Baltimore house) drew to an end, he removed the mask and took a bow.

I gasped and pointed dramatically. "That's Mister Suit Man! That's Mister Suit Man!"

"You lyin'!" Kenya shouted in disbelief.

"Damn girl…you shoulda pulled him when you had the chance," Candace observed. "But at least now

A. M. HATTER

you know what he's got...*and* what you'll be missing!"

The audience cheered and screamed and threw money at him in all ways possible. Fives, tens, twenties hit the floor like roses adorning the stage actor. As he exited the room, he turned, looked me dead in the eyes and winked. *Naw...that wasn't for me, was it? ...Nawww, he's just doing that for the audience.*

"Did you see that? Oh my God! He looked dead at you, Vic!"

I waved Kenya off, "Naw, he just did that for the audience. There are probably twenty other women that think he winked at them."

"No. He looked at *you*, Vic. *I* could see it, *Candace* could see it...hell, that gay guy over there saw it, too!"

I looked at the next table. He tried to sneak a point at me as he talked to his girlfriends (actual women). They attempted badly at inconspicuously looking over in my direction.

"Damn, I guess he did," I said. Then I thought for a sec and rescinded my statement, "Nawww...that was just for show."

"Whatevah. You just don't wanna admit it 'cause you might get too happy," Candace remarked.

I just rolled my eyes at her, "Whatever, man. He didn't look at me."

Two more performers took the stage before the venue opened for dancing and started charging general admission for entrance. (But Mr. Suit Man should've been last because the last two were undoubtedly very

LOOKIN' IN THE MIRROR

good, but neither was as good as Mr. Suit Man.) The deejays changed and everyone got up to dance. Workers moved quickly through the room collecting chairs and tables to provide more space for the dance floor.

The deejay hollered, "You guys ready to getcha freak on???!!!"

Everyone shouted in unison, "YEAH!!!!"

"Well I'm gon' set it off wit' the old school for ya!"

The deejay put on that Jacksons song, 'Shake Your Body (Down to the Ground)'. So, me being a connoisseur of anything Michael Jackson related, you know a sista had to go out and shake her body. The deejay was popping out the greats: Mike, Prince, Kool & the Gang, Shannon… That fool even played some *Johnny Kemp*! And when 'Planet Rock' rolled through, man… You know *everybody* thought they were back in the eighties and shit! Knowing they never knew how to break-dance, but all of a sudden everybody can pop-lock, thinking they're Re-Run in this bitch…O-Zone and shit, talking about, "ORLANDO!! Street-dancer!!!"

But anyway, it was cool, but you know after a while, he *had* to bust out the go-go, which is fine but I can't do a *whole night* of it. I can listen to it for a while, but damn…mix it up a little. Still, I was having a good time until a couple of old farts came out of the woodworks to dance with me. I don't know why, but anytime I go out—I could be in a room *full* of guys that are 25-34, but the *one* geezer in the joint wants to be up on me. And if it's not him, it's the wack-looking guy with the hard-on that wants to dance really close and rub his member on my backside. (Guys, if you have an erection—or even if you're simply not "packaged" right—don't dance with anyone until you handle that. It's really annoying.)

Anyway, everyone's getting his or her groove on, right? Then I saw Mr. Suit Man up in the deejay booth. Minutes later, he was right behind me! *I guess he was winking at me*, I thought.

"What's your name?" he asked.

"Victoria." (Keep in mind we're on the dance floor in a club playing very loud music; we were yelling.)

"That's a sexy name."

"Thank you. What's yours?"

"Vinny."

"Nice to finally meet you, Vinny."

"Mayn! I wanted to talk to you that day I saw you at wurrk, but I had to meet someone upsturrs and I got off on the wrong flo'."

"Girlfriend?"

He looked at me and smiled, "Naw. Somebody werkin' wit' me on a prah-ject."

"Cool..." I nodded.

He handed my twenty back to me. "Can I take you out?"

I tried to hold back a grin beginning to creep across my face. "Sure," I replied all smooth-like, but I think he knew I wanted to do the '80s Toyota jump.

"Mayn, I've thought about you ever since that day. I'm glad I saw you again."

"Same here," I replied, cheesing my ass off.

LOOKIN' IN THE MIRROR

He turned me around, facing away from him, and wrapped his arms around me. I happened to look up just as he thought I wasn't looking, and I saw him give some kind of signal to the deejay. Slow song.

"You know what," the deejay said, "I'm kinda feelin' a slow jam right now…let's see if y'all feel it, too!"

He did a little scratching and screwed the song that he'd been playing to slow the mood, then popped on the slow jam. *Come…closer. Feel…what you been dying for. Don't…be afraid, baby. Touch it…and explooooore.* Screeched across the room.

That muthafucka requested Scandalous! I knew he was setting me up. That's, like, the only slow song a deejay can play at a club without people getting mad. Amidst my shock, he turned me back around and put my hands on his butt, then wrapped his arms around my shoulders.

(((Squeeze)))

Mmmmmmmmmm. Niiiiice buttocks…rrrrrrrrrrrrrrrrrrrrrr.

What else was I supposed to do?

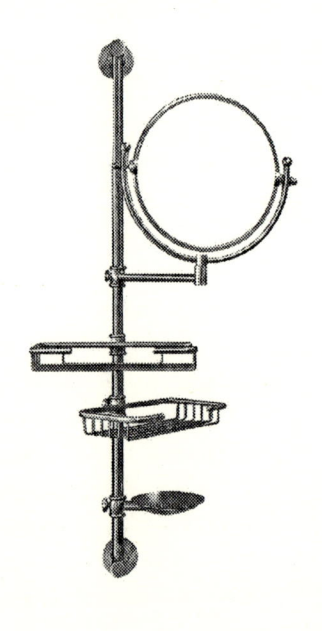

Saturday, April 20

LOOKIN' IN THE MIRROR

(((Ring, Ring!)))
"Hel-lo?"
"Man! You ain't up *yet*??"
"Aww, hey Dante. What's goin' on, man?"
"Shoot, nothin'. Try'na find out whatchu gettin' into tuhday."
"What time is it?" I asked.
"Eleven," he replied.
"…I hadn't planned anything. You know, I just got back from D.C. yesterday."
"Really? Business trip?"
"Yeah," I answered.
"That's cool. How'd it go?"
"It was good, it was good. I met a lotta people. The meetings went smoothly… It was really good."
"Oh, okay…"
"What's on ya mind, kid?"
"Umm…nothin' really. I mean, well, we got this assignment in social studies about what we wanna be when we grow up. But I don't really know."
"Soooo you were thinkin' you'd put down what I do," I said as I got up to brush my teeth.
He snickered a little, "Yeah."
"Is that because you really wanna do what I do, or because writin' that would be easier?"
He thought for a second. "…I don'know," he replied.
"Well, lemme ask you this: what do you feel you're good at?"
"…Well, I'm good at basketball…"
I spit into the sink. "Okay, and what else? Are you good at anything in school? Math, reading, art?"

"I like to draw."

"Okay, then. You could be an artist," I said.

"An *ar-tist*???"

I tried to explain the best I could with my head tilted back, tryin' to balance a mouthful of toothpaste suds, "Man, not an artist like Michelangelo. I mean a *graphic* artist. Like Carlos and Nouri."

"What do they do?"

"They design…you know, anything that needs visual representation." I could tell by his silence that he needed more to go on, so I continued, "Okay, [spit] you got books in school, right?"

"Yeah."

"Well, a graphic artist had to design that book cover. The company that made that book needed graphic artists to organize the text and pictures inside. Uhhhh… They do company logos, like the Nike Swoosh. Or, uhhh, when you see advertisements in magazines or on billboards—even computers and chairs—all those are designed by different kinds of artists. And you could do that," I explained, brushing again.

"Ohhhhh. Dang. I didn't know artists did that much," he paused, "Do they make a lotta money?"

"Sometimes, but not all the time. A lot of 'em have pretty okay salaries, but they're not bankin' unless they own their own design company."

"Oh."

"Or you could be a cartoonist and work for a comic book company or a newspaper, or a video gaming company."

LOOKIN' IN THE MIRROR

"Man, I thought all artists did was sculpt or paint."

"[Spit] Some do. They might work for companies that mass-produce paintings and stuff. Or they might make their money purely from holding art shows or gettin' contracts to do pieces for people. But that's not really smart unless you're big-timin'," I explained.

"Hmm. Okay."

"Did that help?"

"Mmm, yeahhh, I guess so."

"Soooo, is that what you wanna do?" I asked.

"Well…it's okay. That's somethin' I *could* do, but…"

"You still wanna play ball and get a fat contract, huh?"

I could almost hear the big cheese land on his face, "Yeaaaahhhhhh."

I swished a handful of water through my mouth and spit it out. "Okay, dude. I just hope you know what you're gettin' into."

"Yeah, yeah, I know… They play a lotta games and I'll be on the road a lot. I won't be able to trust everybody and I'll be tradin' in my privacy."

"Hey, I'm just try'na warn you," I replied as I dried my face and hands.

"I know, man."

(((Ding, Dong!)))

"Hey, somebody's at my door. If, uh, you wanna come over, call Will and ask him if he's comin' this way and if he can stop by to pick you up 'cause I don't think I'll get out today."

A. M. HATTER

"A'right," he replied.
"Bye, man."

I opened the door. It was Mia. She rushed right past me, like she was walkin' into her own house.

"I can't stand her! I can't stand her! I don't know what to do, Gerald! I'm gonna kill this broad!"

"W-w-w, HUH?"

"Gerald, I'm tellin' you. This woman is tryin' to ruin my marriage!"

I grabbed her on both shoulders, "Hold up, slow down... What woman?"

"Sean's mother."

"Ohhhhh. What'd she do?"

"I just found out today that she's been lyin' to my face all this time!"

"Wha'd'you mean?"

"She's been tellin' Sean—ever since we fuckin' *met*—that he should leave me!"

"Whaaat?"

"I mean, what the fuck! We've been married for *five years* now!"

"Why would she say that?" I asked.

"I don't know! I've been tryin' to figure that out, myself! I've been askin' myself, 'Did I ever say anything that might've made her mad?' I thought maybe it's because we haven't had a child yet. I know she *really* wants a grandchild. But it just doesn't seem like reason enough...I can't figure it out!"

"Well, how'd you find out that she felt that way?" I asked.

LOOKIN' IN THE MIRROR

"This mornin', I was leavin' to catch this furniture sale, right?"

"Yeah."

"I locked the back door and got in the car, but then I remembered that my wallet was still in my other purse, so I went back in the house. Sean was in the computer room, which you know, you have to pass to get to our bedroom."

I nodded, "Yeah."

"I guess he didn't hear me come back in because he was talkin' to her on the speakerphone," she took a breath, "So I'm walkin' by, when I hear her say, 'Son, you know you could've done so much better. I don't like you with her. She doesn't mix well with our family.' I'm tellin' you, man... I didn't know whether to cry or break down the door."

"Damn, Mia. That messed up... What'd he say?"

"Well, he told her to leave him alone and stop talkin' about me—which was the only thing that kept me from kickin' the door down and cussin' her dirty ass out."

"Well at least he stood up to her. You would've felt a lot worse if he agreed," I pointed out.

"Well, yeah," she giggled, "but that doesn't necessarily ease my mind!" She sighed and fixed her eyes on me. "Gerald, you just don't understand how relentless this woman is. Last year, she and his aunt—her sister—got into it somethin' kinda heavy 'cause his aunt used to be in this abusive relationship. And one night, the aunt's husband came home actin' a fool, started beatin' on her and knocked her unconscious, but he kept on beating on her. I'm tellin' you, this woman almost *died*. Her five-year-old son had to call 9-1-1 to save her from his dad. After that, she decided to leave him. Do you know what Sean's mom told her?"

"What?"

"There's no reason a woman should leave her husband and that she should work things out."

"WHAT???? She actually *said* that???"

"Hell yeah! And not only that, but when his aunt moved into another house, provided by this battered women's organization, she told the husband where the aunt moved!!!!"

My jaw dropped. "Hell nawww! What's *her* problem?"

"I have no idea. She's just fuck-ing nuts."

"Did anything happen to the aunt?"

"Almost. But she was in the bathroom when he knocked on the door. The little boy looked through the blinds to see who it was and called the police on him. But get this—when the police took him into custody, they found a gun *and* a knife on him. He was gonna shoot the little boy and stab her."

"Man...I guess she'd rather have a dead sister than a divorced one, huh?"

"Hell, you'd think it," she replied.

"So, I guess they aren't on speaking terms anymore, huh?"

"Ding, ding, ding! You win a brand new car!!"

"Man, your mother-in-law is a lunatic."

"Tell me about it! And she's a freakin' mooch, too! I just don't understand how this woman has a job *and* a husband with a job, but she's always 'borrowing' money from us."

"Huh?"

"Yeah, man! She'll call, 'Lemme speak to my son.' When I give the phone to him, she's like, 'Sean, gimme fitty dollars'."

"Does he give it to her?"

"Yeah! He has it set in his mind that he's supposed to be takin' care of his mom—*which* I'd have no problem with if she was, like, *eighty*. But she's only forty-nine, and fully capable of supportin' herself with her full-time job that she attends Monday-through-Friday. I could even understand if she was handicapped. But the woman has a job and is married to a working husband! What the hell is wrong with her??? I just wish Sean would get some fucking spine when it comes to her."

"Dang, Mia...I don't even know what to tell you."

"There's not much you *can* say to a situation like this...it's just to' down, through-and-through."

(((Ding, Dong!)))

I stood from the arm of the couch and walked toward the door as I returned comment, "Yeahhh... Well, try not to worry about it too much. The inevitability of it is that time passes and things change."

I looked through the peephole and saw it was Carlos.

"Ay, man. What's going on?" he greeted me, with his scruffy Chicano voice as he walked in.

"Not much. You know I just got back from D.C. yesterday."

"Aww, yeah… How'd that go, man?"

"It went really well. I went up there and did my Conan thang," I replied as we stepped down into the living room. "Mia's here."

"That's good, man — Heyyy, Meeeeyahhhh!"

"Hey, Carlos!" she replied as they hugged.

"How's it going, girl?? You skipped a few weeks!"

"Things are pretty good with me."

He sat on the couch across from her. "That's good!" he said, and turned to me, "So, when's ev'rybody else comin' over?"

"Hell, I don't know. I'm just takin' it one minute at a time," I said, diggin' through the refrigerator for somethin' to eat.

"That's cool… Hey, Gerald."

Then, searching through the freezer. "Yeah!" I replied.

"What are you doing next weekend? You gonna be in town?" he asked.

I paused and looked up to think, "Uhhhh, I think I'll be in town, but I'm not sure what I'll be doin'… Why?"

"Man, Alejandra is havin' her quinceañera next Saturday…"

I chuckled, "You don't wanna go, huh?"

"I don't know. Sometimes I feel like, 'No', 'cause you know how my family is. But then, it's my sister's quince and everyone else is all hyped and I start gettin' happy too, y'know?"

LOOKIN' IN THE MIRROR

I chuckled, "Yeah."

"I just hope Uncle Manny doesn't make the deejay play all that Tejano music like he did at my cousin's quince," he shook his head, "MAN! It was *horr*ible! All...freakin'...night, it was [squeaky voice] YAAAAA, HA-HA-HAAAAA! It sounds like circus music. I *hate* that mess."

We laughed.

Man, Carlos almost despises family gatherings. It was funny...once, when we were ten I think, he invited me to his family reunion. It was goin' toward the east, out at this park. They had food, games, and all that. Everything was normal, like any regular family, except all his relatives looked like a bunch of TV stereotypes!

Man, we showed up, his family and a few others are known for being on time, so there were only a few folks there at first; they were the types that look like your "Average American Family" or whatever. (I think Carlos might actually be what we'd call "the bourgeois cousin".) But then, these other folks started comin' up with cowboy outfits on and shit, lookin' like they just jumped out a western! I'm lookin' like, *This is a joke, right?* Then came these short and stocky, dark-skinned guys. They walked up, lookin' all happy like, *Yayyyyy! America!* Then, last but not least, were the "gangbanging cousins," as Carlos puts it. They all had hiked up pants with extra long belts and wife-beater t-shirts...knee-high socks and long shorts, slippers on their feet and fish netting on their heads. The girls had on dark make-up and too-tight clothes. They were straight out of a late-night HBO B-movie. It

A. M. HATTER

was sad. I was *the only* Black kid there and everybody's lookin' at me like, "Who's this kid?"

Nothin' but comedy, nothin' but comedy. He had a couple of fine ass cousins, though. I might need to go to his sister's quince.

Mia laughed, "Oh yeah! I think I met some of your relatives when we were younger... it was Cinco-de-Mayo or somethin', wasn't it?"

"Maaaan, I don't even remember," Carlos answered, lookin' disheartened.

"Check, this Gerald," Mia started rankin' on him (laughin' hard, too), "They looked like Mexican cowboys, man! They had on those plaid western shirts, and these *HUGE* pride-of-Texas belt buckles!" She took a breath. "Man, those mu'gs were big as hell! They were like shields! Like they had Perseus hookin' 'em up on the low-low!"

Me being the 'Clash of the Titans' fan that I am, I *really* wanted to laugh at her last remark, but I could tell that Carlos wasn't enjoying it at all. (Besides, he's my boy; I got his back.) A little bit of laugh slipped out, but I managed to hold it in and try to referee the situation.

"Alright, alright, Mia!" I chuckled a little.

"They're deflectin' bullets and shit—big *super-*Texans!" She stood up, pushed out her pelvis and pretended to line dance. "The stars at night, are big and bright [clap-clap-clap-clap] deep in the hearrrrrrrrt of Texaaaaas!"

But Carlos came back on her—which he doesn't normally do to Mia, "How you gonna rank on

LOOKIN' IN THE MIRROR

my fam'ly, when your dad wore *boot insulation* around the house as *slippers*?"

"Ohhhhhhh-ho-ho-hooooo!" I started to laugh. "Man! I for-*got* about *that*! Yo, your dad used to walk around the house lookin' like Sandman!" I started hummin' the old Sandman Theme from 'Showtime at the Apollo' and fake tap-dancin'.

We were dyin' laughin'. I had to stop choppin' vegetables until I regained my composure.

Her dad was a trip. He's the type of dude to have clothes older than *you*. I remember one time, Mia came outside to play ball with us and she told us about a pair of her dad's *regular*, *everyday*, *basic* cotton briefs that he had for sooo long, they turned *shiny*! (Yes, *shiny*!) It took about three months for us to stop callin' her Rumplestiltskin. She shouldn't have told us about that one. That's one of those things you keep in the house.

"Yeah, man...the boot-liners...that was classic," she replied, lying on her side, gasping for breath.

(((Ding, Dong!)))

I set the knife down and wiped my hands, then started toward the door, "That must be Will & Nouri," I said, and looked through the eyehole. "Yeah."

I opened the door to Nouri and Will as we all did the manly greeting mumbles.

Nouri: "Hey man."

"Hey," I replied and butted my knuckles against his.

Will gripped my hand and pulled me in for the one-armed pat on the back. "Ow."

A. M. HATTER

I gripped him back, "Olé."

They always get excited when Mia's around, like she's Glenda the Good Witch. *We* mumble to each other like we couldn't care less if you're here or not, but she gets all the "Hey Mia!!!!!!!!!!!!!!!!!!!!!!!!!!!!!!!!!!" and ridiculously strong hugs—never mind that it's my house. Not that I'm bitter or anything…I surely don't want any tight squeezes from some hard leg, but it just goes to show that it's hard being a man. We can't express squat.

"Whatcha cookin' dawwwwwwg," Will said like Tommy from 'Martin'.

"Breakfast," I replied.

"Ain't it kinda late for breakfast?" Carlos asked, being smart.

I grinned, "Well take yo' ass down the street and buy *lunch* at Burger King, if it's so late."

Ev'rybody laughed.

They started watchin' the football draft while I finished cookin'. But Mia being Mia, her attention span expired and she went lookin' through my stuff. I'm the one with the problem, but she's the one that always manages to dig her way into my flicks. She's a special one. She always did have this weird fascination with genitals, but not necessarily with the person attached. I remember when we were six, she used to always ask me or Will to take our "ding-a-lings" out. So, one-at-a-time, we'd go behind the bush and show her. She'd look…maybe even lift it up… We didn't know what the big deal was, but she looked all mesmerized so…boys being the ego hounds that we are, we were happy to oblige her strange fascination

LOOKIN' IN THE MIRROR

with our penises—until we realized she didn't really want nothin'. So we stopped doin' that shit. We found out later in life that she did that to all the boys in our crew. It was weird. She never wanted anything. Just to look and see.

Ha! One time, they were all watching one of my flicks—I was up there tryin' to cook in between money shots (you know what I'm talkin' about). Man, I burned one of my omelets. I was mad. I'm a self-proclaimed chef; I don't burn food! It was just a little bit, though, so I put the burned part on the bottom and gave it Mia. Hell, it was her fault. So right now, I have her on flick-restriction. It's just not healthy to be *that* fixated on porn.

Will distracted her rummaging with a story from our old dirt days.

"Hey, Gerald! Man, I saw this girl at the bank that looked *just like* Sheila!"

"Awwww, man...was it her?"

"She might've been," he said, "'cause she looked *straight* at me and didn't say *nuh*-thin'."

"Maybe it wasn't her," I hoped.

"Shiiit, man...I was ready to get to bookin', tho'!" he laughed.

Then Nouri asked, "Who's Sheila? What happened with her?"

I tried to close the conversation, "Nothin' man, nothin'. Don't even worry 'bout it."

But Will was determined to put me on blast, "Bruh! You *gotta* tell the story!"

I grinned, "No, my brutha, I don't."

Then Mia joined in, "Yeah, what ever happened to Sheila? She just…up and left. I remember she was mad at you for somethin', but she wouldn't tell me."

I just kept grinnin'.

"Yeah," Will answered, "she caught him over at Angie Walker's house!" and started laughin'.

Mia looked all shocked, "You did it to Angie Walker??"

I just started laughin' and kept cookin'.

"I *knew* somethin' was up with y'all!" she said.

Will kept tellin' the story, "Man! You shoulda been there! She had his ass stranded! Man, he went over there one afternoon… But Sheila found out from that stuck up bitch—uh, LaKeisha—that he was hittin' Angie, too."

I shook my head, "Man, that was messed up."

"And so Sheila showed up at the house and started throwin' rocks at the window!"

"What??" Nouri said.

"Did she break it?" Mia asked.

"Naw, she was just throwin' pebbles," I answered.

"Oh."

Will continued, "So anyway, they looked out the window—"

"Naw," I interrupted, "at first she was on the wrong side of the house runnin' around talkin' about 'Bitch I'ma kill yo' muthafuckin' ass!' So Angie looked up like, 'What the fuck?' But I was tryin' to, y'know, do my thang, so I was like 'It ain't nothin', it ain't nothin'…lay back down.' But then she smashed my windshield and made the alarm go off."

They started laughin'.

"I bet you got up, *then*!" Nouri teased.

"Maaaaan. I looked out the window, I was like, 'Damn, it's Sheila.' So I went out there and she *fucked* my car *up*! Man, I was so hurt. She was jumpin' in my face and all…I was just tryin' like hell not to body slam her dumb ass."

Will: "Shit, I'da done it! The way she fucked *yo'* car up? She'd've been sleepin' wit' the fishes, dawg."

"What'd she do?" Nouri asked, as Mia gave me a suspicious eye.

"She keyed it up and broke the windshield, knocked one of the side mirrors off—it was hangin' by the wire and shit… Man, yo' car was *trash* when she got finished! I'da knocked the bitch out," Will answered.

"Daaaaaaaaamn. You said you got in a accident, man!" Mia said.

Will replied, "Nobody wanted to tell *you* what really happened, man. All you'da done is look and say 'I told you so.'"

She shrugged, "I sure would've…it serves him right. *I* told him don't mess with Sheila, anyway, 'cause I *knew* the chick was nuts! And *then* he went and fucked around on her!"

Will retorted, "Shiiiiit, you don't understand. That was *Angie Walker*. E'rrrrr'body wanted a piece uh dat!"

I laughed.

"Naw, *you* don't understand! I'm not sayin' don't fuck Angie...hell, if I was a dude, I'da fucked her too! But I'm just sayin' he shouldn'a messed with Sheila. *That* bitch was nuts. She went *all* the way to OU to follow Gerald, man!"

"How d'you know?" Carlos asked.

"Man, she was all in love with Gerald and shit 'cause he was smart. She used to draw his name in hearts when we were in high school and she'd be askin' me to hook her up."

Will dropped his jaw, "Awww, you were blockin', Mia?"

"Naw! I just knew y'all weren't tryin' to be in love and shit. So I wasn't tryin' to put her out there like that. She'd just get her heart broken—like she did! And what happened after that? She withdrew and transferred to Prairie View. She didn't even declare a major when she was at OU. She didn't know what she wanted to do. She was just there 'cause of Gerald. *Y'all* just didn't know 'cause y'all were too stupid to notice *obvious* shit like that."

"That was still funny, though," Will said and started laughin' again.

Nouri just shook his head and smiled. "So what happened? Did you just leave or what?"

"Naw! He couldn't leave! He went back in the house and left out the back, and went up to the gas station and called this guy Lamont from the payphone."

"Who's Lamont? Did I know Lamont?" Mia asked.

LOOKIN' IN THE MIRROR

"Naw, you didn't know him. ...Well, you might've met'm once or somethin'...but we didn't hang wit' him too much. He was one of the locals, all thugged out and shit," he laughed, "Man, I remember like it was yesterday...he called me and told me what was up. I was laughin' at him, then I said, 'A'ight. I'll come getchu', or whatever. Then he called Lamont to come get his car. So Lamont rode with me and we got up there...we thought Sheila had left, but she was still out there fussin' and cussin' or what not...marchin' around like she practicin' for band..." He laughed some more. "Man! That broad *was* nuts. If you had stayed, she prob'ly woulda tried to kill you, dawg."

I just shook my head and let him keep tellin' the story.

"So anyway, when we got there, she started fussin' at us. Lamont got out the car, and he was like, 'Calm down lil lady. We ain't here for you...we're just gettin' Gerald's car.' And then, she pulled a knife out, talkin' 'bout 'Mutha fucka, I'll stab you!' Blasé blah, or whatever."

Nouri cracked up, "You really know how to pick 'em, man."

"But Lamont, shit... He pulled out his nine and was like, 'Now hold up baby girl. You don't even know me like that.' Man, we were already laughin' at the way she fucked up his car, but I was ready to *roll* when he did *that*!"

"What'd she do?" Nouri asked.

"Man, she couldn't do nothin'. She just calmed the fuck down, like he told her in the first place, and left," Will shook his head, "Man, Sheila…boy, she was a trip," he said, smilin'.

"Well, if y'all are finished with story time, you can come get your plates," I said.

Nouri started actin' silly, "You magnificent bastard!"

Mia graded him, "Ahh, 'The Simpsons', good choice."

"I didn't have anything original this time," he replied.

"Did Dante call you, Will?" I asked.

He replied, "Aww, yeah. I told him I'd pick him up tomorrow. I'm takin' him to church with me."

"Oh, okay."

"Are we goin' to the court today?"

"Man, I don't even have it in me. If I do anything, I *might* wash my car," I replied.

"Let's go play some pool later on," he suggested.

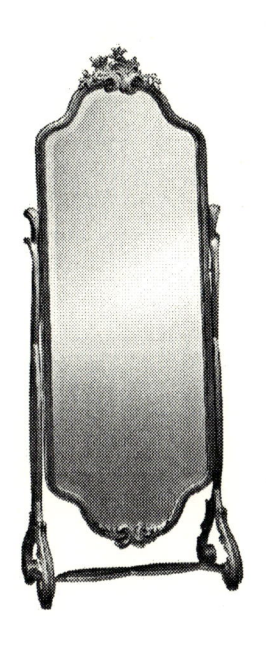

Saturday, Noon

A. M. HATTER

I awoke to find my roommate on the couch, molesting a magazine.

"Hey, come look at this," she said and eagerly waved me over, "If you look hard enough, you can almost see what he'd look like naked."

"Who?" I walked briskly to see whom she was talking about.

"Will Smith."

"Is he...*oh yeahhhh*...wearin' flat-front pants. Mm! I love what they do for his thighs."

"Mmm-hmmm," she concurred.

"OOO, GIRL! I need to tell you what happened last night!" I scared her into dropping the mag.

"What-what-what?" she responded with a huge grin and bright eyes.

"Mr. Suit Man was there."

She gasped dramatically. "For real??"

"Girl, yeah. He was one of the dancers."

She jerked back and snarled a little bit. "He's a stripper???"

"Yeah...and girrrrl...his body was like [angelic voice] whaaaaaaaaaat!"

"Dang, I wish I went with y'all now."

"And he had the smoothest show! He came out like he was Hannibal Lector, right?"

"Uh-huh."

"He was tied up on the dolly and stuff...but when he got loose, he jumped off and acted like a wild man and picked this woman up. He flipped her over and laid her on her stomach, THEN he jumped down and started grindin' on her!"

LOOKIN' IN THE MIRROR

"Oooo...dang. I wanna be that lady," she giggled.

"So then, he—"

(((Ding, Dong!)))

We both looked up at the door.

"Who the hell is at our door this early?" she asked.

True, it was after noon, but in our world that's early because we don't accept visitors before 2pm.

I looked through the peephole. It was Shawn. Under any circumstances, it's very usual for her to be up early. For some reason married people get up early. But she wouldn't dare come over unless it was something at least mildly important. Which I was sure it was because she looked really strange...not nervous, but brewing. She stood on the porch, completely still (not leaning or fidgeting or looking off) with her head tilted. She looked straight into the peephole.

"Open the door," she said just before I had the chance to unlock it. As she stepped in, she looked at me, then to my roommate and says, "I need to talk...I don't know what to do. I'm gonna freak out."

"Well come on! Sit down," my roommate commanded. "What's goin' on?"

I was shocked to see her like that. "Man, you look crazy. What's wrong with you?"

Shawn sat on the couch next to my roommate, breathing heavily. "Last night...Donald..."

"Dah-naaald...?" I glared at her, waiting for her to finish. "He beat you? He's leaving you???"

"No," she paused, "He said he wants to have a baby."

"Wooooooooahhhhhhh," my roommate and I replied in unison.

"He said the 'b-word'?? That's some *shit*!" I exclaimed.

"I know…and I just don't know what to do. When he asked me if I wanted to start tryin'," she paused, then sighed, and continued, "I just froze. I didn't even know what to say…and he just looked at me, waitin' for an answer. But I didn't know what to tell him! …I'm, like, just gettin' to where I wanna be. A supervising position just opened in my department and I applied. If I get pregnant now…damn…I just don't know what to do." She sat forward and put her chin in her palms. Her eyes began to well up.

"Uhhhhhhg!! What is *wrong* with me?? Most women *dream* of being in my situation! Other women *want* husbands who want kids. But I don't want kids…and *definitely* not right now," shifting to a higher tone of voice, "I just can't see makin' the *choice* to interrupt my life. Right now, me and Don can have sex whenever we want—*wher*ever we want. With a kid, that stops. I go out with y'all any old weekend, I work, I work *out*. Damn! My body will go to *shit*! And the whole time it'll be leachin' off of me, takin' my energy and stuff… Tell me how any of that is good?"

I raised my hands in surrender. "Girl, don't ask me. You *know I'M* against children."

Of course the roomie, being the do-gooder that she is, took the optimistic approach. "Well, you do have a point, but I don't think it would be all that bad. Besides, children bring so much joy into your life. Think of all the fun things you could do."

Shawn gave her a look like she was the dumbest person on earth, "Liiike whaaat?"

She shrugged her shoulders and smiled.

"See. Only corny people get all happy about havin' kids. Those people that say stuff like, 'Having children is the best thing that's ever happened to me. Just to get the chance to see the world through the eyes of a child is amazing,'" Shawn said.

I laughed at her because I knew she was talking about something dorky she read in a magazine. I forgot who the actor was that said it.

She continued, "When you say kids, I see me gettin' fat. I see vomiting, mood swings, and no sex... Nine months of being fat and leeched off of, painful labor and irritated breasts, people comin' around tryin' to pet on my baby—and I know I won't want all those people around me, *or* my child. I'll have to get up at retarded hours of the night, and some days, I might not even have time to take a *shower*! Then, there's changin' funky diapers and buyin' expensive baby stuff..."

"Damn. Baby stuff *is* expensive," I added.

"Ain't it? And then you gotta get a lot of it. [Moment of silence] If *I* didn't have to do it, I'd be okay."

I laughed, "You'd just give him the vagina for about nine months, and *maybe* switch 'em back after the baby's born!"

But roommate dissented, "Yeah right. You'd probably get spoiled from not havin' to do shit! You'd get too used to reaching orgasm every time!"

A. M. HATTER

Suddenly, I had an epiphany. "DAMN! I didn't even think of that! That would be the *shit*! I wish I was a man. They have it so easy… LAZY BASTARDS!" I said with my fist in the air and started laughing.

Shawn looked coy, "I get mine, I don'know whutchall talkin' 'bout."

My roommate threw her hands in the air in a surrendering fashion, and leaned back with it. "Well, okay then!!! Go 'head Donald!"

I started pumping my fist. "Roo! Roo! Roo! Roo! Roo!"

She laughed. "But back to the problem at hand," Shawn interjected.

"Well, nobody said you *have* to have kids," I pointed out.

"But if I don't, then he'll resent me. Besides…you're, like, *supposed* to continue your bloodline," she said sarcastically, "I'd let the family down or whatever." Her facial expressions blew off the notion. "And, really, I can't see a life without kids anyway. I just don't wanna physically *have* them."

"You could adopt," said roomie.

"Donald doesn't wanna adopt."

"Well, shit… Your kids are just gonna have to be an accident. That's the only way you'd accept the inevitable, 'cause with Don talkin' about kids, you can only opt out or opt in. If you think he's gonna resent you for opting out, you'll have to deal with the repercussions of that decision, whether it be an open resentment—even divorce, or a subtle resentment that you'll choose not to acknowledge for *years-of-*

LOOKIN' IN THE MIRROR

marriage. Either way, you'll have to get off the fence," said I, the all-wise wizardess of D.C.

"Or I could do like the soap operas and say 'Yes,' but keep takin' birth control!" she joked.

Shawn is hands-down *the* soap opera queen. This chick knows about every character—even the ones from before her time. She can tell you who came on when and for how long. She's one of those people who even knows the characters' birthdays.

"But back to my story…" I turned my head to catch Shawn up, "I was tellin' her about last night when you rang the doorbell."

"Oh, okay. Was it a good show?"

"Oh, *hell* yeah! I saw Mr. Suit Man!"

"For real??"

I fanned my hand at her. "Yeah, but let me tell you the story."

Shawn shut up so I could finish.

"I was tellin' her that he flipped this woman around and started grindin' on her. Then he came right over to our table."

"He recognized you from the other day, didn't he???" my roommate asked with glee.

"He really did. But I didn't even know it was him 'cause he had a mask on. So anyway, he's grindin' his pelvis, right?"

They nodded.

"Then he came over to me."

My roommate's eyes grew wider.

"He started playin' wit' me and stuff… Maaaan," I shook my head, "I just wanted to *lick* him. That's all…just lick'm…. Right on his eight pack."

Shawn looked at me like she just found out I was a 'Star Trek' geek. "Damn. Ohh-kayyy."

"Then he turned me around, where I was facin' away from him and he was like, 'Hold on.' I was like, 'Huh? Hold on?' Y'all, that fool picked me up all fast and started cart wheeling around the room—with ONE ARM! I was straight trippin'!"

They started laughing at me.

"His show was the bomb," I shook my head, "But get this…he took his mask off right before he left, right? And when he was leavin', he turned back for one second, looked DEAD AT ME and WINKED! Kenya was like 'Oh my gosh did you see that?? He looked dead at you!' Girl, even this gay guy at the table next to us saw it. They were pointin' and shit."

"Man, I wish I had gone with y'all," Shawn said, gleeming.

"Me, too!"

"Maybe then Donald wouldn't have started talkin' about havin' a damn baby," she added.

"Man! Forget Donald! This guy had his shit TO-GE-THER, I tell you! How 'bout, when the club started lettin' guys in and clearin' off the dance floor, Mr. Suit Man got the deejay to play 'Scandalous'."

"Whaaaaaaaaaat??? Hell to-da naw!" my roommate exclaimed.

Shawn laughed, "He was talkin' 'bout you and him," she said, alluding to the song lyrics. "Don't be afraid! Touch it!"

I laughed at her. "And then he started dancin' with me."

"Could he dance?" Shawn asked.

"I guess...but I wasn't payin' attention to *that*, 'cause he put my *hands* on his *ass*, maaan!!"

My roommate gasped. "What'd you do??? Did you keep your hands there? Did you squeeze it?"

"HELL YEAH, I squeezed it!! What'd you expect me to do??" I asked with a 'Duhhh' expression on my face.

"Girl, you ain't no good!" My roommate commented. "Guys ain't ready for us. They'd be lookin' in the damn mirror!"

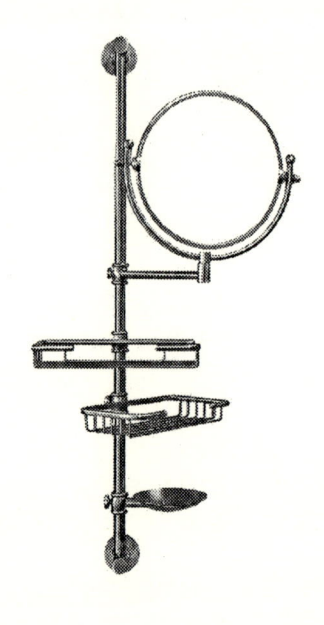

Monday, April 22

Lunch

LOOKIN' IN THE MIRROR

"Hey, I got your email. What's up?"

"Homeboy, you got some work to do this afternoon."

"Why? What happened?" I asked.

"Well, it's really the usual. Carl is pretty cool about everything. He just wants to know how things went while you were in Washington. Tanner is still trippin' about his divorce, so you probably won't hear too much out of him. I think he had a court date this mornin', too, so he might be too distracted. But Chad...woah."

I muttered, "Yeah...that racist mutha—"

"No, Gerald, I'm serious. He is *pissed*. I don't know *what* you did, but he busted in the office Friday mornin' rantin' and ravin' about, um...some fax, or somethin'...? Carl had me hold *all* his calls just so he could calm Chad down. I don't know what the heck you did, but man, you sure did it *this* time!"

I gave her a puzzled look, "Did you hear anything he said?"

"Yeah! He was talkin' loud enough! I remember he said somethin' about 'How dare he be so presumptuous? The position is barely open!' and just, a whole lot of yellin'."

Then it hit me: the fax from John and Barry.

"Ohhhhhhhhhhhhhhhh!" I said.

She looked at me, expecting an explanation. "What?"

"Well, I met a couple of cats up there. Apparently they're some crucial people, y'know, attached to other accounts with the firm we're buyin'. 'Cause I got the feelin' that the dude that used to own it really wanted *them*—in particular—to feel comfortable with the new management. So he introduced them to me, thinkin' they'd be okay for now. Then I found out later from Jannis that they faxed down recommendations for me to become the division head."

"Well that's no big deal. It's not like you told 'em to do it. Why'd he act like that?"

"'Cause Chad's an asshole and a bigot—excuse my language," I responded.

"Oh yeah, how could I have forgotten," she said, "You know what that butthole said to me last week?"

"What?"

"I think it was Wednesday… But anyway, he gon' walk up to my desk and say 'Hey choc'late, you still turnin' me down for lunch?' Oooooh! He just burns me up. I hate that man!"

I just shook my head. "Does Carl know that he's sayin' these things to you?"

"Yeah! I told him after the third time. I looked over it the first time 'cause I just told him, y'know, 'I don't date people in the workplace.' Then he tried again and I thought he would've stopped after that. But the third time was when I told Carl because I also found out that he's married."

"Oh, you didn't know?"

"Not at first, 'cause he just walks around and I never really cared who he was," she replied.

I laughed, "So what'd Carl say when you told him?"

LOOKIN' IN THE MIRROR

"He just asked me to ignore him, talkin' about he's naturally rude and crass, so don't take anything he says to heart."

"So basically, keep your mouth shut 'cause it'll make more stink than it's worth," I deduced.

"Pretty much."

"You should find all his old secretaries and file a civil suit or somethin'. Dude changes assistants every two hours. I bet there's somethin' behind that," I said.

"Maybe...but I'm no Erin Brockovich,"

"A'ight...let'm put a pubic hair on your pop," I retorted.

She laughed.

"Shall I bring your check?" the waitress asked.

"Yes, thanks," I replied.

I saw Tanya reaching for her purse.

"Hey, hey! I got this, girl."

"Oh...thanks," she replied.

"It's the least I could do for warnin' me about Chad."

"Well, I gotta look out for you. If you didn't invite me to that barbecue, I never would've met Nouri," she smiled.

I chuckled. *I'm just glad you didn't hook up with Will. You might be sabotaging me if you did.*

"Well, I'm just glad things are goin' well. I get nervous about friends datin' friends 'cause, y'know, things can go wrong and then get weird," I said.

"I wouldn't do that. We're too cool."

Yeah right. You're a woman. There's always room for revenge.

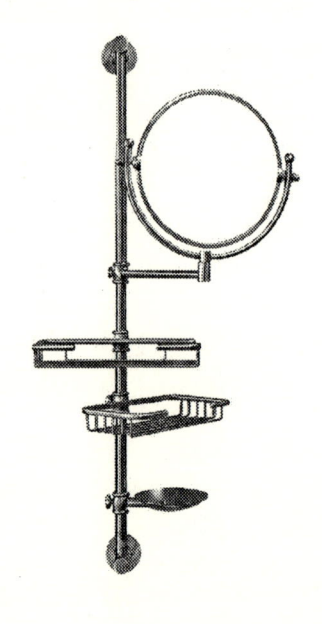

Monday

2:15 p.m.

LOOKIN' IN THE MIRROR

To say I'd been sittin' on pins and needles since lunch would be an understatement. I mean, it wasn't that I was scared or anything 'cause my job wasn't on the line. But you just don't understand how much I hate this man. Chad is such a sphincter. He's the type of guy that—well, let's say you drop a pen RIGHT by his desk…I'm talkin' within the shortest reach of him bein' able just lean over to cordially pick it up for you. *His* punk ass would *look*, but keep on workin'. I know, that's a minor infraction, at the most. But what impression would *you* get from a guy who does that?

Since I'd been back, I'd mainly been goin' over the summary of my trip again, but there were some profit comparisons between a couple other arms of the company that I'd also been workin' on 'cause I had a few ideas that could boost productivity. But as 2:30 neared, I sluggishly wrapped up most of my other work then grabbed my report and notes so I could head over to the conference room.

Jannis told me about a call I'd received earlier as I dragged past her desk.

"I'll, uhh…just hold that message for me," I replied, "Oh, and uh, take messages for the rest of the day, too. I don't feel like dealin' with any mess."

"Okay," she replied with an understanding grin as I continued down the hall to the elevators.

When I entered the conference room, Tanner was there, sittin' at the table goin' over some papers and muttering to himself.

"Ohhhh, that bitch. That bitch, that bitch, that *bitch*. What??? Not the—"

"Hey Tanner. You ready for this meeting?" I asked.

"Huh? Oh, uhhh…you know, I'm sure not," he replied with a drained expression and went back to the papers.

"Are you alright, man? You look—"

He looked up at me. "You're still single, right, Gerald?"

"Uh, yeah," I said waiting for a point.

He shook his head. "Don't ever get married," he said with a forced smile, "Just stay single. You'll appreciate my advice in the long run."

I kinda laughed, "Uhh, okay," I said, pretending not to know what he was talkin' about.

"Women are *evil*. Sure, they're nice to look at, sometimes nice to be with…but don't *ever* get married. They'll suck the life outta you and take everything you have."

"You're getting divorced, aren't you?"

"Oh, was it that obvious?" he replied sarcastically.

I leaned onto the table, "If you don't mind my asking, what's goin' wrong?"

"I don't know man," he sat back from the table, "One minute, it's 'I just wanna get this over with', and things are going smoothly. Next thing I know, she's filing for alimony. She wants this car, that car…she wants the house—she's tryin' to take my *kids*! *I* thought we'd agreed on joint custody," he sighed and looked downward.

I sighed as well.

He started shakin' his head. "You know what?"

LOOKIN' IN THE MIRROR

I looked up.

"I'm not gonna be able to focus on this meeting. I just can't do it right now…"

I pressed my lips together and tried to look sympathetic.

"Ummm. Tell 'em I wasn't feelin' well or somethin'. I gotta get out of here," he said.

"Alright, man," I replied and patted his shoulder, "Do what ya gotta do. I got ya covered."

"Thanks, I appreciate it," he said, turnin' toward the door. He poked his head out, looked both ways and left.

Man. That dude's got it bad. I shook my head and sat down close to the end of the table.

About two minutes passed, and Carl came in.

"Hey Gerald!"

"Hey Carl," I replied with a grin.

"So how was D.C.?"

"It was nice," I nodded, "Yeah, it was real nice."

"Yeah, I like D.C. in the spring. All the cherry blossoms start to bloom. It's *beautiful* up there," he said, takin' a seat close to me, on the table's corner.

"*Oh*, yeah. I'd like a few of those in my yard, ya know?"

Knowin' I don't give a damn about some cherry blossoms.

He damn near salivated, "Aw! You are *so* right! My brother, in North Carolina, has a bunch of those in his yard. And I *love* the way he did 'em. They're all lined up on the sides," he demonstrated with his hands, "curved around the house… Kinda like, if you got an

A. M. HATTER

aerial view, it'd be a half wreath around the house. It's so nice."

"Ohhh, boy. That sounds really pretty. Did he do them himself, or did he get landscapers?"

"Landscapers. My brother doesn't do yard work. He's a pretty boy," he chuckled.

I chuckled back, "Oh, yeah? So you do your own yard?"

"I used to. I miss those days, ya know?"

"Yeah."

"I'd just get out in the yard and nothin' else mattered."

I smiled, "Yeah, I know what you mean…"

"You do your yard?" he asked.

"Yeah. I just can't see payin' somebody to do somethin' I can do myself. All it takes is a little elbow grease, ya know?"

"Yeah, I felt that way, too."

I nodded.

"Then, when everything blooms and grows, you can look back and be proud of your own work," he said.

"Yeahhhhh," I smiled.

And in walked Mr. Negativity himself.

In his good ol' boy accent, "Hey gahz," Chad said, sittin' at the head of the table.

Carl turned and took the seat next to the corner.

"Tanner went home…he wasn't feeling well," I said.

"Yeahh rhyt," Chad smirked, "He's prah-bubbly sweatin' bull-its uh-bowt some'm his greedy wife did."

LOOKIN' IN THE MIRROR

Say what?

Carl hurried to step in and start the meetin', "Okay... Well, we got your report. It was very thorough. I really liked what you picked up, as far as where Blitson Marketing will have room to grow. Uhhh...but I'm curious about the payroll...it's kind of big for what their workload actually is."

"Yeah. I got that feeling too," I replied, "I mean, it wasn't a situation where it was causing a major fiscal problem—at this point in time, anyway, but...the company could definitely shed a few pounds, in my opinion," I took a breath and exhaled, "And they had a high-low thing going on, where they either had a huge project or a whole lot of tiny commitments that bring in a few dollars. Money is money, and it all adds up but," I shrugged, "it was fluff."

"So, where, in particular, do you think we could cut?" Carl asked.

"Executive and general assistants, mainly. Bob, alone, had close to *ten* assistants, and some were junior assistants. It got kind of ridiculous," I paused, "You know, it's funny you asked that. 'Cause there was a whole department, what was it called? Marketing Enhancement."

"What's that?" Chad asked.

"I have no idea," I replied, "And the more they explained it, the more redundant it sounded. It just seemed to me that everything they did was stuff already being done in other areas. I think somebody knew somebody..."

They chuckled.

I don't know why they wanted to meet. Everything I was tellin' 'em was in the report. It wouldn't have been so "thorough" if I hadn't included all that. They just wanted to "have a meeting." Man, people at the top are some of the biggest time wasters in the world. We must've sat there for about an hour and some change, talkin' 'bout junk I put in the report. It was stupid—although, positive—until Chad had to step in with his discontent about the faxes.

"One thing, though, Jairruld… Hmmmmm… We got a cuhhple of fak-sez," he lifted them from his folder, "Ummm, I didn't egg-zactly know how tuh tayyk this… But, uh, if you wanna be-come a can-did-dayt for this poh-zishun, you'll have to wait un*til* the puhzishun o-pens."

Carl interrupted, "Chad, come on…ease up. Don't go there."

"No, I haff to say this, Carrrl. Some-tahms people over-stehhp," he replied and looked back at me, "Did, um, did you ask theze gahz to fax theez in fer yoo?" He squinted. "How did this happen?"

How did this happen?? He acts like I caused a car wreck. It's not that serious.

"Actually, I had no knowledge of those faxes at all until I checked my messages with Jannis the next day, and she told me. I didn't ask them to do anything."

"Oh, oh-kay…becawz… Well, to be ah-nist with yooo, we're considerin' quite a few people uh-head of yoo," Chad said.

"I thought the position wasn't open," I responded.

LOOKIN' IN THE MIRROR

Carl sat there with a flat expression, unimpressed by Chad's antics.

"It's not...but...well, word gets uh-round. There have been a few people to awl-reddy show int'rest," he said.

"Okay...so they can show interest, but I can't?"

Chad quickly replied, "No. No. Now, it's not that, Jairruld. It's just that... See, you're very proh-fishent in your poh-zishun hee-yer. And...well, we don't feel you have ee-nuff ek-speer-ee-ance to head a duhvision just yehht."

So, let me get this straight: I can troubleshoot a whole division's structure, but I can't head it?

I was about to tell his Klan ass to eat shit and die, but Carl intervened.

"Actually, Chad, I don't agree with you there. I feel that Gerald has more than enough experience to head the division."

Chad huffed a little, "H-H-How so? He's nehhver soopervahzd that much staff befohwer."

I just sat there quietly, tryin' to stifle my anger.

"Maybe not, but he's a very intuitive business man, he has people skills, and he's shown this company a lot of loyalty, especially in stickin' with us after he got his M.B.A., when he could've gone to another company and made a huge jump. *I* think he'd be perfect," Carl said.

Chad countered, "But he still has no ek-speer-ee-ance. There are guys wait'n' ohn this poh-zishun that have mannejd staff and headed duhvisions for *eight* years—and mohrr!"

A. M. HATTER

"And they can be considered, too. But you can't count him out just because *[he's Black]* he hasn't been head of a division before. Chad, be realistic. We send this guy out to weather some of our biggest storms, problems in legs of this company that could've possibly *crumbled* a few. If he can face the bad times, it only makes sense that he would work well in the good times, too."

Carl looked at me and shook my hand.

He added, "You know, I'll write you a recommendation, too, if you need one. The dedication you've shown over the years you've been here—gettin' here early and leavin' later than *anyone* else, your attention to detail…you even overdress at the company picnics," he laughed, "I'd be insulted if you didn't try for this position. You *should* be a division head." Then he got up and left.

Chad just had a pouty look on his face. Then he followed.

I just sat there.

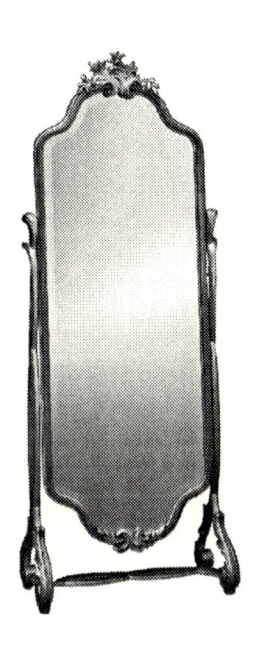

Friday, April 26

Evening

Candace said with a look of concern, "I hope nobody gets fired or anything."

"I think it'll be okay. From what I've heard around the building, it's just a matter of switching ownership. If they fire anyone, it might be the security people and-or the janitorial staff so they can switch to out-source companies and cut down on salaries and benefit packages," Shawn reassured her.

"Man, these are dire times. Nobody needs the pressure of the pink slip," Candace asserted. "Have you heard of Blitson, Vicki?"

I sat in the left corner of the back seat, looking out of the window. We were on our way to a benefit auction raising proceeds for the homeless shelter that we volunteer with every Sunday.

"Hey! Dream girl!" Candace snapped her fingers in front of my face.

"Huh?" I said.

"I was askin' you if you'd heard anything about Blitson, Inc. They're buying our company."

"Oh, uhhh…I think I've heard of 'em. It's weird 'cause they really kinda came outta nowhere, as far as the public spotlight. But older guys who are into watchin' those stock shows tell me that they've got a pretty strong profit base goin' from previous years and now they're usin' it while everyone else is down."

"Mm-hmm," Candace nodded.

"They're pretty much just buyin' a lot of smaller and mid-level companies on the eastern side of the country, whereas other companies are comin' up by gettin' pieces of other giants that are now goin' out of business or sellin' off to finance their debts. I'm

LOOKIN' IN THE MIRROR

thinkin' that Blitson is takin' companies that the giants once did business with, or provide services that everyone needs."

"Are you okay?" Candace asked. "You have this look on your face like...I don't know, it's weird."

"I'm straight...I think I'm gonna start my period soon. Yesterday I woke up for work...and I was just pissed."

They started laughing.

"Man, I was pissed to be up, I was pissed to have to *move*," I smiled, "I didn't wanna go to work. I didn't wanna talk to anybody...man, I was just heated."

"Oh yeah...I've had those days," Kenya sympathized.

"So you're just melancholy today, huh?" Candace inquired, searching for my mood.

My face went uneasy. "Hmmm...I guess so. I feel kinda...blahh, y'know?"

Shawn looked in the rear view mirror, "Have you talked to Theresa lately?"

"Umm...maybe a week ago, why?" I answered.

"Did she decide to keep the baby or what?" she asked.

"Oh, yeah, I guess so. I mean, we didn't really talk about it, but I guess she's keepin' it 'cause she didn't mention a change or anything."

"Ohh."

"Did I tell you that April's getting married??" I asked her.

"WHAT????" Shawn's whole face opened up.
"Yeah!"

Said Shawn, "No! You didn't tell me!!! Who is it?"

"This cat she met in college… Uhhhh, what's his name? I've talked to him a couple of times…" I mumbled, "Dammit, what's his name?"

"That guy you said she met her junior year?"

"Yeah…ummm…damn. I still can't remember!"

My roommate interrupted, "Hey Shawn, are you and Donald okay now?"

Kenya looked surprised, but was confused, "What? What's wrong? Y'all aren't getting a divorce are you?"

"No, girl!" Shawn looked at her ridiculously. "He wanted me to get off birth control so we could start tryin' to have a baby."

And Kenya blew up with elation, "Oh my gosh!!!! Are you serious??? Are you pregnant??"

"Calm down, girl!" Candace said so Shawn could explain.

"No, I'm not pregnant," she answered Kenya then looked at my roommate via the rear view mirror, "We talked and I told him that I'm not ready to have a baby, but after a year or two we can look at things again."

Candace looked at me. My life is always the entertainment because Kenya is the lonesome dove, Candace has a boyfriend, and my roommate—well, she's just as nomadic as I am, but not quite as commitment phobic. Besides, if she's off being transient, then she's more likely with her other friends,

LOOKIN' IN THE MIRROR

whereas I would be out showcasing some new man of mine to the public.

"So how's it goin' with the contenders??" she asked.

"The main ones or the new guys?" I asked.

"The ones that have been around for at least a month," she specified.

"Ummm. That would be…" I thought aloud, "HEY! BENTLEY!!!! THAT'S HIS NAME! BENTLEY!!"

"Huh??" rippled through the car.

"April's fiancé. His name is Bentley Saint-John."

Kenya responded all frowned up, "Bent-ley??"

"Yeah, he's from Barbados or somethin'," I explained, "He talks so cool!"

Looks of disinterest fell on their faces.

"But anyway," I resumed my previous subject, "the contenders are pretty much just Vinny and Lamar."

Shawn made fun of his name by mimicking a line from the gay Lamar character in 'NERDS', "You like me, you really like me!"

"You're gonna let her make fun of your man like that?" Candace instigated.

I shrugged and chuckled. "He ain't my man. They haven't earned that much keep yet."

"So what's wrong with 'em?" she asked.

I paused, looked out the window and over at Kenya in the front passenger seat. I looked down at my lap, then finally at Candace to answer her, "It's kinda weird. You just have to know Lamar…'cause he's kinda overworkin' himself to get my attention. He tries to take too much of my time—hell, I almost couldn't get tonight with y'all 'cause he wanted to come and be up under me all night."

"Damn. Is he needy or what?" my roommate asked.

"I know, right. And Vinny is cool, but it's kinda distracting to talk to him, y'know?" I started laughing. "When we're out together, he'll start talkin', but I can't listen 'cause I'm too busy tryin' to imagine him naked." A proud smile spread across my face.

Shawn laughed. "That's not a bad problem to have."

"No, it's *not*," I agreed, "Not at all…"

"But otherwise, you like him?" Candace asked.

"Well, he's alright. But since he's a stripper, he has to travel a lot so we can't spend as much time together as, like, me and Lamar," I explained.

My roommate looked at me. "Could you see yourself settling down with him?"

"Woahhhhh, woahhhh, hold your horses!" I said, waving my hands at her. "There's no need to get irrational, now!"

Candace laughed.

"Just caaaalm down…you *don't* need to cuss," I said smiling.

Kenya spoke forlornly, "I wish I could find a contender so I can settle down… But I always find these bustas. I need a man that can support me."

My brows squished forward, "Support you how?"

She paused. "You know, give me what I need," Kenya replied.

I was confounded. "We're talkin', *emotional* support, right?" I asked, testing the waters.

"Well, yeah, that too. But I need a man that'll pay the bills too, shiiit."

Still looking as though she had no evident common sense I asked, "But don't you have a job? Why do you need financial support?"

Candace jumped in to save her, "No, she means that she wants someone who won't weigh her down."

"Yeah," Kenya agreed. "And...don't you want someone that'll take care of you?"

"Emotionally? Yeah. For me, that's what marriage is about. Companionship. But I don't need a financial caretaker. I'm a grown ass woman. I'm fully capable of takin' care of myself."

"See, that's why men are intimidated by you. Men have to feel needed and you just strip them of their duties."

"Don't gimme that bullshit! This ain't the sixties. Besides, if a man *only* feels he can offer me money and transmission work then I don't want him anyway. This is a skills-based era and you have to maximize your potential."

"So," Kenya started, "you *want* a man who can't pay the bills?"

"Oh, come on!" Shawn cut in.

"Girl, that's—"

I interrupted my roommate's reaction, "That's the dumbest thing I've ever heard in my life. And why—if I don't wholeheartedly support your way—do you automatically go drastically left, like that even makes sense? That's some stupid ass logic."

"Well, I'm just sayin' that as a strong Black woman, I need a man who can be up to my caliber."

"Meaning what? Makes more money than you," I asked.

"Yeah. Isn't that what you want?"

"Well—" I began, when Shawn cut in again.

"But you aren't always gonna get that, especially in today's economy."

"Shawn, you can't even talk. You already have a man, *and* he's a systems engineer. You *found* your bank."

"No," I defended Shawn, "She's being realistic. It doesn't matter what Donald does. The fact is that in today's economy, it's not guaranteed that you're gonna marry someone that's makin' 1, 2 hundred Gs a year. But to answer your question, it would be nice if I did find some guy with Donald's paycheck. But that's not a requirement for me 'cause I'm only a writer. We don't make that much. We make enough, but it's not luxurious. So why would I irrationally expect luxury from someone else when I don't earn that? I only expect from someone else what I've accomplished—with some degree of separation."

"Degree of separation? Wha'd'you mean?" Candace asked, looking as if she was trying to coach me into schooling Kenya.

"Like, I went to college. Y'all went to college. Therefore, we naturally desire someone else that has attained that level of education, right?" I posed.

"Yeah," my roommate responded.

"But what about guys in—or employed by—the military? They don't necessarily have degrees all the time. But they're not necessarily scrubs, either. What about pilots? Head mechanics? They're not pushing papers at a desk, but they're employed, and makin' good money. You gotta think about all the possibilities out there."

"Okay, but you still need a man that'll pay the bills and support you," Kenya held.

"Support *what*??? I'm a grown ass woman. *And* I got a job. I can pay my own bills. And so can you, last time I checked." I looked at Candace. "Is she ever strugglin' for rent?"

Candace shook her head, grinning. Then perked up and added, "Well, there have been a few times, when she went out shoppin' and I had to cover her."

"Well, hell, that's just yo' fault. You shouldn't've been buyin' up the world," I said to Kenya.

"But see, if I had a good man, I could do that."

"Maaaan. You just wanna freeload. You wanna spend all his money on bills and waste your money on a lotta nonsense," I laughed, "That ain't right."

Shawn added, "We'll see how a 'good man' will like that idea."

Kenya was still intent on proving her side, "So you wanna just pay all the bills *and* take care of the kids and just let him do whatever?"

My roommate rolled her eyes and started giggling.

"Don't laugh at me, I'm for real!" Kenya said seriously.

A. M. HATTER

"Maaaaaan. Come *on*! That's not even *logical*...let alone a reasonable argument." I looked at Candace with my face squinted and then looked back at Kenya. "Dammit, Kenya. You just don't get it..."

"Well explain it to me, then. Since I just don't get it."

I sighed. "Okay, let's say I'm married. All the money *we* earn is *our* money, not his or mine 'cause it'd filter its way between the two of us anyway. So, the way I figure, we'd split up the bills depending on how much we're bringing home. It's just like in college, I always told freshmen 'Don't take more than one or two classes that you're not good at in the same semester.' That way, you balance your good grades with your bad grades and you won't have a breakdown tryin' to study all hard for eighty classes. So, gettin' to the point, unless my husband just *wanted* to pay all the bills—like Donald," I smiled at Shawn as she muttered 'Fuck you' under her breath, "we'd split the bills fairly evenly by considering how large the bills are. And the mortgage would be split in half. As for the children, they're his responsibility, too. There's no way I'd marry a man that wouldn't participate in raising our kids. That's stupid!"

"You act like everything is just fifty-fifty. You got answers for everything. What if he made less money than you?" Kenya asked. "Then you're both strugglin' and shit."

"You know," I said with a thoughtful tone, "I'd rather have a man that made less than me and spent his money with a little common sense and on investing, than a man who just had a truckload of money and

LOOKIN' IN THE MIRROR

blew it all. 'Cause then, where's the payoff? I can't see it, 'cause he spends it all on stupid shit." Remembering her 'struggling' comment I added, "Besides, if I'm living like this on my own, then adding a salary can't hurt. So we wouldn't exactly be strugglin', as long as we spend within our range. See, that's people's problem today. They wanna buy a Lexus, when they know they can only afford a Honda Civic."

My roommate finally got a chance to say something, "See Kenya, you're assuming that things are gonna be easy if you just find a man that makes more than you. But what if he got laid off?"

Seeing an opportunity to make a couple more points I jumped in, "I know! And he was the one payin' *all* the bills while you were wastin' your money; now neither of you can support the house or the kids. And whatcha gonna do? And that's why I couldn't be a stay-at-home mom, either. That shit with Enron, man. I heard this one guy killed himself over that. So now his wife can't get his life insurance—"

"Mm-hmm, 'cause you can't collect on a suicide," my roommate said.

"And even if she has a freakin' doctorate, she's been sittin' outta the workforce for I-don't-know-how-long, and the world has all this new technology by the *day*. Now what?" I paused. I looked at Candace. "I just can't see a grown ass woman with all the talent and freedom in the world, just *not workin'*. No reason whatsoever…just *not workin'*." I looked at Kenya. "Or being employed, but talkin' about needin' support."

Candace replied, "I feel you."

"You know I'm gonna write about you now, right? You've inspired a rant."

Kenya was silent.

"So don't be surprised if you see a Jay Phillips about this very discussion," I said, laughing at her dumb ass.

I knew I was the only one savagely pursuing her with the specific intent of trouncing her ideology, but hey…it's a stupid notion. And the discussion would make for a good rant. I'm sick and tired of hearing women say they're strong and independent "new millennium" women, but holding on to dependent-ass, childish belief systems. Kenya called herself being mad that I said I'd write a rant about her, but oh well… We only had to endure her silent treatment for about five or ten more minutes until we got to the benefit. (Not that it mattered because the rest of us had a good old time talking amongst ourselves.) Sadly, though, finding that I had a bona fide halfwit in my crew wasn't the shock of the evening.

When we got there, we checked in and all that. The place was nice—well, it was your average hotel ballroom. No big deal. We showed up in time to eat, not that we really wanted hotel food, but hey, it was food nonetheless. (Blehhq) These banquet things are all the same: mingle, sit, intro, eat, program…blah, blah, blah. The actual auction had a couple of *nice* men up for grabs. The rest were just okay-looking. But to a room full of thirty-and-up women, it really doesn't matter as long as you're not butt ugly and you have a job they can respect. Oh, and if you can cook or fix

LOOKIN' IN THE MIRROR

stuff...women go bonkers! Those are two *major* buzzwords.

So anyway, the auction was over, everyone breaks out to join in the dance. The deejay started playing 'The Electric Slide' to get everyone on the floor. All the Black folks jumped up, along with some White and Asian folks who were inclusive enough to know that old ass dance. Then, of course there were the people who weren't exactly in on the deal and couldn't really dance, but wanted to participate anyway. I like them. They don't give a fuck what they look like, but they get out there and give it the old college try anyway. That's so cool. You just can't get that kind of enthusiasm out of Black folks. They're always too busy trying to look cool. The deejay was pretty cool, though. He played really good songs from a few genres *and* time periods. (Try to beat this: Cher/Believe, Mary J./Real Love, Village People/YMCA, BeeGees/Stayin' Alive, 'The Casper Slide', Biggie/Mo' Money Mo' Problems, Dirty Vegas/Days Go By, and Pink/Get This Party Started, among others.) So overall, the dance was pretty funky.

The problem presented itself when I was on the dance floor.

I'm out there getting my shuffle on and all—I swear I didn't sit down the whole night—when I felt this finger tap on my shoulder. Man, I turned around and it was Lamar's fucking ass! I couldn't believe it. Few women I've known in my lifetime have ever been as shocked as I was right then. As a matter of fact, shocked is an understatement for the simple fact that it doesn't also convey the levels of fear and pisstivity that were registering at that very moment as well. But there he was, looking like he did a good thing, cheesing like he'd been away for six months and I couldn't wait to see him again.

"What are you *doing* here???" I asked.

"Well, I started missin' you," he put his arms around my waist, "Then I remembered what hotel you said the benefit was at, so I put on my best and came to surprise you."

"Uhhhh, *no*," I said, and backed away. "This is *not* cool. I told you that it'd be me and the girls, not me, the girls, and Luh*mar*."

"Aww," he stepped back, "I apologize. I didn't mean to cramp your style."

I just stared furiously.

"Please don't be mad at me."

"Look, I'm not in the position to discuss this rationally, so I'm gonna remove myself from your presence. And don't follow me!" I replied.

I muttered, "Freakin' psycho," within earshot as I turned away.

He reached for my hand, "Victoria, I'm sorry."

But I wriggled from his grasp and disappeared into the crowd. Really, I just walked to the other side of the dance floor and started dancing behind these two fat people. Then, of course, some geezer grabbed my hand. *Ugh!* I swear he looked 54, trying to sell me on being 32. Yeah, he has old man gut, gray hairs in his mustache, yellow eyes and wrinkles—oh yeah, and the signature old fart hat—but I'm supposed to believe that he's just a few years older than I? He must think I'm Billy Bo-Bo.

Later on, after the event was over and we were headed home, Shawn told me that Lamar spoke with her. She cut me off to explain that he'd seen us together before the party really started, though he didn't really know which friend she was. But, it didn't really matter because he just went up to her, asked her name and if she knew me.

Their conversation was one with mediocre depth, mainly serving his interest of finding out more about me. But Shawn, being the top dog that she is, kept him at bay by telling him long and protracted stories that drifted off of the subject, but made sure to mention my name every now and again just to make him think he'd eventually find out something important. He also apologized to her profusely just so that she'd remember to tell me how remorseful he was about the ill-thought surprise he planned. Anyway, she brought all this news to my attention to warn me about one thing: he said he's really interested in me and thinks we may have a future.

That was *not* the shit that I remotely wanted to hear. I was still trying to figure out why he thought it'd be cool to just show up at the benefit without my invitation. What in the hell was he thinking?

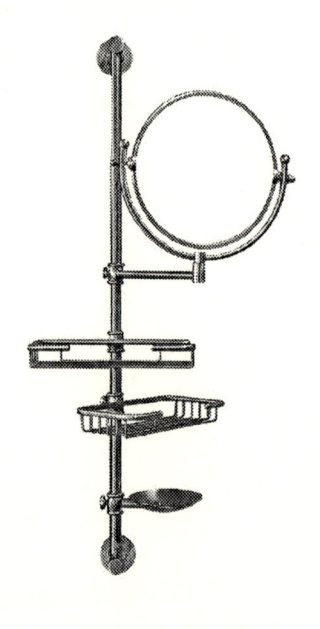

Saturday, April 27

Alejandra's Quinceañera

LOOKIN' IN THE MIRROR

"Hey, Mr. Menendez! How ya doin'?"

"Gerald! What'd I tell you when you left for college?"

I looked at him curiously.

He patted me on the shoulder, "Call me Luis! You're a man, now! No more of this 'Mr.' business," he smiled, "Okay?"

"Okay," I nodded.

We dodged the partygoers as we walked. "It's good to see you again! Thanks for coming."

"Oh, no problem! You know I had to come and celebrate Alejandra."

"So what have you been up to? We haven't seen you in so long."

Carlos's mom walked up, "Gerald! It's been too long. Where have you been?"

"Oh, I've just been workin', travelin'...mostly business stuff."

She smiled, "All work and no play, Gerald..."

"Rosa, leave the man alone," Luis said.

She laughed and ignored him, "So when will I get a wedding invitation?"

I laughed, "Aww, man, uhhh...I don'know. I don'know."

Luis intercepted, "Woman, leave'm alone. We have to make sure our other guests are happy," and nudged her away.

It was weird being at another Menendez function. I felt weirdly old, but young, in some strange phase between the elders and Alejandra's 'NSync-loving friends. I know it's gotta be about three years since I'd really been to one of their gatherings...maybe more. The last quince I went to was Gabriella's, and she's, like, twenty-five now. I think the very last thing I went to was one of Carlos & Andréa's anniversary parties...about three or four years ago.

A voice rang from behind me, "Hey there, gringo."

I turned to find open arms and a smiling face, "Gabriella!" I said.

We hugged then I stepped back to look at her.

"Ya veo que siempre estas muy sensual," I flirted.

"I see you're still very sexy," I flirted.

She laughed, "Oh, stop. I'm in my work clothes!"

"With that figure, it doesn't even matter," I replied.

"So where have you been? I was beginning to think you didn't like us anymore," she said.

I smiled and brushed it off, "Yeah, right... Man, I'm glad you came. I didn't know if I'd get to see you."

"I know. I was so mad because I had the day off," she said, noticing one of her coworkers nearby pickin' up some of the hotel plates. She continued in Spanish, "Pero este gerente corrupto quien tenia que trabajar mi turno hoy dia perdio el horario y so tomo el dia libre. ¿Miras esa muchacha alla?"

She continued in Spanish, "But this crooked manager that was supposed to take my shift today 'lost' the vacation schedule and took the day off. You see that girl over there?"

She tilted her head in the employee's direction.

"Si," I replied.

"Yes," I replied.

"Ella es la novia del pendejo ese, por eso es que estoy hablando en Español."

"She's the asshole's girlfriend. That's why I'm speaking in Spanish."

I laughed, returning comment in Spanish, "Hombre, eso esta jodido...¿No se puede tenerle confiaza a nadie en este trabajo, verdad?"

I laughed, returning comment in Spanish, "Man, that's jacked up...you can't trust anybody at this job, can you?"

"Odio este lugar, en un par de meses, escuche, que va haber una posicion de gerente en otra sucursal y voy aplicar. Espero obtener el trabajo. Quiero irme lejos de esta gente. Son estupidos y me ponen nerviosa, estare tan feliz cuando termine mi Maestria en Negocios y pueda aplicar for una posicion mas alta."

"I hate it here. In a couple of months, I heard that a staff manager spot is opening at another branch. I'm going to apply for it. I hope I get it. I wanna get away from these people. They're so stupid and they get on my nerves...I'll be so happy when I finish my MBA and I can apply for something higher."

I patted her on the back and replied to her in English, "It'll be okay. Just look at it this way: at least you were able to make it."

"Yeah. You're right," she said, "I need to make the best of it...even though it's kinda weird to be around all these prepubescents," she laughed.

Carlos walked up, "I know man. I feel all old and shit."

Their uncle, Manuel, walked up. "Pardon me," he said turning to Carlos, "Hey, are they going to bring out some more food, or is this the last round?"

Carlos replied, "I think this is it, Uncle Manuel. We only have the room for another forty-five minutes."

"Okay," he replied.

Gabriella interjected, "Hey, Uncle Manuel. Do you remember Carlos's friend Gerald? He was the best man at the wedding."

He squinted at me for a short second. Dude had *definitely* knocked back a few glasses of the old aqua vitae. "Oh yeah! Gerald! It's been a long time! Where have you been?"

"Pretty much, just working, Mr. Menendez. I've been working a lot," I replied.

"Huhh?"

"I said I've been working a lot!"

"Ohh! Good, good! A little work never hurt anybody! You keep it up," he said as he started to walk off, "But don't be a stranger. Make time to see us!" Mumbling at the end, "We're your family, too."

"Okay, I'll do that," I replied.

"Good to see you!" he replied as he staggered off.

We laughed. Manuel was always the family lush.

"Glad to see nothing has changed," I laughed.

"Oh yeah…good ol' reliable Uncle Manny."

LOOKIN' IN THE MIRROR

Alejandra stopped by briefly. "Hi, Gerald. Thanks again for the present."

"No problem, Alejandra. I'm glad you like it," I replied.

Then she walked off with her friends, just smilin'.

"What'd you get her?" Gabriella asked.

"An antique jewelry box," I replied.

"Oh, that's nice," she said.

Carlos seemed beyond bored, inching toward antsy. "You ready to go, man?"

"Umm…yeah, I guess so."

"Good, I wanna go to the movies," he said.

"Cool! You wanna come with us, Gabriella?"

"Yeah, that's cool with me. What are we going to see?"

Carlos shrugged, "Shhh…hell if I know. Just come on…"

"Okay," she said.

As we started toward the door, his face changed to a confused expression. "Where's my wife?"

"I think she's with mom," Gabriella answered.

I chuckled. "We better wait, then."

"You ain't lyin'. I'll never hear the end, if we go to the movies and don't tell her about it."

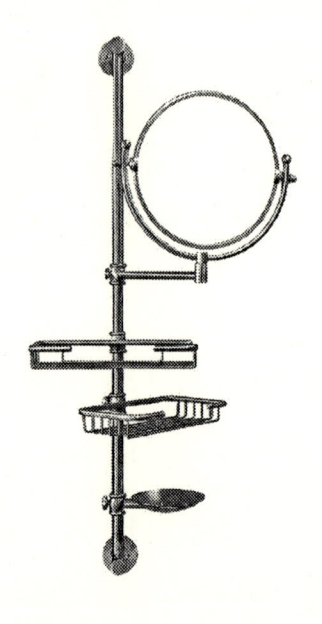

The Next Day

LOOKIN' IN THE MIRROR

I had been awake for a couple hours, but I just laid there.

Wide awake with nowhere to go.

I didn't move, lettin' time roll by while I flipped through dull Sunday mornin' programming—televangelists, infomercials, and colorless 80s movies on cable. My back felt like it was six inches into the mattress. Even the air felt heavy. Then I reached over to my nightstand and pulled the top drawer out. I pulled out a letter that I'd been keepin' for weeks. It was from Denise.

It was on her special stationery—the kind made of soft paper with a slight texture that feels like really expensive resume paper. With my fingertips at opposite ends, I rotated it around in my hands, turning it again and again. I'd flip it over, look at the address. Then I'd flip it over again and look at the lipstick stain over the seal, and back around again. Just seeing her name, "Denise," as mundane as it is, brought back memories—fond memories—that, even though I'd spent the last seven months (one week and two days, but who's counting?) licking my wounds, still couldn't be erased. Part of me wanted to throw it away, but the curiosity was eatin' at me. So after twirling the letter for about five minutes, I finally gave in and opened it.

It carried her other signature, I didn't even have to open the envelope that much to catch a whiff of her peach scented perfume—the kind that smells like it would taste like a Jolly Rancher, but disappoints you when you suck on her neck and taste chemical. It was folded neatly, almost like an invitation, but wore her thickly inked, calligraphic handwriting. I swear, she writes like she's holdin' lead pen. You'd think there'd be holes in the paper.

> *Dear Gerald,*
>
> *Please forgive me for leaving you the way I did. There is nothing that I can say or do to justify it or make it up to you, but I am asking for your forgiveness.*
>
> *Over the last six months, what I did has replayed through my mind over and over. I can't forget how much I must have hurt you, and it makes me sick to my stomach.*
>
> *A good man like you doesn't deserve what I did and*

(((Ding, Dong!)))
Huh? Who's at my door on Sunday at noon?

I dropped the letter on the bed and kicked the covers off. The doorbell rang again as I trotted down the stairs. When I got to the door, I looked through the eyehole.

Oh, hell naw, I thought. I punched in the alarm code to turn it off, and opened the door.

"Hi," she said.

I replied, "Hi," but my thoughts ran more like, *don't you have anything better to do?*

"I-I uhh…I'm sorry to show up unannounced, but I didn't get a response from you."

"Yeah, I've been busy. I really *just* got around to readin' a lot of my mail."

"Oh," she said, "So, uhh…can I, come in?"

I opened the storm door and let her in. She went straight to her spot right in the middle of the couch. Eight months ago I'd have sat right next to her,

LOOKIN' IN THE MIRROR

but this time I sat on the loveseat just to the side and stretched out.

"So, uhh, what's on your mind?" I asked, tryin' to get to the point of her visit.

"Did you read the letter?" she asked.

I grabbed the remote control and turned on the TV. "Why don't *you* tell me?" I replied.

She sighed, "This is really hard for me..."

Life's a bitch ain't it? I thought to myself, as I flipped to CNN.

"I came over because I'm asking for your forgiveness. The way I left was really, *really* sorry. Cowardly. I didn't wanna hurt you, even though I did."

I just looked at her.

"If you could find it in your heart, I'd appreciate another chance," she said.

I grinned. "Why, so you can walk out again?"

"No, I wouldn't do that, Gerald. I wanna stay. I wanna stay for keeps. I wantchu back."

"What??"

She scrambled to find words, "Gerald...you don't understand. My momma...you know she didn't want me living with you. She kept telling me that you controlled too much and that I—that I should have my own place so that I could be independent," she hung her head, "Man, she's crazy...I never shoulda listened to her."

I controlled too much? I sat up and looked at her like, *what the hell are you talkin' about?*

"I never told you, but my dad left while we were together. And my mom was pretty much on her own. So it just got me scared and she really didn't help the situation."

"So, lemme get this straight... I opened doors for you, pulled out your seats, treated you like a fuckin' *queen*. I did *nothin'* but help you. I put you through beauty school. I helped you do your business plan so you could get the capital to start your own shop—*my* name ain't *no*where on the lease, and you got scared that I was controllin' too much?"

"I just felt that I should get my own place, though. I didn't wanna be like my mom."

"What would make you think I'd do somethin' like what happened to your mother?"

She shook her head and shrugged, "I don't know…"

"Were you fuckin' some other guy?"

"Huh?"

I responded sternly, "You heard me! Were you fuckin' some other guy?"

She answered quickly, "No! No! I'm tellin' you, no. I never would have done that. I was just brainwashed, Gerald. My momma kept telling me that I needed to get from under your thumb."

She wasn't makin' any fuckin' sense, but I humored her theory anyway. "So, you just got up one day and decided to move. No letter, *nothin'*. And you just couldn't find *any* reason whatsoever to come talk to *me*," I asked with a sarcastic calm.

"My momma kept tellin' me that if I said anything, you'd convince me to stay. Look Gerald, I know this sounds weak, but I'm being honest. I just want another chance."

"I don't know, Denise. You on some bullshit, and I'm just not tryin' to hear it right now."

"Gerald. Just listen to me…I want the chance to treat you like you *want* to be treated."

Who is she? Father-MC or some shit?

"I just wanna start over. Be right to you, be your friend. There were a lot of things I did that were selfish and jealous. But I don't want to be that way anymore. I want us to be real. I want to be the way you and Mia are."

"Last I remember, you didn't like Mia too much."

She replied, "I was just jealous. You have a bond with her that I didn't have with you. But I've come to respect her place in your life. She's like your sister and I'm cool with that," she paused, "Look, I'm trying to get you back. All that other stuff that I used to be mad about, I don't care. The way you used to stay on the computer all day sometimes, playing 'Quake'. I'll take it. I don't care anymore. I just want you back."

She got up and stepped toward me, "Well, it's up to you," she said and leaned to kiss my lips. Her mouth brushed mine, but I tilted my head away.

"If you choose to leave me alone, I'll understand and…well, I'd have no choice but to respect your decision," she smiled nervously, "But, um, I just had to let you know how I feel…and if you give me another chance, I'd do my best to make sure you don't regret it."

Then she left.

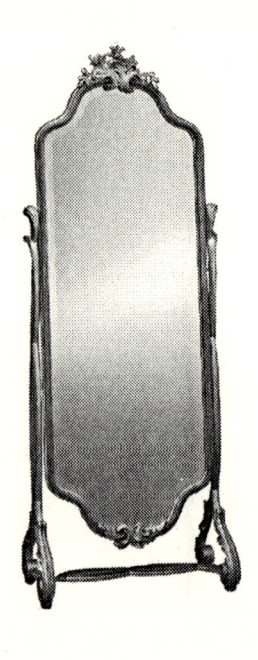

Thursday, August 1

LOOKIN' IN THE MIRROR

My day began with me deep in thought. In fact, my rambling brain made me ten minutes late for work because 1) I wouldn't stop checkin' myself out when I put on my new underwear set, and 2) for some reason I was ardently compelled to review the last few months of activities, so I was lolligagging. But hey, Socrates did say that the unexamined life is not worth living. (Though, a case could be made that I examine a little too much or a bit too often.)

It's amazing how time passes so slowly when you're young, but suddenly you're in your late twenties (ahem, er, uh...*young adult stage*) wondering where May, June & July went. The last truly memorable event was back when I met Vinny, the suit man. Oh, yeah...and the church lady from the time I went to that place in Georgetown with Lamar. Truly two times to remember! But I had trouble recalling all the time between then and August first that virtually breezed by. I remembered a few girls' nights at the sports bar...some "art shows," that damn male auction, but not much else. Then it hit me: the reason why I was so compelled to review the last few months was that I'd dated three other guys (in addition to Vinny & after Lamar) and each had been eliminated. And it's my custom to periodically take inventory of my encounters to evaluate whether or not I caused problems or if anything could've been salvaged, had it not been for my impetuous ignorance. However, in retrospect, I can truly say that two out of three were not my fault—and even the solo case is just a maybe.

Mr. Maybe was this White guy—no, he was a fine ass White guy. He was tall and fairly wiry, well,

A. M. HATTER

no… not wiry because guys with wiry bodies are some lanky mo-foes. He would be classified as athletically slim: chiseled but not really padded, with *great* legs. And his derrière was the bomb, might I add. (He was probably a pretty good soccer player at some point in time.) He had dark, disheveled hair like Steve Nash, big dimples, and (dun, dun, dunnnnnnn!) a goatee. I was infatuated. The only problem was that he was kind of dry. Really nice guy, but he hadn't a preference for anything *in life*. I mean *anything*. If I asked him what he wanted to do, he'd ask me what *I* like to do. The conversation was…*level* at best, but not passionate. It didn't have any bite, any get-up-and-go… Hell, it didn't even have any tilt-up-and-sit. Dude was just dry. But I loved his hair. And his legs…*man*. He looked like he'd be in a jean commercial.

Then there was this Australian Black guy. Two thousand cool points just for the accent alone! I met him at the grocery store, when he asked me where to find the spice aisle. We'd already been checking each other out in previous aisles, but when he spoke, that put the nail in the coffin! It was really cool to hear him talk, but it was kind of hard to carry a real conversation sometimes, simply because of the differing slang and the thickness of his accent. That was a cool experience, especially since I can say I dated a Black dude from the Down-under, but his attitude wasn't too hot.

We went out to a restaurant where—oh my gosh, we had this waiter named LaMonday (no bull) and in this other seating section there were three ghetto ass Black women. (My roommate always did tell me that it's hell to wait on three Black women—and it's

LOOKIN' IN THE MIRROR

always three. Not four, not two, but three. They always act a fool and they *never* tip accurately. But then, when she was waitressing, she never wanted to seat anybody Black because of "our" tipping habits. She made that known to all the management and staff, and justified herself by saying, "It's not racism because I'm Black, too!") Those chicks made *so much* noise! I was embarrassed for the whole ethnic group—at least, I *would* be if I wasn't calling myself "other" now.

Man, those women were so disrespectful and you could tell that they were only ordering a lot of stuff and changing things so the server would get it wrong and they'd get their food free. They called the waitress back so many times *I* wanted to help her. But that didn't work because she did almost everything right except bring more of some condiment "fast enough," and some "mysterious taste" ruined one girl's dish. So she spoke brashly at the server and told her to remove her dinner from the check, but strangely the mysterious taste became apparent only after she ate all but a quarter of it. So, of course, she couldn't remove the dinner because it was almost totally eaten, but things escalated until the manager came; when, naturally he merely reiterated what the server said. So the girl huffed and puffed, but finished her dinner and neither one of them tipped the server. But, so many people witnessed the girls' atrocious behavior that even people from other sections walked by and left a dollar or two. So because of those three ghetto chicks, the girl got close to thirty dollars off that one table. (And people wonder why nobody likes Black folks. Tell ya cousins to quit playin'.)

A. M. HATTER

But back to Mr. Dundee, we went out to that restaurant and there were a couple of gay guys who walked in and ate dinner—like anyone else. But he just couldn't get over the fact that they were there. He thought it was so disgusting that they "parade around like nothing's wrong with being *that way*." (What's with this "parade" word? Like they just march in everywhere on instruments, playing some Village People tune, sporting gay exotic dancers donning thongs with ballet cups inside. And I heard Australia was supposed to be a tolerant nation. I think he's been in America too long.)

Then he asked, "Do you agree with the way they live?"

I shrugged munching on a breadstick, sitting there looking like I couldn't give a rat's ass (which I don't) and replied, "Well, I'm straight. Why would I care what gay people do?"

To which, he replies, "But that's unnat'ral. [Blah, blah, blah.]"

Staring blankly, "And that would be my business because?"

"I just don't think it's right," he said.

"Just don't look at 'em then. It's not like they're over here trying to recruit you." Then I laughed. I personally thought it was funny to picture, like, a gay recruitment officer or something. *Ha! Me and my imagination!* ☺

He didn't find it as funny, though.

So I had to let him go because he was entirely too agitated about them for that to be healthy, or even normal. [Sigh.] I can't possibly imagine being *that*

LOOKIN' IN THE MIRROR

bothered by a person or group that I have nothing to do with and has no knowledge of my existence. But that's all right because while he's over there stewing over nothing, I'll just be hetero-mind-my-own-damn-business-and-*eat*-my-stew. How about that? Things would be so much easier if people would just look in their own plates.

HA! Look in your own plate...ironic. Check the next story.

Anyway, as I change soapboxes, the other guy was this...I don't know, moment of intrigue? He wasn't even my type. I can't stand vegetarians—*or* vegans. I just can't understand the logic. I think it's asinine to *totally* cut a food out of your life. *Especially* meat...and chee-yeee-yeeeese. I'm not for eating meat every day, because that's not healthy either. But hell, there's nothing like sitting down to a well-cooked sirloin. *Mmmmmmmm. Sirrrloin. Rrrrrrrrrrrrrrrrr.*

All that crap about "saving a life" is stupid. (And I bet half of those "animal rights" activists wouldn't lift a hand to help *a human being*. Dorks.) To be a vegetarian is killing plants. Why are their lives not as valuable? Just because they don't move around and make voluntary noises? Who says that's a sign of life? Scientifically, plants are classified as living. And I bet those PETA retards have nooo problem cutting the grass, right? Besides, cows don't do shit but sit around grazing all day. Kill them, eat the meat, use the hide and ground the rest up for fertilizer. As long as nothing's being wasted, it's a good process!

ANYWAY, the vegan man (Vee-Gan Maaaan!!) was this cat I met in the District. He's really cute, but dresses like a clown—or a Hare Krishna with dreads and a backpack, basically. I was down at this record store, one of those places that has a lot of albums that you can't find anywhere else, and we started making eye contact. I don't know if his contact was intentional, but for me, it was more like I'd look up and happened to catch his eye. I don't like when that happens.

So after we did the look-and-look-away thing a few times, he got to where he was on the other side of the shelf from me. We started talking and he asked me out... I'm thinking, *Free meal!* So, naturally, I said yes. He asked me if I minded going to a vegetarian restaurant. I told him no, and he asked if I ate animal products. To which, I replied yes, but that it didn't bother me that he doesn't. So we went out to this cool little place squeezed between a few other attached businesses on the block. We were having a good time, talking about everything under the sun: music, art, sports, video games, comics, movies...and the food was really good! So I thought I'd be nice—you know, supportive sounding—and mention it. But that little kimono-and-Asics-wearing goofball took it as a chance to convert me and started up trying to sell me on his vegetarian lifestyle and shit, talking about I need to purify my body, cleanse my spirit and let go of those animal chemicals. I'm sitting there like, *Fool, shutcho ass up*. And just as I prepared to cordially tell him that I wasn't interested, this geek lights a fucking cigarette! His explanation was that "It's a plant; therefore it's natural." *Yesssss, I see your point Mr. Vegan man. Let's take a natural plant and add all these natural carcinogens and herbal nicotine because addiction soo natural. Yeah, I've heard of that natural addiction thing before… It happens to crack babies all the time. Freakin' dickhead.* So then, I had to inform him that I don't date smokers and that was the end of that.

Lamar called but I let the voicemail get it. He's desperately trying to get me back. He emails every week to apologize more and tell me that he understands the concept that I only wanted to be friends. Only, I don't want to start our routine again, where he'll be okay for a minute, but revert to his old get-her-to-like-me tactics after, like, two weeks of being good. Then, after two weeks of him annoying me to damn death, I'll let him know that he's smothering me. Then he'd back off again and we'd start over.

On the other hand, with exception to the above, I did like his convenience—minus the name Lamar. (Really, what kind of name is Lamar? Luh-mahrr. Ugh.) But after that benefit auction fiasco, he *had* to go, which created a significant gap in my schedule. He, by far, had been hogging more of my time. He was very aggressive about setting dates with me; quite often, he'd ask about meeting again right at the end of the date. I would normally have become pretty cautious about that type of behavior, as it could be a sign of a jealous man who wants to keep you from any other guys. But he has some distinct woman-like competitive qualities about him and I simply felt like he was just angling. Boy, was I right. But I'm always up-front that I am a very active dater. Nobody's keeping me away from any men. I've been boy crazy since I was, like, two.

But he definitely had to go. I was fucking up my game with him anyway. He's only a level seven contender—he would've been a level five because he's smart and stuff, but he wouldn't quit bugging me; however, he got to enjoy level four status because he was always available when I was bored. Whereas, Vinny is a level five contender, but only gets to enjoy level seven status because (1) he travels a lot and (2) he's not quite as versed as Lamar.

But Vinny, by far, has held my attention. Well, not in any *real* sense. It's not like I'm looking at him as keep-him material, but he just really, *really* entertains my eyes. And that's such a welcome escape, though, very distracting when you're face-to-face. He laughs at me because he's caught me staring before. So I just learned to stare at his eyes. But that didn't work for long because I still don't listen very well.

Anyway, Vinny is cool. But I feel for him because he was downsized and that's why he started stripping (er, uh…"exotic dancing"). He's from Memphis, so he kinda talks like Nelly and he says "mayn." He has a passable level of substance and possesses a lot of style, so he fills in where Lamar didn't—especially in the voice area. Maaaaan… Vinny's voice will turn a nun into a porn star. But Lamar sounds like the Boston version of that light-skinned guy from 'Mo' Money'.

And sex appeal… [Drum roll] …ONE STAR!

Beyond being late, my day was going pretty well. Sherry was off on vacation. The preacher lady was out doing research. I'm at my desk like, *Cool!* Anita even came by and gave me some good news:

thanks to Rick & Terry getting us some exposure, their company wanted to add DeFi to their collection and she brought me the complimentary productions for us. *Yeah! Now I can bust out my own designs! Woo-hooo!*

And then there was that thing with people calling me when I want to get work done. I don't get it. It never fails. When I'm bullshitting, nobody knows me. But when I'm *trying* to work I'm always bombarded with frivolous calls from people who I haven't talked to in a while or people who feel their inconsequential issue is soooo important that I need to listen—like Theresa. But this time she didn't keep me on long, plus she had good-ish news: she's not pregnant. She miscarried. I'm not sure that everything was on the up-and-up, considering that she's the type that would do something to *cause* that. But hey, if it'll keep her out of early motherhood then so be it. She's SO not ready, and if it'll prevent her from being tied to that asshole Derek for the remainder of her years, then, hell, I'm all for it. *I still hope she told him, though. But I bet she copped out.*

Besides, the world could use one less spawn. It's quite interesting that she gave me news of her miscarriage as I was working on my piece about population control. Not that she was sad about the miscarriage—because she clearly wasn't, but (like what I wrote in my article) people in general irritate me because they wanna find cures for every ailment, like that's even…damn, pick a word: possible, logical, necessary, desirable.

I could see finding a cure for, say, menstrual cramps. We don't need that shit at any point in life.

But other shit—stuff that kills people? I'm not seeing it. Don't get me wrong, I'm not saying it's good to have cancer or HIV/AIDS, and I'm sure it's more than horrible to watch a loved one die from either one. But if *nobody* in the fucking world had anything that would kill them, there'd be too many fucking people! Do you know how many babies are born every *day*?? SHEESH. You think urban sprawl is a problem…imagine if everyone spread out! *Grand Canyon Apartments! Move-in Special!*

The way I see it: People getting killed? Population control. People starving? Population control. People in war? Population control. If nothing else, call it evolution. Either way, nature is going to balance itself out as best it can. Birth & death happens. It's the natural cycle of life. Everybody that came in is eventually going out; it's just a matter of how.

Men or women who can't have children: sorry, but doo-doo occurs. Still, you can adopt or make a very meaningful mark on the world some other way.

Those people that fatally wound themselves *by accident*? Come on, man. You don't see us living people playing with weapons.

(Or any other death worthy of being listed on DarwinAwards.com.)

But menstrual cramps? Yeah, those can go.

Is there a cure for stupid people? They procreate too damn fast. They're having a dumboning effect on the population. Hey, wait…I need to get on the ball or else I'll be evolved out of the game!

Just as that thought ran through my head, a nice young man that I wouldn't mind procreating with called. (Just so you know, I'm being facetious.)

"Hey Vinny!" I responded to his "Hello." I always knew his voice; there was nothing else like it.

"How are you?"

"I'm fine. Working on some articles."

"Oh really? What're you writin' about now?"

"Population control."

"Oh. Are you anotha one of those Darwin-ers?"

I laughed, "Yeah, just a little bit, but I'm writin' more from the angle of Thomas Malthus. I'm kinda into both of them, though."

"Hmm, okay then," he answered just before he started laughing.

"What are you doin'?" I asked.

"I'm readin' this email that my homegirl sent to me… Some white girl wrote to this magazine, talkin' 'bout how she hates that Black women shoot her mean looks and make snide remarks 'cause she datin' a Black man, and she askin' Black men to explain why White women are so coveted."

"What? *Coveted??* That's ballsy."

"And that ain't the half of it!" he said eagerly.

"What else did she say?"

"She talkin' 'bout her fiancé told her that he dates White women 'cause the options among Black women are slim… …and… Aawww, hell naw… This broad go'n say maybe Black women should take notes on how to treat they men. I can't be-*lieve* this!" He laughed. "She *wanna* get beat down!"

A. M. HATTER

I just laughed. "She's stupid. First of all, if her fiancé gave her any answer as to why he dates a specific ethnic group, that's the wrong reason. It should be about her and her only, not about what other people act like... And who really looks at interracial couples anymore? That shit's so old now."

"True... ...So, you don't curr about Black men datin' White women?"

I replied nonchalantly, "Not particularly. Hell, chances are, they wouldn't like me anyway. I'm Black. Besides, I'm greatness. They wouldn't know how to handle me."

He laughed. "Girl, you're too much," he paused, reading more of the email, "What I don't like is her assumption that this one Black guy speaks for a nation of Black men, *and* she's making statements when she knows nothin' about what's going on in Black society. She shouldn't talk about what she don't know."

"Well, yeah, I guess that's true. But anyway..."

"AWWWW, MAYN! Somebody responded to'er! And he straight slashed her, too!"

"Oh, really? What'd they say?" I don't know why I asked. I wasn't the least bit interested in some dating propaganda between Black people and White people, which—knowing how things tend to go with that—always leads to the slavery debate...it never fails.

Trying to calm down, "Yeah, this Black dude...and he straight slashed her. I hope she read it, 'cause he put her in her place," still laughing, "He was like, Black guys like White girls 'cause they give it up quick and they docile and easy to control!" he said and laughed some more.

I was shocked by the letter's brashness. "Damn, he put it out like *that*???"

"Yehhh, mayn! I'm kinda glad, too...burst her damn bubble. She was a lil bit too cocky for me, talkin' about shit she don't know."

"I wonder if she did read it, and what she thought."

"And ya boy got historical on her, too, talkin' about how Black women taught them how to season they food and how the slaves nursed and raised they children... [Short, spiked laugh] He told her don't think that 'cause you're white, you're a goddess! He straight dissin' her!"

Oh, how easily impressed... Note to self; ideas for rants: 1-Who gives a fuck about interracial couples, 2-Unless you've personally endured slavery, quit bitchin', and 3-People who are in awe of hot air.

"I wonder how many guys do date White girls for that reason."

"What? Because they're easy?" he asked.

"No, because they're perceived to be docile," I replied.

"Mayn, that's almost every guy I've known who dated one."

"Really??"

"Hell yehh! I used to work with this guy a couple years back, mayn. He didn't say it, but like, from his actions, we knew that's what it was about. 'Cause he would tell his girl somethin' and say 'No back-talk.'"

My head jerked back. "No *back-talk*???"

"Yehhhh!" He chuckled. "And we were lookin' like, hell naw! So I knew that had to be it 'cause, you can't just tell a sista no shit like that. Come on, nah."

"Man, I wish somebody *would* tell me 'No back-talk.' Man, what the *hell*??" We laughed. "And that ain't even cool! I mean, that's like talkin' to a five-year-old. Why would you wanna talk to your *spouse* like that?" I wondered.

"It's like she don't have any self-respect, lettin' him talk to her like that… See, that's why I couldn't date other women, mayn. They just don't act the same…when I come home, I want a woman that'll shoot the breeze…knows my slang…got a big ol' ass," he laughed, "And'll kick my son's ass if he brings some ol' sorry ass girlfriend home, like *my* momma did."

I laughed. "Oh, your momma tripped about the girls you dated?"

"Hey-ll yehhh! Mayn my momma didn't even like me with light-skinned *Black* girls! She was like, 'Why you always datin' light-skinned girls? Give the dark sistas a chance!'"

"Is your momma dark?" I asked.

"Not really. Well, not dark like me. She's like, ummm…dark brown, I guess."

"Oh, I was about to say, 'cause usually dark women are the strongest about not wanting their sons to date light-skinned chicks or White chicks."

"Yehhhh. But it wasn't just that. She didn't want me to have some ol' docile woman up under me, y'know?"

"Uh-huh."

"When I was, like, fifteen, moms sat me down and she was like, 'You're not gonna grow up and marry some flaky woman who's gonna be ya do-girl and call it a day. Hoes can do that.' And then she went, 'What if you died? She's in charge of your kids and all your money goes to her. You have to be able to trust her to take care of business if things don't go as planned.' And that *really* made me think about who I finally choose in life."

"Yeah… That was good advice."

"But, uhhh, changin' the subject," he laughed, "When we goin' out again? I mean, I know I asked you for this weekend last week, but lobbyin' for yo' time is like bein' at an auction."

I laughed, "What?? *Lobby*-in'??"

"Muhfuckas be like, 'Five minutes, five minutes, five minutes, ten minutes, ten minutes, ten minutes, Oh! One hour over hurr in the red! One hour, one hour, Oh! Two hours, orange shirt! Two hours, two hours, two hours—Sold! To the man in the orange shirt!"

I died laughing at his characterization of me, as if I'm even that in-demand.

"You need to quit," I exclaimed, still laughing at him.

"You know I'm tellin' the truth. I don't know why you try'na act modest," he paused, "Mayn, let me tell you about this homeless dude I saw."

"Uh-huh."

"You know I just got back from doin' a couple shows in New York, right?"

A. M. HATTER

"Yeah."

"I was walkin' down the street one night, headed back to the crib and I saw these two ladies up ahead of me gigglin' at this vagrant."

"Why were they laughin' at him??"

"Wait, lemme tell you. I looked over at the homeless dude and," he started to laugh, "he was posed up on the wall," he started laughing louder, "Like, you remember how the tin man looked when he ran out of oil?"

"Yeah."

"That's how he looked," he snickered.

"Okay…" I said, starting to giggle.

"So, one of the women told the other one to throw some money in his hat, and when she did, he gon' walk over to his radio and turn it on and start dancin'!!!" He kicked out a loud, open-mouthed laugh.

I laughed along with him.

"But, naw, check this: when their time was up, he gon' turn off the radio and freeze back up!"

I laughed more, "Hobo the Human Jukebox, huh?"

"Mayn, for *real*!"

I continued laughing, "See, that's why I like New York. They have some of the most entertaining characters there."

"Mayn, you ain't lyin'. 'Cause that was some funny shit rhyt thurr."

"I'll never forget, I was on the train, right… And, like, *right* as the doors were closing, this ol' dirty man hopped in. But he had a saxophone, so I was

LOOKIN' IN THE MIRROR

thinkin' 'Ugh,' 'cause I was thinkin' he was gonna go around askin' for money in exchange for a few notes."

"Uh-huh."

"But he was like, 'I need some money to *eat*! So, if I don't get some money right now, I'm gonna blow your ears out!' And then he started playin' really loud and off-key! It was all 'Waaaaank! Weeeeeeerrrrr! Aaaaaaaaaaah! Eeeeeeeeeeeee!"

He laughed. "Awwwwww mayn! Did anybody give'm some money?"

"Yeah, this woman in the back gave him some money after a while and he just went into the next cab."

He chuckled, "You didn't give'm no money?"

"Nope…I didn't have far to go anyway. I was just gonna deal with it. You forget I grew up with brothers."

He chuckled a little harder, "Hellllll nawww. Shawty said she ain't givin' up no money!"

"Nawww, buddy," I replied.

"Lemme ask you a question," he said.

"What?"

"You're a really different type-uh chick—"

I interrupted, "I ain't that different. That's just what *you* think."

"Yes you are…I mean, you like all these kinds of music…"

"A lotta people like multiple genres of music. That doesn't make me some kind of cultural melting pot," I debated.

"Well…yeah it does. I mean, you like all this music, you know a lotta history and philosophy. You were born in the south, went to school in Cali, now you live on the upper east coast. You're different. Nobody can classify you," he said.

"Okay…so what's your question?"

"Who can get witchu? I mean, what type-uh dude are you lookin' for?"

I replied flatly, "I'm not."

"Whatchu mean?"

"I mean, I'm not lookin'," I answered.

"What? You don't want a man? Like, ever?" he asked, sounding concerned.

"It's not that, necessarily…it's just that I'm not looking. Whatever happens, happens. But I'm not gonna go out huntin' and shit like I don't have a life."

"Damn. That's real," he replied.

I sat on the phone quietly, making faces in response to his ever-so-profound reply.
Ooooh…"That's real"…I'm so enlightened.

"So, like," he began, "do you ever feel lonely?"

"No," I stated.

He paused, "Come on, nah. You don't *ever* get lonely??"

"*No.*"

"How?"

"Whatchu mean, *How*?" I asked.

"—*HOW*, mayn. I mean, ev'rybody gets lonely ev'ry now and again!"

"No. I have friends and I live my life excitingly. If some dude wants to join me, then that's fine. But if I *never* get married and do all that storybook shit, then what? I'm still gonna be alive, right?"

LOOKIN' IN THE MIRROR

"Yeah."

"Okay then. It's not like I'm gonna jump off a bridge. So, I'll just keep livin' life the way I do—doin' what I love, doin' whatever the hell I want, writing, and acquiring money."

"'Cause you're the anti. Damn, you're hard, girl."

We laughed together.

He gave me that name, 'The Anti', because he says I'm a natural rebel. I'm against everything considered normal for my age group, my ethnic group, my gender, and any other way to classify me. According to him, I should walk around with a white T-shirt and a minus sign on it "'cause there ain't nothin' positive about" me. Funny. Very funny.

But, hell, I must not be too negative, because he still wants me. ☺

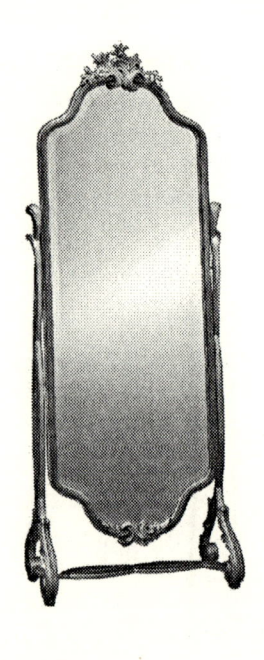

The Next Day

LOOKIN' IN THE MIRROR

I leaned back in my chair to take a breather from my computer. The tip of my head reached just outside of my cubicle and I just happened to turn my head in time to catch the mailroom dude with the nice ass walk by.

Hot damn! Every time I turn around, there's some fine ass man in my view. I don't know what scent I'm giving off, but I hope it sticks around for a while! And, for about a week or two, I've been stacking phone numbers like a famous rapper or some junk.

Oh yeah! And, I saw this dude on the freeway the other day, when I went down to V-A to visit my brother and his family. It was kind of a cool situation because we kept sneaking peeks and throwing grins at each other when he or I passed in traffic; but it was catch-22 because it's like, *Try to communicate and you wreck. Watch traffic and miss out on the hottie.* So…I had to miss out on that one. I don't need any car accidents in this mo-fo. But it was really cool at the end because as I was exiting, I looked back and he was looking right at me and we both smiled and waved goodbye. So sweet.

I wanted to write about it, but there wasn't enough of a story there. Well, not in my opinion anyway. I could make mention of it in a piece about something else, but it'd fit in more like rambling than with an effect that I wanted. Dammit. I get so distracted sometimes! I'm at my desk, trying to work on damn near 80 story ideas at once. Okay, well, about three or four really. But nothing was coming together. I'd start a story and just as I passed the second or third stanza, where you shift into a real flow, the steam dissipated. I had enough for a bunch of shorts, but not a whole piece.

And I kept wandering into dreamland about this guy that I frequently see walking on the way to work. He's…*so* lovely. Just stunning. Picturesque. Aesthetic. He has these *bee-you-*tif-full eyes, and quite possibly the most *gorgeous* smile I've *ever* seen on a man in all my years. *Ahhhhhhhhh*. He's just heavenly. But I only see him every now and then; when I do, he's always on the other side of the super busy street from where I'm walking. There have only been a couple of occasions when we've consciously looked at each other at the same time. Still, I never get to talk to him because he's on the other side, walking in a different direction and I don't have enough time to randomly follow someone to get their number and make it to work on time. Even so, I never know when he'll be out there again. He doesn't show at the same time every day. Besides, beauty like that should be left alone. He's probably an asshole or something. I don't want to ruin the fantasy.

Another beginning popped in my head. I really even got to the end, but it was still really short. I could've filibustered to make my inches, but I have this thing about not producing fluff. Fluff is my antithesis. (Although, an argument could be made that all editorials are only fluff anyway.) And as I read over it again and again, it sounded more like babble or steam that I was just trying to blow than like real writing. So I just put my "work" away and decided to answer email. That's what I do when I can't think of anything with substance. So, I blew a kiss to the dread-

LOOKIN' IN THE MIRROR

locked man on the *Essence* magazine cover hanging on my cubicle wall and got to work.

The first letter was from this airhead woman that I swear writes me an email every damn week about stupidity between her and her boyfriend. Well, really it's her. She's the type that swears up and down that she trusts her beau, but then goes through his shit. It's insane. The newest letter was about how she feels second place when it comes to sports because her guy ignores her when the game is on.

Now, it's shit like that, that bugs the hell out of me. Those bogus little ninnies who can't wait a few hours for the game to go off before they go whining about how the two of you "need to talk" because [blah, blah, blah] earlier that day. Then they get mad when you don't pay attention. Hell, nobody comes bugging *them*—getting loud in front of company—during *their* favorite TV show, talking about something *totally* off the subject and generally stupid and pointless. Conversely, if you're sitting in front of "the game" *all* day, *every* day, that's just called neglect. There's something to be said for a little thing called balance. [Sigh.] Not everyone can be as poignant as I.

Another mail type that I don't like is the "Who/What is your favorite?" mail. It's sort of a double-edged sword because you're supposed to enjoy your readers. However, the only reason people ask is to either hate me because I don't like the same thing they like, or to love me a little too much for liking a few of the same things they like. Either way, it's not cool and I don't usually answer it. But, I got

A. M. HATTER

tired of dodging the letters. So it became the topic for my next column: 'Jay's Phavorites'.

Of course, there's always the basics: food, color, name, number, book, movie, etc.

Uhhh, Pad Thai noodles, purple, mine, 7...uhh, Choose Your Own Adventure Books, and...damn, favorite movie? That's a lot. I'll have to come back to that one.

```
        Hey Jay, you're always talking about
sports. What are your favorite sports
moments and who are your favorite players?
```

Football (2)—when Bo Jackson took down The Boz, and when Barry Sanders shook all eleven Bears players in the Thanksgiving game...naturally.

Bo Jackson, Barry Sanders, Warren Moon, Jerry Rice (duhhh), and...Lawrence Taylor (minus the addiction)

Basketball (non-Jordan)—when Rodman showed Shaq who the man is. I miss Rodman. He was gangsta. And I liked the back of his book.

Jordan—of course, everyone wants to point at the moment that will forever haunt Craig Ehlo, but my personal favorite was the 63-point game, that Boston claimed they'd prevent, where he blew Danny Ainge, Dennis Johnson, AND Larry Bird out of the water, like, "Get back, you can't touch me."

That was gangsta.

My favorite B-ball players are always defenders because they're the backbone of the team. I like backcourt people (note: Muggsy Bogues, Steve Kerr, and T-Mac—among others), but defense rules. That said, my favorite players are Dennis Rodman, KG, and Alonzo Mourning. Mmm. Consistent like a David Robinson flat top. Plus, 'Zo is fine as hell.

LOOKIN' IN THE MIRROR

Classics, like Dr. J, Magic and Bird for instance, go without saying.

Dear Jay, my boyfriend and I are having a difference of opinion. He says the woman is supposed to "submit" to the man. I say these are modern times and things have changed. What do you think?

Submit what? Really. Are you applying to a school that he has founded?

On a serious note, friendship between two loving adults *should*n't involve control over either party, nor *should* one person's say carry more weight than the other's; realistically, though, people possess three things that get in the way of such equity: opinions, egos, and complexes. But if the two of you have enough love and respect (things that are rapidly dissipating these days) for one another, then you will "submit" to *each other*, rather than one to the other—regardless of gender.

All that aside, I can't find myself ever blindly following *anyone*, because people are stupid.

To the evil racist *(<<do you see that???)* **that writes the Jay Phillips column:**

Silver spoon assholes like you talk from your high horse about wellfare and what poor people should do but all your doing is hiding behind your newspaper. I dare you too read your goverment artical in public where all of us "ghetto" people can kick your ass.

First off, whenever you're going to blog someone, make sure that you check your spelling, grammar, and punctuation because you, not I, look like an ass. (You might wanna try Botox.) Expounding on that, HEY AMERICA! "Your" denotes possession; "you're" is a contraction of the subject/verb "you are." Get it? Got it? Good. I hate that.

A. M. HATTER

Secondly, I assume that by "racist" you mean against minorities and that you've probably read both "Good Government in 12 Easy Steps" and "Let's Get Ghetto Out of Here." But I'll ask you to do some research on me and find out that I, too, am a minority. Further, my anti-welfare feelings haven't the slightest thing to do with any ethnic group whatsoever, and A LOT to do with the fact that I don't want the government taking taxes out of my check to pass off to some opportunistic college student that realized they're eligible. Moreover, I don't feel that it's my responsibility to provide (without consent) money out of the check that I work five days a week to earn so that some dumbass that couldn't even stay still enough to finish high school can buy bread and support three children that they irresponsibly conceived. Nobody helps me buy food. Hell, It's hard enough to swallow being taxed to pay the Chief Secretary's junior-junior assistant 85k a year, or to support these bogus teacher unions. But that's off the subject.

What do you want from me? An apology? Sorry, I can't give that for believing that everyone should earn his or her keep. If you want to live off the government, then you should work for the government. And if the government is going to tax me, it should be for a road, not to help some loser that didn't have the good sense to stay in school instead of having kids when she was twelve. Pardon me, for expecting good sense or ambition (maybe even some self-control) out of people.

```
Hello to the Jay-meister! Who are
you favorite comedians? What are your
favorite comedies?
```

My favorite comedians, in no specific order: Bill Cosby, Chris Rock, George Carlin, Bill Maher, Paul Rodriguez, Bernie Mack, Ced the Entertainer, Keenan & Damon Wayans, Jon Stuart, Dennis Miller, Robert Townsend, Adam Carolla…okay, that's enough.

LOOKIN' IN THE MIRROR

Oh yeah, Jeneane Garofalo, Phil Hartman, Jimmie Fallon, Steve Martin

My favorite comedies—again, in no specific order: The Color Purple, Forrest Gump, Hollywood Shuffle, Austin Powers, Wayne's World, I'm Gonna Git You Sucka, The Three Amigos, Pootie Tang

(Honorable Mention) TV Shows: Ren & Stimpy, Herman's Head, Living Single, Saturday Night Live or Mad TV, In Living Color, The Simpsons, Southpark, Ally McBeal

Hi Jay, I know a million people probably write you and ask what you like. I wanna know what you absolutely hate.

"Reality TV", Viacom, people with low standards, radio play lists, focus groups, men with perms, gold teeth, stupid people, financially irresponsible people, people who use racial slurs (and try to justify it), AOL, when rappers who can't act get movie or TV roles, Microsoft, and (finally) when TV people try to hype up a personality or model like they look sooooo good, but they're really not that cute.

Jay, you are the most insensitive #&^@!* on the planet...

Sheesh, this is gonna take all day...

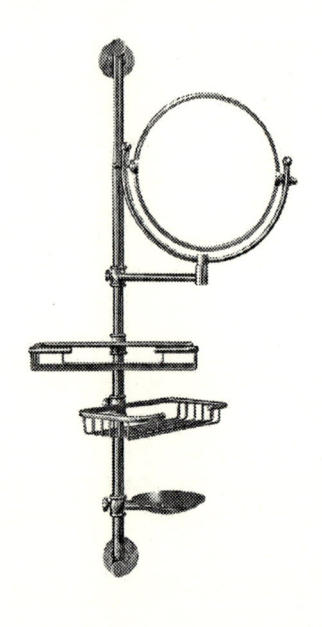

April 30

Tuesday Morning

LOOKIN' IN THE MIRROR

"Pull your pants up, home skillet," I said to Dante as we walked toward the school.

"Man, why you try'na to have me lookin' corny?" he asked.

"You don't have to wear 'em on your chest, man...just pull 'em up a little," I replied.

I looked at Will. The situation was all too familiar: Will and I both had some serious high-top fades in our day (Kid'N'Play *who*?), and we knew a barber who was gonna hook us up with the latest back-of-the-head art, but our moms weren't havin' it.

Will intervened, "Look, bruh, just pull ya pants up."

"Man, now all the girls gon' laugh at me," Dante remarked.

Will tried to turn the situation around, "For wearin' your pants the right way?"

Dante looked straight ahead.

"Nahhhhhhhh... Now, if you wore your pants like *this*," Will tugged on Dante's back belt loop and gave him a shallow wedgie, "*then* they'd laugh at you."

"Awwwww. Come on maaan!" Dante responded.

We laughed at him tuggin' his pants out his butt.

* * *

We got into the building and went to his class. There were very few role models live and present

A. M. HATTER

besides us. It was kind of sad. Will and I just looked at each other. It's a damn shame that on Role Model Day, there were only five adults visiting, out of thirty-four students.

We waited through two of his classes until the third one, social studies, when we were to be presented. I hadn't realized that Dante really had become quite the wiz kid (although by 'hood code, you're not supposed to show it for fear of outshining someone else). But I took it as a personal accomplishment that he was one of three students that the teacher would default to when the other kids couldn't answer. Especially since Black boys have more problems in school than other kids.

The presentations began, and each student had some kind of poster of who they wanted to be like. One girl had J.Lo, another, Queen Latifah. That was cool. *Tamara wanted to be like Queen*, I thought. But they don't know the Queen that we knew, with the Black suit on and stuff, lookin' all tough. You couldn't tell my sister *nothin'*. She thought she could kick *e'ry* boy's ass after 'Ladies First' came out. I wish there were girls who wanted to be like Claire Huxtable. Now, *that's* a role model.

The boys weren't far off from the girls, naming everybody TV-related from Puff Daddy to Allen Iverson—but no political figures, of course. The funny thing was this one boy, who brought a picture of Sanaa Lathan and said he wants to be like whoever is her boyfriend, "'Cause she's fine and is real, real cool and knows about stuff that guys like."

"I guess I can feel that," Will whispered.

LOOKIN' IN THE MIRROR

The other three adults present were a mother who is a shift manager at a hotel, a cousin that owns a restaurant, and another mom that drives a bus. The thing I liked about them as role models is that since they're not in high-profile fields, I know that the marks they make on their respective children are more meaningful. Those are people that were invited 'cause those kids look up to them and respect them. Like the bus driver mom...she either had to take off from work or wake up early, if her shift is at night. She gave her daughter time out of her sleep or her paycheck so that she wouldn't be there without a live figure. *That's* respect due.

We went, pretty much, last. (There were only a couple of kids that were after us.) They liked Will because he was funny. He cracks jokes and stuff...your all-around-clown type of guy. They asked if he was a comedian, then they said he should be. They were totally lost when he told them he was an advertising account executive. And I got the same look of incomprehension when I said my title, special services rep. Well, no, *his* was more like a general look of curiosity. *I* got a whole classroom of kids with blank ass stares, and eyes that said, *Okay...what the hell is that?* Not that I hadn't expected it. I get it enough from adults alone. To me, it sounds like a hyped up title for a fluffer.

Overall, though, it was a cool experience. The best part about it was when all the young teachers wanted to meet us. A couple of successful bruthas, who could speak with proper diction? We were like chum in a shark tank. And Will, man...he had 'em

A. M. HATTER

eatin' out of his hand. That guy probably won't calm down 'til he's forty-two. He can sell *anything*. I'm tellin' you, *anything*. He could probably sell dashikis to Darth Vader.

I remember this time in high school when we were at the mall. We were sixteen. We saw these fine ass girls walk into…Foot Locker, I think it was. There were three of 'em. Man, they *had* to be, like, twenty-one, twenty-two. He walked up to 'em—man, I *still* don't know what the hell he told 'em, but two weeks later, he brought me a tape (a *tape*) of him at their apartment, gettin' triple-teamed. He had their asses *linin' up*, *WAITIN'* for their turn. At that point, I knew that *that* dude was a mutha fuckin' trip.

Anyway… There was this cute, quiet teacher standin' in the corner munchin' on celery and carrot sticks. I peeped her when she came in to watch a couple of the presentations. On the outside, she looked like 'Little House on the Prairie', but homegirl had ass like a donkey. I took mine stealth 'cause I didn't want any irresponsible vibes flowin' around, considering that I was there in the capacity of a role model and there were a bunch of kids around. So I just walked up and thanked her (as a rep of the school) for havin' Role Model Day, and told her that I thought it was a really good activity. It turned out that she was one of the people that conceived the idea. As I shook her hand, I slipped her one of my "Have dinner with me" cards, and said that we need more people like her to get children thinkin' about their futures. If she wants dinner, she'll call.

LOOKIN' IN THE MIRROR

HAVE DINNER WITH ME

Gerald Boudreaux
713.115.8706

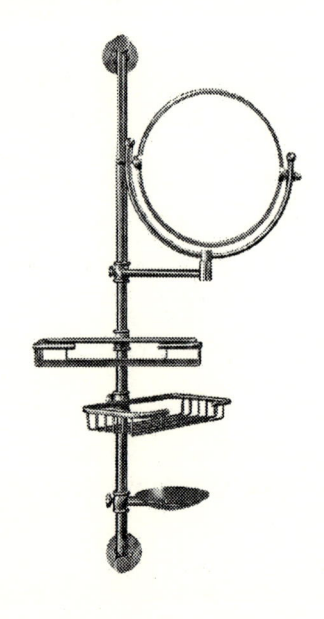

May 21

Lesson 1: Never stare directly into the booty.

Man, it was a struggle and a half, tryin' to get ol' girl—the teacher—to agree on somethin' to do. I offered to take her to dinner; she said she eats out too much. I brought up some movies that were out; she didn't wanna see any of them. She doesn't like to walk in the park, she didn't wanna rent movies, go to the club—nothin'. I was about ready to let it go, but I figured I'd back off a little bit and just talk. Let her get to know me, y'know? So we conversed (yes, it's con*verse*, not conversate) off and on for a few weeks, maybe a month; I let her get comfortable with me. It was all good.

So then, I let *her* make the move as far as when we'd go out. And, like I figured, she eased up on the date options. She finally figured she could start eatin' out again or whatever, 'cause she decided she wanted Chinese. So I took her to this nice Hunan restaurant in town. I like the ambiance. I was thinkin' of takin' her dancin' afterward—if we had made it that far. But man, I should've taken her hard-to-please attitude at the beginning as a hint. *Why do I always have to give these broads a chance?*

The whole evening was probably doomed from the beginning, and I should've picked up on that, by the way she came to the door. Not to say she was ghetto, but uh, stiletto heels and leopard-print spandex wasn't quite what I expected from a teacher who

A. M. HATTER

dresses like a pilgrim. I'm up there, dressed like a grown man is supposed to dress, and she got on clothes like those old women who try to act like they still got it, lookin' like Klymaxx. When she opened the door, I thought she was gon' tell me she had a meetin' in the ladies' room or somethin'. I don't know why I even try! I should just quit my job, buy some oversized vehicle with gaudy rims and drive around the corner all day blastin' Juvenile.

But anyway, I did the best I could in spite of things.

At least she didn't smack when she talked.

When we got to the restaurant, they seated us…the wait staff was really good, by the way. Which brings us to the second thing: I assumed that by her requesting Chinese, she at least had some idea of what she liked. But we looked at the menus and she's actin' like we're *IN China* or somethin'. I was like, *Can you not read?* She didn't know what she wanted, she called the waiter back a million times to ask him all these childish questions about the food. I started feelin' like, *Here ya go, bruh. Sit down…have dinner with us.* It's not even like Chinese is all that complicated. Who doesn't know how to order sweet'n'sour chicken? Or hey, here's an idea: sesame. Poof! A whole new meal! She's up there actin' like she never ate Chinese food before.

And then she finally ordered—somethin' with beef, I think—but decided she didn't like it. Started frownin' all up… "This looks raw," she said, "I thought it was gonna be cooked." The food was clearly cooked. At least, to me and the wait staff, it seemed

LOOKIN' IN THE MIRROR

cooked. Oh yeah, and it was spicy, but she didn't know it, even though the menu said "spicy" right in the food description. But, you know, these days you can't just go around expecting to meet women with common sense.

On the other hand, it could've been a lot worse. I could've been publicly humiliated by a churchy nutcase who didn't know how to dress; but that's neither here, nor there. At least this one had conversation. But if she wasn't fine, I'd have been pissed.

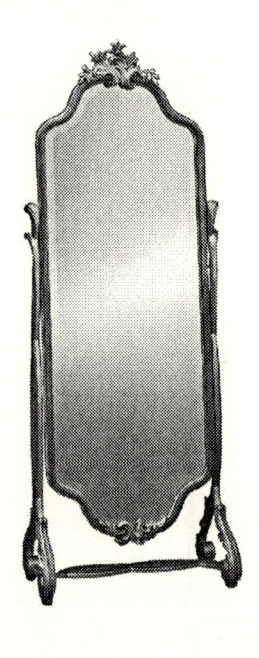

Saturday, August 3

LOOKIN' IN THE MIRROR

Shawn and I met at a local food joint to catch up. The day was clear and really nice. There was a slight breeze nudging the trees just outside the window back and forth. Every now and again, one would tap the window and unsettle my nerves like something was going to break through and do harm to me. The Saturday afternoon traffic was really thick and it was a little hard to hear Shawn, though the table-for-two put only inches between us. We sounded like people on cell phones with mediocre reception.

We were seated against the back wall where we could see everyone who came in. She sat properly, facing me with her legs together, pulled under the table; whereas, I, the everlasting uncouth, sat with my legs facing outward and slightly parted, my back leaned against the stone pillar behind me and my right arm draped across the chair back. It wasn't a slovenly type of sitting, just comfortable. With a burnt orange linen pipe-legged pantsuit, I felt that I had that type of freedom.

"Man, we haven't kicked it in a *while*! Where you been?" she asked me.

"Girl, I've been under the ground lately…just workin'."

"Oh. Tryin' to get ahead? Or you freelancin' again?"

I replied, "Well, I *was* building up an archive to get back into freelancin'… I was just gonna mass mail all over the place, but then I met this publisher when I was out at lunch with Big Turk about a month ago. Actually I met him *through* Turk…'cause apparently, he had been tellin' the publisher guy that I'm this super great writer and junk. So he actually kinda set me up. But me and dude started talkin'…and now I'm writin' a book!"

She spit her ice back into her cup. "You're *what*???"

"Yep…*me*. …*I'm* writing a book," I grinned.

"I'm shocked! Miss anti-real-literature???"

"Mmm-hhmmm," I nodded.

"Damn! What kinda rug did he pull over *your* head?"

"Shit, I don't know…he really just brought to my attention that I've built quite an archive, between the website that I built back in college and what I've put in at the journal."

"Yeah."

"So, I wouldn't even have to write much of anything. I *might* write some situational stuff to say what inspired what piece and so forth, but…for the most part, it's just collecting the 'best of' stuff."

"Oh, okay. That sounds cool… I know it's right up your alley, 'cause you don't have to do much more than what you do now!" she chuckled.

"Shhhhhh…hell yeah! You know, I'm all for slackin' off," I laughed back.

"O-*kay*! Man, I wouldn't mind being a full time book writer. I'll take full advantage of not havin' to go to work!"

My answer followed a jovial push of breath, "For real. And you can proudly tell people 'My job is a work in progress.'"

My head leaned on the base of my left palm, where the hand meets the wrist and I traced the back of the chair with my right index finger, running over all the surface imperfections.

"Have you thought about what you're gonna name it?" she asked.

I stopped playing with the chair and looked her dead in the eyes, teasing her with my classic sneaky smile.

"You wouldn't believe it if I told you," I replied and started laughing quietly.

She looked at me as if to say, *Awww man...here we go again.*

"Ohhhhhhh, man. What is it? Just tell me now."

"It's—"

"Wait," she interrupted, "should I prepare myself?"

"Dude. You know me. Wha'd'you think?"

"Ohhhh, boy," she sighed, "okay... I'm ready...I think."

I started laughing again. "I don't know if America is ready for my rampant, unbridled hubris. I really don't."

She continued the laughter. "I don't think America is ready for the word hubris!"

I looked at her with a happy-shocked expression, "That's what Turk said!"

"Okay, okay! What's the name? Tell me."

"Okay," I paused and looked to my lap, licked my lips and tilted my head to where I looked at her sideways. "It's called, 'I Must Be A Genius' and in parentheses, '('Cause I Can't Find Anyone With Common Sense)'."

Shawn put her nose into her palm and shook her head.

"Hell naw," she said and gave me a puzzled look. "It's funny, you'd think people would hate you for writing as arrogantly as you do—but they only like you more for it."

"MMMMMMMM," I growled, "Nawww, not *everyone* likes what I say. There was this woman not too long ago, that wrote in, talkin' about how she didn't like what I said in the population piece about people who can't have children. She said I was harsh. But I'm like, wha'd'ya want me to do about it? I can't make infertile people have kids. Don't get mad at me 'cause shit happens. Deal with it; life goes on, y'know?"

"What did she expect? A retraction? It's like, 'Uhh, helloooo? The piece is already published. We don't care what you think'," she confirmed with support.

"O-*kay*! She was just lookin' for someone to be mad at and I'm not gonna be her scapegoat. Hell, if you're lucky enough to have infertility be your *only* strike in life, *trust* that there could be worse. I mean, you *could* be infertile *with* cancer, or a quadriplegic, or born with no arms and legs, HIV, blind…or a man with a little dick…or a midget—not that any of those are even comparable, but y'know, she could've been in other undesired situations."

She shook her head and laughed. "You found a way to put a quadriplegic in the same argument as a man with a little dick."

LOOKIN' IN THE MIRROR

"If he's unlucky enough, he might be a quadriplegic *with* a little dick," I retorted.

Her jaw dropped. "You're a lunatic. I'm convinced."

"RIGHT! And the sooner you realize this, the better off you'll be," I said as-a-matter-of-factly and got up to use the restroom.

I slid over the tiled floor with my sandals, barely picking up my feet. From the corner of my eye, I noticed a few heads turning as I passed by the other patrons. Even if they weren't looking at me, it didn't really matter. In my mind they were. ☺

The place wasn't big. It's more like a big Wendy's, but they serve simple sit-down food dishes like salads, chicken clubs and spaghetti. Sitting in the back, you can see virtually everything that goes on, with exception to this huge median of plants in the middle of the refectory. So anyway, I made my way around the massive partition of foliage when I saw this *good…looking…guy* standing in line! I felt like ya boy in 'Artificial Intelligence', when he cocked his head to the side and started spitting game. *The mack juice is running!*

Actually, his whole crew—there were three of them—looked pretty straight. But the one I first noticed was the one that happened to turn around as I rounded the partition. We made contact immediately. The moment was so well-planned you could put music to it… Something like…'The Boy of Ipanema'. Yeahhhh. The one with Rosemary Clooney.

He looked at me with those special eyes. Then his homeboys turned around and started grinning as well. But it was just me and the first dude. For about thirty seconds, we had our own little existence. It was *magic*! (Duhhhnnn! Duhn-duhhnnn! Duhhhnnn! Duhnn-duhhnnn! Can you feel it!)

He came up to me; asked me how I was doing and all. I'm acting all cute. (Why is it that when a guy comes to talk to you, you get all child-like and start grinning and shit like no other guy has ever approached you before?) I gave him the doe-eyes. They love that. They just grin at you like you're so innocent.

He took my hand at the tips.

"I'm Shareef."

"I'm Victoria."

"It's nice to meet you, Victoria."

"Likewise," I replied, holding steady with the grin.

"You are so beautiful, Victoria."

I giggled, acting like I'm so modest, "Thank you."

"You prob'ly get that all the time, though."

I giggled some more, trying to avoid a true answer.

"Huh?! Huh?!"

I laughed some more.

"Go 'head and say yeah… it's cool. I know brothas just blow ya head up."

Still giggling, I nodded a little to get him off my back but covered part of my face so I wouldn't look cocky.

"That's a'right, though, 'cause it's true!"

LOOKIN' IN THE MIRROR

Dammit, would you move on to something else???

"Thank you," I replied then I glanced over his shoulder.

"Oh, let me stop being rude," he turned to where I could meet his friends and introduced them from right to left, "This is Tarrell, and this is Andre."

"Hey guys," I said as I shook each of their hands, "I'm Victoria."

"Hey."

"Ha'ya doin'," they said in consecutive order.

"I don't mean to be rude, but I was headin'...to the..." I explained.

"Oh. Oh, cool. Umm, just holla at me when you come out," he said with a cocky smirk.

"Okay."

So I went into the bathroom and handled my business. When I came out, the guys were about to sit down. The cashier had just given Andre his change.

"Hey lady," Shareef said.

"Hey gent."

"So, uh, where you sittin'?"

"Actually," I looked in the general direction of the back, "we were about to leave. I was just, you know, doin' my business before we left." I inched toward a table blocked by the plant partition. That way, they couldn't see if I left or not; further, I just didn't want them sitting with us anyway. It would just give Shareef more time to goo-goo in my face and give me more of his corny mack vibe.

"Oh, okay," he said, putting down his plate, "maybe we can hook up some utha time?"

"Yeah, that's cool," I replied.

He got out his cell phone and I gave him my number—the cell of course.

"This ya home numba or ya cell?" he asked.

"Yeah, my cell. That way you can always reach me...I keep it with me at all times."

They always buy that bullshit. Really it's just so they can't track my home number to an address, on the off chance that they'd try some shit like that. Plus, when I program their number in my cell, if I don't like them after the first call, I can send them to my voicemail quick and easy.

He handed me his business card.

"Eric?"

"Oh. Yeah. That's my real name."

"Your *real* name?"

"Yeah, I'm changing my name to Shareef."

Don't ask, Vic. Don't ask!

I shrugged, "Oh. Okay. Well, I'm gonna head back to my friend now."

He shook my hand and smiled graciously.

"It was nice meeting you," I said to his friends.

They waved and grinned as best they could, with food crammed in their cheeks.

A funny thing happened on the way to the table: Shawn introduced me to a guy who'd been sitting with her, waiting for me. *Come on, Usher...sing it for me... How do I say, 'Hel-looo, I just wanna talk to you'!*

I stood physically closer to Shawn, in case the other dude looked around the plant partition to see where we were sitting because my positioning would

LOOKIN' IN THE MIRROR

give him the idea that the new guy is Shawn's friend, rather than competition. But the new guy was sitting with her before I got there anyway, so one would naturally assume that he's with Shawn.

"Hey Vic. This is Rob. He said he likes the way you walk," she said.

Well, hel-lo there, thick brown man.

I blushed and shook his hand, "Hi Rob."

He stood. "Hi Victoria," he replied and kissed my hand.

"So you like the way I walk, huh?"

"Yeah. You got this…glide. Like…you're not even walkin'. It's like you're standin' on a motorized cart," he said and grinned.

The image made me laugh. It actually reminded me of an episode of 'The Fresh Prince' where Tom Jones came floating into the living room on a cloud of smoke as Carlton's fairy godfather.

I chuckled. "Motorized cart, huh? I got the Spike Lee effect goin' on?"

Shawn and Rob laughed, too.

I shook my head at him and looked at Shawn, "Hey, I'm ready to go. Let's blow this joint."

Rob walked with us outside, talking freely to both of us. I pretended to be occupied with something in my purse so that I could lag just a step and a half behind. Positioning is everything in the mack world.

I finally looked up, "Hey, y'all go on to the car. I see somebody I met one day."

I wanted to walk over and tell Shareef goodbye, plus provide any PR that was necessary in case he did look around the partition.

A. M. HATTER

Shareef (I mean Eric) wiped his mouth. "So ya out?" he said, rising from his seat.

"Yep. I just wanted to say bye and all."

He nodded with a grin. "Cool, cool," he replied, leaning toward me, "Call me later, a'ight?"

He backed me into the wall and I pressed my elbow against his stomach. "Boy get back. Whatchu doin'?"

He grinned mischievously and whispered, "I wanna kiss those round lips."

I looked at him crazy and gave him a hard nudge with my elbow, "Boy, sit down and eatcho food."

He laughed and sat down.

Then I swept through the table, gripping their hands like a guy, showing no difference in treatment (except when I pinched Andre's cheek to balance out the dynamic between me and the group) just in case Rob might be watching.

"I'll see y'all later," I said, heading for the door.

Rob stopped me in my tracks as I neared the car, "See, there's that walk."

I blushed again. "Man, now you got me all conscious of my walk. Leave me alone," I laughed.

"Well, I'm about to go," said Rob, "I gotta tutor this little boy in my complex."

He leaned to hug me, then hugged Shawn. "I left my number with Shawn. I didn't wanna mess up your game and all," stepping backwards toward his car.

LOOKIN' IN THE MIRROR

My face beamed. "What, a sista can't have male friends now?"

He laughed, "I'm jokin'. You're all right, though. Gimme a call later on."

"Definitely!"

Rob jogged to his car.

Shawn looked at me and shook her head.

"What?" I fronted, innocently.

"When did you meet them?"

"Who?"

She unlocked the car. "Those guys in there! You know who!"

"Today," I said, giggling.

"I thought you met 'em 'one day'?"

"I did. Today... *One* day."

"I knew your ass was up to no good. That's why I busted you out!" she said laughing.

"Whatchu mean??"

"Girl, I gotta give it to you, though. Guys really don't pick up on that shit. He was out here talkin' 'bout, 'Oh, I thought that was competition. They're just friends. Does she know a lot of guys?' So I just told him what was up."

My jaw dropped. "I can't believe you did that! How you gonna bust me out like that?? Man, that ain't cool!"

She just laughed. "Naw, I told him at first, but when he looked at me like he really believed me, I just played it off. That's why he joked with you about runnin' game."

"So what'd you tell him?"

"I just said, 'Naw, she just acts dude-like so it looks like they're just cool. But really she's trying to holla.' But then he was like, 'For real?' And so I just said, 'Naw. I'm just playin'. She just knows a lot of people.'"

"Man, that's fucked up that you put me out like that. You coulda had me all messed up! And dude— what's his name?"

"Rob."

"Yeah... Rob was *cute*! And thick, too!" I sat there looking salty for a second.

"So which one of them were you talkin' to?"

"The one with the lips."

"Oh. Yeah, that one was...yeah."

"Yeah," I grinned proudly, "he was. But I don't think I'll holla back...he's goin' through that doofball name-change thing."

"Oh, the I'm-trying-to-prove-I'm-Black-so-I'll-take-an-African-like-name?"

I snickered, "You already know. Man, why'd he introduce himself as Shareef and give me a business card with Eric on it?"

She laughed, "Aww hell. He's a dumbass!"

"I know right. And he's probably one of those that thinks he can read hieroglyphics, too."

"Amen Ra, reincarnate?"

"You'd think. Plus, I think he's young...he gon' back me up to the wall talkin' about he wanna kiss me," I said.

"Are you serious??!"

"Hell yeah! I was like, 'Boy sit down.' That fool..." I trailed off.

LOOKIN' IN THE MIRROR

"He's prob'ly twenty or somethin'. They all looked kinda young anyway."

"I know...young ass game. He had *no* mack. The only thing he has goin' for him is his looks."

"So why'd you talk to him?" she asked.

"I don't know...'cause he was there. Somethin' to do, I guess. He was pretty."

She laughed, finding my aimlessness amusing. "Man, when are you gonna chill out? I mean, you can't act like we're still in college forever," she said.

"I know, man...it's just...I don't know. I like guys...datin' guys. Hell, datin' is cool. I like this."

"Yeah, but you can't date forever."

"Watch me!" I said, laughing.

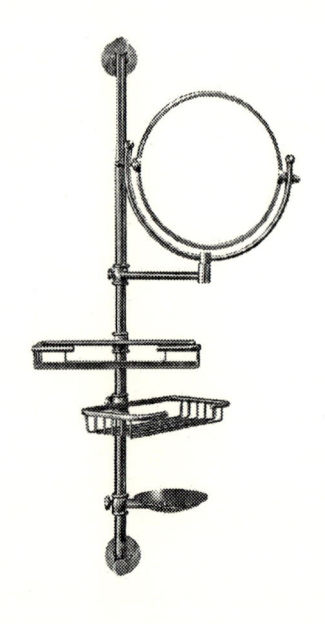

May 30

Thursday Night

"Hello."

"What-up, bruthaman! Black'n'tan! Peter pan wit' a pension plan!"

"Awwww! What's up, Ant?"

"Sweatin' to tha oldies, dawg. It's hotter than Kenya at noon with *no* clouds," he said.

I laughed.

"So, what's up, Geek? What's goin' on down there?"

"Sweeps," I said, progressively more frustrated and bored with the TV.

He laughed. "So, lemme guess…tittie bars aren't all they're cracked up to be, and…Hustonians don't drive the speed limit?"

I chuckled. "You forgot about the story where they get up-close-and-personal with the news staff."

"Oh! Of course! What would our lives be like if we didn't get to see our local camera man eatin' breakfast?"

"Yes. I feel so informed," I answered, slumped over on my couch, munchin' on cashew halves AND PIECES. (I had to capitalize that. It was on the can and I had to make sure you knew. You might've thought all of my store-bought cashews-in-a-can were whole. I wouldn't wanna mislead you or anything. You might sue me.)

"Oh, I almost forgot…" he said.

"What?"

"Happy Birthday, man."

I chuckled. "Ain't it kinda early for that?"

"Yeah, but I'll be out of the country until the end of next month—maybe longer," he said.

A. M. HATTER

"Oh, okay. Where ya goin'?"

He yawned. "Uhhh, France. There's a guy over there that wants me to ghostwrite for him."

"Uh. Okay. Good deal."

"Man, lemme tell you what happened today, I had a couple parents double-teamin' this kid," he laughed, "This boy in my class started actin' up…"

"Yeah."

"So I told him to change his card to yellow," he said.

"HA! You still use the green card, yellow card, red card system?"

"Yeah, man…I never realized how effective it is until I started teachin'."

I snickered at him some more.

"So anyway, the little boy got up with an attitude and changed his card. Then he snatched his hand down and accidentally knocked over my candy jar and it broke. So then, I stood up and told him to apologize to the class for actin' up and to clean up the mess. But lil man keeps actin' hard and goes, 'I ain't'."

"Uh-uhhhhh!" I started laughin'. "He's smellin' himself, ain't he?"

"I don't know what his problem was, but I wasn't dealin' with that so I pressed the intercom and had school security pick him up from my class. And a while later, I went to the principal's office to follow up. But it was funny 'cause his mom was in there yellin' at him. But lil man wanna act tough. Boyyy, he said somethin' smart to her and, *man*! She grabbed him by his shirt and put him against the wall! I wanted to *die* laughin'!"

"All right momma! That's what I'm talkin' 'bout!"

"But then his dad showed up, 'cause she had to go back to work. So we all filled him in, and he told the boy to apologize for actin' stupid and breakin' my jar. But he just folded his arms and kept on frownin'. Pops wasn't doin' the negotiation thang, so he took the boy across the hall to the bathroom...bruhman *to'* his ass *up*! You could hear'im cryin' all down the hall! Me and the principal were in there rollin'."

"Yeah! Woop his ass pops! See, that's what I'm talkin' 'bout! Don't spare the rod! Shove-it, down-his, *throat*!" I laughed, "Bad ass lil boy..."

"I know," Ant said, "But get this: we were technically supposed to stop him or call the police."

"Ain't that some mess?"

"I know...all the damn politics, man...gotta be politically correct, can't give homework on the weekends, gotta pussyfoot with the stupid kids, you can't punish 'em," he paused, "Maaaaan, it's just more reasons to wear condoms," Ant laughed.

"You ain't lyin'," I laughed back. "So what else is goin' on in da A-T-L?"

"Not a damn thing, man. I'm gettin' tired of this stupid ass town."

"Why do you say that?" I asked.

"Shit, there's enough to say, just talkin' about these lazy ass parents. Man, it seems like folks just don't even *try* anymore...but I am *so* sick of these *ignorant ass* politicians. And it just amazes me how country these people fail to realize Atlanta is. They will argue you *down* about bein' so citified. But they don't even want their transit rail to be convenient. They got, like, *two* stops goin' each direction, and it barely hits out west. Folks keep sayin' they don't want 'the bad element'."

"Mmm," I grunted. "But don't they always trip about their air quality?"

"Yeah! And public transit would seem like the logical answer, but they got their heads so far up their asses about keepin' Black folks out of their neighborhoods that Marta is losing money and even has to shut down some of its stations."

"Straight up? Damn, that's backwards."

"Tell me about it. And I'd jump on the transit every day if it came remotely close to my house. But hell, if I gotta drive, or ride the bus thirty minutes to the station, I might as well drive to work—or wherever I'm goin', 'cause it doesn't go anywhere near my school, either."

"Yeah, yeah…talk that yang. You know you love Atlanta," I contested.

"Nahh, not really. It… It just sucks less," he said, using his persuasive tone. "'Cause I don't wanna move out to Cali…I couldn't afford to live. And I don't wanna go back to New York, for the same reason. Plus, their winters are too damn harsh. I *ain't* goin' back to Texas, and Florida got hurricanes. Then there's Detroit, Chicago and DC, but it gets cold up there. So Atlanta just sucks less," he reasoned.

"What about Arizona?"

He grumbled. "Maaan, ain't enough Black people," he said.

LOOKIN' IN THE MIRROR

I laughed. "Hey, did I tell you I'm puttin' in for a job in DC?"

I happened to look up, and my picture of me and the gang on the mantle jumped out at me.

"What? Naw, you didn't tell me. What's goin' on with that?"

"We have a division head position opening when they close the deal with a company up there. And I'm gonna put in for it."

He chuckled. "Hell, the way you talk about Blitson, you might need to put *out* for it."

I laughed back. "Yeah, that's true. And there's a guy, right now, tryin' to cockblock the position. He even tried to write me up for mishandlin' *his* report that I had *nothing* to do with!"

"So how'd he write you up for it?"

"He said I'm not showin' company leadership or somethin'...I have a lack of teamwork 'cause I should've volunteered to help with his report. Hell, I'm already writin' reports on business trips, seems like, every two days as it is! But I gotta do this, *too*... Yeah, right. I ain't volunteerin' to help *him*, with shit."

"Damn. That's what's up. But good luck on that. You need to get out of Houston."

"You ain't lyin' man. It seems like every time I turn around, somethin' wack is happenin'. And the women here are just *tired*."

Then, it seemed like this tiny little wallet of Denise just jumped out of my couch and poked me in the leg. I dug it out of the seat and threw it on the lamp table. I think it fell off and went into the trash.

A. M. HATTER

"You don't have to tell me. I got out as soon as I could. Shit, I turned eighteen and got the hell outta dodge," he boasted.

I snickered. "You sound like Anita, talkin' about her hometown."

"Well, sometimes it's like that...you get to where you need a change and...you just go. You make a new life, have new experiences... You grow up and never look back. For me, I've always said 'never ride the same train twice', and I don't intend to."

I started lookin' around at all that I'd collected over the years. Things that I've had since childhood, since college, since moving into my family-sized house. Old bills stackin' on the coffee table. The exhaustingly comprehensive, scrupulous and meticulously gigantic record collection that I've amassed and come to pride myself over. My flatscreen plasma TV. The PS-II, original Nintendo & Sega systems neatly wound and stored in the rack under the TV. My turn-of-the-century gourmet kitchen, lush bedroom fit for a king...and no queen.

"Yeah..." I paused, "Hey, Ant..."

"Yeah."

"Lemme holla at you some other time. I'm 'bout to lay it down."

"Oh, okay man. I'll let you go, then," he said.

"Later."

I went to bed, tryin' not to think about it, but the question popped in my head: Next month I'll be thirty-*one*. What have I *really* accomplished?

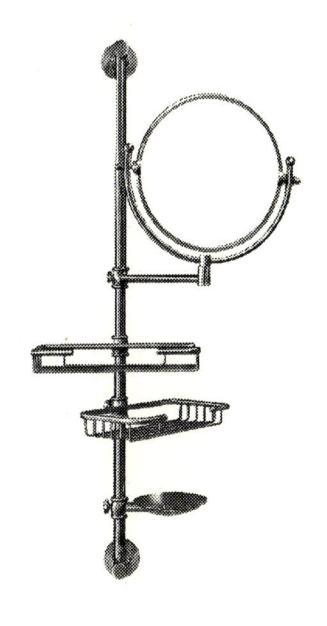

June 6

Thursday

"Hey, Gerald," Dante whispered, "What lens is this?"

"That's the zoom lens," I whispered back.

"Which one do I get out?"

"Leave it alone until the teacher gets here," I answered.

It was the first session for a summer photo class that I enrolled us in. Every summer I try to get Dante in some kind of class so that he stays active, but mostly, artistic classes that will develop his natural talents. Especially since school systems don't do much to cultivate artistic minds. Carlos had the hardest time when we were growin' up.

The instructor for this class turned out to be really good for Dante. He's a fast-talkin' dude that points out a lot of details and jokes a lot. From the point he walked in, he had Dante at the front, helpin' him with class demonstrations. That's good for kids. They can't do the sit-down-and-listen thing for too long. I wanted to laugh, though, 'cause the guy looked like a White version of J-J (from "Good Times"), but dressed like the folk singer dude from that MTV show "Daria", and sounded like Julia Childs, if she was a man that talked fast.

There wasn't much that we accomplished in this session 'cause some people didn't have their equipment yet—despite the fact that the catalog explained what you'd need for class. We had our stuff about two weeks ago. Carlos and I went to this pawnshop to get the camera. I took Carlos along for the knowledge. Since he's in the graphics field, I figured he'd know better than I would which camera to get for Dante. And he told me to hit a pawnshop 'cause they really don't know what kind of equipment they have. Really, it's all Greek to me, but Carlos got all excited 'cause they had a whole Pentax setup (camera with a standard lens, professional flash, tripod, and a telephoto lens) for just under a hundred bucks, with tax, just 'cause it was manual. I imagine that Carlos won't have a problem keepin' this up if I do get the job in D.C. He knows a lot more about the training that Dante needs than I do.

But anyway, the guy comes in the classroom all hyper, talkin' loud and tellin' jokes. He set his camera bag on the floor and threw his books on the desk. Then he started grumbling about how people always wanna buy the weakest photos that you take. Cue story: he's takin' pics for this grand country wedding out in Pearland and he got a perfect silhouette of the groom and bride standin' under a tree, the wedding party slightly blurred in the background (a trick that photographers create, using f-stops or somethin'), and "vivid landscaping" filling in on the sides. But the people didn't want it 'cause you couldn't see their faces, and they said it looked like clipart. And since he's a professional, you can imagine that he was kinda pissed about the people sayin' his work looked like clipart.

Then after he got off that, he realized a lot of the people didn't have any equipment. He came prepared to teach, but started clownin' folks for not havin' their materials. Besides, a lot of the people in the class didn't have any experience using semi-pro or manual cameras anyway. There was, maybe, one other

A. M. HATTER

person who had a manual camera, and one person with a digital. Then the rest of the people who brought stuff had regular cameras—the kind that you take on a family vacation. So he had Dante pass out diagrams of a camera that showed the names of the parts. And since he already had Dante up there next to him, he used our camera to demonstrate where the parts are in real life.

He also let the class see his portfolio. He had nice work. There was one picture in there of this girl that kinda looked like Denise. And I don't know why, but for some reason I flashed back to this argument we had a few years back, when she fussed at me for buyin' wheat bread. She harped on me for a *good* minute, talkin' 'bout how I should know she doesn't like wheat bread and it was inconsiderate of me to eat the white bread, knowin' she doesn't eat any other bread. I really didn't know. It wasn't a big deal to me. It was bread. I could see if she was allergic to it, but I don't see a big difference between wheat and white, other than wheat being a little bit sturdier. And that's why I get it. But she swore up and down that wheat is so nasty and there's some huge difference. Then she went out the next day to go get some white bread, which she banned me from even lookin' at. So I learned to get white bread for her if there was no bread in the house, but I didn't know she needed a specific brand, too. She only eats Iron Kids white bread. Not Rainbow, Wonderbread, Sunbeam, white wheat, she needs Iron Kids. And that's it. In fact, she was like that with a lot of stuff: her lotion—well, no, I can understand lotion, but also her ketchup, syrup, juice, yogurt, cheese, waffles, frozen dinners, vegetables…I'm now realizing

LOOKIN' IN THE MIRROR

exactly to what extent I can't stand high-maintenance women. Bad relationships will do that to you.

But back to the class...

I think it'll be a good experience for Dante. He got to be useful, be teacher's pet and all. He's the center-of-attention for the primarily adult class (a couple of people brought their kids). Me and the teacher have him hyped that he's learning stuff "wayyyy before" when most people learn this stuff, which, to a certain extent, is true. But mostly, I think he's hyped 'cause of this ten-year-old girl in there. She's all cute, got his nose wide open. I saw 'em makin' eyes at each other during class. But I don't think he'll miss the material 'cause the teacher invited him out on some of his less-serious photo projects. So he'll prob'ly learn it anyway. And if we work it right, he and the little girl can practice together sometimes. Her mom is married, but hey, both of us don't have to miss out.

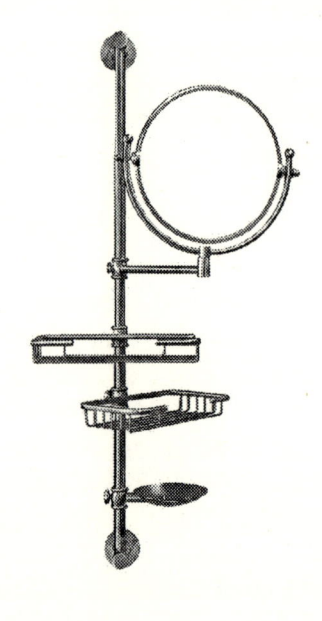

June 9

The Following Sunday

LOOKIN' IN THE MIRROR

Man, when she wants you, she has the most intoxicating presence. It's not 'cause she gets extra-dolled up, or the perfume; it's the way she comes at you. And she knows me. She knows my weaknesses. She knows that if she calls and asks enough questions, she can find out where I'll be, what I'll be doin'—or if I'll be doin' anything at all. She knows that if she comes over on a Sunday mornin' after I've been out of town, I'll be loungin' around the house. So she did.

See, when she wants somethin', she'll catch me off-guard so that I'm too wrapped up in whatever attitude she's provoked for me to react the way I naturally would. So, knowin' this about her, I kept my eyes open for any requests, any stories that might begin with "I need a favor," and the usual. Like a broke relative.

When she came in, I had just started changin' out a washer on my kitchen faucet so I went back to workin'. She said, "Hi, how are you," and all that jazz, but she went to watch TV instead of sittin' by me and talkin' me to death, which I found to be kinda weird. The way she walked in, it was almost like she was reclaiming her kingdom. The nerve of her.

But here's the problem: I accidentally cut myself on this knife sittin' on the counter top. Which, you know, opened the door for her to play nurse.

"Aw, shit!" I said, which alerted her ears to my frustration.

Then, like clockwork, she walked up the steps into the kitchen and grabbed my other hand. She sat me down at the kitchen table and trotted off to get the first aid kit from the back bathroom. Almost like my momma in action, she treated my dinky wound—actually, more like a poke—and bandaged me up. I was all better.

"Thanks," I said.

"You're very welcome," she replied, "That's what friends do."

Friends? Friends don't walk out on each other.

My left cheek raised slightly. I didn't wanna be mean 'cause she was being nice, but I wasn't particularly welcoming to the traitor in her, so I didn't really know how to react.

She looked dead into my eyes and slid her fingers into my palm, cupping my knuckles in her other hand. "It was kinda fun takin' care of you…it felt like old times."

She smiled softly and glanced away, then back at me. At my mouth.

I tried like hell to avoid her eyes. She got x-ray beams in'nem joints. No matter what I'm thinkin' or feelin', she knows. And she'll push it. She'll test it. I didn't want that. I wanted her to leave…but I didn't. And she knew it.

It had been eight months since I'd had a loving woman's attention, her touch, her understanding. Eight months since a woman's presence had been in my house—besides Mia, and she doesn't count. It had been eight months since anyone held my hand and looked into my eyes. Eight months since anyone touched my cheek and slid her hand around to that spot on the back of my neck, then up the back of my head. Eight months since a woman rubbed my chest, or my shoulders, or my arms, my legs… My heart didn't want to react to her—to let her back in. But she worked all the points, all the right moves. Even the sound of her voice had me dancin' like an Indian snake while she brought up all the best memories she could remember. She always had this way of using this one perfect pitch that rides the line between your mom readin' you to sleep, and a one-nine-hundred girl.

My brain shut down. My heart was split. My body did the obvious number. I wanted some warmth, and I knew she was bad news, but I needed to feel somethin'—anything, and there I was, sittin' there like a stray animal that wandered out of Death Valley into a water park. She wasn't exactly what I wanted, but she'd do for now.

Friday, August 16

LOOKIN' IN THE MIRROR

She took a sip of her virgin daiquiri and set it on the table.

"Lemme tell you about this chick at work—I don't know what's wrong with her. It's like she just *has* to be able to call someone her boyfriend. She settles for *all kinds* of bullshit and no matter how bad he's treating her, she always goes 'Y'all, this might be the one!' And I'm like, you were just cryin' on the phone with him an hour ago! You know? I mean, well, I think it, but I don't say it. You know."

I gave her a confirmation nod so she could continue.

"I don't think she knows that I can hear her whimperin' through the cubicle," she paused and drank from her daiquiri, "All these women are in such a hurry to get married…I don't get it! Then they get with some bum and wonder why they ain't happy. Or why they're gettin' a divorce a year later. It's stupid! And I don't see what the fuckin' rush is to begin with!"

"O-*kay*! Lemme tell you about this guy I've been talkin' to…he was tellin' me last night how chicks are gettin' dumber and dumber…more are crazy—and *nobody* has self-respect anymore." My brows twitched downward and I exhaled. "A while back, he tried to cut it off with this girl he used to date, right? And he tried to be nice, but she just wasn't gettin' the message. So one day, he goes 'Look, I'm not feelin' you…I don't wanna talk to you anymore.' She asked him why, and he told her 'Frankly, I think you're stupid.'"

"Damn, he had to get harsh with her," she said.

"Yeah, y'know," I rolled my eyes, "Some folks just won't take the hint…but that's not *half* of it!" I started laughing. "He ended the conversation, tells her 'Bye' and hangs up." I paused and looked at her with a flat expression. "She gon' call back."

She winced. "Why?" she asked.

"Girl, I don'know! She's all, 'Wait, let's talk about this!' But he's like, 'There's nothing to talk about. I'm sorry things didn't work out, but we don't click.' He tried to get her off the phone nicely, but then he just had to hang up on her. But she kept callin' back!" We were both laughing by this point in the story, as I changed my voice to accentuate how stupid the girl sounded. "Then she was like, 'Why you keep hangin' up on me??' 'Click', 'Ring-Ring', 'Stop hangin' up on me! We gotta talk about this!' Man…chicks are re*tar*ded! He was like, 'Man, I know I'm not the most wonderful man in the world for her to act like I'm the last guy she got a chance with!'"

"It's all this 'shortage' propaganda," she answered. "Women get caught up like they'll never find anybody to settle down with." She shook her head. "At this point, I don't even care about gettin' married. I don't even know if I *wanna* get married."

"Whether I get married or not is not the issue…I'm not gonna look stupid over anybody. All this 'Wait, let's talk about it.' Yeah, right. Just let it go. But *marriage*… Hell, I'm just fine being single. I'm like, 'outta sight, outta mind'."

She nodded.

I sighed. "Oh! Speakin' of stupid people, lemme tell you what happened at work yesterday! Me

LOOKIN' IN THE MIRROR

and Turk went to lunch, right? You know that story broke about Blitson, Inc. buyin' up a lotta mid-sized companies on the eastern half of the country—"

"Yeah," she responded.

"So we're sittin' there eatin'…chew-chew-chew, munch-munch-munch…the news anchor had just ended a story and teased for the Blitson story after the break. So they go to commercial and we're steadily eatin'… When they came back, the woman led into the story—I mean, she *just got finished* with the lead, right?"

She nodded.

"She got to, like, probably the third or fourth line and even introduced the first key name in the story. I looked down to take another bite… How 'bout the cafeteria worker took her happy ass up to the TV and changed the channel!"

"Aww, man! I hate it when that happens," she responded.

"But that's not it, man! I'm up here tryin' to be enriched with knowledge, updated on current events and financial information—stuff that might help me in choosin' stocks."

I nodded. She nodded. I continued.

"This asshole changed the channel to fuckin' Ricky Lake!"

"Awwwwww *hell naw*!!" she exclaimed.

"Yeah! And you *know* it was one of those shows talkin' about 'My Man Bet' Not Be Cheatin' On Me' or some shit. We just got up and went upstairs to our desks. That shit just wasn't called for. I was insulted."

"And the first person on there was some Black dude with a loud ass shirt, right? Talkin' about 'See, wuh ha' happen wuh'," my roommate joked.

"Girl, you must've seen the show!" I replied facetiously.

Some of the male patrons in the sports bar repeatedly passed by us.

"Uh-oh girl, they're try'na get your attention," I said, fooling with her.

"Naw, those are *your* men."

I scrolled through my palm pilot. "It *is* time for me to restock my phonebook. My last group has dwindled down to, like, three guys," I said.

"Oh! Oh! Those wouldn't be contenders, now would they?" she asked.

"Girl, naw. These are just the ones that haven't pissed me off yet. But I'll let you know when I have a contender."

"I have a question."

"Shoot," I responded.

"What are they contending for?"

I was stumped on that one. I honestly use the word as a meaningless term, but for me to call guys I like contenders would mean that they'd have to be in the running for something. It's a reasonable deduction, but I just never thought about it.

"Ummmm. You know, I don't know. I actually use the word as some hollow term, but…well, I guess they'd be contending for more time from me, as opposed to the standard I-got-time-to-kill-and-you're-convenient type date. They're really just the guys who take longer to annoy me or piss me off." I stopped,

LOOKIN' IN THE MIRROR

thinking I was finished but quickly added the other contender-death-type, "Or bore me to death."

She looked down at her fries, "Oh. Maaan, I thought I was finally gonna get you to admit somethin' about marriage."

I knarled my face up and clawed my fingers. "CURSES!!!!" I hissed.

She laughed and sipped on her drink some more.

We checked out a couple of guys walkin' by. "Damn, he's kinda fine…check *him* out," I said. "He's got that…*mature* solid frame, like…'I'm sexy and 30-somethin'. Damn, and a nice ass. I can dig *that*!"

She looked up abruptly, "What brought you to the whole 'I don't wanna get married' thing?"

I thought for a second, flashing an expression that seemed like I got a whiff of something malodorous. "Well…a number of things, really." I paused to think. "I think the first was when I turned nineteen. My mom was like, 'This month at your age I just got married.' And that tripped me the fuck out! Y'know? I was only startin' my sophomore year in college. I couldn't *possibly* imagine being married already! That's crazy! [pause] Then, my senior year, I realized 'Dang. A lotta chicks in my class are married or engaged…but I'm young as hell. I still got a lotta life to live! If I settle down now, I'd be married for a long ass time! I wanna travel and club and—Shit! There are a lotta guys out there!' So, I had to reassess that whole serious thing. Like, you said…what's the fuckin' rush?"

"Yeah. Yeah," she responded.

"I mean, the idea of marriage was cool and all, growing up—until I realized that I was old enough to *do* the shit, y'know?" I laughed, but she sat there with a look on her face that showed her thoughts like tickertape across her forehead. "What's with that look, man?" I asked.

"Well, it just seems like…you're tellin' me the truth, but not everything you're thinkin'. I mean, it's got to be more than that… At any given time, you act like you have no interest in guys whatsoever, except to waste your time with'm."

I nodded. "Pretty much!" I said and laughed.

"But people don't take on attitudes as drastic as yours unless they're tryin' to avoid somethin'."

"Yeah…being serious!"

"But I know that can't be all! We're talkin' about *you*! And there's *always* more than one or two reasons! You'll have stuff argued down to a pinpoint logic. I know there's gotta be more than just fear of being serious or accepting age."

"Like what?" I asked, playing the part of a true skeptic.

"Well, like…hell, don't you *ever* wanna get married?"

"Man, please. I get claustrophobic at the mere *thought*." I leaned forward, lowering my voice to a grumble. "At twenty-one, I'm sittin' up thinkin' about the whole concept of marriage, right? Then it hit me: this person is supposed to be the *last* person you're with for the *rest* of your life. I just can't see being with somebody for thirty, fifty, seventy years. That's cray-zee! I can't even make up my mind on what I wanna *wear*. How am I supposed to *choose* my partner *for life*??" I shook my head. "It's my responsibility to be some guy's *sole source* of sexual gratification." I shook my head again. "I can't even see that. And he's *legally allowed* to be in my space at *any* given time. And that's weird enough, but that's not even the scary part." I glanced away and back at my roommate. "Say you find someone you click with, treats you well and all that jazz—your fuckin' knight in shining armor, right? He can go to the store one day and…I don'know…get hit by a car and be paralyzed from the neck down. My cousin's husband got shot and killed a *week* after they got married. You can imagine how much that sucked. And what about psychosis? You're happily married for twelve years and your spouse becomes schizophrenic. What the hell do you do then?"

"Damn. I'd hate to be you. You'll drain all happiness out of anything."

"But that shit can happen! What? Would you rather be blindsided?? I mean, you can never be truly prepared for any of that, but you have to accept that the shit *can* happen. I just don't even wanna deal with it. I'm like, 'Hey, keep that over there.'"

"Have you ever been in love?"

She caught me off-guard.

"Awwwwww hellllllllllll. Not *that* question," I exhaled heavily and rolled my eyes.

"Come on…give up the goods. What's under that cold exterior?"

I looked at her the way an agitated wife looks at her husband just before she calmly tells him he's getting on her nerves. Then I waited to see if I could just get away with no answer, but her eyes stayed fixed on me, obviously letting me know that she wasn't letting go of this question.

"You can play quiet all you want, but I'm not gonna forget. And if you don't answer tonight, I'm gonna ask tomorrow or next week, or—"

"Well, kinda…once," I admitted, staring across the room at the people around the bar. "There was this boy who stayed down the street from me. We were little at the time—y'know, eight, ten, so forth."

"That was your *only* love??? Oh no!"

"Hush. Let me tell the story, dammit! You wanted to know!"

"Woahhhh…seer-ee-us!" she teased.

I sipped on my water. "So anyway…my family moved to this new neighborhood on the south side of Atlanta so we could go to this school our parents really wanted us to go to down there—I was, like, seven. We moved in and got settled. I went outside with my dad one day to help him wash the car and he was sayin' that I needed to play with some of the kids in the neighborhood. But I didn't know those folks. Then these boys kept riding up and down the street on their bikes and invited me to come play with them. …So I got my bike out and rolled."

"They were tryin' to flirt, huh?" she asked as I took a big gulp of water.

"Well…not overtly, but the guy who was the leader did like me. At first, you couldn't tell who the leader was because he was one of those kids that had subtle power, but knowin' his personality, he was the

LOOKIN' IN THE MIRROR

leader. They always looked to him when they were like, 'What do y'all wanna do now?'"

She giggled.

"Excuse me, ma'am," I flagged the waitress.

"Yes," she replied.

"I'd like another glass of water."

"I'll have that for you in just a second."

"Thank you." I turned back to my roommate. "So anyway, we eventually hooked up. But it wasn't like we exclaimed it to the world...we just started hangin' around each other more and more. Then we got so tight where if you saw me, you saw him and vice versa. Some of the others started callin' us peanut butter and jelly. I had to be jelly 'cause I was the girl. They eventually shortened his to peanut."

"Awwww that's so cute!"

"Yeahhh, yeahhh...shut up. So anyway, we were together until about the sixth grade. I tell you, we were *in love*. You couldn't tell us *nothin'*. He and I were like, a standard. You just expected us to be together. Then, one summer, he went to his grandma's house in California and he sent me a letter while he was there. It was the sweetest thing you could ever ask for, and at the end, he told me he was in love with me."

Her eyes got really big, "Whaaaat?? Aw man! You had him hooked, girl."

"But my dad took a job in another state and we had to move."

"Awww maaaaaan! Were you sad?"

"Ex-*treme*ly." I fidgeted with my empty glass. "Damn...*where* is that water?"

"Was that the job in Illinois?" she asked.

269

"Yeah. At first he and my mom considered the long-distance thing, where he'd come back home every weekend, but he didn't like that. Plus, that's a helluva drive!"

"You ain't lyin'!"

"So we all had to move."

"Oh, yeah. I remember you told me that before. Man, more people need families like that—even though it still sucks that y'all had to move."

"Yeah. Well, we stayed in Illinois for about three or four years, but he didn't like being up there, which was cool 'cause none of us liked our school. The kids would make fun of our accents and this group of boys would always beat up on Marcus—you know, my brother right under me."

"Ohhh, poor Marcus. I thought you said he was a bully, though?"

"No, that's my older brother, Brian."

"Oh, okay."

"It was especially hard for me 'cause I was dealin' with my break-up and I just didn't have interest in anything at the new school. I really missed him. He was my *best friend*," I looked down, "And it just hurt a lot to not have him anymore."

"Y'all didn't keep in touch?"

"Uhh, *hello*? I was in the sixth grade. I couldn't just sit on the phone rackin' up charges, and the letters only lasted so long."

"That sucks."

I shrugged.

"Here's your water, ma'am."

"Thanks," I nodded at the waitress and took a gulp of my water, then continued with my dreaded story. "SO THEN, we moved back to the south side of Atlanta, but it was a different neighborhood."

"Did you go back to see if he still lived in the same house?"

"Well, no. I didn't have my driver's license yet and I couldn't just say 'Hey mom, I wanna go on a goose hunt to see if my old neighborhood boyfriend still lives there.'"

"Sounds to me like you just made excuses for not tryin'."

"No. I had no idea where he was or if he still lived in the area! For all I knew they could've moved back to California! But it turned out that he was at the high school where they enrolled me."

"Woah!!! That's some meant-to-be type shit! Did y'all hook back up?"

"Nah…I fucked it up," I answered.

"What???"

"Let me fin-ish! So I'm at the new school for a couple of months and I hooked up with this bad boy-type dude."

"Oh. One of those go-nowhere-in-life types?"

"Yeah, pretty much," I replied, laughing.

"I had one of those, too. Ugh…"

"Girl, it's all right. We didn't know any better. Besides, really I just liked that he was silly and always told me I was fine."

"Maaaaaan. You suck," she giggled, "Superficial ass."

Setting my glass down after a drink, "Well, what can I say? So anyway, I remember the first time I saw him again…I was like, 'Hey…that's him'," I told her with a reminiscent grin, "We spoke. Said, 'Hey', and stuff. Pretty much just standin' there grinnin' and kickin' the dirt and shit." We laughed. "I started seein' him around every now and then. He'd grin at me…sometimes say stuff that would bring up old memories."

"He was tryin' to holla—"

"Girl, I didn't even see it. I was just *stu-pid*! I don't know how I missed it! I mean, NOW, I'd recognize that as a way to bridge the gap, but back then, I thought he was just bringin' up old shit. Especially since he always manages to bring up this one time when he claims I got him in trouble. He's been blamin' that crap on me for a hundred years now."

She started laughing. "Girl, why'd you get him in trouble?"

"I didn't, man! See, we were outside with the crew, right?"

"Yeah."

"And we're walkin' around the neighborhood and there was this area behind our subdivision that was undeveloped. It was just straight country area—trees and rocks and shit."

"Y'all were some ol' ruffian kids!" she hooted.

"Man, we got dirty, like, *every* day! And don't let it be summer, man! It was routine to almost break somethin' before dinner!" I cracked up. "So, we're outside one day, just walkin'…talkin', then he slapped me on my butt at the same time that I was tryin' to step over a rock, but I didn't quite make it so I tripped and fell and scraped my elbow. I knew he didn't mean to hurt me, but this nosey old woman in our neighborhood saw it happen, so when I went home to clean my wound, she went and told his mom and his mom was waitin' for him with the belt when he got home."

"Ahhhhhhhhh! I bet she to' his ass up! Ha-haaaa!" she said with glee.

"I think she did. His momma was *not* to be fucked with!" I laughed. "But he always thought it was me who told on him."

"Why'd she have to be nosey like that?"

"Man, that woman was an old bitty. She didn't like that I was a girl hangin' with a bunch of boys. She thought that I'd be outside doin' stuff I didn't need to do—which I was, but she was thinkin' we'd be behind bushes and tress gettin' it on, like we're just nasty or somethin'. But I'm like, she must be the nasty one if she thinks little kids would do it in the dirt. 'Cause *we* weren't even thinkin' that far."

She giggled, "That must've been somethin' *she* did! Oooooo, the old lady was doin' the grown folks behind the bushes!"

I chuckled back. "Ewwww, that's nasty man. You just gave me a bad image... Man, UUUH!!"

"Sorry," she giggled. "So what happened when y'all were in high school?"

"Oh, oh yeah. Well, it all came down to this one day. A lot of the students would hang out in the practice gym during lunch period. Some kids would play ball, others would sit on the bleachers, tryin' to look cute. Anyway, we were sittin' on the bleachers, talkin'. *Deep* in conversation. I wish I could remember what we were talkin' about. But then, outta nowhere, he kissed me on the cheek…and I froze. I didn't know what to do!" My gulps started getting bigger.

"Why?"

"Well, 'cause…I have a really strong loyalty factor—and true enough, my loyalty was misplaced at the time—but, the fact was that I had a boyfriend and I'm all serious like, 'I'm not gonna cheat on him.' So, when he kissed me, a million things ran through my head. [Gulp] I wanted to get with him 'cause he was my first love, but I had a boyfriend and I didn't know what to do. And for some retarded reason," I looked confused, "it never occurred to me that I could just break up with the buster and go back to my heart."

"So what'd you do?"

[Gulp] "Well…after he kissed me, I made this cute expression and said, 'What was that for?' He was shy, so he just shrugged his shoulders. I looked down for a hot second, and looked back up 'cause I was about to say somethin'. Then, out of the *pure blue*—I don't even remember if I knew he was there! *That's* how sudden it was! My dirty boyfriend waltzes up, kisses me SQUARE on the mouth…and led me off by my arm."

She glared at me in utter disbelief, disgust, pain *and* suffering. "I am so mad at you. I am *so* freakin' mad at you! Daaaamn," she paused and looked away then looked back at me, "Daaamn! I *can't believe* you dropped the ball like that, Victoria!"

"*Dropped* the ball? Girl, given that situation, I basically *threw* it! Man...I broke my *own* heart that day. And that night, I went home and called Shawn and said, 'Today, I made the worst mistake of my life.'"

"For real?"

"Yes," I nodded, "At *sixteen*, I knew that *that* day would automatically supercede *every* other fuck-up that I'd come to make. And to this day, that's the only thing that I acknowledge as a true fuck-up. He's the only one that got away."

"What's his name?"

"Almer Duane Taylor," I said with that reminiscent tone of voice.

She jerked back, "Al-mer???" she said with a grimaced expression and started snickering. "What kinda name is Al-mer?"

I smiled back, "I know, right. But you just don't understand. That was the *better* name!" I said to start the story, but rolled out my own crescendo of laughter.

Her head jerked back again, "The *better* name????"

I tried to calm down, "Girl" [Laughter] "Okay..." [Laughter] "Okay! Okay!" I pounded my fist on the table.

She looked at me with this slight grin, but her eyes beamed, *Tell me the damn story!*

"Alright..." I paused to get my wind back, "See, when he was born, his parents, like, had it out about his name 'cause his mom was strictly against juniors or seconds and thirds and stuff."

"Uh-huh."

"But his dad wanted to name him after himself." I started laughing again.

"Whaaaaaaaaaaat??!!! Tell meeeee!"

"But his dad's name was," I blurted out more belly aerobics, but mustered enough wind to get to the end; although I barely made it past the middle name and ended with that high-pitched voice that you get when you're running out of breath. "It was… …Almer Lee-o-phus Tay-lor!!!!" Then I kicked my head back and let out one of the most ghetto laughs I've ever sounded off in public. But hell, that was funny. People have no business having names like that. I pitted my face into my forearm.

She palmed her face with both hands, shaking with laughter. "Lee-o-phus???"

I looked up. "Yeah!" I gasped. "And he had three brothers named Clee-ophus, Ray-ophus, and *DELL*-ophus," I managed to squeeze out.

About twelve years later, after the gut pounding that the name gave us, we calmed down to mere giggles.

She pressed her hands over her cheeks, trying to keep from smiling.

I wiped my eyes.

Then, we were breathing hard…

And I explained the rest of the story.

"Alright, so he wanted Duane to have his name, but his mom was planted firmly against the middle name—"

She started snickering, "Hell, I would be, too!"

"Stop! You're gonna make me start laughing again!"

"Okay, okay...go ahead," she said, still holding her face straight with her hands.

"So she managed to get him to agree to Duane as the middle name, in exchange for Almer as the first name, citing that his friends would rag on him for havin' a name like Leeophus."

"Smart mom."

"I know, right... But hell, I wouldn't've named him Almer, either. I'd have gotten the name papers and done them later when he wasn't around."

She giggled. Then she started on her warpath again. "Wow...the one that got away. Have you seen him, do you know what he does now?"

"I haven't seen him since we graduated from high school. But word has it, he's doing something in music...prob'ly tryin' to rap or somethin'. Hell, that's what everybody else at home does."

"What would you say if you saw him?"

"Ummm...I don't know...I guess, I wanna apologize—although I don't really know what purpose it would serve. It would be kind of unrealistic to expect anything... Hell, he could be married by now. We're twenty-eight."

"You need to find him and tell him."

[Gulp] "Huh??? *Why?*" I asked.

"'Cause you need closure. This is like a story with no ending! A *good* story, at that! The two of you could be, like, destiny and totally miss your chance 'cause you're actin' scared."

"But if it's destiny, then we'll get back together anyway. It might be destiny for us to hook up in old age."

"You still need to tell him. Can you get in touch with his family?" she asked.

"Man, please. I could just see it: 'Hey Duane, I've never forgotten about fallin' in love with you when I was seven. How 'bout we try again now that it's twenty years later?'" I looked at her skeptically. "…If we had anything in high school to draw from, then *maybe* it'd be the *slightest bit* relevant. But now? Who just holds a torch for a flame from when they were seven?"

"You."

"Ha, very funny smart ass."

"I know what you're sayin', Vic, but you can't let that stop you. Obviously you *are* holdin' a torch for him. You need to address this so you can move past it or claim what's yours. Hell, he might be your soulmate and you're just puttin' it off."

"You act like you know for sure that he's carrying this inane romantic obsession with our past, too." I paused and mumbled, "Listen to me, *our past*—like it's some kind of illicit affair." I continued mumbling, "Like he'd even remember," As she responded, "He might be."

"Might?" I rolled my eyes. "Like I said before: who just holds a torch for an age-five-love—besides me?"

She shrugged and giggled.

"See, I'm the only person retarded enough to even think about this as an issue. No, *you* are! 'Cause *I* was totally fine with this before you brought it up." I drank from my cup again. "Man, this is ridiculous. I'm not talkin' about it anymore."

"Isn't your reunion this winter?"

"Shhhhhhh!"

"You might see him there…you could tell him then."

I chugged the rest of my water and slammed my cup down. "Man, what'd I say? This conversation is *over*. Now it's time to peep talent. I know I didn't come to this damn sports bar to talk about *Duane*. …And fuckin' *marriage*!"

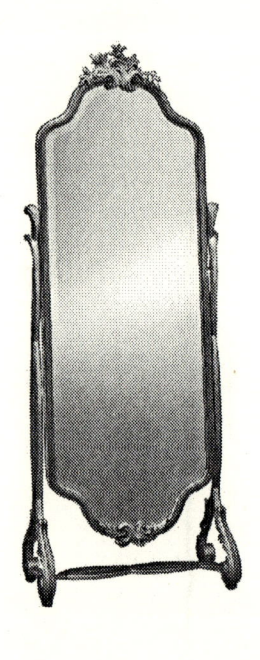

Saturday, August 17

LOOKIN' IN THE MIRROR

Even though we stayed up pretty late after we left the sports bar, I still woke up fairly early the next morning...well, early for me anyway. Usually I wake up somewhere between noon and two, which is bad considering I'm twenty-eight. I really must get out of this young-and-single routine. I tell people I'm twenty-four all the time so they won't look at me crazy (and for some reason they believe it), but I must admit that it's time for me to let go of this state of perpetual adolescence. But, hell, guys can do it and nobody questions them! And if I did wake up at—say 8 a.m., what would I do? Saturday mornings aren't chock-full of activity. They aren't jam-packed with adventure.

*I could go to the volunteer center on Saturday mornings, too. Hmmm...that's more productive than what I do now. I'll have to look into that. But then, when would I catch up on my sleep from our Friday night endeavors? ...Well, I don't have to go **every** Saturday morning. If we're out late Friday night, I'll sleep in and if we're not I'll get up Saturday. Yeah...that'll work. Nahhh...I'll sleep in. I already go to the homeless Shelter every Sunday. I can give myself Saturday mornings.*

What really woke me up early was Candace ringing the doorbell. I don't know why she was over so early, but knowing us, it didn't matter anyway. *Wait, yes it does! Ringing the doorbell at nine in the fucking a-m on a Saturday! What the hell is wrong with her? She knows the program!* And then, my aunt happened to call, too, but that was an hour after Candace came over. I was still in the bed, pretending to be asleep and hearing everything she and my roommate talked

A. M. HATTER

about—including Duane. (Don't people know how to use their inside voices anymore? Sheesh.) Anyway, my aunt didn't really want anything... Well, she did, but I wasn't trying to hear her advice on how to catch a man. She's up here telling me to go to the grocery store on Sunday afternoons because that's when the men are there. Oh yeah, then I'd *really* be shopping. How desperate is that? Besides, that's not when single people shop. That's when married people shop. Single people shop at night. I should know; I'm single. ☺

After I got off the phone with her, (Wait, am I supposed to care that I'm twenty-eight with no husband? She talks to me like it's a shame or something.) I finally went downstairs, when I heard my roommate whisper to Candace, "Shh-shh. Watch this."

"I wanna hear more about ol' dude!" she said as I stepped off the last stair.

"*HUH*??" I replied.

"Your friend...what's his name? Elmer—Almer?" she answered.

"Duane," I said.

"Oooooh! Who's Elmer?? Who's Duane???" Candace asked with her eyes bucked open.

Great, this is all I need. Now Candace will never leave me alone about it. Damn, I'm glad everyone else isn't here. This would be hella embarrassing.

"Man, why are you askin' me about that again? Why won't you leave me alone?" I questioned.

Candace interjected again, "*Who's* Elmer!? Is he a *contender*??"

LOOKIN' IN THE MIRROR

With a mischievous grin, my roommate partially filled Candace in on the situation, "He's her long lost love."

Candace looked at me like she just won a car, "LUHHV????? YOUUU????"

She looked at my roommate, "HERR???"

She shook her head, "I can't believe this shit," and turned off the TV, "Come on wit' it."

"They grew up together."

I plopped into the lounge seat next to the door, staring at her while she stripped me of my privacy. It felt like the dream where you go to school naked. *Why is she doing this? What the fuck is her problem? Why won't she leave me alone? I knew I shouldn't have told her anything. People always think this shit is funny. She thinks this is cute, but it's not at all amusing. Asshole.*

"Woowwww…in-ter-es-ting…I wanna hear this! Do tell, do tell!" Candace added, cheesing ear to ear.

"No. I don't wanna talk about it."

"Ooooh, even better! Somethin' she doesn't want us to know!"

"You *would* take joy in that, Candace."

"I'm just jokin', girl. If you don't want me to know, that's cool. [Pause] We'll just talk about it after you leave!" they laughed.

"Seriously, though," my roommate conceded, "can I tell her?"

I gave her a lifeless shrug, hatred brewing in my stare. "Have at it, you've already started the story," I replied.

Hell, she'd already raided my privacy. Why'd she even bother to ask? I might as well bring down my taxes.

"Okay, well, she met this dude named Elmer—" she paused and looked at me, "It's Elmer, right?"

I muttered, "*AL-mer*, but we called him Duane."

"Okay," she started, "Almer-Duane is this boy she's had this lifelong crush on. They met when she was in elementary school…"

Strike one, I thought to myself. She didn't lay the groundwork correctly. She provided no atmosphere. Plus, I didn't meet him in elementary school. I was just elementary school *aged*.

"And they were, like, in *love*. Like, *deep* love, right. They were together for a long time but her family moved."

"Maaaaan…you ain't tellin' it right," I interrupted.

"Yes I am! That's what you said!" she contested.

"Kinda, but you're not tellin' the whole story. It's all boring and fast. Plus, I didn't meet him in elementary school."

"I didn't say y'all met in elementary school."

"I know, but the way you said it wasn't clear enough. Did you think I met him at school, Candace?"

"I didn't really think about it, but now that you ask, yeah."

"See."

"Well, *somebody* just tell me the damn story!"

LOOKIN' IN THE MIRROR

I surrendered. "Fine, I'll tell it," I glared at my roommate, "You did this shit on purpose. You ain't foolin' nobody."

She smiled.

Even though my solitude had been invaded, I so love telling a story. It's just...the sheer focus that descends upon someone when they wanna hear a story—the whole story—the truth and nothing but. I become the maestro of minds, the commander of attention, the master of ceremonies. But most of all, I love to tell a story because I am a verbal artist, illustrating every turn and rocky terrain of emotion. I leaned forward and they faced toward me like kids sitting Indian-style for story time...and I began.

"Okay, it's 1981. I'm seven years old. My family had just moved from Dekalb County to the south side of Atlanta so that me and my brothers could go to this school down there. It was a cool neighborhood...Atlanta suburbs back then were really country, instead of just 'shrubbed', ya know?"

They nodded for confirmation and I continued.

"There were some old people in most of the houses, but some of the other houses had teenagers so it wasn't just a *really* quiet neighborhood, but it wasn't loud either—like the folks next door. Anyway, we got all settled in... Some days later, I was outside with my dad on the weekend helpin' him wash the car and he was tellin' me how I needed to make some friends in the neighborhood. But I don't just go out and make friends...I'll go do my own thing before I just randomly walk up to people. But anyway, we're out there and these boys my age from up the street were riding their bikes and invited me to ride with them. My dad said it was okay, so I rolled. But one of their friends—Duane, wasn't out there..."

"Hey! You didn't say that last night," my roommate charged.

"I know, 'cause I didn't wanna tell the story in the first place so I skipped over some stuff."

"But *Candace* gets the whole story."

"You're sittin' here, too, right?"

"Yeah."

"Then shut up and let me tell the story. You act like I volunteered the information!" I fell backward into the seat. "Hell, I'd rather be upstairs in bed, but everyone in the fuckin' world wanted to come over or call this morning," I grumbled.

My roommate play-whispered to Candace, "Damn. See how mean she gets. She did that last night, too."

Candace laughed at us bickering like old people, then asked, "How do you remember all this?"

"It's not really that I remember everything that happened...I remember some stuff—well, no, I remember a lot of it. But mostly, I remember the way I felt about certain things and that helps to fill in the blanks."

"Damn, well, you must've felt a lotta stuff!" She cackled. "'Cause you're describing *every* little thing possible!" She gave my roommate pound. "I know you *must* still be in love with this boy, 'cause I would've forgot this junk a *long* time ago!"

LOOKIN' IN THE MIRROR

My face shifted to annoyance, "Do you wanna hear the damn story, or what? 'Cause I'm not volunteerin' for y'all to bust jokes."

They began to calm their laughter, but giggled a little more.

"Okay, okay... go. We're listening," Candace said.

"What was I even talkin' about?"

"Duane wasn't there," my roommate supplied.

"Oh. Yeah. So like I was *saying*, before I was so rudely interrupted...Duane wasn't out there because he had a sinus cold or whatever—from when the season changes. Meanwhile, me and the guys were kickin' it...I even met some girls on the next block. I heard from here and there that there was another boy that was sick, and that he moved from Cali a few weeks before. Some of the girls said he was cute." I leaned forward, resting my elbows on my knees.

Candace looked on with the biggest smile and my roommate sat, looking dreamy-eyed.

I ran my hand over my hair and proceeded, "He was sick for a few more days, but the gang came over one day to pick me up. The doorbell rang and my mom was like, 'Vicki, the boys are outside.' I'm like, 'Okay momma!' She sent them around to the garage 'cause that's where my bike was. I'm throwin' on my shoes tryin' to get out the house...I opened the garage and went outside. They're like, 'Hey, this is Duane'." I paused once again and gave them a very focused look.

"Damn, Vic. That boy must've been somethin' kinda fine for you to be lookin' like this!"

"Man, that was the most beautiful kid I'd seen in my *life*."

They just sat there grinning.

"Well, he wasn't just extra fine or nothin', but he was really cute. Man, the sun was hittin' him *just right*, and his skin looked like it was *glowin'*. He had these *beautiful* lips—the kind with that hard edge on 'em…and a cool ass afro. Man, he had the brightest eyes and the prettiest smile I'd ever seen… …*AND* he had an *accent*!! Shoot! I was *through*! *HAD* to have'm. I'm *seven*, hangin' up the player coat like," I pounded my fist on my chest, right over my heart, and threw the peace sign, "I'm outchall! This is for life!"

They started crackin' up. "You sound like when guys talk about a teacher they had a crush on," my roommate teased, "But I guess you were right about it being for life 'cause your ass is sittin' right here still crushin' on him twenty years later!" and she laughed harder.

"Oh! You got jokes now! Last night you're all," I changed my voice to a wimpy tone, "'You need to find him and tell him.' Now you wanna laugh at a muhfucka. I see how you wanna be."

Candace—by now lookin' confused, "Okay, I feel lost. Was that the end of the story? 'Cause, if it is, I don't understand what y'all are talkin' 'bout. I mean, it was really sweet and all, but I don't get what all the secrecy was about and all the 'Find him and tell him'."

"Naw, that's not all…" I looked at her, "See, this is where it gets dirty… Me and Duane weren't an instant thing, it was more of a gradual thing 'cause over time, we just started hangin' with each other more and more. As we got older, we did homework together…blah, blah, blah. Our friends nicknamed us Peanut Butter & Jelly."

Candace laughed.

"I *love* that! It's *so* cute!" my roommate said.

I rolled my eyes. "Well, anyway, some years later, my dad moved us to Illinois. It was really hard for me because those boys were my rat pack and Duane wasn't just my boyfriend, he was my *best* friend. We spent *a lot* of time together."

"Awwwwwwww," Candace taunted.

"Yeah, yeah, yeah… Well, we stayed there for about four years, but my dad didn't like it up there so we moved back when I was, like, sixteen. So now I'm in high school…and I saw Duane at my new school. I was all dazed like, 'Wow, that's him'," I illustrated with a light smile, "I still liked him, but I didn't know how to come at him. It had been so long, y'know? I didn't know if he still felt the same way. But then, I ended up goin' with this ol' buster-ass dude who'd been givin' me a lot of attention or what not…"

"She liked thugs back then," she interrupted, causing Candace to give me this sour expression.

I countered with bugged eyes and a clenched jaw muscle, but continued, "And later on, Duane started droppin' some hints to me by bringin' up nostalgia—which I didn't even recognize as tryin'-to-holla because I was young-and-stupid."

"Oh no… Don't tell me you fucked up. *Please* don't tell me you fucked up."

"I fucked up."

"Day-um, Vic! I told you not to tell me!" Candace laughed, then released a hard sigh. "What happened?"

"It came down to this one day when we were kickin' it during lunchtime. We're all engrossed in conversation, when—out of nowhere, he kissed me on the cheek. Which freaked me out 'cause I had a boyfriend! So I tried to figure out how to navigate the situation, but out of the *pure-fuckin'-blue*, my boyfriend just—poof!—appears, kisses me *square on the mouth*, then led me off by the arm."

"And you never said anything? You *never* tried to talk to him?"

"Nope. ...Well, actually, after me and Mr. Thug went outside, we exchanged a few choice words and he walked off. Then I went back to find Duane but he was gone."

They both moaned like sad puppies.

"And normally I'd have seen him at least once more in the hallway or somethin'—"

"But you couldn't find him?"

"Never saw him," I said, "I went to all the places that I thought he'd be—I even sneaked out of my last class to try to catch him walkin' outta his class when the bell rang, but he wasn't there. And even though I could've said somethin' the next day—the next week, the next year...I just never said anything. I still had a crush on him, but after so long, I thought he would've looked at me like I was stupid if I brought it up."

LOOKIN' IN THE MIRROR

"Vic...you're a dumbass," Candace attested, "And now *we're* lookin' at you stupid for not settling this back then!"

"That's why I didn't want to tell the story, *re*tard...and also why Ms. Happy Movie over here wants me to find him and tell him I made a terrible mistake eighty years ago and that I still want him back."

Quite on the optimistic side she replied in support of my roommate, "Well...you never know..."

"I never know??? OH MY GOD! You guys are ri-*dic*ulous! Do you know how long it's been???"

"Well, you said you were sixteen, right?" she asked.

"Yeah."

"...'Bout twelve years, then," she replied.

"And you don't see *anything* crazy about just walkin' up to him today and confessing my 'undying love' for him?"

Candace looked at my roommate and began to waver, "Well...I can see your point, but..."

"*BUT*??" I winced.

She looked at me with her head tilted.

"Okay, *BUT*... and by the way, you can't steal my expression. That's patented."

"Girl, shut up," she grinned, "But I was sayin'—before I was so rudely interrupted," she looked at me, "that I can see your point, but one: you're never gonna feel like it's totally resolved unless you say something. Two: you really *would* never know if he feels the same way if you don't say anything; and three: it sounds to me like you're just makin' excuses to not say anything just on the off chance that you might actually reveal some feelings. And we all know how you are about possibly being vulnerable. Hell, that's probably why you got with that thug dude, instead of holdin' out to see what might happen with Duane."

Roomie chimed in, "Good point! I never thought about that!"

"How so?" I asked...she really did have a good point, though I hate it when people know me so well—especially when pegging my flaws.

"Well, if you were anything like you are now, you probably took the easier road—the thug—'cause you knew you didn't really like him. *So* you never would've been at risk of gettin' too deep; whereas, with Duane, you probably would've been head over heels in love—and possibly married by now."

"Uuuuugh. You said the 'M'-word. You better quit cussin' at me, man."

My attempt to drag her off-course proved futile. "Where is he now," she asked.

"I'm not totally for sure, but I think he's still at home, doin' somethin' in the music business."

"Didn't you say your class reunion is this winter?"

I gasped, "Not you, too!!" I swear, any other time nobody ever listens to me, but this would be the one thing everyone just happened to notice. "Was that, like, the only time everyone was glued to what I was saying?"

Candace responded, "Well, I just remembered 'cause, at the time, I was thinkin' we could add it to our list of trips this year."

LOOKIN' IN THE MIRROR

"Oh, y'all wanted to go?"

My roommate replied, "Yeah!" As Candace simultaneously began her explanation, "Well I did, but I didn't, 'cause I was thinkin' it would be cool to travel, but I've been to Atlanta and it really didn't interest me to meet a bunch of corny folks you went to high school with, but now, yeah…I do wanna go, just to make sure you talk to Duane."

I rolled my eyes at her Duane comment, but it kinda touched me that they'd support me like that—not that I'd let *them* know or anything.

"Oh, well, I'll check into the tickets or registration prices for the reunion, then."

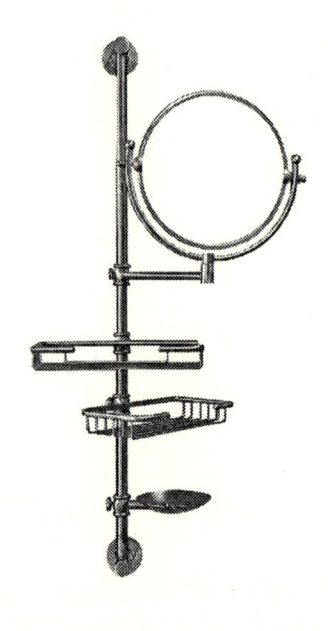

June 14

Early Evening at the House

LOOKIN' IN THE MIRROR

Somethin' weird is goin' on. I don't know, maybe it's the age thing finally settin' in, but I've been noticin' stuff missin', or moved to places where I didn't think I last put 'em...it's like in that movie, 'Amelie'. How that dude would wake up and his slippers were switched, his toothpaste was on the wrong side of the sink and stuff. It's just like that. But it's my *clothes*. I guess maybe I left some stuff at the cleaners and just forgot, but I don't even remember *goin'* to the cleaners. And this particular night, it seemed like I was hearin' noises. I must've gone through the house eight times, investigatin' some nondescript ding or tick. Lately, I've been thinkin' I'm goin' crazy.

It got to a point where I just had to let myself go. So I popped some popcorn and chilled on the sofa for a while. It was about...6:17, maybe. I started watchin' some TV; turned on my TIVO so I could catch up on my soaps from earlier. And things were quiet. It was just me, my popcorn and Y&R. A little less than and hour later, I was caught up on the show and I was down to the greasy corn seeds at the bottom of the bag. Well actually, the popcorn was gone in the first fifteen minutes of the show. But anyway, I wiped my hand on my joggin' pants and started to reach for the remote when I felt somethin' comin' close to me. Like, a shadow or some body heat.

So I looked down toward my feet and there was a man, about 5'9 or 5'10 dressed head-to-toe in black clothes, no other color visible but his eyes. So I jumped up and threw the remote at him, then I noticed somebody standin' behind me. So I swung around to maybe catch the guy in the eye with my fist, then my elbow, but he jumped back, and another came outta nowhere. He got me in a full nelson and wrestled me to the ground on my stomach. They put a papertowel in my mouth and put duck tape over. Then they duck taped my feet together at my ankles and put a bandana over my eyes. The three guys worked together to bring my arms behind my back and they tied my wrists together with duck tape as well, which was smart 'cause I was a Boy Scout. I can get out of any knot with my eyes closed and my fingers glued together.

But anyway...it seemed that nothin' would help me now. These night marauders had me subdued on my stomach in my own house, without the slightest mention of wanting anything. They didn't vandalize any of my stuff, they didn't call anyone, they didn't really beat me up, they didn't seem to steal anything—except me. And I couldn't move. Ving Rhames in that gimp suit flashed through my head. I tried to remain calm, though. I laid there tryin' to figure out how these cats got into my house without me knowin'. No windows were broken, they didn't bust in the door. It was almost like an organized hit. *But since when am I that important?* I wondered. I couldn't think of anyone I'd crossed, beaten up, stolen from, or even offended enough to wanna do this to me.

I didn't feel the third guy with them anymore. I wondered where he ran off to. The other two got me up from the floor. One spoke to the other in Spanish. But he had a different accent, not like the accents that I'm used to hearing at Carlos's family functions.

"¡Te jodio con el control!" he laughed.

LOOKIN' IN THE MIRROR

"He got you with that remote!" he laughed.

"SHHHHHHHHH!" the other said.

"¿Que??? No habla Español. Te apuesto que no sabe lo que estoy diciendo," he said and poked me, "¿No es asi voz? ¿Como?" He laughed. "Ya ves, te lo dije."

"What? He can't speak Spanish. I bet he doesn't even know what I'm saying," he said and poked me, "Do ya, pal? Huh?" He laughed. "See, I told you."

I stood motionless. I hoped that one would maybe mention a name. Maybe they'd talk about their plans in Spanish so I'd find out what they were gonna do with me. The garage door sounded, and the third guy came back. The three of them carried me to the car and threw me in the trunk. It was a long ride. A very long ride. And cramped, too. I felt bags behind me. And they played really loud tejano music the whole way.

At first, I kinda knew where they were goin' 'cause I could feel the turns. But after a while, I think they started makin' aimless turns so I wouldn't know where they were goin'. They changed lanes a lot, too. Then, after a while, the speed picked up. A lot. They had to be on the freeway somewhere. It was such a long ride. I started thinkin' about my family and all the people that would be at my funeral. My mom, my dad, Terrence...his stupid wife that, at that moment, I started to miss. My nephew. Never being able to see Tamara in a professional game. All my friends: Mia, Will, Carlos, Nouri, Ant, Schaefer. All the things I'd never get to do, like go to Egypt, Italy, go rock climbing, have a family of my own, take 'em to Disney World & Six Flags. I thought about Anita and her friend who writes the Jay Phillips column…their fashion line. Denise. Jannis, Tanya, Carl, Tanner, Chad. *Could Chad really hate me enough to pay some random Hispanic cats to abduct me?*

I remembered the time when we jumped these dudes for messin' with Gabriella. And this time when Will & Schaefer went streaking through Mia's sorority party in undergrad. I started laughin' to myself. *I always wanted a dog. I should've gotten one. Is my will in order? I think it is.*

It seemed like an hour, at least, and I felt the speed slow. There was a series of stops, then finally one. Car doors opened and closed. I heard footsteps. They opened the trunk. They grabbed my legs and swung me around so I could sit up, then they pulled me out. For some reason, I heard laughter. One of 'em sounded like Will's laugh. They took off the bandana. It was Will, Carlos & Nouri. I was at the airport.

"Happy Birthday," Carlos said.

I just looked at them as Will cut the duck tape off my wrists and ankles.

Nouri grabbed the bags out of the trunk. One of 'em was my bag.

"Come on man. We're gonna miss the flight," Carlos said, grabbin' his bag. He went around to the driver's side and kissed Andréa goodbye.

I stood there, lookin' confused. I took the duck tape off my mouth (boy, did that hurt) and spit out the wet wad of paper towel that they stuffed in my mouth. Then I cussed their asses out.

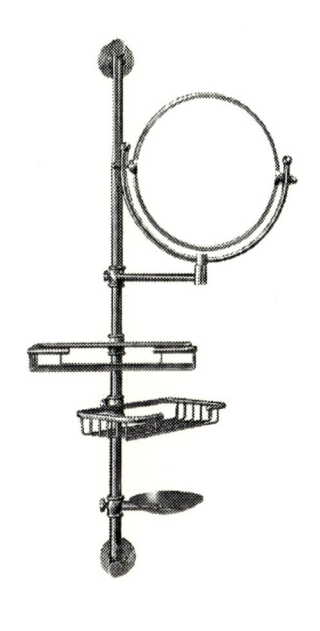

The Next Morning

Birthday Weekend

Will answered his cell phone in the adjacent room.

"Man, I knew somethin' was goin' down, but I didn't expect all this," I told Nouri.

He laughed. "I know you were scared when we came and got you outta yo' house!"

"MAN! I didn't know *what* was goin' on! All month, I was noticin' stuff was missin'…last night, I kept hearin' little noises…I thought I was goin' crazy!" We all laughed. "Next thing I knew, I looked up, I just saw some bodies standin' over me in black. I thought I was gettin' robbed! Y'all scared the shit outta me."

Will laughed. "Yeah, we were smooth wit' it. You didn't *even* see it comin'!"

"Yeah, you didn't see his fist comin' at your head either," Carlos laughed.

Will replied strokin' the side of his head, "Whew…that one almost took my head off. I'm just glad I saw it when I did…it woulda done more than just graze me."

"How did y'all get my keys and stuff, though?" I asked.

Nouri cracked a grin, "That's the good part about datin' Tanya. It was all her idea. Then she got with Jannis, and it all started comin' together."

"Man, *that's* why Jannis kept actin' all weird…man, that's crazy," I replied.

"That's what I said. When Nouri first came to me talkin' that noise, I was like, 'Man, are you crazy?? His daddy from New Orleans! I ain't try'na get shot!'" He paused and grinned at Nouri. "But he *had* to pull

LOOKIN' IN THE MIRROR

the double dare out, so it was on and poppin' after that." He laughed.

I shook my head. "So all y'all kept comin' in to get my clothes…"

"Yeah, Mia worked that out. I wasn't try'na touch ya drawls'n'shat," Will said.

I laughed. "…Okay…and Jannis made sure my schedule was clear…

Nouri nodded.

"All y'all chipped in on the tickets…"

Will nodded.

Carlos finished the puzzle, "Gabriella got us the hook-up on the hotel."

"Man, I was wonderin'! I'm lookin' like, 'We're beachfront…*somebody's* comin' out some cheese!' But I know y'all cheapos ain't comin' outta no beachfront money! And a *suite*, too??!"

They laughed.

"Man, just know this: *e'r'thing* on this this trip is on *some* type-uh hook up," Will asserted, "Whether it's by knowin' somebody, or flirtin', or Spanish inquisition…we're gettin' *whatever we can* for a lower price or free. And if not, it'll just be on ya boy."

Huh?

"…What boy?"

(((Knock, Knock! Knock!)))

I looked at him kinda funny, and Carlos answered the door.

A voice yelled from the doorway. "What're you DOOO-IIING!!!!!!"

"What're *YOUUUUU* DOO-IIING????" Will yelled back.

301

A. M. HATTER

They all shouted in unison, "AHHHHHHHHHHHHHHHHHHH!"

I just sat there and laughed.

"What's up, man. Didn't expect me, didja?"

I got up to hug him. "What the hell're you doin' here, Schaefer?"

Comin' out of the one-armed pat on the back, "It's ya birthday, man! Didja think I forgot?"

I looked at him confused, then I looked at Will, Nouri and Carlos.

"Your secretary got my information out of your rolodex...her name is Jannis, right?"

"Damn...that girl is unstoppable. What the *hell*?" I mumbled.

"Well, everybody's dressed?" Kev asked.

I shrugged. "Yeah, man, we've, uh, we've just been sittin' here."

"Okay, well, let's synchronize our watches...I know y'all central time boys prob'ly think it's eleven-thirty," he smiled.

Carlos's neck snapped back, "Aww, yeah! Damn, I forgot about that!"

"See there. Where would y'all be if I wasn't White?"

We laughed.

Nouri interjected, "Hey, I'm Iranian. I can be on time."

"Man please. Don't try to play that foreign shit. You're just kinda light-skinned," Will retorted.

We laughed.

"So, uh, are we gettin' this party on the road?" Kevin goaded as he walked toward the door.

"Dang, bruh rushin' us out the door and shit!" Will smiled.

"It's *Miami*, man! What? You wanna just sit here and look at *each other* all day?" He paused and looked back with a slight grin on his face. "Besides, I got some ladies meetin' us at the café down the street," Kev explained.

Will eyes widened. "Oh, straight?"

Kev nodded.

"Shit, nee-gro! That's all you had to say!" Will said, walkin' out behind Kev.

"Where'd you find some women that quick?" I asked. "You ain't got game like that, bwah!"

"Muthafucka, I'm *Kev*. Pimpin' ain't dead; y'all bitches just *scared*."

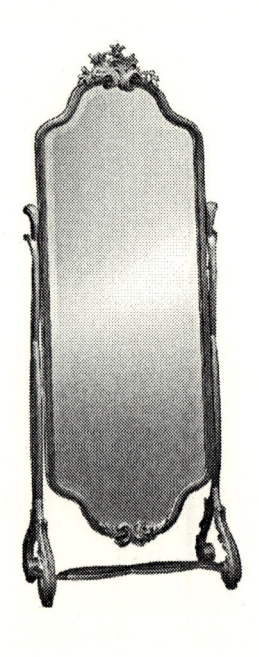

Monday, August 19

LOOKIN' IN THE MIRROR

My at-work cohort, Anita, dropped by my desk to chat on the way back to the tech office from a job she just finished. She told me about some guy in another department that had just been fired for downloading porn. Then she shared with me the shock of meeting a White guy who's Nation of Islam. Imagine *THAT*! I was like, "So, what does he do? Sit around hating himself?" (Funny!) But then, Turk walked up with this ominous expression on his face. I thought he was about to tell me his mom died or something. I was almost scared to talk to him.

"Hey, Ben..." Anita looked confused.

"Hey, girrrl."

"Er'you alright?" she asked.

"Yeah. Why wouldn't I be?" he replied.

"Oh, no reason...you just look kinda...I-doh-know, solemn."

"Hmm. Nah, I'm alright."

"Okay. Well, I'm goin' back ta my desk."

"Okay, girl," I said, bidding her adieu.

"See ya later," he added, resting his buttocks on the edge of my desk.

"So what's goin' on?" I asked him.

"You're gonna be mad at me."

"For what? What'd you do?"

"I'm leavin' the journal. I just put in my two-week notice."

"What???" I reached toward him with an outstretched hand. "Nooooooooooooo!" I grabbed his forearms. "You can't leeeeave meeee; I looove youuuuu, maaaaaan!" I finished my theatrics by rolling over to him, still in my chair, and wrapping my arms around his waist. "I'd be nothing without you." I whispered dramatically and jerked backward.

"Oh, buck up, kiddo," he said with a Humphrey Bogart voice, "You'll be okay…you'd be better off without the likes-uh-me."

My right hand rose to his jaw, as I stood from the chair, my fingers sliding into the hair at the nape of his neck. My accent shifted to one of those film noir actresses, "Oh, Jaunny. Don't you darrre say thaht. You know I simply cahn't live without you. I woodent know up from down, left from right." I turned away suddenly. "Oh, Jaunny, cahn't you see!" And faced him again. "I'm in love with you!"

Having become Rhett Butler by now, "Frankly my dear…I don't give a damn!"

I had to break character on that one…it was a well-timed line. But he couldn't beat a karate line: "BULL-SHIT, Mr. Hand Man! You come straight out of a comic book."

"Awwwww! You pulled out the Bruce Lee on me!"

"If we kept going, I'd have pulled out some 'Last Dragon'…" I bragged.

"Ha!"

"Nawwww, I'd've put you *down* on 'The Punisher'-one! You ain't *even* ready!" We smiled and got quiet.

"Man…I'm gonna miss you," he lamented.

Crossing my arms, "It serves you right for leavin' me, man."

"Now, you know I can't stay here. I'm goin' nuts as it is. Alton's gonna give me an ulcer."

LOOKIN' IN THE MIRROR

"Yeah. He *is* kind of an asshole."

"Kinda?" He gave me an acerbic look. "But still, I can't be one of those people who get old and still have the same job. That shit's ridiculous. We're not in the fifties."

"Good point. You *have* been here for a while. What's it been? Like—"

"Seven…eight years," he answered.

"That's not so long."

"Yes it is! Try working two *weeks* with Alton, and you'll see."

"So, what're you gonna do?"

"Umm…I'm not sure right off. I've been emailing a little bit. There's this three-month gig that I can help out with…a non-profit that helps disadvantaged children."

"Is it paying or are you volunteering?"

"Well, a little of both, 'cause it doesn't pay very much… But I still got the restaurant, so I'll be fine," he paused, "Oh! Jamel told me you were there not too long ago. He told me to ask you who your friend was and to hook him up," he said to me, looking happy.

"My friend??" I had to remember what even happened when I went, to place what he was talking about. Then it hit me. "OH!!!" I said, then went lackluster, "Maaan, I was with Shawn."

His expression morphed from happy to limp, "Ohhhh," then to a half-smirk, "well, I guess it's back to the drawing board."

"Ooooo! Man, I don't think I told you about that day!"

A. M. HATTER

"What? About the two guys you macked?"

I frowned.

"Jamel told me that, too!" He laughed. "In fact, I would tell you what he said about you, if I didn't think it'd blow your head to smitherines!"

"What??!!" I looked intrigued. "Come on, man! What'd he say?"

"Nah. I'm not tellin' you."

"Why not?"

"'Cause your ego is already *this* damn big!" he explained, holding his arms wayyy out.

"He wanted to get with me, didn't he?" I watched intently, trying to draw a reaction.

But he just sat there playing poker face, "I told you I'm not tellin' you."

"Uhhh, huh. That's what it is. He wanted to holla, but when he saw the true game of The Mackalicious Pimpmama, he got intimidated and backed down. *That's* what it *is*!" I cackled like a mad scientist.

Again, with the poker face, "If that's what you wanna think."

"Well, what else would it be, if it's supposed to make my ego big?"

"But back to my new job…You know, they're gonna pay for me to travel."

"Really? I'm jealous."

"Yeah. I don't think I'll be traveling that much, but I'm guessing that I'll be really busy. That's how it usually is with new organizations that don't pay you a lot."

LOOKIN' IN THE MIRROR

"Yeah, that's true. You hold multiple positions and stuff. They got you runnin' around like a chicken with its head cut off."

Then, for just a hot second, I looked defeated.

"What?" he asked.

"How will I see you?"

"Awwww, we'll see each other!" he leaned over and pressed my head to his sternum. "It just won't be as often as now. Besides, this gives us so many more opportunities to play ranch packet."

We both laughed wildly. See, ranch packet is this game that started about…hell, almost a year ago. I was at his restaurant one day and I was craving a salad, something fierce. So I put my salad together and grabbed a packet of ranch sauce, thinking that's what I wanted. But a few steps later, I saw a packet of Caesar and grabbed that on the way to my seat.

When he came in a little later to walk around and visit with his loyal constituents, he naturally came to my table and we chatted for a little while.

As he left, I was like, "Hey, take this back up there on your way."

But since he's a hardhead, he tossed it back to me and said, "You can have it."

But what am I going to do with a packet of ranch sauce that I don't want? So when I was leaving, I made it a point to leave it on the counter right in front of him and go, "Keep the change."

To my dismay, he grabbed it just before the register girl got to it and waited until I was ready to get in my car. Then he ran out like he forgot to tell me something. So he came up to the car, ranch packet in sleeve, and made vigorous idle conversation with me. After laughing my heart out at the useless, nonsensical banter that we usually volley to each other, I figured it's time for me to go. (Mostly because we went back and forth imitating Mike Myers as Dr. Evil; though, nobody got better, only louder. So when people started looking at the two weird folks that kept going "Mwa-ha-ha-ha-haaaaa," I knew it was time to go.) Lo and behold, a week later I found that damn packet in my back seat!

I had almost forgotten that I had it, but I remembered to take it in to work one day and I put it in his desk when he went to the bathroom. About a month after that, he's at my cubicle carrying conversation with me like normal, and slips it in my coat pocket. I didn't even realize I had the damn thing until I was at C&K's looking for my keys as I was leaving. So I interoffice mailed it to him—even marked it urgent, like it was important.

But his next strike was good—really good. One: because he let about two months pass by, and two: because he used my magnanimous ego against me.

At that point, it was maybe June or July and he had this guy I didn't know from another department call me from the security desk like I had a delivery. So I went down and picked it up... He handed me a cute little box, wrapped in reflective paper...said the tip was already taken care of like he was a real courier. He even had me sign for it!! Turk really did his homework. The note attached read, "From a secret admirer." I thought I was so special, just knowing it

LOOKIN' IN THE MIRROR

was from Vinny or Lamar, or my White guy. But to my dismay, I got to my desk and opened the box only to find...

That *damn* ranch packet! Uuuuuuuuuuuuuugh! I had to appreciate the planning though. That was a bomb ass hit.

So that weekend, I went to this bazaar and found this do-nothing book for fifty cents. So I flipped to, like, page twenty and cut a rectangle in the middle, about an inch and a half deep, and put the ranch packet inside. I waited about...a month or so, until the "secret admirer" strike had gotten a little bit old, and I started telling him that I was tired of the game and couldn't think of anything. I laid enough groundwork for him to let his guard down and I nestled the book right between a few trite books toward the end of his desk arrangement.

Three weeks later, he swaggers into my cubicle at lunch like usual, but with a story about how confused he was to see a book he didn't remember buying; particularly one entitled, "My Ass Is First Class." Then, flipping through, only to find (Dun-Dun-DUNNNNNN!!!) the ranch packet.

After that, he kind of pissed me off because he went into my CD case and took 'Make Yourself' (Incubus, my favorite group), 'Doggy Style' (My favorite by Snoop), and my Barry Manilow greatest hits, leaving the ranch packet behind. I guess he was supposed to be marking that he took them as well as telling me it's my turn. But that junk wasn't funny. I don't play about my CDs. So a sista had to get rowdy and take homeboy's favorite PlayStation game, leaving the ranch packet in the game's slot in his disk tower. I bet it was really funny to turn that tower around and catch that packet where his game should've been.

The ranch packet, that's funny. This does provide more opportunities, though… What's my next move? I gotta get him back for leaving that thing in my purse.

Ohhhhh, I know. I'll get him good…

The phone rang.

"Hello?"

"Hey girl. You busy?"

"Not really. Me & Turk are just talkin'."

"Oh, tell him I said 'Hi'."

"Okay." I looked up at Turk, "Shawn said 'Hi'."

"Ohh! Tell her I said 'Hey'."

Going back to the phone, "He says 'Hey'."

"Girl, why have Candace and your roommate been askin' me about our reunion? They're like—"

Turk interrupted, "Hey, I'll let you take the call. I'll talk to you later," he whispered.

"Okay, bye," I whispered back.

Shawn continued, though I missed a small chunk of what she'd been saying, "so she's askin' me all these questions about guys we knew and all this stuff. I'm like, 'Where is this coming from??' Y'know? I mean, I don't just have a nagging interest in anyone they used to know. They're just actin' weird."

"Dag, I don't even wanna talk about the reunion. I had no interest in goin' until they said they wanted to—which was weird, 'cause, I mean, they're not gonna know anybody. What would they do?"

"I know!"

"But they wanna go and shit...so I told 'em I'd try to find invitation info and all. Try to get Brian to hook us up with tickets again."

"Man, I don't wanna go," she complained, "I can't stand talkin' to people that I haven't seen in a long time, 'cause then they ask you a bunch of questions. And I'm like, if I cared for you to know, I'd have kept in touch."

I laughed. "O-*kay*! ...But you know they're not gonna let this go, right?"

"Yeah."

"So...what? Candace & Kenya at your folks' house and my roommate at mine?"

"I guess so," she sighed, sounding beaten.

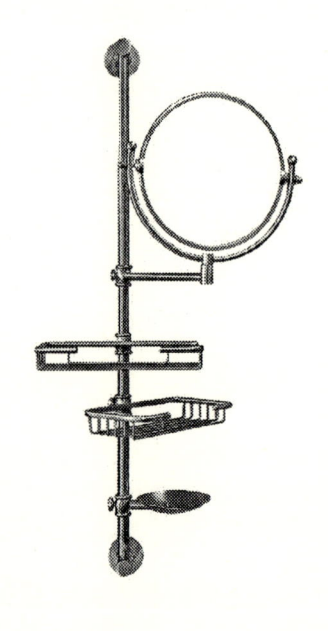

June 25

Just After Work

LOOKIN' IN THE MIRROR

RHOyalHighness: sup
Bou-G: not much, man.
RHOyalHighness: really? That's not what I saw.
Bou-G: huh???
RHOyalHighness: what's up w/ Denise's car bein @ ur house?
Bou-G: ...
RHOyalHighness: yeah…uh-huh.
RHOyalHighness: so, what? Y'all back 2gether?
Bou-G: naw, not really
RHOyalHighness: so what's goin' on?
Bou-G: she was just over here. we were talkin about old times and stuff.
RHOyalHighness: all night?
Bou-G: damn, u spyin on me or somethin?
RHOyalHighness: LOL! U'd love that, wouldn't you?
RHOyalHighness: naw, I was over at my cousin's house—remember, they stay a block from you?
Bou-G: oh yeah
RHOyalHighness: and I was gonna drop your medu netr cd back to you. I was over there a while, but her car was still there when I left.
Bou-G: U're the one that got my cd???
RHOyalHighness: ha…yeah
Bou-G: yeah, I want that back
RHOyalHighness: uh, duhhh, that's what I was trying to do. but ol' girl was over there
Bou-G: what'd you think about it, tho?
RHOyalHighness: it was pretty cool, man…especially that one song…
Bou-G:???

RHOyalHighness: whatchu talkin bouuuut, whatchu talkin bouuuut, sho is talkin loud!

Bou-G: oh, yeah...that one's pretty catchy.

RHOyalHighness: where'd you get it?

Bou-G: I got it when I went up to Oklahoma to see Donovan...he went to school with some of them. He's always talkin' about some guy named E.B.

RHOyalHighness: oh, okay...how *is* Donovan?

Bou-G: he's good...you know him, tryin' to be the next Bill Pickett

Bou-G: he thinks he's Marvel Rogers

Bou-G: brb

Ampuloso1: Hey Mia, guess what I found out.

RHOyalHighness: what?

Ampuloso1: 1-Jorge is graduating this august, 2-Cesar got accepted to OU

RHOyalHighness: Uh-oh! Alma Mater!!

Ampuloso1: yeah, he'll be on our old stompin grounds

RHOyalHighness: what's his major?

Bou-G: hey, what's up Carlos

Ampuloso1: Marketing, I think

Ampuloso1: not much, man

RHOyalHighness: Jorge went to U of T, right?

Ampuloso1: yeah.

Bou-G: Jorge's comin out?

Ampuloso1: yeah.

Bou-G: good shot!

Ampuloso1: Andrea says hey, everybody

Bou-G: hey, girrrrrrl

RHOyalHighness: what up DRE!!

Bou-G: hey, I talked to kev the other day

RHOyalHighness: oh, really?

LOOKIN' IN THE MIRROR

Bou-G: yeah. He's gonna hook me up w/ a realtor up there
RHOyalHighness: oh, okay...cool.
Ampuloso1: so you're really serious about movin', huh?
Bou-G: yeah...I need to do somethin' different, ya know?
Ampuloso1: yeah, I feel ya
RHOyalHighness: ...I really don't want you to go, but then, I guess it's about time for u 2 do somethin different
Bou-G: yeah...
Im_Will_I_Wont: What's up y'all?
RHOyalHighness: hey will, what's up?
Im_Will_I_Wont: What's new with you guys?
RHOyalHighness: nothin here...but Gerald—well, I'll let him tell you
Bou-G: oh, thanks mia
Ampuloso1: ooooh, gossip! Lol
Im_Will_I_Wont: what?
Bou-G: Denise is back
Im_Will_I_Wont: :-1
Ampuloso1: well I guess we won't see u for another 4 years
Im_Will_I_Wont: Bruh...come on now. What's the deal?
Ampuloso1: say it ain't sooo
Bou-G: we're not back together
Ampuloso1: <<<<<wiping brow
Im_Will_I_Wont: She let you hit, though, huh?
Bou-G: lol, yeah
Ampuloso1: hmmmm
Im_Will_I_Wont: Give it time...
Bou-G: damn...y'all must think I'm stupid or something

RHOyalHighness: when it comes to *her*—yeah!

Bou-G: fuck u, mia

RHOyalHighness: seriously! that girl had you whipped! And you *know* it!

RHOyalHighness: I can't believe you even allowed her into your house!

Im_Will_I_Wont: Mia, chill.

RHOyalHighness: she walked out on you, G!

Bou-G: yes, I remember

RHOyalHighness: DO YOU??? cuz I can't tell!

Im_Will_I_Wont: Mia!!! He's a grown ass man.

RHOyalHighness: until he gets around *her*! apparently I'm the only one who remembers how he fuckin' disappeared when they were together.

Ampuloso1: <<<raising hand. I remember.

Im_Will_I_Wont: mia, goin' on a rampage isn't gonna help right now.

RHOyalHighness: he didn't know us anymore

RHOyalHighness: couldn't hang out at the house…couldn't call, couldn't damn send a b-day card!

Ampuloso1: not even flowers! (LOL)

Bou-G: naw, that was just you, mia…you know she didn't like you. i used to hang with everyone else, tho.

Im_Will_I_Wont: Well, actually, dawg…You did kind of disappear. We'd see you, but not very often.

Ampuloso1: my family thought you moved or something

Im_Will_I_Wont: Even the chapter started saying that you were on "work detail."

Bou-G: damn. for real?

LOOKIN' IN THE MIRROR

Im_Will_I_Wont: Yeah, man...it was kinda heavy back then.
RHOyalHighness: see
Im_Will_I_Wont: Shut up, mia
Im_Will_I_Wont: Look, bruh...I'm still your boy to the end and all
Im_Will_I_Wont: but...I don't like her. Straight up. That's the way I feel
RHOyalHighness: I second that opinion
Im_Will_I_Wont: I just always felt like she was bad news
Ampuloso1: I *still* feel like that!
Im_Will_I_Wont: But if she's what you want, I can't say anything. It's your business.
RHOyalHighness: you better be glad Antoine ain't in here!
Im_Will_I_Wont: Awww man! That's for sure!
Ampuloso1: he'd melt the keyboard!
Bou-G: it's cool...
Bou-G: I gotta go, tho. I'm takin Dante to photo class.
Im_Will_I_Wont: A'ight. Peace.
RHOyalHighness: see ya later
Ampuloso1: think about what Will said, man. Don't do it.
Bou-G: yeah.
Bou-G: bye

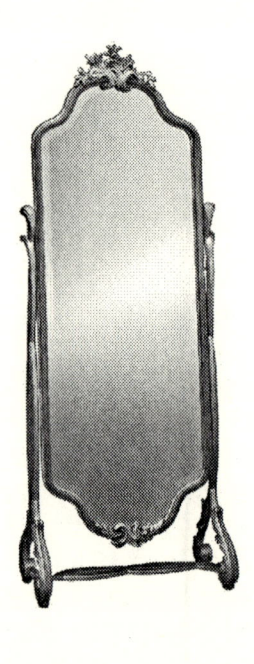

Saturday, October 19

New Orleans, LA

LOOKIN' IN THE MIRROR

Sometimes it amazes me that I even hang with these chicks. I've always been one to hang out with a bunch of guys, but now it's all women. It's weird as hell. At times it's cool, but I'd rather hang with guys because they don't get all emotional about the tiniest little things. They don't call you up and say, "We need to talk." They don't have posse gripe sessions…it's simple: don't trip unless it's a big deal. And really, how many make-or-break situations can you run into with one or two friends? (If you find that you have a lot, then you might not need to be friends anymore.)

But then, the thing with guys is that they like you and you're cool to have around up until a certain point. Then, they just want to be around guys—or they F around and hook up with some chick, and you can't be around while they're getting their groove on unless you want to participate. On the other hand, she might be a longer termed presence than that, which you're totally fine with. But no matter how nice you are, your homeboy's girlfriend will *never* accept you. They're always too insecure.

At first it took some major adjustment to get used to being around women on as consistent a basis as my GP (Girl Posse) used to kick it. At times, I found myself ready to go nuts because they—my roommate and *Kenya*, especially—are so fucking sensitive. I'd say things that I really meant in jest and they're all "What do you mean by that??" or "That's mean, Victoria!"

Oh! Like this one time—I'll never forget! It was about two years back. We were at C& K's house when the door burst open. There's twenty-four-year-old Kenya, storming in all exasperated, asking if her butt jiggles when she walks because earlier that day some dude giggled and said, "It's jigglin' baby! Go 'head, baby!"

Shawn, who probably would've said something along the lines of "It doesn't matter 'cause I ain't lookin' at your ass," was in the kitchen making a sandwich and not paying attention.

Candace just laughed.

My roommate the do-gooder replied, "Noooo! Why would he say something like that??"

But I, with my big mouth, snickered at her absurdity and said in a pimp-type voice, "It's shakin' like jelly!" Then I added an old man cackle, kind of like the old tired steam engine that would go kaput on those ancient Looney Toons episodes (back when Bugs Bunny had a round head). *I* thought it was comedy! ☺

They didn't find it as amusing, though. ☹

I don't know what she was tripping about. I mean, like it's not going to jiggle. Her ass is as big as a Macy's balloon. Simple physics says what? And why is a jiggle a bad thing? Guys love that shit! But then, guys like anything soft with nipples and a coochie (most times, just the coochie). And it really doesn't matter what kind of case it comes in; there's always a customer willing to buy if you know how to market it right.

Anyway… It was really cool to be on the trip, clowning with my GP again since we'd been on hiatus for a month or so. Sure, I'd hang with Candace one day or Shawn the next, and they'd hang with one or two others; but all of us hadn't been together for a while because of boyfriends. *(Rolling my eyes) That friggin' word...ever the freakin' cramp in my style.*

It's not that I hate men or anything, because I soooo deeply appreciate them and what they have to offer for my viewing pleasure! But it's kind of hard to be friends with gal pals who are in relationships. Sure, they'll *tell* you that nothing's going to change, but then they stop doing certain things that they used to do because they're trying to build that damn trust bullshit. Then they can't hang out with you as much because the significant other wants to spend time. And men turn into such babies when they don't get enough time! Then they try to mix the two worlds, but it never works because you represent a possible version of who the significant other's dear love (your friend) used to be; plus they can't comment on stuff that you (I) really want to discuss—like some guy's incredibly rotund rear end. *Rrrrrrrrrrrrrrrrrrrrrrrrrr*. (Man! I wanted to throw a whole bag of quarters at his ass! By the handful...so I could see them bounce off into the distance in slow motion like some Matrix-type shit. *Wooowwww...*)

So there I am, stuck in social purgatory and forced to overdevelop my dating game. I've become quite the chronic dater because of friends with boyfriends. In fact, I'd have cut all of my so-called contenders off six months ago, if I wasn't so freaking bored lately and they weren't so convenient. It's normally my policy to drift off after two dates; that way I've gotten my entertainment and they don't start feeling like it's going anywhere (translation: don't expect anything from me).

A. M. HATTER

But anyway…Jackson State vs. Southern University @ the New Orleans Dome… Cool trip!

It was Candace and Kenya's idea because they're avid JSU alumni and absolutely adore their HBCU band. Plus, Candace was all serious about initiating me into the ways of "The Boom." She about had a baby when she first found out that I had never seen an HBCU band play. To me, it was never a big deal, since I and my brothers attended UCLA, where my dad went. But since she attended and marched in the band at Jackson State, and her parents before her, it was just impossible to perceive a person—a Black native Atlantan, in particular—who had just *never* seen an HBCU band in action, which is supposed to be something of a jewel. So they made sure that I was free this year to come with them for the big rival of SU vs. JSU, set in New Orleans, because I'd missed the trip for the last few years.

So anyway, we had to get to the dome all early because, apparently, people start packing the place early with this rivalry. (Man, we were up there with the freaking janitors and shit, three hours early and it was *still* crowded!) The air was thick and humid, kind of misty and sprinkling. It had that hot, wet feel that makes you semi-miserable; yet, we saw folks outside tailgating. The bands were there… *Man*! They weren't playing about the bands. When they march in, everything's about style: from the plumes on their hats to the way they wear their pants and spats, to the way they move as they march. All this shit is *too serious* with these folks!

For instance, Southern U wears their pants high to show off their spats or something...and they have this thing where they jump on every eighth step. But the cool part is that when they jump, the cymbal players raise their arms up and there's this shiny row of bronze glimmering at you. Then there are the dancers—and that's a *big* thing with these groups. If your dancers aren't shapely, cute, kicking high, and executing moves (trust that it's really as much about the dancing as the aesthetic lineup), then your girls *will* get clowned. Southern is, apparently, known for having tall, light-skinned chicks with long hair on their dance line. As Candace tells it, they have these height requirements for each section so that everything is uniform.

Jackson State, on the other hand, comes in more like a train. They charge in on their theme song, 'Get Ready' by The Temptations, and the trombone players (in front) tick their heads back and forth synonymously with the stepping foot. During the changeup, however, they swing their heads (while still playing the instruments!) in a circular motion. I guess that train thing is their persona...Candace kept yelling out "The Funky Freight Train."

They don't have any height requirements for their band that I could tell, but each section had a specific assignment, which they call "catching the flash" (more on that in a minute). After they finish playing 'Get Ready', they start in with this really, *really* long cadence called 'Series'. (She never explained why it's called that...she was too mesmerized with her band, and it was so inconsequential that I never remembered to ask.) And during 'Series', each section will do something like hold their horn a specific way or turn a specific direction—anything to occupy your eyes; but the drum section, in particular has their own choreography or something. For such a simple instrument, those cymbal players sure do a lot with them!

    Their dancers, the J-Settes, seemed like the 'School Daze' opponent to SU's dancers, The Dancing Dolls. You guessed it: The Dancing Dolls are light, The J-Settes are darker; "darker," meaning anywhere from mocha-cream to black as hell. And I don't know where these schools find these chicks, but fuck videos! Fuck the fashion mags! *These* are the chicks that give you the image complexes because they're real life! They don't have the luxury of relying on PhotoShop. They're marching in with these sculpted calf muscles, thick thighs, bubble-gum rumps and tight ass waists, topping it all off with a set of perfect hand-sized tits jiggling every time they clomp the ground with their dancing girl boots. What are they feeding these chicks? Oats and carrots?

    The JSU-SU game is a really huge rivalry. In fact, the way it was told to me, this pairing should be the SWAC's (Southwestern Athletic Conference) real claim to fame.

    "Forget the Bayou Classic 'cause Grambling always loses!" they said.

    Speaking of losing, Candace and Kenya had been on a high all day because Jackson State had been losing the SU battle for a long while, until they started beating them two years ago. Those chicks…man, you'd swear they were on speed or something. Neither one of them could sit down. EVERY FRIGGIN MINUTE, they were up, singing along with the band—which, by the way, they absolutely *had* to sit by. I wondered if they went for the game or for the band...I'm thinking the band.

I could've sworn that every song they played was Candace's "Favorite song!!!" One minute she's going, "Ooo! Ooo! 'Black-N-Blues'! That's my song!" Then it's "Ohhh! 'Africano'! That's my jam!" Along with, (what was it??) Mr. Magic, Seven Day Weekend... Give It To Me Baby, Don't Stop 'Til You Get Enough (with which, I concur) and, hell, a whole lot of other junk. I don't know how those kids remember all those songs...and right off the tops of their heads, even if the band hasn't played it in a while.

Oh, and don't let a section from the other band stand up and play as a challenge, because then it's on. They go back and forth, playing—not songs from the band's general repertoire, but their own collection of section music. The baritones have their songs, and the trombones have their songs, and the trumpets... Man, these folks will take it all day! It's like being around a bunch of 'Star Trek' geeks at a Sci-Fi convention. And the fans will even join in! At other games, Candace said, people will bring in fog horns or these long plastic tube horn things and blow them in the rhythm of a song they want the band to play. I'm sitting there like, *So this is how they request music in the boondocks, huh?*

The funniest thing was this White guy running around in his briefs and a silk cape, climbing up on the

A. M. HATTER

railing sounding like dirt road and alcohol, yelling out, "Yeeeeeeeaaaaaah! Yeeeeeeeaaaaaah!!!" Man, folks lose their fucking minds in New Orleans.

Then, one of Candace's old band friends that still lives in Jackson came up and talked to her. Some dude named Jeremy that she called Saddam Hussein. In the band, they don't greet each other by their real names. They go, "[Ridiculous name]!! What's up, man!" [Hug] She said they called him that when he was a crab (first year player) because he looks Middle Eastern, which is true. Given in context, the name actually is really funny—and quite fitting—because the guy really did look like Saddam Hussein.

I asked her what her crab name was, and it took Mr. Hussein blurting it out for me to learn that they called her Mrs. Butterworth, "'Cause she's thick—and rich." When the trumpet upperclassmen made her do her skit (a sketch to make the upperclassmen laugh), she'd have to put her hands behind her head and sway her hips at the same time that she said "thick" and "rich." With her being the only girl in the trumpet section, they had her doing *all* the major female movie lines like Eartha Kitts' role in 'Boomerang': "Maaarrrrrrr-cuuussssssss…I'm not wearrring any pahn-teeees!" Or Olive Oil: "Ohhhh Pop-eye!" And this other one, which she openly claims as her best work: the WHOLE SCENE from 'The Color Purple' where Miss Sophia confronts Celie in the field, which people know as "You told Harpo to beat me?" (I truly don't think they knew that they were making a comedy when they did that film.)

LOOKIN' IN THE MIRROR

In between seeing JSU stomp the shit out of Southern (in the actual game), I caught random dialogue here and there about some dude in the band that's super old, like 28 and shit. Of course, that's not old in the grand scheme of things, but next to kids coming out of high school...that's old as H_2O. So his crab name is Bob Hope, because what? Bob Hope's as old as space. But they call him Abraham when he's around his crab brother, "Moses," aptly named because dude had quite an extensive beard.

I looked at Jeremy as they talked about the beard boy, "That's one of your Taliban friends, ain't it Suh-dom-hoo-sayn?" (They never call him by Saddam or Hussein, they run it together like one word.)

They laughed.

"You sure she didn't go to school with us?" he quipped, meaning that I'm a smart-ass like them.

Other names I picked up over the course of the game: "Sheila D."-a drummer, named so because she really sucked on her drum when she first came in and wasn't half as good as Sheila E.; "Benny Hill," a saxophonist who walks exceptionally fast; "Banana Peel Tone," a dude named Tony who's high yellow, dresses like a pimp and has a perm; and Booty Lips, a tuba player with some big ass lips (no pun intended).

The ways they ridicule these folks are so funny that the situation itself is rendered helpless. Saddam Hussein told us about this guy (Bo-Bo) who's roommate caught him jacking off in their hotel room during one of the band trips. The next day on the bus, some upperclassmen got a few of the guy's crab brothers together to sing in BARBER SHOP

A. M. HATTER

QUARTET HARMONY to the tune of MARY HAD A LITTLE freaking LAMB, "Hmmmmmmmmmmm. Bo-Bo ja_cks off in bed, off in bed, off in bed / Bo-Bo Ja____cks off, in, be_____d...He jacked off la___st ni____ght."

    These people are lunatics.
    They need to be comedians.
    They need to have their own variety show.
    Anyway, if the game and all it's theatrics wasn't enough, there's plenty after the game. Regulars call it "the fifth quarter," where the bands battle it out for another dose of braggadocio. Besides, JSU had a score to settle because Southern popped a nice little piece on them in their halftime show breakdown. Man, I heard the talk; everyone thought SU was doing their regular stuff until they got to the last of their four squads (which, again, is normal for them) and said, "Let's do it JSU style!" Then proceeded to do a JSU routine. I'm not a band geek, but I had to give them their props. I thought it was pretty funny, just in understanding how competition goes. And those cats from SU stayed hyped *all through* the game: the jillions of fans, the band—hell, the freaking *cheerleaders* get more crunk than a Trick Daddy video.

    But *then* came the sorority sisters! Oh, man! All it took was one 'Eee-Yip' from deep within the crowd and Kenya and Candace got all happy. They were jumping up and down...throwing up their hand sign (which, I make fun of all the time by calling them Murder, Inc., although I'm sure their sorority probably had it first), doing this obnoxious call...hugging folks

LOOKIN' IN THE MIRROR

they didn't even know like they were best friends and crap. All that shit is too weird to me.

I have never seen so many people so happy to be at a freakin' football game, but not necessarily for the game itself. They're happier than old people at church during the greet-your-neighbor part. This might have to be an annual trip. Especially if it's in New Orleans, so we can go to the gay bar on Bourbon Street and see the scantily clad men again. ☺

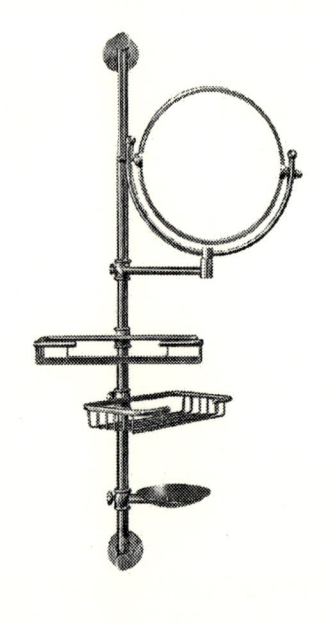

July 6

Saturday Afternoon

LOOKIN' IN THE MIRROR

Saturday, I went over to my parents' house. The usual Saturday meal with the gang at my house was preempted for the holiday.

"Hey, where were you last night? I called you at midnight and you weren't at home," my mom stated flatly, like I was suddenly fifteen again and owed her an explanation.

I stared at her like she was off, "I was out... That's what single, grown men do on Friday nights."

"Alright! Get smart. I'll show you what grown is," she replied.

Hm-hm, hm, hmm! What's she gon' do?? I thought and laughed to myself.

I kissed her on the forehead. "Yeah, I love you too, momma," I said and walked into the house, on a beeline to the kitchen.

"Heyyy man!" I greeted my brother with a hug (er, uh, the one-armed pat on the back, rather). "I didn't know you were in town! When'd you get in?"

"Real late last night. Momma tried to call you," Terrence said.

"I know. She cut me up at the door, talkin' 'bout 'Where were *you*'," I laughed.

"Oh! Uhhh...your present's in the car. I'll get it for you later," he said.

"Awwww," I smiled, "lil bro got me a pwehh-zent."

He rolled his eyes at me. "You gon' get some of this now, or what," he asked about the barbecue before he put it back into the oven.

"Aw, yeah, lemme get at that," I replied grabbin' plate. "So uh, where's W—" *Ooooooh! Not*

Wanda... Dammit, what's that girl's name? "Um, Yolanda," I asked, tryin' to play off the slip by takin' a bite out of a chicken leg.

He glared at me for a sec like he knew I was gonna call her Wanda, then replied, "She—she, uhh—I mean, her mom came through, so she stayed home."

"Ohhhhh, so *that's* why you came home!"

He laughed at me.

I chuckled some more. "I was about to say! You never cared about the fourth-of-July before. Why you so eager to get here now?" (He was always too mellow for holidays; their only purpose in his life was to get out of school. He's one of those guys that's so cool he's almost comatose. You'd have to damn near launch a nuke to get a rise out of him. And even then he'd just say, 'Aww, man. That's fucked up,' soundin' like Snoop.)

"Man, I can't stand her old lady. Lemme tell you what she did last month," he said.

I sat at the table shakin' my head, knowin' I was about to hear some mess.

He leaned against the counter. "Yo had this big plan for Father's Day and all, so she asked her mom to come and take Sherard for the weekend," he looked down and scratched his head, "that woman came to the house wearin' a cat suit."

"Whahhh??" I frowned up. "You mean the…" I waved my hands up and down my body.

"Yeah," he replied.

"That's just wrong."

Then he started laughin, "Now, you know Yo got some ghetto inna…even she was like, 'Mah,

LOOKIN' IN THE MIRROR

whatchu wearin'?' She, like, fitty-six wearin' a cat suit, man. What is *that* shit?"

"I could see her in it, too...big, boxy ass..." I paused, realizin' the torture I'd just submitted myself to. I shook my head and shoulders violently. "Uuuuh!"

Terrence laughed at me.

Dad walked up from the basement. "Ay, y'aul...where ya momma at?"

"I don't know...down the hall somewhere," Terrence replied.

He stood there lookin' puzzled, "Uh..." then started walkin' toward the oven, "Any food left?"

"Yeah," I said, "but the potato salad's almost gone."

"Mmmph," he grunted, pickin' out some leftover barbecue.

Terrence and I looked at each other curiously. Dad's not the type to be in a funk. Mom must've pissed him off.

He turned around with his plate full and took a hunk out of his hotdog just before trying to talk, "So how's it goin' wit' the job?"

"Uhhhh...shhhh..." I sighed. I really didn't wanna think about work. "It's cool, I guess."

"Uh-huh," he replied skeptically, eyeing my expression.

"Well, you know, it's the same ol' stuff: Carl's cool, Chad's a racist, and Tanner has emotional problems. Nothin' out of the ordinary," I grinned.

Terrence grinned, "You still try'na move ta DC?"

"Yeah…Yeah…but, uhh…Chad's tryin' to do ev'rything he can to keep it from happenin'," I replied.

Terrence just nodded and Dad looked at me.

"Well, son, I tolja dis day would come. Now it's time to see whatcha made uhh. This is where you gotta use ya connections to get by dat knuckahead," Dad explained.

I nodded, "I know…it's just…you know, it's frustrating."

"Yeh, well, dat's the world," he replied.

My cell phone rang.

Terrence left the room.

"What-up, What-up! Yeeeeaaaaaaah! Yeeeeaaaaaaah!"

"Anita?!?!"

My dad perked up, "Ay, that's Anita? Tell her I said, 'Hey'."

"My dad said, 'Hey', Anita."

"Oh! Tell him I said, 'Hi'. And Happy Fourth."

I relayed the message and got back to the point of her call, "So, what's up with you? You're all fired up."

"Bruh! I'm goin' bananas in this joint! You just don'know!"

"Well, what's up?"

"Gerald, thank you so-so-so-so-so-so-so-so much for givin' me money for my fashion line! You wouldn't be-*leeev* the good news—well, you would, but I'm just excited!"

"Anita. Calm down. You're rambling."

LOOKIN' IN THE MIRROR

"I know. I know. *Wooo*. Okay. Uhhh, well, I told you how me and my coworker met with some fashion industry cats a while back, right?"

"Yeah," I replied.

"Well, they slipped a few of our pieces into this fashion show that they had goin' to test reactions and to kinda gain interest from their peers—"

"Woah…you need to be careful about that. They might try to steal credit for your work. Did you get a contract with these people?"

"Well no, but—"

"Hmm, Anita, you need to talk to a lawyer," I warned.

"Jair-ruhhld! Lemme tell you the story!"

"Okay, okay!"

"Well, they called back and said their company is interested in adding our stuff to their line. They even want to buy our name and invest money into launching us as a brand!"

"Wow…that's really good! I'm proud of you!"

She put the phone down and started yellin' for a minute.

"Okay, I'm back…"

"So, when do I get my money back?"

She laughed at me, "Well, we're gonna meet with some lawyers and stuff pretty soon about settin' everything up. So you'll get your money back, don't worry."

"Okay…as long as you're meetin' with lawyers, though. I want you to protect your interests. You got money for the lawyers?"

"Yeah. I'm good," she replied, "Vicki's got that covered."

"Oh, okay. Well, if you need me, just call."

"I know. Don'tchu worry 'bout *that*!" she laughed.

I chuckled. "I'm happy about your success, though. I'm really proud of you."

"Thanks. But it's all because of you, man," she said.

"Well, you had a pretty good pitch. Plus, I know you ain't about bull so, I couldn't turn you down."

"I'm glad you didn't. I don't know *where* I would've gotten the money for the seamstresses," she paused, "Hey, have you read my friend's website?"

"No. Which friend?"

"The one I'm working with! Remember, I told you she writes at the company I work for, too?"

"Oh! Oh yeah… Yeah, I caught a couple pieces…she's pretty funny. That's a cool little site she's got goin'…how long has she had it?"

"Pssssh…I don'know…since she was in college or somethin'."

"Aww, okay."

"Well, I'm gonna get off this phone," she said, "I got some friends in Maryland that are barbecuing and I wanna hit that up before I get too lazy to get out."

"A'ight, then. Talk to ya later."

Dad resumed conversation. "Ya know Tam'ra's get'n in tuhnight."

"Uh. Nah, I didn't know that… Why so late?"

LOOKIN' IN THE MIRROR

"Well, she comin' in from Europe. She'll be heeah 'til Toozdee," he replied.

I nodded. My mother walked in.

"Alfred, you know, your brother called," she said passing through, to the utility room.

"Which one?" he asked.

"Clarence. He wants us to come to Thibodaux for Thanksgiving," she replied.

"Awww. Shit. I ain't goin' tuh no damn Tibbadoe. He betta take his ass ta momma house. I'll see him in N'w'Orlens, like I awlways do."

"Stop being mean," she said.

"Ain't nobody bein' mean. I just know I ain't goin ta no Tibbadoe! His crezzy ass always want somebody ta come out to da cuntry," he looked at me, "Ruhmemba dat time he wanted us to go to da beach down in Grand Isle?" He gave my momma a crazy look. "*You* know Cla'ence crezzy."

"Man, I don't wanna go to Uncle Clarence's house. They always start fightin'," I said.

"Aw. I didn't tell ya??"

"What?"

Ending on an upbeat, he replied, "He ain't beat'n on Fifi no mo'."

A crooked grin slid up the right side of my face. "What happened?"

"Shit. She got tired of'm. He came home one day, raisin' sand, and Josephine took that black fryin' pan and clocked'm upside da head," he explained, "Evah since den, he doh'mess wit'huh no mo'."

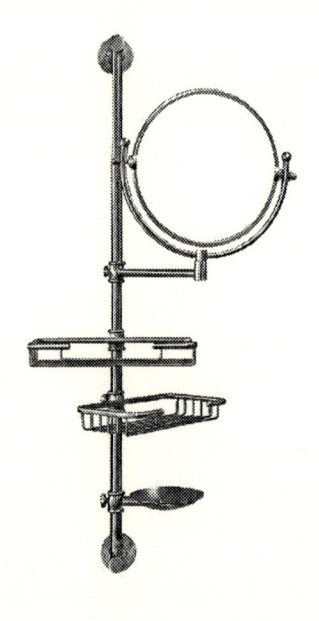

That Evening

LOOKIN' IN THE MIRROR

Everybody came over my house that night after all the barbecues to watch B-movies. All the usual suspects were there plus Tanya & Andréa. Then, like my dad said earlier, Tamara came in town. Denise wanted to come (although, I don't know why, considering she's not the B-movie type. She went with us to the rental store to pick out some titles and she gon' pull out 'Girls Just Wanna Have Fun'...she *really* doesn't get it), and for some crackhead reason, Terrence's wife "Wanda" (okay, Yolanda) came in town too.

A n d j o i n e d u s.

So anyway, everyone else started showin' up about 8, 9 o'clock. Carlos and Terrence were in the den down by the TV, talkin' about an article in one of my issues of 'Worth' magazine. Nouri, Tamara, Tanya & Andréa were down there, too, but they were half-payin' attention between them and watching TV, or they started talkin' to each other about something on TV. Yolanda and Denise were sittin' at the kitchen table—talkin' up a storm. You'd've thought they were old college buddies that hadn't seen each other in a couple of years. (It always bugged me that my then-girlfriend got along so well with a woman that disgusts me to exhaustion.) Man! I wanted to crack up when Mia came in, 'cause I knew she'd pass a stone when she saw 'em. She walked in, laid her eyes on those two, maaan... She shot me a look like she was gonna telepathically throw me through a window. Even her husband, Sean, had to do a double-take. And it was kinda awkward seein' him look at me like, *I...thought...y'all...broke up.*

A. M. HATTER

I was in the kitchen makin' a sandwich and Will was standin' by, tellin' me what happened in the last frat meeting. I miss out on a lot 'cause I'm always traveling or spendin' time with Dante. But, y'know, I make it to whatever functions I can, and they know I'll hook 'em up with whatever I can provide.

But anyway, Mia came up to the kitchen to talk to us when she finished with Nouri and Tamara, and she asked us what movies we got.

"Look through the bag," Will replied.

She thumbed through the titles in the bag at the end of the counter and busted out laughin'.

"The Blair *Clown* Project???!!!"

"That's the shit, ain't it?" Will said.

She turned the box over. "Hey! Jason Mewes is in it!"

"Yeah, that's why we got it," I replied, "I *want* the one with Kevin Smith...there's a special edition version with him in it."

Denise came up and put her arm around my waist. "Who's Kevin Smith?"

Will isn't too fond of her, so he looked down at his feet tryin' not to laugh. 'Cause, like, we're all big movie (and occasionally comic book) geeks, so for someone to ask us who Kevin Smith is, is like askin' a Star Wars nerd "what's the big deal about Yoda?" Well, maybe not *that* deep, but anyway, I tried to break down the talent that is Kevin Smith into something simple she could understand.

"He wrote a few movies we like," I explained.

"Oh," she said, tryin' to dodge the silence that descended on the four of us during her presence.

LOOKIN' IN THE MIRROR

Will caught a light bulb over his head, "We shoulda gotten Leprechaun in the Hood, man."

"But we've already seen that," Mia replied.

Denise slipped in, "What's Leprechaun in the Hood?"

But Will talked over her, "But that shit was *too* funny!"

I whispered the answer to her, "It's a cheesy movie."

Will and Mia imitated a line from the movie, "'A frrriend with weeed is a frrriend in-deeed.'"

Sean walked up and added on to their statement. "Naw, y'all shoulda gotten 'Hercules in New York'."

I hadn't heard of that movie. "What's that?" I asked.

Mia interrupted, smilin' and shakin' her head, "Ohhhhhhhhhhhhhhhhhh..."

"It's, like, the *first* movie Arnold Schwarzeneggar *ever* did—and it's *un*dubbed," Sean replied.

"Oh shit! We gotta do that next time," I glared at Will, who nodded back at me.

"Why didn't you tell us about that?" Will asked Mia.

"I forgot, man...I don't even know why. I just never thought about it. But I just saw it, like a few months ago anyway," she shrugged.

"Well, we still did alright," I pointed out, "When I bought SuperFuzz, the dude that sold it to me told me it was tight, and we got The Circuit 2. I mean, you just can't beat a movie that has Lorenzo Lamas and Billy Blanks' brother in it!"

Will laughed. "Nothin's better than late-night HBO, bay-bee!"

Nouri called from the den, "HEY! ARE WE GONNA WATCH SOME MOVIES OR WHAT??"

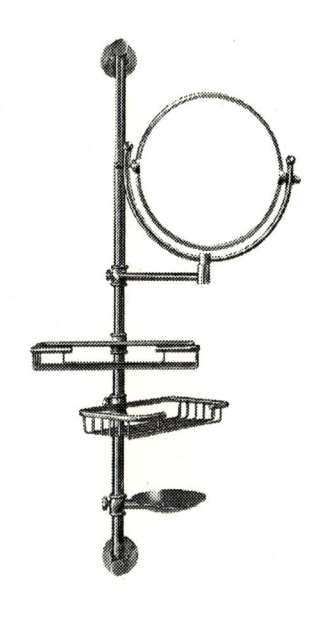

July 9

Very Late

A. M. HATTER

Don't you hate it when you're goin' to sleep and you get right to that point where you're fallin' into a good sleep, everything is quiet, you've gotten to that *one* spot where you're extra comfortable, your eyes are closed, your body feels like it's sinkin' into the bed, and you're just about to start droolin', then somebody wakes you up? Then, you're wonderin' who the hell is ringin' your doorbell at e-leven-fif-teen-p-m on a Tuesday. And to top it all off, they have the nerve to be impatient with the doorbell.

People today. They just don't know how to act.

At first I wasn't gonna answer it. I knew it wasn't anybody *but* Denise, thinkin' she can come over whenever, however and for whatever reason she feels necessary. She doesn't seem to understand the fact that grown folks have things to do besides revolve around her and bow to her every whim. All that's beside the point with her, though. It's whatever *she* wants, *now*. So I laid there. I was too tired for her shit. But the longer I laid there, the more the bell rang. The noise was relentless. So after, maybe, a minute or so I finally slid the covers off and turned to get up.

This better be good, I thought as I dragged out of bed, comtemplating how I'd tear into Denise's worrisome rear end. *Am I her personal servant or something?? Here for all her childish needs? I know it ain't nothin' important*, I mouthed off to myself. Almost the worst thing to do is wake me up from sleep. You can wake me up from a nap, if I'm not too tired, but if you wake me up from *SLEEP*, when it's *TIME* to sleep??? Shoot…let's just say that you don't really wanna be around me.

LOOKIN' IN THE MIRROR

(((Ding, Dong!)))

I stormed down the stairs. *DAMN, she just won't let up! I ain't lettin' her in. I'm sendin' her right back home. I don't care what she says. Childish ass. She is so selfish. She thinks she can do whatever she wants.*

(((Ding, Dong!)))

"I'm comin'! I'm comin'! Hol' on!" I yelled at the door.

I'm too old for this shit! She thinks she can come over whenever she wants, wakin' folks up. I'm not dealin' wit' her dumb ass tonight. No sir. I got a thang or two for her stupid ass. Wanna wake somebody up. Knowin' I gotta go to work in the mornin'. And I was sleepin' good, too.

I punched in the code to the alarm and opened the door. My head jerked back.

"Hi Gerald," she wimpered. Her eyes were bloodshot and puffy, cheeks, damp from tears and her face was all frowned up.

"Mia...what's wrong?"

"I need a favor," she said. I opened the storm door and stepped to the side. I noticed she had a couple bags with her.

"Wait, hol' up...what's goin' on?" I asked, helpin' her with her bags.

"I don't know...I don't even know why I came over here. I don't know what it would help," she said and fell onto the sofa.

I left her bags in the foyer and joined her on the couch.

"What happened?"

A. M. HATTER

She shook her head. "I don't know if you remember, but back when me & Sean were about to get married, he co-signed on an s-class jag for his mom. And I told him back then, don't do it, 'cause I don't trust her. She just doesn't have good sense. But that's his momma and he just won't listen when it comes to her."

"Uh-huh."

"He was like, 'No, she said she gonna do' this and that…blah, blah, blah. She put down some money, but it's still sky high…plus she got this astronomical interest rate."

"Right."

"So now, it's three years later, and the woman just stopped payin' the note. No real reason…she just stopped payin' the note," she explained.

"What??"

"Yeah!" She blew her nose. "And now the loan has shifted to us. We gotta pay this month's note plus two months of back payments!"

My jaw dropped.

"The car note is, like, *eight-fifty* Gerald!" More tears dropped from her eyes. "I don't know what to do! We don't have that kind of room! Twenty-five hundred dollars, at the drop of a hat! What the fuck!" She grabbed her tissue and wiped her nose. "She did this shit on purpose, Gerald! I know she did! Why would she just stop payments? I bet she didn't even tell her husband! And he *still* doesn't see that that woman's a fucking nutcase! We've been fighting *all night*! He just won't accept that he has to draw a line with her."

"Some guys are just tight with their moms like that, Mia."

"I know that, Gerald! And that's normal. You and your mom are tight. So is Terrence, Will, Carlos...*all* y'all are mommas boys! But the woman is purposely sabotaging our credit! She's insane! And he *won't* see it! I knew when he signed for that damn loan that this would happen. I knew *something* would happen! But he wouldn't listen to me! He's dead set on believing that I just don't wanna get along with his mom for no reason," she paused, "I should've taken that as a sign."

"Woah, woah, woah...don't say that."

"Don't say that??? Don't *say* that??? If you were married to a woman that was this cracked out on her daddy, had you sufferin' through stuff you could've avoided, *and* let the fuckin' electric bill get past due, how would *you* be feelin' right now???"

"Are the lights turned off?"

"No, but that's only because I got home early and checked the mail first. He usually gets home first, but I came home today and found a *second* late notice in the mail! I'm like, 'Well, shit! Where's the first one??' So I asked him about it, and *that's* when he wanted to let me know what was goin' on. JUST NOW. Really and truly, he's been makin' partial payments for about *six months* now. On a car she didn't even need! Tell me, what's wrong with a Tercel? Or a Civic? Or a Saturn? Huh? Hell, she ain't that big. He coulda put her in an Echo," she paused and mumbled, "Shit, all she *deserves* is a Kia."

I laughed.

A. M. HATTER

"I got enough stress at work! I don't need *this* shit when I get home!"

"Have you considered sellin' it?"

She looked at me with wheels turnin' in her head.

"And make a lump sum payment? I mean, you'd still lose about a G or two compared to the bluebook value, but you wouldn't default on the loan, and you'd get it out of your hair."

"Well…that's a good idea, but I'd still have to get him to agree to it, which would be hell," she said.

"Well, yeah, but it's an option… You could sell it to her husband," I smiled.

Her voice cracked, "An even better idea!"

I put my arm around her shoulder. "It's gonna be okay, girl. Just calm down and think about what it's gonna take to get this behind you. Focus on problem *solving*, not the problem itself."

She teared up again. "But that *is* the problem. 'Cause he won't listen to solutions."

"Still, it's not gonna go away tonight. So there's no point in gettin' all worked up," I said.

"I know," she said wipin' her face, "…I'm sorry that I came over this late and woke you up. I could tell you were sleep."

I smiled. "Well, I can understand. But if you were Denise, I'd've been mad."

She sniffled and laughed.

"…Um, I have to be honest with you," she looked at me, "I don't know how long I'm gonna need to stay."

"Huh?"

"I mean, if I'm imposing, then I'll leave tomorrow."

"Oh…well, it's no problem…you know you can use that room over there," I pointed to the guest bedroom across from us, "It doesn't matter to me."

"Thanks. I really appreciate it…I just can't be around Sean right now. Not after treating me like this."

"Does he know you're over here?"

"I don't know…probably."

"*Prob*ably??" I said, "Look Mia, I don't wanna say this, but I don't know if this is the best place for you to be."

"Gerald, I don't have anywhere else to go," she paused, "I guess I could go to Will's…"

"Oh, *hell* no. He *really* wouldn't want you over there," I replied.

She laughed and rolled her eyes. "I know, like I would do it to Will."

"You can't go over your cousin's?"

"I'm not tryin' to have all my business spread all over the family. Besides, the first thing she'd do is say 'I told you so'—'"

"HMMMM, sounds familiar!"

She laughed. "Shut up! …And the second thing she'd say is there's no room 'cause her mom is stayin' with her now. Her mom is schizophrenic."

"Oh yeah. You told me about that…"

"So, that's why I'm here…"

"Well, I still want you to call and tell him where you are," I said.

"Okay. Yeah. I get it," she said sarcastically, "But it's probably not as serious as you're making it. I told you we settled that a long time ago."

"Did he say he didn't care?"

"Basically."

"He cares. And I bet you it'll bug him that tonight, when you got pissed off, the first person you ran to is me," I said gettin' up from the couch.

She rolled her eyes.

"Just call him. Let'm know you're here. I'll feel better," I said, and took my ass back to bed.

July 13

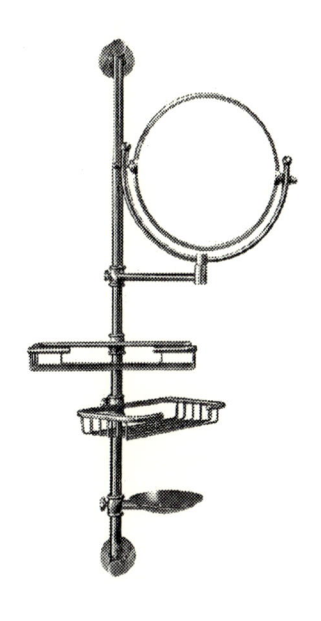

Midday

A. M. HATTER

I sat on the stool, thinkin' to myself, *I'm glad this is over.* Not that Mia, herself, had been a headache. Mostly, we rarely saw each other unless we were catchin' an evening show on the tube. But a person can only take so much of the phone ringin' and all the loud arguing when it's time to go to sleep. Thank goodness that it didn't have to come down to me askin' her to leave. I'm down to help whenever I can, but I need my peace, y'know? But I think, in a way, she knew it too, 'cause she came to the house early from work Thursday and told me she'd be leavin' on Saturday. It's prob'ly better that she only stayed a few days anyway. It would've been hard for her to have to rehash everything to explain to the fellas why she's stayin' with me. That's one good thing about the whole situation…nobody knew except for me, her and Sean.

I grabbed a magazine off the tank of the commode; I heard Mia knockin' around downstairs, packin' up, zippin', draggin' her bag to the door. A couple minutes later, I heard some pots clanging. *Ohhh, yeahhhh! Homegirl's gonna cook!* I thought to myself. Then the doorbell rang. My heart sank. We'd gotten so far without havin' to tell any of the guys about this. I hoped that she had already put her bag in the car. That way it wouldn't look like she stayed over. She's just here for the regular Saturday bonding. But I didn't hear Will or Carlos or Nouri. The voice was really faint, but it sounded like a woman. Then the door shut. I calmed down for a sec, 'cause I figured it might've been a door-to-door person. But I went ahead and started wiping so she wouldn't have to answer the door, and also 'cause I wanted to know who it was that came. The strange thing was—and it was hard to make out over the TV—it seemed like there were still two women's voices. But they were just mumbles from where I was. I got up to flush the toilet, and opened the door. As I washed my hands, I heard one voice yell, *"BITCH!!!!"*, followed by a really loud boom.

Oh, shit...Denise! I thought and ran to the stairs.

And there they were: Mia in her bra and panties with her robe wide open, hangin' from her arms, her headwrap on the floor, and her hair in every direction with Denise in a headlock, smackin' her upside the head. Denise, fully clothed with smeared make-up, punched Mia in the back to make her let go. But it must not've been one of those kidney punches 'cause Mia just swung around and clocked her in the forehead. Then she lunged into Denise and grabbed her by the throat, backing her against the wall. Denise grabbed her wrist and put her other hand in Mia's face. My first instinct was to grab some popcorn and let 'em fight it out. *Can we get some mud up in here?* But I resisted temptation and ran down to break 'em apart.

"HEY! HEY!" I yelled.

After hurdling down the last five steps, I picked Mia up by her waist and moved her behind me.

Denise pressed her hand to her neck tryin' to play all distraught and victimized. "She's trying to kill me," she said, "I knew she had it in for me."

Brava! Brava!! She should go to Television City and audtition for Y&R!

A. M. HATTER

"Bitch, you betta be glad all I did was putcho stupid ass on the wall!" Mia yelled back.

And then her true colors came to light, "Oh, don't even talk to *me*, bitch! YOU betta be glad Gerald was here, I'll kick yo' little ass all over this room! *BITCH!*"

"Well come on, then!" Mia stepped forward.

I extended my arms to keep them apart. "Shut up, Mia! Go finish packin'!"

"See, bitch, you betta be glad!"

Mia responded, stepping backward, "Whateva, you weren't gon' do nothin' no way!"

"Mia, go," I growled.

"Whatchu want then, *bitch*???" Denise taunted.

"You sho didn't do nothin' when I had yo' triflin' ass on the wall!"

Denise lunged forward, into me, tryin' to get at Mia. "You betta watchyaback!"

Mia stood there, grinnin'.

"Watchyaback, nah! Watchyaback!"

I leaned into Denise, backin' her against the wall. *And the wall said, "Nice to see you again!"*

"Whateva," Mia waved off Denise, "Stupid ass ho," she mumbled on the way to the guest room.

I glared at Denise. Then I turned and went to the kitchen, shakin' my head.

Her footsteps hastened and I looked back quickly to see what she was doin'. She came hurling at me like she was gonna hit me. I stepped back and grabbed her wrists.

"HEY! Whatchu doin'???" I said.

LOOKIN' IN THE MIRROR

"HOW CAN YOU DO THIS TO ME????" she yelled, starting to cry.

"Do *what* to you? What are you *talkin'* about???"

She sniffled. "How long have y'all been sleeping together?"

I turned and wiped my hand over my face. "Maaaaaaaaan..." I said and started digging through the refrigerator.

"DON'T IG-NORE ME, GERALD!!!!!!!!"

I stood and looked her straight in the eye. "Lower, your, voice."

"LOWER MY VOICE??? Fuck that! WHAT IS SHE DOING HERE, GERALD???"

"We grew up together. She can come over here whenever she wants."

Her eyes bugged out. "When-*ever* she *wants*???" she chuckled, with tears streaming down her face, "Ohhh! So it's like *that*??? How long have y'all been fucking, Gerald?"

I stepped over and leaned against the counter with my arms folded across my chest, laughin' at her. "Why do Mia and I have to be havin' sex?"

"Wha'd'you mean, why do you and Mia have to be havin' sex? She DOESN'T HAVE ANY DAMN CLOTHES ON!"

"Okay, so she slept over."

She gestured like, *Well there you go.*

"But that doesn't mean we're having sex," *You cro-magnon ignoramous.*

"WELL, WHY IS SHE HERE, THEN??"

"I can't tell you that," I replied.

Her eyes bucked open and her jaw dropped. "YOU CAN'T *TELL* ME????"

I just looked at her. "Raise your voice one mo' damn time."

She sniffled. "I'm sorry," she paused, "But we're in a relationship. You're supposed to be able to tell me anything."

"First off, *sex* doesn't make a relationship—"

She rolled her eyes. "Yeah, I know, I'm still on trial."

I grimaced. "Secondly, I don't have to tell you what's goin' on with Mia. That's her business."

"And that's another thing! Why is it that Mia thinks I'm your booty call??? Is that all you think about me??"

I shot her a stale expression and turned to go sit on the couch.

She pushed me on the shoulder. "Gerald, don't ignore me!"

I turned quickly and grabbed her tightly by the wrist, speaking through my teeth, "Look. Mia and I are *not* having sex. We grew up together, she's entitled to come over. *Get* that through your damn scull. *TWO*, how can you be *my* booty call, when *you* come over to *my* house for sex??? *Quit* being so fuckin' *stu*pid!" I said and threw her wrist down and turned to continue my walk to the den. Then I turned back quickly, and pointed my finger at her. "I don't wanna talk about this again."

She nodded and followed me to the couch. She grabbed a tissue from the box on the lamp table and sat next to me.

LOOKIN' IN THE MIRROR

Mia came out of the guest room and asked me to help her with her bags. While we were outside, she told me Will called on her cell to see if she was "goin'" over my house, but she told him I was with Denise. So no Saturday bonding for me.

When I went back in, after Mia drove off, I went straight upstairs, leavin' the crybaby on the couch. But about an hour later, she came upstairs too.

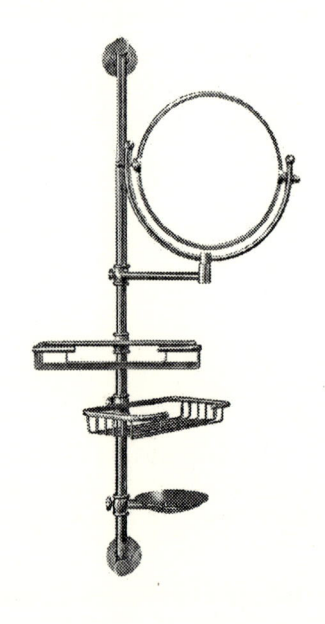

Tuesday, July 30

LOOKIN' IN THE MIRROR

AND THEN, life has a way of kickin' you in the pants.

I'll tell you, it ain't enough that my momma's always ridin' me about settlin' down and givin' her some grandchildren, I gotta work with a jerk hell-bent on stifling my career, my best friend's marriage is crumbling, and my ex won't let up on tryin' to run my life. But then, everybody's got problems, right? I should be so lucky to only have these.

But man, it's just not fair.

There's this woman that I'd been chattin' with over the internet for somethin' like a month and a half to two months—I can't remember exactly, it may have been longer. At first we were emailin', then instant messagin', and then we swapped phone numbers but we were still I-M-ing, too. And the whole time, we were really clickin'. I mean, she'd say somethin', then I'd be like, "Yeah!" It seemed like we agreed on everything. It was crazy. Well, y'know, we didn't agree on *every*thing. But most chicks nowadays are dumb as rocks; you ask 'em their opinion on the state of welfare or just mention somethin' as simple as how quickly the Mavs turned it around, and they give you this look like they're about to spontaneously combust. You wanna apologize for havin' made 'em think.

But Lisa's tight, so even if we do disagree, there's still a level of respect there. There was this one evening when we were arguing about the realistic application of socialism in the U.S., and you know how conversations will travel and warp into different issues or whatever...shoot, we were chattin' almost all night. It's funny, we started off *dis*agreeing, but ended the chat agreeing 'cause we ended up talkin' about how mass marketing is the new tool of genocide (ie: what's been done with hip-hop), welfare as a handicap, how we need to have better financial sense, and bruthas needin' to freelance or start our own businesses to avoid vulnerability to layoffs.

I *liked* her. I was diggin' her, for real. She's real and just...*cool*; we've talked about past relationships and stuff...what we learned from 'em...what we've come to expect from other people at this phase in life...personal flaws—the *real* stuff, y'know? And she looks all right. I mean, she ain't *fine*, but she's *definitely* not ugly. I'd say, on a scale of one-to-ten, she's the overall package, where everything is in the six-or-seven-area: her body's straight, her face is straight, she's got good conversation... She's a little bit bigger than I'm used to, but I can hang wit' a lil baby fat. (Just a little, though. If you're 5'3 / 190, you need to walk—literally.) *And* she dresses like a grown woman! Wayyyyyyyyy better than the teacher, and that Sunday School catalog model from 1983. (I still can't believe she wore that dress in public.)

So we went to lunch one day to meet in person for the first time. This was, like, three weeks ago, I think. She happened to be in my area for a meeting—she's a tech consultant—so we hooked up at this place down the street from where I work. I was kinda nervous because she's actually the type that you wanna act right for. But I had on my favorite casual business suit—well, it's not really "casual", it's really just the color 'cause it's kind of a brown-ish, olive, gray color,

LOOKIN' IN THE MIRROR

so it's not as "official" as a blue suit, but it's appropriate for work. And, anyway, I was comfortable.

It was close to one o'clock, I got up from my desk and did the once-over in the mirror on my wall: checked my fly, checked my teeth, my hair, my nose, my nose hair...everything was straight. All was well and a brutha was happy to see that she looked the same as her picture; she hadn't gained a hundred pounds since she took the pic EIGHT YEARS AGO, like some broads will do. But when we leaned in to hug, I caught a whiff of somethin' scandalous.

Is it the restaurant? Somethin' in the air? I thought. *Damn, I knew I shoulda gargled! I hope it ain't me.*

I smiled and tried to keep my speech to a minimum, at the very least, I avoided words with Hs just in case it was me. But the more she talked, I realized it was her.

It's not fair, I tell you. This woman that I had exalted on high, pledged two months of my time and interest to. I even told Mia about her. And she's plagued with halitosis. A real bad case of it, at that. The kind that floats. It came kickin' across the table. The food kind of suppressed it, though. But it wasn't a bad lunch. I had fun. She just had bad breath. I figured, *maybe it's a bad day...we all have those every now and again. She might've just had hunger-breath...she deserves another chance.* So I took her out to this dinner club a few days later. My spirits were kinda mediocre 'cause that first impact was kinda rough, y'know? But I hoped that this time would be better.

It wasn't.

A. M. HATTER

Man, she got bad breath like a dude. It's depressing. The *one* time that I *want* a girl to keep talkin', I don't want her to open her mouth. I started chewin' a piece of gum, and put it away, then offered her a stick like I forgot to ask if she wanted some. I was extra-relieved (you just don't know) when she fell for the bait, but it didn't totally get the bad breath out. I mean, it wasn't doin' the kung foo thang so much anymore, but it was still kinda off. Breath that persistent doesn't go away with one little stick of gum. This is a Manhattan Project for Dentine, Trident, *and* Wrigley's. They all need to work on her.

And throughout the whole episode, I just kept wondering, *doesn't she know? Hasn't the dentist or one of her friends told her?* I mean, you can't have breath *that* bad and just *not know*. That scent *gotta* be burnin' her nostrils, too. It's pretty wicked.

Nevertheless, I tried one more time to see if *maybe* there was a part of the day when things were workin' out for her. So I invited her for breakfast one mornin' before work. I'm thinkin' that she's fresh out the bed, she's just brushed her teeth, things shouldn't be that bad—which, they weren't. But instead of being good breath or even normal breath without funk like the rest of us, it was just normal funky. It wasn't kickin' like the other times because they were later in the day, but since she has halitosis, her day is comprised of degrees of funkiness, sorta like a grayscale. It starts off at a little funky, then gets funkier, and gets worse as the day progresses. And that kinda made me realize, *Damn! Mornin' breath for her must be damn-near immoral!* It ain't just kickin', there's an actual foot comin' out that bitch.

So at the end of breakfast, I sat with her in the car, and with a heavy heart, I compassionately broke the news to her that I'd been truly captivated by her friendship, intelligence and company, but that I couldn't continue to see her 'cause of her "dental problem." She knew exactly what I meant. Then she started cryin'. And I held her. I felt so bad. She told me that she'd gone to the dentist, discussed it with her doctor, changed her diet several times, and ordered every new product on the market, but nothing worked. I almost started cryin' with her. Well, not *really*, but I felt that bad about it. It was a sad situation, but we parted ways in a refined adult manner. We still email each other every now and then.

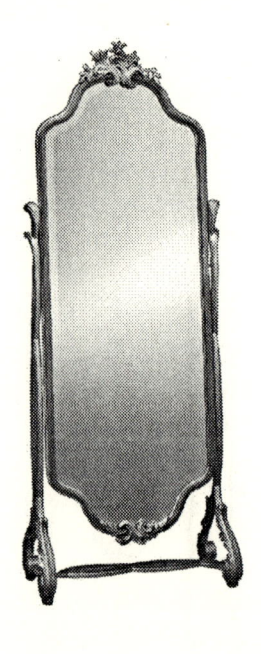

Saturday, October 26

LOOKIN' IN THE MIRROR

I Wish You Well

It's been a long time since we last talked.
But I want you to know that I care.
I see you're doing well:
Makin' moves and causin' sparks...
I just wish I could be there to see it.

If I think of you every day of my life,
I ask myself, "Is it out of love or guilt?"
Do I obsess much?
Probably so.
But if I didn't think of you I'd be sad.
'Cause my thoughts are activated hopes for you to do well.

I couldn't be there to see you take that major award.
I wasn't your first kiss, or your first date.
But I was almost the great love of your life.
I wanted to be.

But understand that even though I let you get away,
You're truly one in a million.
So be strong, and walk with pride.
'Cause my thoughts are with you, and I know you'll be great.

So I guess it's true, what they say...
That if you love them, you can let them go.
'Cause I respect you,
And I am proud of you.
Even if it's from afar.

So shoot for the top, I say.
And don't be afraid to push the limits.
'Cause I am thinking of you.
And you will be great.

A. M. HATTER

Turk and I met for the first full weekend since he left Sidewalk Journal. What used to be regular meetings for lunch throughout the week and I'm-bored-let-me-bug-you sessions at either of our desks, turned in to quick hey-how-ya-doin's on the celly and *maybe* a bite to eat here or there. He'd been out traveling like Thomas Crown since jumping on with the nonprofit, so I'd barely seen hide or hair of him in good while.

I went to his house for another installment of memorizing my poem in Hebrew translation for his son's Bar Mitzvah. Lucky for me recitation is an innate talent, because my attention wasn't really there. I probably sounded more like some kind of zombie because even now, I barely recall going over the material. I had a lot going on in my head, considering my usually placid disposition; so much that I was able to tune out Turk getting heated on the phone. He had to cut my practice short to catch a phone call that, to his dismay, kept him subjugated for about twenty minutes or so.

"It never ceases to amaze me how stupid she pretends to be," Turk said, returning to his Macintosh-blue beanbag.

"Huh?"

"Liz. She keeps calling me asking these juvenile questions about Roi's Bar Mitzvah like she doesn't know what's goin' on."

I stared at him blankly as he dug his hindquarters into the seat.

"She's a thirty-six-year-old Jewish woman with *three* brothers! But she expects me to believe that she

LOOKIN' IN THE MIRROR

has no recollection of the Mitzvah process," he scowled, "I told her to call my mother. She can drive *her* up a damn wall."

I chuckled. "Ben, you're silly."

"I'm serious. I don't wanna deal with her crap. I know she's only doing it 'cause she thinks I care that she's changed religions."

"For real? What is she now?"

"Buddhist."

I chuckled again.

"Yeah...for years she got in my ass about going to shul on time and told me I was going to hell for eating an orange *ONE* Yom Kippur, when I was *six-teen*. Now she's sportin' a Buddha and a rock garden."

"Oooo! You broke your fast! You're goin' tuh HELL!" I laughed.

He smiled. "Yeah, I'll be dancin' a jig down there with you."

"Nope, I'm a gentile. We go to a different hell, so nyahhh."

"Well, *I'm* gonna change to Catholicism so I can go to Purgatory, and *you'll* be stuck in hell! So nyahhh," he stuck out his tongue.

I smiled, eyes still glazed over.

"What's wrong with you?" he asked.

I shrugged. "Prob'ly my period. Ain't the first of the month next week?"

It's the first-of-the-mooooooooooonth!

Get-up, get-up, get-up, get-up, get-up...Wake-up, wake-up, wake-up, wake-up, wake-up.

Hee-hee!

You know that was the cut; don't even act.
"Don't give me that," he replied skeptically.
"Wha'd'you mean?"
"I don't know…it *could* be your period, I ain't no expert…"
"*But…*" I prodded.
"Usually when your period comes around, you get confused and over-analytical…but that doesn't explain why you're all spacey." He looked harder at me. "See! Look at you! You're not even listening to me now, are you?"

He flicked a knot of paper at me.

"Man, what'd you do that for?" I replied, irritated.

"*What* is *wrong* with you??"

I sighed. "Nothin', really. It's just this situation with my roommate and Candace."

"What, they're fightin' or somethin'?"

"No…they're pressuring me to…to, uhh…I don't know, *resolve* an open-ended experience from my past, I guess you could call it."

"Oh, the boy you never fell out of love with?"

I gawked at him. "Huh?"

He chuckled. "You didn't think I knew did you?"

"How *do* you know?"

"I went through those spirals in your desk once."

I was confused. He could've been talking about anything.

LOOKIN' IN THE MIRROR

"There was a poem you wrote…talkin' about how he's the one that got away and you wish him well in life or something… It was really nice. I liked it."

My jaw dropped. "What??? I can't believe you did that! Why'd you read it??!!!"

He looked shocked. "I don't know… I was originally lookin' for a pen, but then I saw that you had a ton of spirals so I just picked one up and thumbed through it, being nosey. I *really* thought they were rough draft articles, at first. That's why I looked in the first place."

"That is so embarrassing. I can't believe you read that."

"Why?" he asked. "It was good."

"*'Cause*, man…I don't know…it's just embarrassing."

"You're still kickin' yourself for lettin' him get away, aren't you?"

I slumped over, onto the sofa cushions. "Yeah."

"Is that why you're embarrassed?"

"Kinda, but not really…"

"You still love him, don't you?"

"No."

"Yes you do."

I got agitated. "Man, leave me alone. Why are you bustin' me with the twenty questions?"

"Why are you so embarrassed about it? You should embrace your love."

"But it's from when I was *two*, man. It's not real."

"Oh. You're Love'N'Basketballin'," he replied simply.

"*Oh*! Well *now* I under*stand*!" I mumbled caustically.

"Well, just because it's from a long time ago doesn't mean you feel it any less."

"I resent the fact that you've simplified this to box office antics."

"Well, you know what they say: art reflects life…and be glad that it's a good movie. You'd've been offended if I said a Jennifer Lopez title."

I snickered a little. "But how do I explain being in love with a guy I technically don't even know anymore? I mean, I haven't so much as shared words with him since…hell, some time in high school."

"You don't have to *ex-plain* it to *any*body. It's nobody's business. *You're* just uncomfortable with it because you think it's not normal. …But if you think about it, if nobody else had that experience, then nobody would've written 'Love'N'Basketball'."

I fell silent.

"True," I replied. That's the same reasoning that I used on Shawn when D.L. Hughley came out with his Pee-pee Dream joke, and she tried to clown me because I knew what he was talking about.

"And what would you consider more real? That six-month calamity from a couple years back, or this kid you apparently care about—with whom you could, probably, at least be friends with, even now?"

I chuckled and nodded my head. "That wasn't a calamity. That was boredom."

"Yeah, yeah…you were wasting your time—I know that. He was nowhere near your level."

"Who *is*, though? I mean, *really*?"

LOOKIN' IN THE MIRROR

He fashioned his arms like the frame of a mirror and replied in monotone, "No one, your highness. No one is comparable to your greatness."

I flashed a smirk.

He fell silent for a few seconds. "Going back to your dilemma, though: would you *really* rather grow old, knowing you never told him how you felt?"

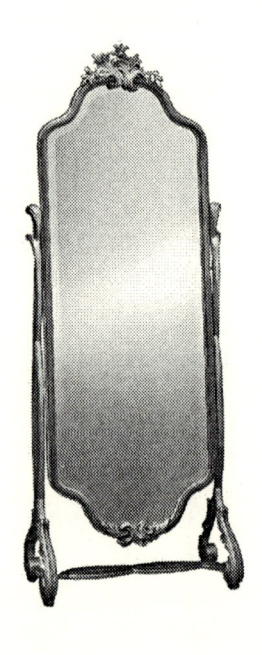

October 27

LOOKIN' IN THE MIRROR

After laying in the bed running my brain to death, I joined myself for my "daily affirmation" of posing scantily clad in the mirror; after which, I went downstairs to watch some football...still in my undies. But first I ran aimless circles in the kitchen for about twelve years, with no results. Finally, I plopped on the couch to some vanilla-cinnamon oatmeal and a small glass of white zinfandel (don't ask).

Why am I watching Indianapolis & Washington? I mean, really! Got one team that hasn't so much as spelled "play off" since NINETEEN-NINETY-TWO (Joe Gibbs... they need you!), and the other hasn't been successful since SEVENTY-TWO, but just doesn't suck As Much because they had ONE nice run in '97 and because they just got Tony Dungy. Dammit! I'm stuck. And basketball doesn't come on again 'til Tuesday. SHIIIIIIIIIIIIIIIIIIIIIT!!!!

Okay, panic attack over.

Halfway into the third quarter, my roommate returned and found me in my bra & panties.

"Just got done with your daily affirmation, huh?"

"Well, actually it's been a while. I've just been sittin' here watching football."

"Oh," she said passing in front of the television. "I don't see how you watch that."

"Sit down. Watch with me."

"Nahhhhhhh. Football's boring. It takes too long."

"Man! You crazy! Football is the bomb! You just need to know where to look," I said.

She hung her coat in the closet and kicked her shoes off, then settled on the floor in front of the couch, adjacent to my legs.

"Okay, so where do I look?"

"At their asses, for starters," I replied with a smile and a short giggle, "C-views are the best! Wooooooooh!"

She smiled back curiosly, "What's a see-view?"

"It's a shot from behind the line as they start a play. It's alllll ca-BOOSE! Sometimes I call it the hiney hike," I smiled.

She laughed at my absurdity and started watching with me. The sex appeal factor seemed to appease her for a minute, but after a short while, she grew tired of me grunting and jumping while she remained lost. "What's going on, man? I don't get this."

"H-H...Hold up...I'll explain...in-a...minute." I waited for a time out to give her a simple breakdown of football. "Okay, basically, what you're doin' is just watchin' their strategy. It's all about outsmarting the other team so you can get to the end zone."

"Okay."

"So, they line up—that's the line of scrimmage, right?"

"Yeah."

"The guy in the middle holds the ball and throws it through his legs to the quarterback—that's called the snap."

"Man! I'm not a *mental patient*! I know all that part."

LOOKIN' IN THE MIRROR

"Okay… so… what don't you understand?" I asked.

"Well…" she thought, looking off, then at the TV. "Hell, why does it take so long??"

I laughed, "Ohhhhh, okay!" I laughed some more.

"What's so funny?"

"That's what all women ask."

She frowned and rolled her eyes. "Yeah, yeah, yeah. And all-knowing Vicky, such the super person."

"Hey, don't get mad at me because you don't know football," I said and laughed at her some more.

"Okay so—"

I looked back at the TV to see what I missed. "Dammit, man! They suck!"

"Who are you rootin' for?"

I paused, "Umm, I'm tryin' to go for The Skins, but…they both suck. Really I couldn't care less who wins."

"So why are you watchin'?"

"Because…hell, I don'know," I shrugged. "I like seeing men. Men running, men in tight pants. Do I need any other reason?"

She laughed. "I guess not."

"But to answer your question," she looked at me like she forgot what she asked, "the reason why it takes so long would be the downs. 'Cause every time they start a new set, they can revert to first down several times."

"Okayyy…"

"See, in each 'set' you get four downs—or, um, chances to make a touchdown, right?"

"Okay, yeah."

"Okay, so here's a situation: it's the first chance—or down, they get at the line of scrimmage and snap the ball—blah, blah, dude runs and so on."

"Mm-hmm."

"And if the runner gets *at least* ten yards when they tackle him, then his team gets to stay at first down."

"Why?"

"I don'know. Doesn't matter. Don't ask."

She laughed. "Ohhh-kayyyyy."

"Dad never explained that. So I just take it for what it is…so anyway! You know when they put that yellow line down—like right there," I said, pointing at the screen.

"Yeah."

"If they get the ball past there, they get first down."

"Oh, okay. So that's why everyone cheers even though nobody got a touchdown."

"Yeah," I answered.

"Ohhhhh! Okay! I'm leeeeeeeeear-ning! I'm leeeeear-ning!"

I chuckled. "But do you know why it's a good thing?"

"Because the team gets more chances to make a touchdown."

"Uh-oh! Uh-oh! By golly! I think she's got it!"

She was so proud, but then she looked confused, "That's all?"

"No," I replied.

LOOKIN' IN THE MIRROR

"Damn. Okay," she settled down, "I'm ready teacher."

"Okay, so it takes ten yards to get first down. If you don't get ten yards, you go to second down and so on. But at any point, they can convert back to first down if they make it past the yellow line—or at fourth down, it turns red. But a lot of teams don't try that after the third down because you've, hopefully, gotten your touchdown or you'd rather just go for the kick and get three points instead of risking first down and not making it."

"And you said there are four downs in a set?"

"Yeah."

"What happens at fourth down?"

"If they get to fourth down, they have three options: one, make a touchdown, two, let their nuts hang and go for first down, or three, kick a field goal and make three points. If they don't get to first down again, or score by touchdown or the field goal, it's the other team's turn. They lose possession of the ball."

"Damn."

"Right," I said.

"And that's why it takes so long?"

"Yeah. Pretty much. 'Cause if you got a good team, then they'll keep gettin' first down."

"Or a lot of touchdowns."

"Right. But if the other team has a better defense, then your offense won't get to keep first down or be able to score."

"Okay...I think I'm getting it."

"You're with me so far?"

"Yeah."

"Okay. You wanna know more?" I asked.

"What's a two-point conversion? Guys are always saying that."

"Okay…a touchdown is six points by itself, right?"

"Yeah."

"But after the touchdown, you get an opportunity to tack on up to two points."

"Why?" she asked.

"Maaaaan, does it matter?"

She laughed.

"So, a two-point conversion is where the team that just scored opts to run the ball into the end zone for an extra two points, rather than kick through the field goal for the extra one point."

"Oh. So why don't they do that more?"

I exhaled. "Well, it would seem more logical, but then you run the risk of some fat guy sackin' your quarterback or a good defender blockin' you and not gettin' the extra score at all; whereas, with kicks," I shrugged, "they get blocked sometimes, but it's not as risky y'know? I mean, as long as the line does its job and the kicker kicks high and straight, then you got the extra point."

"Yeah… What's a safety?"

"A safety is like, the last line of defense. They're the ones that have to go after the receivers. So they have to be fast. And they'll put a hurt on you, too!" I laughed.

She was mesmerized. "Man. You know a lot about football!"

LOOKIN' IN THE MIRROR

"Naw, not really. I just know the basics...enough to watch and not get lost. Man, there are cats that know shit about football from before they were born. They get down with the referees and shit... I can't be like them. I got shit to do."

"For real, though."

Still staring at the TV, "Damn... The Skins just might win today," I said, surprised.

"How'd you learn all that?"

"Um...you just watch, really. Most guys have been watchin' for so long that they just know. When you've been watchin' since you were, like, five and shit... you can pick out plays and see calls. So, I mean, it just takes time."

She looked at me sideways with a skeptical look on her face, "So you've just been watchin' since you were five, huh?"

"Naw, not really. I was too busy playin' outside and runnin' around the house. But sometimes my dad would fuck around and get control of the TV and I'd watch with him. So I'd sit in his lap and he'd explain what was goin' on during the commercials. But I still didn't really care. I just liked when the guys would take off running. And they'd get the touchdown and dance or somethin'. And you know the Bears were off the chain back then! They were dancin', rappin'—sellin' perfume!" I started cracking up. "Shit, The Fridge and the Bears were *everywhere*!"

"*That's* who Refrigerator played with?"

I replied, still kind of laughing, "Yeah. The Chicago Bears, boy! They were *all over* the eighties. And the funny thing is that they only won one year!

A. M. HATTER

Well, they kept makin' the playoffs up until, like, '90 or somethin'. So they were pretty straight."

"Dag, and I thought they were just the bomb… takin' every Super Bowl from eighty-two to ninety!"

I laughed. "But they've been *horrible* ever since… Although, they're one of those natural game teams—they still play in the dirt, so I can appreciate them for that. Not like these punk-ass turf teams with the jacked up knees."

"Oh well…I've never been a fan."

"Me either."

"Do you have a team that you like?"

"Not really. I never really built up an allegiance. I just rooted for whoever my dad liked, which was pretty much Chicago, Greenbay or the Falcons…until I got to college and started writin' sports for the campus paper. Then I had to pay attention to stats and stuff, so I *really* got into it, then. But being that I'm an 'ATLien', I gotta be down for my dirty birds!" Then I jumped up and started doing the funky chicken and my roommate started laughing at me.

"But don't Atlanta teams suck?"

"Hey, hey, hey! We got the Braves…and Home Depot man and Mike Vick are tryin' to clean some folks' clocks!" I started throwing my bows and doing other dirty south dances.

"Uhhh, it's not real cute for you to be doin' the funky chicken and throwin' your bows in your underwear, girl. What if somebody walked in?"

"Who's gonna walk in with the door locked??? This ain't a sitcom."

"So! Go put on some clothes!"

Started for the stairs, "You know I'm fine. You're just jealous of my impeccable beauty."

"You look fruity?? Huh? What'd you say? You got cooties? You itch in your booty? Is that what you said?"

Laughing, "FUCK YOU!!!" I yelled from the top of the stairs.

"NOPE! SAVE THAT FOR ALMER!!!"

Awww, she ain't right! I laughed. "LEAVE ME ALONE! WITCHO PUNK-ASS!"

She just laughed at me.

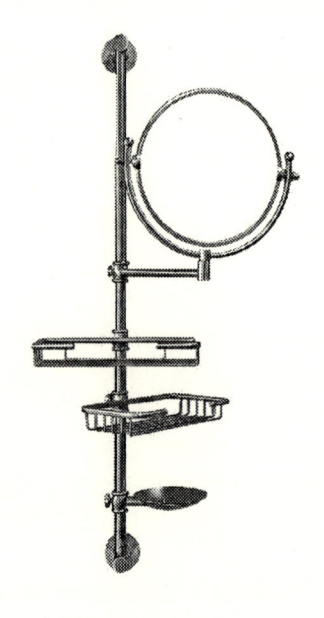

Friday, August 2

LOOKIN' IN THE MIRROR

Jannis was in my office readin' the Jay Phillips website with me. That site had us rollin'. She was talkin' 'bout those things you do when you first start datin' somebody and try to hide that you gotta fart or take a dump. Then, there was this other one that was real cool, called "Good Government in 12 Easy Steps." It's a pretty long article, a six-parter to be exact, but you gotta see some of her pointers. So I'll try to give you the bullet points:

1) No income tax. Money people earn should be money they keep.
2) Enact a flat sales tax, which is applied based on what you buy: luxury taxes (cars, jewelry, etc.) are higher than necessities taxes (food, school supplies & clothing).
3) Legalize prostitution, all drugs, and reclassify alcohol and cigarettes to the same category. Then enact a 15-20% vice tax. (It's not our business what you do with your body or life, but if you want to be an addict, you have to pay for it.) Use that money to pay for public schools and hospitals. Plus, require all facilities that serve drugs to provide a way home for their patrons, or at least confiscate the patron's keys before they partake. Drug sellers & businesses will require specific licenses just like bars today.
4) All public offices will have minimum wage salaries. "Public service" isn't glamorous. So this rids the system of seat riders. They no longer have the ability to vote on their own wage or pay raise, and nobody can hold office longer than two consecutive terms unless requested by a petition and approved by vote.
5) Based on their violation, all prisoners are required to provide work that benefits society—whether on a farm, in construction, in the military, or inside the penitentiary itself. Lawbreakers cannot be allowed to "pay" a debt to society by living off its taxes. Further, if they are ever proven innocent, there's

at least a dollar amount that can be recouped by the errantly incarcerated person since they can't get their life back; and skills gained in prison can be used in the working world. Once released, all can vote again.

6) Naturalize aliens. It's not like they don't work; make their asses pay taxes! (Oh, wait, there's no income tax in my system...but then, it's not like anyone will listen to me, so, like I said: MAKE THEIR ASSES PAY TAXES!)

7) Schoolbook texts shall be approved by the current information accepted by corresponding organization. That way new mathematic theories, for example will be up to date.

8) No tax dollars shall go to dumb scientific studies like monitoring cow farts, or to floundering corporations.

9) The government's only job is to protect the constitution, the rights of its citizens, its land, and commerce. It cannot rule on personal matters like gay marriage, or sexual relationships unless it violates a being's rights.

10) Welfare & public housing are no longer allowed. The only free support—like welfare now—is available for people who physically or mentally cannot work. People on welfare or in public housing now would live in self-supported communities, similar to a reservation. Everything in those communities is provided on a barter system by the residents' work, whether it's food, cleaning, carpentry, etc. All the residents have to chip in to keep the community up and provide food for their families.

11) Do away with the Electoral College and enact true democratic voting. If a candidate wins by *one* vote, that's the freaking winner.

12) If a child is more than one year behind in school, he or she cannot acquire a driver's license until they have achieved at least a 2.8 gpa. Tort reform. Campaign reform. (These are totally unrelated, but I couldn't go past 12.)

LOOKIN' IN THE MIRROR

That Jay Phillips...she's no joke. In this other article, she was *doggin'* BET *out* and said that 'Soul Train' should be put out of its misery. (In a footnote, she said she'd love for 'Apollo' to stick around, but the new Sandman is kinda wack, they need a better host, and a tougher audience.) And then she was sayin' that rappers *are* irresponsible—not for rappin' about lowbrow content, but for not being the change that they want to come about. Which is cool, but this is the funny part: she named Nelly and Lil Bow-Wow as having the reach and popularity to launch educational videos like "CorreKt Grammar" with Nelly (note: the K is also backwards) or "A Lil History with Lil Bow-Wow." But if you think about it, it's not like it'd hurt their careers. Children's entertainment has major, *major* longevity. Then she went off the handle—and Jannis agreed—about all these hip hop/pop superstars investing so much money into wack, repetitive gear supposedly supporting the women with full hips, but didn't do anything to fill the underwear gap. She had me laughin' my ass off. That chick will write *anything*! And I'm tryin' to figure out exactly where she or her paper will draw the line. I mean, she chastises public officers, entertainers and people that she *knows*. Personally. She uses words like "crackheadedness" and "bucketheadity." They let her cuss, she talks about drawls...this chick is nuts!

Goin' back to the underwear article, though: she noted that she couldn't care less about pantylines 'cause she hasn't met any men who truly give a damn about 'em (I know I don't) and women's thoughts don't get listed on her agenda. Then she goes,

"Besides, if my pantylines bother you that much, quit looking at my ass." *LOL!* Thongs (as Jannis suggested) "are okay for seduction because they're about to come off anyway (*LOL!*), but are out of the question as underwear because drawls just aren't meant to be that far up your crack on g-p. And they kind of defeat the purpose of wearing undergarments anyway (women should know what I mean)." Then we were comin' to this part where she was talkin' about how she tried some boycut panties, thinkin' that they'd provide the sexiness that bloomers and period panties (as she calls them) wish for, and the support that bikinis lack, but her cheeks sucked 'em up like soup! So her search for the best panty has led her to makin' her own underwear. *Ohhhh, I get it! It's a plug for DeFi!*

That was hella cool.

Then Denise called and Jannis went back to her desk.

"Bayyyy-beeeee…howw arrrrrrre youuuuu?"

I hate when she sings her words.

"I'm a'right," I replied, still laughin' at the website.

"What are you dooooing?"

"I'm readin' that website I told you about…the one with the writer in DC."

"Ohhh, yeah. I read some of her stuff after you showed me that site," she said.

Still readin' the site and holdin' a big smile, "Oh really? What'd you think?" I asked.

"I didn't like it too much."

"Really? Why not?"

"She seems kinda stuck up…I mean…some of her articles were okay, but she wasn't the bomb or anything. Mostly, I just really didn't like the vibe I was getting."

She was killing my high. "Oh yeah? Why do you say that?"

"Well, it seems like she's always talking down to people...and...I don't know, she's just really arrogant."

"Oh, well...you're entitled to your opinion..."

My quiet began to anger her. "Why are you so quiet?" she asked attitudishly.

"Mmmm, I'm just readin' this website. It's funny," I replied and started to laugh.

"I don't understand how you like that site. She thinks she knows everything."

"Well, it's her opinion, so she's entitled to whatever she writes, but I pretty much agree with most things that I've read on here. And it's just really funny."

"How can you say that? She's so insensitive. And I was really offended by that article she wrote about hair salons. She made it seem like everyone who does hair is the same, and then she said hairdressers are always really religious. Is that supposed to be a bad thing???"

I had to hold in my laugh on that one 'cause I read that article and everything she said was right. But the article was about how she went to a lot of salons in a small time frame, 'cause she would hang out with friends while they got their hair done, and she noticed a lot of the same characters in the salons. Then she pinpointed each and every familiar personality, with each specific variable, which didn't go above two or three. For example, she said that there's always at least one guy working there, which is either quiet and ambiguous, or loud and very gay. If there are two guys, one is straight and keeps to himself, and the other is loud and gay. Anyway, the article hit the nail on the head and Denise is just mad 'cause she probably saw herself in it. Probably as "the one who always talks about her boyfriend or other people's business." Not that I remember verbatim or anything…

Anyway, I was tryin' to find a way to get off the phone with her. She didn't want anything and I could tell she was tryin' to start a fight. It was obvious that we had different points of view about the website, so she could've moved on, but she wanted to bring me over to her side—which, you and I both know, ain't hap'nin'. I tried to find an angle where I could toss a paperclip at Jannis. But she had her headphones on and couldn't hear my repeated emails. Then, luckily, Tanner walked in. For some reason, ever since that meeting after my first DC trip to Logan Marketing he's been clingin' to me like I'm his best friend. A personal counselor or somethin'. I don't get it. But I've been puttin' up with it 'cause of the thing with Chad.

I need all the allies I can get.

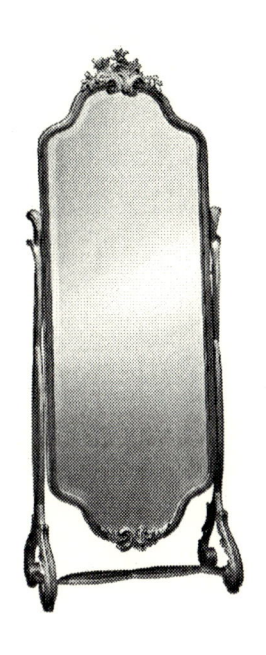

November 19

A. M. HATTER

"Hey Rob! What's goin' on, man?"

"Nothin' much. What's up with you?"

"Squat, dawg. I'm inside tonight."

"Whaaaaat? The superstar is stayin' in tonight??? Woah! Hell must be frozen!"

"Yeah, man! Just me and my bowl of cereal tonight," I replied.

"Hey, are you goin' home for the All Star game? You know it's in Atlanta."

"Oh yeah…I don't know. I might…but man, I can only imagine that traffic… Shit, I don't know, dawg. I'll have to think about that."

"Me and some of my frat are rollin' down," he said.

"*Dri*ving???"

"Yeah," he answered.

"Naw, man. I gotta pass on that one."

"I feel you. But, I gotta suck it up…this is MJ's last stand. I *gotta* see this, y'know?"

"AWW SHIT!!"

"What?"

"Man, I spilled my cereal! Dammit!" I released a hard sigh.

"Awww…"

"I was *all* ready to sit down and work it out, too. Man, damn! Let me call you back, man."

It was a calm Tuesday evening, pretty uneventful; I didn't feel like getting out. Lamar called while I was cleaning up my cereal, but I let the voice mail get it. Then, *(10, 9, 8, 7, 6, 5, 4, 3, 2, 1)* he called my cell phone. I picked up…it was time to use the old-fashioned psychology routine.

LOOKIN' IN THE MIRROR

"Lamar."

"Victoria…I told you I'm sorry. What else can I do?"

"Look, Lamar. It's not that I don't want you. I'm not throwing you away like a dirty paper towel. I just think…that…you should move on. I don't deserve you."

"Don't say that. Why do you think that?" he asked.

"Because, I'm not ready to commit the way you deserve. You need someone who knows what they want and who's ready to treat you the way you need to be treated. I'm just too childish to appreciate the attention that you give. Let me go. Find a real woman."

There was a long silence.

"Lamar?"

"I'm here. Can we still be friends?"

"Well, I think you need to find your true love before we rebuild our friendship. Otherwise, I might stagnate your progress. And I don't wanna hold you back from happiness."

He paused, "Well…if that's the way you feel. I understand."

(((Ring, Ring!)))

"Well, Lamar, lemme get that…it's a family member."

"Okay," he replied, "bye."

(((Ring, Ring!!)))

"Yeah!" I answered.

"Hey. Vic?"

"Yeah."

A. M. HATTER

"Ohhh," Shawn laughed. "Man, what's wrong with you?"

"Man, I just spilled my cereal. I'm pissed. And it was my last bowl, too."

"Awww, man. That's crucial."

"FUCK," I yelled. "Plus *La-mar* called again."

She laughed and started mocking him, sounding like the dude from Mo' Money, "Am-ber! Am-ber! Amber, come back here!"

I returned laughter. "I used the psychology routine on him."

"It won't work. I bet it won't. That shit is too corny!"

"We'll see."

"Whatcha puttin' on it?" she asked.

"Man, I'm not even tryin' to bet."

"Yeaaaahhh…chicken. That's 'cause you know I'm right."

"Whatever man! Nobody can beat my game! Besides, it's not *what* you say. It's *how* you say it."

"Like you said…we'll see."

We were quiet for a minute as I cleaned up the last bit of cereal.

"So what's up?" I asked as I was throwing away the last paper towel.

"Huh?" She sounded like she'd gotten into whatever TV show she was watching, but then snapped back. "…Oh! Ummm…you got those tickets yet?"

"Yeah. Brian called me yesterday and told me everything is set."

"Okay, 'cause Candace called me again askin' about the reunion."

I replied, "Man, they're trippin'."

"Exactly. She gon' start off with the regular stuff…she was tellin' me about an art show she went to recently…"

"A real art show or my kinda art show?" I asked.

"A real art show."

"Oh, okay."

Shawn continued, "So anyway, after she finished with that story, she started with the reunion junk and then started askin' about people we went to school with…who we hung with and all that crap. Like I couldn't tell that's where she was headed in the first place."

"Oh, by the way," I cut in, "I can't find my parents, man. But I got the key, so we can all stay at my folks' house. I'm guessin' they're on another trip."

"Okay. Well, anyway, she was askin' if there were any guys that you went with in high school that maybe we could fix you up with now."

"WHAT???!!! Aww, *hell* naw!"

"I know, right. So I was like, 'No'."

"Yeah… They have this cockamamie idea that me and Duane *belong* together 'cause we were first loves."

"What??? Okay…yeah, they are *really* trippin'," she commented.

"Well, next month, it'll all be over."

She sighed, "Yeah…"

"But let me go…I wanna write some stuff."

"You are *always* working! What's wrong with you? You work more than anybody I know. You even work on the *weekends*!"

"Hey, I can't let all this talent just sit and fester. You gotta put greatness to work!" I laughed.

She put on the corny psychologist hat. "Overworking yourself…I sense that you are compensating for something…Tell me about your relationship with your mother…"

"Girl, shut up," I laughed, "I'm gettin' off the phone to *work-on-my-book*, of which, I have to have the first draft *by April*."

She laughed back at me. "A'ight, girl."

"Bye."

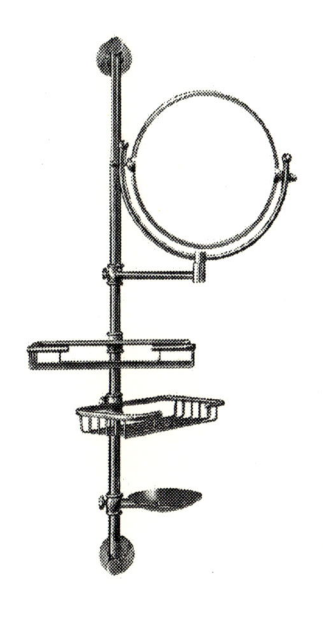

September 24

A. M. HATTER

It's gotten to the point where I look forward to going to the Jay Phillips site. She is one of the most mentally attractive women I've read. If nothin' else, she's just really funny. After I checked my email, I read a piece from her archive. It was one of her really old articles; the date said "4.15.95".

> Personality being a factor in a relationship goes without saying, but in this evolving social climate, the move toward "everyone is beautiful" has done some damage to the reality that appearance does, in fact, matter.
>
> Lately, I've been the target of some scrutiny because I have a close male friend who has something of a crush on me. Though, in my eyes, we are strictly platonic. And apparently the fact that I don't find him the least bit attractive rubs some people the wrong way, particularly because I know myself well enough to say why I'm not attracted to him. I suppose, though, if I were to stumble over my words and mutter, "I don't know" in response to their question, I'd be more credible?
>
> Perhaps if I were born with Xy, rather than the double X, people would be more accepting of my tastes in the opposite sex. I noticed, from hanging around several guys while growing up, that they were never questioned about why they didn't like a girl. But if he answered, "she's ugly," or "I like small chicks," he's free to have that preference. People say "Okay," or even agree with him. On the flipside, chicks I've known who say I don't like 'Male Exhibit B' because he's too tall, or short or because he's overweight or because he's just not attractive, are expected to make a way to like him.
>
> The naysayers will tell you that you're "limiting yourself" or "being superficial." "Ohhh, it's about personality! Looks don't matter," they say. Like hell they don't! I say, "Why don't *you* try falling for someone who you're not attracted to?" Oh, you're

LOOKIN' IN THE MIRROR

having a bit of trouble now, eh? We're not talking about you; it's about me?

I think I have it now: as a non-smoker I have the right to not date smokers, for example; however, if I'm merely not attracted to a guy because he's obese, I'm to make myself like him.

But let's take a trip down Dittohead Lane, where everyone does what the majority says, regardless of what they really feel. And let's assume that I did hook up with this friend of mine merely because my friends say I should. When the relationship calls for romantic solace and I can't give him what he needs, aren't I doing us both an injustice by pretending love—or even faking *like*?

Granted, it can be shown where you get used to someone or you eventually become attracted to people that you weren't initially attracted to. But shouldn't the dating come at that time, and not before?

"Are you readin' that website again?" Mia asked.

"Uh, yeah," I said clicking on another article.

"I swear, one day I'm gonna walk in on you jackin' off to that shit."

I laughed, "Man, you trippin'. Getcho punk ass on."

She plopped onto my futon. "Is she really that tight?" she asked.

"She really is. Just the other day, I read an article where she was talkin' about the Run TMC squad at Golden State. This chick is no joke."

"Well, it's a good thing you're movin' to DC, then, huh?" she said with a hint of melancholy.

"Man, I *gotta* meet this girl…"

"What if she's ghetto? She lives in DC…she could easily be a Baltimore 'round-the-way girl," she chuckled.

"Naw, she ain't ghetto. Not the way she writes. I mean, she'll use slang and cuss—or, use the abbreviations—but then she'll use," I used my fingers as quotations, "'big words', too. You just don't get that kind of range out of somebody ghetto."

"Man, please. That just means she's a good writer. It has nothin' to do with her being ghetto."

"It does if she wrote a piece about how she can't stand ghetto people," I responded.

"Okayyyyy! Alrighty then! *That* might mean somethin'," she nodded, "…but, what if she's a mud-duck?"

I paused. "…I *think* I can get past that," I replied.

She gave me a look like, *Shut yo' lyin' ass up*.

"What if she's all fat'n'nasty-ugly, just uuugh?" she asked.

"Naw, Anita woulda mentioned somethin' like that," I replied. "She'd've been like 'She's real fat'n'nasty-lookin', but she's cool as hell.'"

"Oh, okay…"

I looked at her strangely, "You tryin' to change my mind or somethin'?"

"No," she responded, "I'm just surprised at how much you like this chick and you don't even know her."

"I know man… It's kinda crazy, y'know? I mean, I don't know her, but like, I do…'cause you can see how a person thinks in the way they write and what they write about. And she just seems…real cool," I paused. "Like with this article I'm readin' now. I mean, I can see her point, but considering what she writes about now, it's kinda superficial. So, like, I can see how her material has grown."

"But what about Denise?" she asked.

I ignored her and kept clicking through the site.

She laughed. "Gerald, don't ig-nore me!!!"

I looked at her with one raised eyebrow and went back to clicking.

"So y'all are on the outs again?"

I remained silent.

"What happened this time?" she asked, rolling her eyes.

"Man, I ain't thinkin' about her dumb ass," I replied.

"Yeah, right...'til she sweetens up to you, then you'll forgive her and you'll go through the whole routine again."

"No. I'm serious. I'm not thinkin' about her dumb ass," I repeated firmly.

Then she looked at me, with a faceful of glee. "Does this mean it's over??"

"You don't have to look so happy," I replied.

"And *you* don't have to act like you're not. We both know you've just been goin' through the motions with her."

I looked down at the keyboard and did a site search on 'video games'.

"So what tipped the boat?"

I sat for a few pauses, debating whether or not to tell her the story. But I figured, *fuck it. I'll end up tellin' her anyway.*

"Man," I started, "you know I was real busy, like, a couple weeks ago, right?"

A. M. HATTER

"Yeah," she replied.

"Well, Denise called on my cell. She was whinin' about I've been neglectin' her or whatever. *Even though* I went over to her house, dead tired, and watched some sappy ass Sandra Bullock movie with her like we're in a relationship or somethin'—we were only supposed to be 'friends', accordin' to her!"

She looked at me like, *you dumbass. You know you weren't just friends.*

"Hey," I shrugged, "that's the pitch she made to me. I can't help that she gave it up," and I laughed.

"Awwwww, hell," she interjected.

"Well I apologized anyway. I was try'na get her to shut up, pretty much. But she couldn't take that. Then she started trippin', talkin' 'bout I don't care about her."

Mia rolled her eyes.

"Yeah. And you *know* that led to an argument."

She grimaced and replied, "Of course."

"She's fussin' at me, talkin' 'bout I'm only usin' her, I only come around when it's late—like I've *ever* been that type of dude to her. I was like, 'How am *I* usin' you??' *She's* the one always comin' over *my* house to have sex! But I'm only usin' her. Even though I put up with her crazy attitudes and all her stupid shit—hell, *she* left *me*! And I took her funky ass back…but I'm usin' her."

"I hate when chicks do that. They give us a bad name."

"She talkin' 'bout I don't luuuuv herrrr, 'n' I'm neh-glec-tin' herrrr, doggin' me out 'cause I'm outta town a lot. So I was like, 'Look, you knew I traveled a lot when we met. You knew I had the same fuckin' job when you came back talkin' about you want another chance…ain't shit changed.'" I sat there lookin' aggravated. "She talkin' 'bout, I travel a lot more now 'cause I'm tryin' to cheat on her," I squinted for a second and released, "She said last time she called on my cell, she heard a woman in the background."

"What woman? Me?" Mia asked.

"Man, I don't know! I was like, 'Woman???' Man, that bitch is *crazy*. She's makin' shit up."

"She couldn't be talkin' about me. She's knows I moved out," she theorized.

"…You know what? Now that I think about it…I bet it was the week I was in Vegas for that seminar," I nodded, "Yep, I bet it was. 'Cause I remember I was sittin' at the roulette table and she called when one of the waitresses came by and asked me if I wanted a drink. That *had* to be it…man, that week, she called me *every ten minutes*, Mia. No bullshit!"

She returned a confused look.

"And if I didn't answer the phone, she'd start grillin' me on why I didn't answer my phone—never mind that I was in Vegas on *business*. God forbid, I might be in a seminar," I griped.

"You still love her, though."

"Man, fuck her. I don't have time to deal wit' her whinin', keepin' tabs on somebody. I'm a grown ass man."

I looked back at the computer and saw the search results:

Remember this? 10.14.98 It said.

A. M. HATTER

The two of us spent the remainder of the evening laughin' at the stuff she listed.

1. Saying "PSYCH"
2. the words to "Diff'rent Strokes" & "Good Times"
3. wearing biker shorts under your skirt
4. yearning to be a member of "The Baby-sitters Club" and trying to start a club of your own
5. when football wasn't on turf
6. you were "the man" if you had a Huffy or a 10-speed
7. when it was actually worth getting up early on Saturday to watch cartoons
8. wearing a pony tail on the side of your head
9. when parents would discipline their kids
10. making your mom buy one of those clips that would hold your shirt in a knot on the side
11. forget Barbie…it was all about "Jem"
12. the words to "The Mysfits" part of the "Jem" theme song
13. Choose Your Own Adventure books
14. the profound meaning of "Wax on, wax off"
15. "Transformers" vs. "Gobots"
16. lunch pails
17. those plastic sunshades with slits in the eye part
18. Atari (along with Pinball, Donkey Kong, & Space Invaders)
19. slap bracelets
20. Swatch watches (and all of the face guards)
21. saying "NOT" after every sentence
22. thinking She-Ra and He-Man should hook up
23. playing "Barbie & G.I. Joe"
24. Jellies and Kangaroos
25. Skates with plastic wheels (or any skates before the in-line trend)
26. "Dont worry, be happy"
27. slouch socks (and wearing, like, EIGHT pairs together in alternating colors)

LOOKIN' IN THE MIRROR

28. "Miss Mary Mack, Mack, Mack...all dressed in black, black, black..."
29. "And knowing is half the battle..."
30. the original class from "Saved By The Bell"
31. Contra
32. knowing someone who knew someone who could beat "Mike Tyson Punchout"
33. when dances had names
34. ProWings & Keds
35. jams
36. when generic foods weren't trying to front like they're name brand
37. horrible special effects
38. "Fraggle Rock"
39. when football players could celebrate a touchdown—for *real*
40. when there wasn't a disorder for everything
41. Oregon Trail & Spy Hunter
42. the Micromachines man
43. Lincoln logs
44. mullets, flat tops, high tops, shags, Jheri curls, teasing & feathering and every other bad hairstyle from the 80s
45. Debbi Gibson hats
46. putting a key on one hoop earring
47. Tron & Automan
48. the Evil Kineval wind-up stunt cycle
49. M-dada (actually titled, "Din-da-da" by George Kranz)
50. Apple IIa,b,c,d,e,f,g... and those HUGE floppy disks!

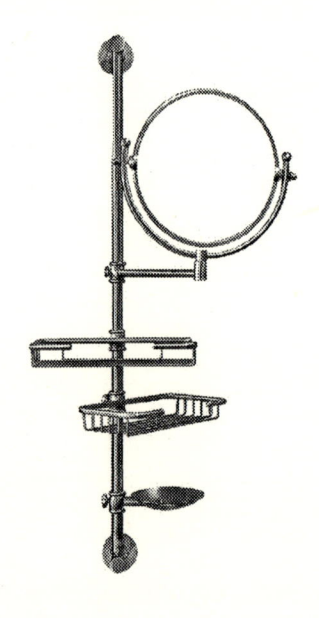

October 3

LOOKIN' IN THE MIRROR

"I'm glad you came tonight," Denise said, smiling.

"Yeah, well…I was free, I was hungry and you called. So, you had good timing," I replied.

She *definitely* brought the representative with her this time, though it didn't really help my demeanor. It had gotten to the point that everything she said irked me. If she'd been anyone else, a man like me would tell her what's up. But since we'd been playin' a charade for the past few months—her, more than I, 'cause she thinks she has game—I was completely justified in playin' along with her conspiracy to set me into her evil clutches and regain her dragon's grip on my life. On the other hand, she offered to drive and pay for dinner. I didn't need a whole lot more convincing than that.

Her face dropped. "What's with the attitude?" she asked.

I looked up from my linguine pescatore and replied, "What attitude? I don't have an attitude."

"Well, it just seemed like you snapped at me," she said.

"Oh," swallowing some pasta, "my bad, then," I said and went back to my food.

"Where were you the other night?" she asked softly.

"What night?" I asked. *How the hell she gon' ask me 'Where were you', like she's my woman?*

"Thursday night. I called but you didn't answer."

I shrugged my shoulders.

I don't know why she acts like she has some authority over where I go and what I do. I must have 'Sucker' written on my forehead. Between her and my momma, I don't know who's worse. But I don't care if my momma asks me that. She's my momma. She can do that. It's different.

"And you didn't answer your cell phone," she added.

I shrugged again. "I don'know. Probably at the gym or out with Will & the rest."

"You're usually at home about ten, though."

"So?"

"Well, I wanted to talk to you."

I looked at her. "Well, I wasn't at home. Whatchu want me to do about it now?"

"Daaaang! I was just askin' where you were!"

"Calm down. It's not that serious," I replied.

"Are you sure you don't want anything to drink? You seem kinda tense."

Ah-ha! Tryin' to get me to drink! I knew she was tryin' to pull somethin'!

"No. Thank you. I'm cool," I answered.

For the past…I wanna say *month*, she's been actin' *extra* nice; tryin' to find excuses to call, makin' up reasons for us to be alone somewhere—anywhere. In little under three weeks—18 days, to be exact—she made 216 calls, left 162 voicemails, and 108 emails—no, 432 if you count all my email accounts. Needless to say she's a bit of a bugaboo. But there I sat, at the restaurant where we met, tryin' to dodge her questions about where I've been, berated by her lackluster conversation.

LOOKIN' IN THE MIRROR

She thought I'd be vulnerable to the memories. Ever since we sat down, she kept bringin' up old times. (Yeah, that's her method.) I laughed along with her, but things I've noticed since she left me started comin' to mind. I thought about the times when she called *all day long* and nearly drove me crazy. I thought about the times when she'd ask me where I went and got mad at me 'cause I was out with the guys, even though she'd previously agree to "free days." How she'd drink all the orange juice and leave a swallow at the bottom, but wouldn't run to the store to get more, knowin' there was nothin' left to drink—at all. I thought about all the messages she'd leave with Jannis when she was lonely, or bored, or mad, or amorous, or heard some new gossip while she was at work (hair salon, remember?). Yeah, and how there'd be some discussion in the salon that day, and she'd call to get my opinion, but would get mad and actually start some long-lasting feud if I didn't answer the way she wanted. Particularly, this one time when she pretended to want a threesome to see what I'd say. She thought I'd say, "No, of course not! I only want you, baby!" so she could go back and brag to her little shop friends. I know the game. I *knew* she was fakin'. Ain't no Black woman gon' walk in the house one day and just ask you about havin' a threesome for no apparent reason. So I jacked her up and said, "Okay." Boy...she was burnin' up about that one for about six months. That was too funny; ya shoulda been there.

Man, I was whipped. I have to admit. But I can just charge it to the game, 'cause at least I'm not stuck in a situation like Terrence. Somewhere between her

A. M. HATTER

story about this woman's children actin' bad, and one of her client's nappy hair, I remembered when I saw him during this year's fourth-of-july and it got me to thinkin': *I don't wanna be in his situation, stuck in a ghetto relationship. I don't want a mother-in-law that disgusts me. I don't want Denise raisin' my kids. I don't want Denise.*

I fell out of love with her a long time ago, and now, I don't even like her. She thought I'd be vulnerable to the memories. But as they say, there comes a time when we must move on.

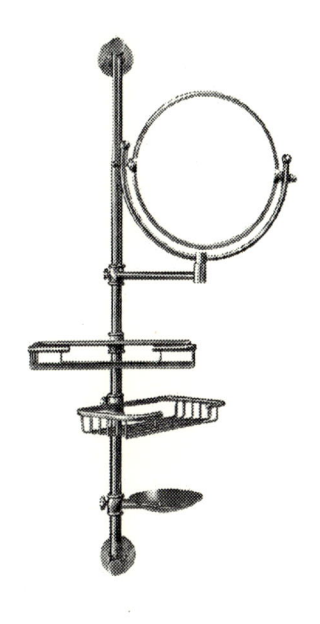

After Dinner

A. M. HATTER

"Stop looking at your car," she said, "You're not trying to leave, are you?"

She stared into me like she imagined me as a glazed ham. She had the 'big eyes look,' and draped her arms over my shoulders, draggin' me by my neck into her apartment.

She locked the door and slid around me, and wrapped her arms around my waist. "You know, it just occurred to me that you've never slept over here before…why *is* that?"

"Oh, I haven't?"

She shook her head.

I looked at her like it was news to me. "I never really thought about it."

We sat on the couch and she leaned back. She threw her feet into my lap.

"Rub my feet for me," she grinned.

My head fell back.

"Pleeeeeease," she smiled and batted her eyes.

I looked at her yellow toes, freshly manicured and neat, with white tips.

I sighed. "Aaaaaa'ight," I replied. So I started rubbing her feet.

"Hey, do you remember that time we went to that Spanish restaurant where you got the waiter to bring us that cake for free 'cause you could speak Spanish?"

I frowned for a few seconds. I had no idea what she was talkin' about. And then I remembered. "Ohhh, you mean that time we went to Fago?"

"Yeah, I think so," she nodded, "That place with the meat."

"Yeah, yeah...it wasn't the waiter, I knew the manager."

"Ohhhh," she smiled, "you are so talented."

"Why are you looking at me like that?" she asked.

I shrugged and kept rubbing her foot.

"Wow...I can't believe that I almost didn't talk to you...had I stuck to the guys I was normally attracted to, I would've missed out on a really sweet guy," she said.

"There you go with that expression again," she said.

I just grinned and shook my head.

She paused and rubbed her other foot up and down my chest. "We've had so many good times together...you've done so much for me. I never would've seen or experienced half of the things that we've done together with someone else."

"Why you say that?" I asked.

"Be-*cause*! I mean, well, maybe I'd have met somebody else with goals and stuff...but the guys I used to date were just really good-looking and *sorry*."

I laughed quietly.

Then she slid her feet away and crawled over to straddle me. She looked deep into my eyes. "Make love to me," she said, and pressed her lips to mine.

I pressed the small of her back and she spread her legs farther to sit on my crotch. We went back and forth pressing our lips between each other's, tasting each other's saliva, and lickin' each other's tongues. She leaned into the kiss and wrapped her mouth around my mine. Her tongue reached in and slid back, back to hump of my tongue. And we rolled our tongues around, dippin' in and out, lickin' lips, tongues, the roofs of each other's mouths. She tilted forward, pressed her hands against my chest and raised her head. With my tongue, I trailed down her neck, to that spot where the collarbones meet, then slid over to the side and closed my mouth over her neck. My hands slid down to her butt and gripped both cheeks in the back. She rocked slowly back and forth over my lap, grinding in, tryin' to feel my dick. And I rubbed my hands back and forth over the entire span of her hips. She started to moan lightly as my mouth continued to suck on her neck. I lifted her skirt and shoved my hands under the back part of her panties, my fingertips resting at the crack of her ass. Her pubic hairs teased the tips of my end fingers.

She lowered her face to kiss me again, but I tilted her over onto the couch and crouched over her. I ran my hand up the bottom side of her entire leg, and planted my mouth on her thigh. I pressed into it. And ran my teeth over it. She reached down and grabbed me by the back of my neck to bring me back to her mouth. I raised her leg to my hip and she wrapped her legs around me. I leaned slightly to the side and started to unbutton her dress. She had on a front-access bra that seemed to pop open as soon as I touched it. I looked down at the two brown points below. I ran my right hand from her butt, across that point right below the pelvic bone, to the gap of her inner thigh—and back. Then I scooted down and wrapped my left arm around her waist; I pushed my hand into the small of her back and she arched up like a good girl. I ran my tongue up the middle, from her belly button to her sternum. I stayed there, at the sternum, lickin' and suckin' from one side to the other, kissin' her yellow-toned skin to tease her nipples. I ran my right hand up her side. Her legs tightened around my waist and she clawed the back of my couch, anticipating my next move. *Follow me, to the right* → I licked around the bottom of her breast, makin' a half circle and looped up to her neck. She beat her fist into my back.

"Gerald! Stop playing, boy!" she giggled.

I looked at her and laughed back.

"You know you're wrong!" she smiled.

I kissed her lips, then her chin, then on her thyroid, down her sternum. I cupped her right breast and planted my mouth on it. I sucked it like a baby. Her moans mixed in with the suckin' noises comin' from my mouth. I clamped down on more breast and shoved it in my mouth, then pulled back, lettin' it slide slowly from my lips. Her nipple snapped back to her chest and I paused to watch it jiggle. Then I went to the left side and licked her whole breast, around and around. Then I sucked it. I stayed on it. She palmed the back of my head with her left hand, and pushed it to her chest, and I sucked harder, rubbing the other breast with my hand. Her legs waved in and out; then she slid her feet up and down the backs of my legs. And with both arms, she hugged my head.

I slid my right hand down from her breast, pushed the crotch of her panties to the side and parted her lips. She was so wet. I could smell it twenty minutes ago. The whole thing was pulsating. I softly stroked her clit with my forefinger and thumb, and she pushed her pelvis up just slightly. She wanted me. But I wouldn't let her have it just yet. I switched back to her right breast and continued suckin'. Up and down, I gently rubbed my thumb over the top of her clit. My other fingers gripped her thigh.

She motioned for me to turn over so I leaned to the side to see what she wanted to do. She scooted from under me and propped her kneepit on my shoulder. Then she pulled me closer and licked on my ear. I stuck my fore and middle fingers inside her pussy. Her walls were so swollen and hot, I could already feel her on my dick in my imagination. Palm up, I stroked that "ball" at the top, just inside the opening. After about a minute or so, I pushed past it into the sinkhole right behind it. She wrapped both arms around my neck and started moaning like a puppy as I massaged the top wall. She started rubbing around, and must've realized that she was nearly naked and I was fully clothed.

She sucked on my neck as she unbuttoned my shirt, grindin' back on me, the more I stroked with my fingers. I started to press against the sides, bending my knuckles and pulling in and out. Her head kicked back and she yelled, grippin' my collars tightly. She pulled me toward her. I continued workin' with my fingers, but I pulled her up so I could suck on her tits again. But she pushed my head away.

"Get up," she said.

So I stood, wondering what she wanted to do next. She started unbuckling my pants, so I kicked off my shoes. My pants fell, and she stared at my man, stickin' out from my boxer briefs. She rubbed her

LOOKIN' IN THE MIRROR

hands on my butt, and I pulled her up from the couch by her shoulders. She removed the remaining clothes from her body, and I bent down to put her over my shoulder.

She laughed. "Boy! What are you doing???" she said, as I carried her from the couch to the kitchen and sat her on the table.

"Lay back," I said, pulling the chair out.

I sat down and propped her thighs up. She put her feet on the posts of the chair back. I grabbed her hips and pulled her to the edge of the table. I smelled her: heat and flesh. I heard it bubblin' and cracklin' like rice cereal. The pussy was talkin' to me.

She giggled. "I feel like I'm getting a pap."

I grinned. "Yeah, I'd call this a vaginal exam."

And she closed her thighs on my head, playin' around. I pulled them apart and she giggled at me. I smacked the side of her thigh. With both hands, I felt her, from the creases of her cheeks to the pits of her knees. I started suckin' on the inside of her right thigh. My hands went running. All over the place, it didn't even matter. She put them on her breasts as I kissed down her thigh, into her gap, just a half-inch from where she wanted me to be. And I stayed there, suckin' on that pit just to the side of her lip. But then I ran my right hand up her leg, extending it upward as I licked from that pit all the way to her ankle.

I sucked on her knee pit, on her calf, and on her ankle. I put her leg back down and sucked on her belly button. She pushed on my head, but I pulled her hand away. I rubbed my nose in her pubic hair, smelling her heat. I kissed it. And again. Then I spread her lips and, with my tongue widened, I licked from the bottom to the top, flicking the tip of my tongue on her clit at the end. Slowly, I flipped my tongue back and forth over her clit, then kissed it, and licked the sides. She smelled so good, and sounded so sexy when she moaned. I dug my tongue into her vagina and rolled my tongue around inside her oyster-tasting flesh. Her pubic hairs rubbed around my mouth as my lips pressed against the pink. I moved my tongue around, lickin' the ball at the top. Then I pulled out and licked the outside again. I sucked on her and she started rockin' against my face.

"Ohhhhh, I wanna fuck," she moaned.

But I kept sucking. She wrapped her legs around my head.

"Stop, stop, stop," she said and leaned up.

I wiped my mouth off as she got off the table. She took a second to calm down and I just looked at her.

"What's wrong?" I asked.

She looked up at me. She turned me around and pushed me toward the bedroom.

She pushed me onto the bed and I turned over, watchin' her ass jiggle as she walked to the door to close it. She turned back to me and took grasp of the band of my underwear, pullin' 'em off of me. Then she got some flavored lube out of her sex drawer and laid between my legs. She pressed against my inner thighs for me to spread 'em further and squeezed the lube into the palm of her right hand. She lifted my balls and licked 'em from back to front, wettin' my entire sack. Then she took my left nut into her mouth and started to

LOOKIN' IN THE MIRROR

suck on it. She jacked me off while she sucked on my balls. If ever a man wanted to cum right then, it was me. She sucked on it so nicely, caressing it with her tongue as she sucked one, and rubbing the other with her free hand. And when she was done, she licked from my sack all the way up to the tip of my dick. I could feel the heat of her breath on my head as she hung in the balance, almost like how a roller coaster cart goes over that first hill. Then she swung her hair to the side, cupped my balls, tucked her lips over her teeth, and took that head like a champ. Her head bobbed up and down on it, while she circled her tongue on the bottom side. She sucked it hard, slow and smooth, while she stroked her hand up and down at the base. Her mouth smacked and slurped as her head moved up and down, her low-toned moans vibrated on the head of my dick; her left hand was still rubbing my balls. She continued for about ten or fifteen minutes and she added more force on the down stroke. She started suckin' harder, she stroked faster. My dick got harder. The pulses beat quicker. She knew I was about to cum. She reached under me and grabbed my butt, and forced her head down on it. She stroked her tongue more, and sucked more, and slurped more. She did it harder, and harder.

"OHHHHH, SHIT!" I yelled.

She kept on suckin', lettin' my cum shoot into her mouth. Then she took it out of her mouth and put it to her face. It went on her cheeks, on her lips, in her eyelash, and almost up her nose. When I finished, I looked down at her, lookin' like a pastry. She wanted me to look. She waited. 'Cause she looked straight into my eyes so I could see her throat muscles move up and down. Then she wiped what cum there was off her face and rubbed it on her body.

She laid beside me.

"Turn to your side," I told her.

I pulled her in, where I could spoon her, and she laid her head on my right bicep. I pulled her hair out of the way and started suckin' on her neck, playin' with her body as I did so. Then we'd lay there. Then we'd start feelin' on each other, which would turn into more kissing and licking, and more touching. I sat up and patted her on her rear so she'd sit up. I got behind her and pushed her forward. I scooted back and put my face in her pussy. I grabbed her thighs and pulled them outward. I licked and stuck my tongue in and pulled it out and licked some more. I sucked the crease in her skin, where the ass meets the thigh, and I rubbed all up and down her thighs and ass. I kissed her pussy and licked it some more. But then my neck started to hurt. I hate when that happens 'cause I love seeing her ass in my face. So I reached under her and grabbed her by the waist to lift her up so I could flip her forward. (On her back, legs at the headboard.) I got on top of her and put my face in her stuff again. I wrapped my arms around her and her legs squeezed around my neck. On the other end, she started suckin' on my dick again.

Once I got hard again, I reached over to her sex drawer and pulled out a condom. I put it on and I turned her around on her back and slid in. I stroked her slow and hard. She oooo'd and ahhhh'd, while diggin' her claws into my back.

I stopped strokin'. "Dee…ah, ah…Dee!"

LOOKIN' IN THE MIRROR

"Huh?"

"Your nails," I said.

"Oh! I'm sorry," she said and pressed in with her fingertips instead of her nails. She kissed on my neck as I started again, and she slid her hand down to my butt.

I raised her leg and started diggin' into the side.

"OHHHHH! OH, GERALD!" she yelled. She grabbed for the sheets and pulled at them. I switched to the other leg and dug in the other side. Then, I scooped my arms under her shoulders and drilled in slow and forcefully. I pushed in and pulled back. I could feel her feet sliding back and forth on the bed as I thrusted in and out. She tried to scoot, she tried to crawl, but she wasn't goin' *no*where. And then, the bottom fell out.

Her walls opened up and I went to work. I stroked her slow, then hard, then slow *and* hard. We turned to the side and I wrapped my arms around her, cupping her breast with one hand and her stomach with my other. I put her on top facing me. Facing away from me. Facing away, leaned back. I bounced her up and down on top of me. We did it against the wall. On the floor. In the kitchen. Against the counter. In the sink. We went *back* to the bed. She laid on her stomach, and I worked her mid-tempo. Then faster. Then I pulled her butt up and grabbed her cheeks. I put my thumbs right in the crack of her ass and spread 'em. She put it back in and I pushed and pulled her. She grabbed the pillow and started screaming into it. I pushed in harder...and harder. Faster. We got into a good rhythm, my nuts swingin' back and forth against her pussy. Her butt cheeks smacked against my thighs.

A. M. HATTER

Both of our thighs were wet with her juices. Then I grabbed her at her pelvic bones and pushed her to the bed. I pulled out and shot all over her. She turned over and scooted down to catch it on her face. Then she sucked the rest out.

    I fell over.

    She wiped her face on the sheets.

    She crawled up to me and exhaled. "Baby, that was sooooo goood."

    I nodded.

    "Damn, you feel so good," she said.

    I just smiled.

    Then I got up. I hooked my underwear on my foot so she wouldn't see what I was doing. I dragged them to the living room, where I started puttin' on my clothes.

    After a couple of minutes, she yelled from the bedroom, "HEY! WHAT ARE YOU DOING? COME BACK TO BED!" and giggled. But I didn't answer. So she came into the front room, wrapped in a sheet, where she found me almost fully dressed. If she was white, she'd have gone pale.

    "Where are you going?" she asked.

    "I'm going home," I replied.

    She giggled nervously. "You can sleep over here. You don't need to go home."

    "Yes I do."

    "Right *now*?" she looked at me.

    I looked for my keys.

    "We just made love…don't go," her lip started to tremble.

"No, I'm leaving," I said, grabbin' my keys and walkin' past her to the door.

She followed me, cryin'. "Gerald! Don't go! Why are you leaving???"

I unlocked the door, then looked back, "Oh, and I should tell you...I'll probably be leaving Houston, so, uhh...you should find someone else."

She covered her mouth and dropped to her knees. "Why are you doing this to me? Why didn't you *tell* me???"

"I am telling you. I'm telling you now...which is more than you did for me."

And I walked out.

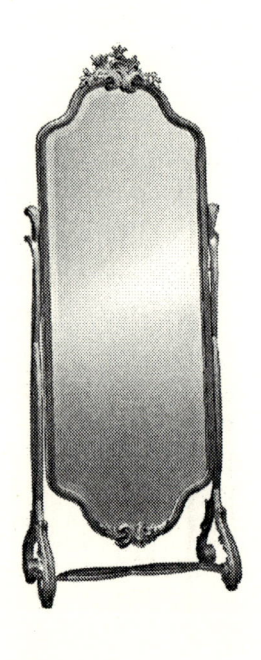

Saturday, December 28

Atlanta, GA

LOOKIN' IN THE MIRROR

My girl posse took the reunion by storm. WOAH! Did we make an entrance or what??? Me, my roommate, Shawn, Candace, and Kenya entered the banquet room on flying carpets or some shit!!

Kenya wore this black number with a wide v-neck that draped her hips ever so lightly, reaching mid-calf with three-quarter-length sleeves, in shorthaired velvet. She had her hair French rolled with her baby-hair out. For shoes she chose sexy black heels with a conservative toe opening, and put on glimmering black and silver dangling earrings with a matching link necklace.

Shawn wore a light beige polyester blend uni with wide legs and a short jacket to match, accenting with a gold chain belt. The uni had a boat neckline and a teardrop opening in the cleavage sector. She wore a very short haircut, similar to old school Toni Braxton; adding old gold leather slingbacks and large gold stud earrings.

Candace exploded on the scene in a very long, flowing maroon dress with a straight neckline, the back drooping almost to her ass and a split up to her nose. Add steep heels to match. Spiraled hair, semi-pinned for that slightly disheveled look, and a three-diamond dangle on each ear. She seemed kind of overdressed, but she looked *good*!

My roomie went with a very long burnt auburn wrap dress, emphasizing her thin waistline and an afrocentric pattern using brown, maroon, black and beige. She crowned herself with a tall turban and had her locks spilling from the top. She wore sleek brown mules with a one-inch heel and accessorized with a brown cloth choker, tooth-like earrings, and wooden bracelets.

Yours truly appeared on location in a fiery purple tango dress with thin straps (high split & asymmetrical hemline—I love that dress!). I had my hair done in very wide waves to resemble the old time waves from Madame C.J. Walker times, and added fake eyelashes and an eyeliner mole. I went with a very deep wine-colored lipstick and accessorized with a simple teardrop shaped zircon that fell just above the apex of my plunging neckline. The shoes I wore came from a second-hand store and looked like dance teacher shoes—you know: black, ankle strap, medium-height wide heel, pointed toe. Classic!

Candace, Kenya and my roommate signed in as guests of mine and Shawn's. The chick that signed us in was just like the sign-in chicks that are in the reunion movies: loud and obnoxious and they always wanna catch up by telling you way too much information.

"Shawn??? Shawn Thomas??? Wow, superstar! You look great!!"

"Thanks," Shawn replied, glancing up briefly and signing the book, purposely neglecting to correct her about the last name.

The chick—I forget her name—looked around for another familiar face and saw me behind Kenya. "OHH—MY—GOSH! Vicki! Vicki Phillips! [Gasp] You look terrific! You're wearing a dress! I can't believe this! I need to find everyone so they can see!" Her expression morphed into one of those proud grandmother expressions for when the first child graduates or something. "I am so happy you got yourself out of those workman suits. You have such a beautiful figure."

I was not happy that she spotlighted me like that. It's not that damn serious that I'm in a friggin' dress. I mean, what the fuck! Am I supposed to be socially inept or something?

"Thanks," I mumbled awkwardly and looked around.

"And she's modest! Look at her! She's the shy beauty!" she continued.

After they all signed in, they went to the banquet room entrance to look for a table where everyone could sit. As they lurked in the doorway, you could see people's eyes tracing every step they made. It was kind of cool the way things worked out because I was last to sign in so I got somewhat of my own entrance. They left the doorway just as I entered it and I heard one guy gasp.

"Vicki? Vicki Phillips??" he exclaimed.

"Quinton! Woah! How are you??" I replied as we hugged.

"I can't believe you're in a dress! I always wondered if you'd ever get tired of wearing auto repair suits."

Is that all anyone remembers about me???

He laughed and added in a calmer tone, "You're very pretty tonight."

I smiled, "Thank you."

"So, what are you doing now? Are you still in the area?"

A. M. HATTER

"No, I moved to DC. I write for a journal up there. It's kinda like 'Creative Loafing'."

"Oh really? So you bash the president and stuff?" he laughed.

"Well, yeah, but not always. I have a rant column, so I'll shoot my mouth off about stuff that happens in my life, as far as dating or running into stupid people…sometimes politics…other times I'll answer questions that people write in with. Some people have even asked me for advice!"

"Well, okay then, Miss Landers!"

I giggled at his joke and moved to cut off the conversation, "Well, I'll catch ya later. I need to find out where my guests have run off to."

"Alright, then. It's good seeing you!" he said as I smiled and walked away.

Luckily, the posse saw me when I turned around to look for them. They waved to get my attention. I was happy to sit down because I wasn't really interested in mingling…my only interest was to finally get rid of this nagging obsession with Duane once and for all. All I expected was to apologize and walk away.

Well, to be honest, yes, there was a deep hope that he'd take me in his arms and break out with this confession that he'd missed my presence in his life all that time, but I knew that fantasizing would only make things worse. I had to stick to my motto: "Expect the worst," which means he'd laugh at me because he's probably happily married with two kids; "hope for the best," he'd admit the same void and sympathize with

LOOKIN' IN THE MIRROR

me, even though he got over the situation 80 years ago and he's happily married with two kids.

"Who are you looking for?" Shawn asked and waited for a response.

"Yoooo-hoooo!" Kenya chimed in.

"Hey! Vicki! Wake up!" Candace said and nudged me with her elbow.

I jerked around, "Huh? What? What's up?"

"What are you looking at?" Kenya asked.

"Nothing in particular," I replied, "All the people."

Plenty of classmates came to our table to talk to Shawn and I—mostly girls we didn't like back in the day who suddenly became our friends apparently. They asked questions and talked to us as if either one of us cared to even see them, let alone share information. Like this one girl, Tina Winters. Back in HS, it was like her whole life was dedicated to humiliating us, but moreso, me in particular. I guess it was because we were naturally cool with the football team, whereas, she had to fuck them—and of course they never respected her after that. Hell, the way we heard it, she was horrible in bed and her fellatio was like getting oral from a St. Bernard.

Honestly, though, I couldn't care less about her. I just couldn't believe she came up to speak; in her shoes, I wouldn't have. On the other hand, it was funny to see that she's fat with six kids and still had this…semi-jheri-curl-type thing goin' on. Hardly recognizable was she: the chick who was God's gift to people in general, and the girl who tried to bust me out at the senior awards banquet by asking aloud, "Hey, did you ever find a thong?? I understand that problem, 'cause panty lines are so gross!" I never found out how she knew I even had trouble finding a thong that agreed with me.

Then, the other half of the unwanted visitors was a bunch of guys who just wanted to know who our guests were. It's beyond me why they don't just try to talk directly to our friends, rather than wasting Shawn's and my time by acting like they wanna catch up and then, sliding over to the subject of who our guests are. I mean it's so stupid! I'm sitting there like, *they ain't slick.* I knew what they wanted when they walked up! They had that "damn, she's fine" look on their faces. Wasting my damn time. Why didn't they just ask to be introduced to our friends?

Anyway, by the time the dinner started, we were hungry as hell and my roommate was getting on my nerves, whispering to me about Duane. The bad thing was that it didn't even start by C-P-T, we just had to be extremely fucking early to get a table that would seat all of us together.

We endured a good wait until the emcee came out to start the ceremony. There was a big dedication to all the classmates who died—one being the class president; therefore, our master of ceremonies for the night was the class vice president. Since the five-year update reunion—which Shawn and I didn't attend—there had been one new death, bringing the grand total to four. The first three were caused by car accidents. The other was a bystander death at the hands of a gas station thief.

LOOKIN' IN THE MIRROR

In between presentations, the sound people played music that was popular when we were in school and the emcee read things like what clothes were popular and the senior superlatives…the wills of the football team…some of the more memorable commercials of the time. Somehow they even got an act from our senior talent show to perform. While it was cool that they could still do the dances without breaking a hip, it wasn't one of the better acts of that show. Even back then the momentum lagged at several points in what's now called "hip-hop dance" choreography, just as it still did.

    The slideshow was featured after the group via PowerPoint presentation. The posse would not stop cracking on this pic that Shawn and I were in, calling us JJ Fad and Oaktown 3-5-7. I had the high-low mushroom cut with a tail, and Shawn had a finger wave on one side with her hair curled in layers on the other. Of course Shawn & I matched all the boys, wearing overalls with one strap hanging. The other girls wore big shirts and those leggings with the lace at the bottom or biker shorts. Yeah…those were the days. That slideshow was nothing short of an award-winning comedy. Even the people who were embarrassed laughed. You just couldn't help it. That hair…what were we thinking???

    The show ended and the emcee announced an afterparty associated with the reunion in a neighboring banquet room. All the people were lined up, trying to leave. As I gathered my things, I happened to look up and spotted Duane. My heart started racing. The moment of truth presented itself. My roommate must've been watching me because she seemed to know that I spotted him.

"You see him don't you?" she whispered.
"Yeah."
"Go talk to him!"
"I will, man. Just…give me some time," I said, trying to get her to leave me alone.
"All you've had is time! It's been over ten years, since it happened! Just go talk ta him."
I glared at her, "I will. Now leave me alone."
"I'll distract them while we head over to the dance. You just go handle your business."
I grabbed my purse and headed in his direction. I felt really weird…like a stalker, watching him leave the banquet hall and go into the bathroom. (I don't do obsession very well…I get all self-conscious, like everyone knows.) I tried to look inconspicuous, waiting near a group of people in the foyer who failed to grow out of their teen stage, talking about who they hated most in high school. Is there anything worse than a bunch of grown ass men and women that cling desperately to the fashions of their adolescence? They looked like friggin' REO Speedwagon fans! And one of them had a *mullet*! It's almost 2003 and this dude has a *mullet*!

"Oh, there goes Sandy Buckner. I hated her. Do you know what she did to me??" said one woman.

"Yeah I remember, Jen. She's a real bitch," one guy answered after laughing, "You know, I heard she's twice divorced, with four kids—and none of them are by either of her husbands!!"

LOOKIN' IN THE MIRROR

They all cackled and snorted... Apparently there is something worse—people who won't let go of past fads *and* obsess on adolescent contention. I mean, come on! Is this the Biff-McFly rivalry?? They reminded me of Brad Pitt's character on 'Friends'. I couldn't wait for Duane to come out, if only to get away from those yin-yangs.

But wait...I'm obsessing on a freakin' crush from twenty years ago! How pathetic am I?

When I saw him leave the bathroom, I walked by like I was heading toward the phones.

I gasped, "Duane! ...Hey!"

"Aww, hey girl! How's it goin'?" he responded.

"I'm doin' well. How about you?"

"Things are pretty good for me, too."

"That's good," I answered.

"When did you get a mole?" he asked.

I laughed, "Tonight when I put my eyeliner pencil to my face."

He grinned at my reply. "You look nice. A big change from those body shop uniforms."

"Very funny, smart-ass. But, thank you."

We stood there with awkwardness between us, not wanting to leave, but not having anything to say. I was shocked to see how attractive he became—not that he was ever ugly...just that he's such a man now; after all, it is that 26-28 stage.

"How's your brother?" he asked.

How's my brother??? I thought. *What kinda question is that? He never really knew my brother. And which one??*

"UHHMM, he's doing fine! He graduated from college last year."

"Wow," he said, "I remember when he was, like, eight!"

I laughed, "I remember when *you* were, like, eight!"

Grinning again, "Yeah…we go way back," he looked away for a sec and looked back. "You still in the area?"

"No. I moved to DC. I do a column for one of those sidewalk journals."

"Oh, okay…that's cool," he answered, nodding. "You like it?"

"Yeah, it's a good outlet for me! I get to talk about whatever's on my mind and shoot my mouth off. People get all mad sometimes…it's funny 'cause I don't expect anyone to really listen or take me seriously." I paused. "Man, sometimes they remember what I say with such detail! It's amazing! *I* don't even remember what I write that well!"

"Yeah, people can get kind of fanatical about opinions and stuff."

We stood there again with the awkwardness. Then I went for it.

"Hey…I don't know any way to bring this up other than to just say it."

He shrugged, "Then just say it."

My words trailed, almost as if I sang them, "Doo youu re-mem-berr in the tenth graade wheen—"

"Yeah," he said softly, looking me dead in the eyes.

I grimaced. "What?" I asked, testing him.

He barely blinked. "The day you dissed me," he replied so easily, expressionless, and shifted his weight from one foot to the other. "Mm-hmm…What about it?"

I was shocked. My mouth dropped open. I couldn't believe he titled the day! "You gave it a *title*???" I stared at him. "Oh my gosh! I mean…it makes me feel really bad to know that's how you see it."

He shrugged it off, "Well…that's the way it happened."

"Damn… Well, anyway… Uhhh, I only brought this up 'cause I want you to understand that I've never forgotten about it, aaand I've never forgiven myself for lettin' Roscoe get between us. …I wasn't tryin' to diss you. It's just that I had a boyfriend and—I don'know, I was really dumb for missing my chance to at least rekindle our friendship." I looked down, fiddling with my fingers, then back at him. "There were a lot of issues surrounding the way I felt at that time…some, excuses…but, ultimately, I just want you to know that I'm sorry for droppin' the ball and never tellin' you how I really felt. And," I shrugged, "I'll always care."

That had to be the only time his eyes weren't beaming onto mine. "Okayyy…" he said, nodding.

I interrupted, "I mean…I know this is, like, really irrelevant considering that it's been almost fifty years since it happened, but I regard that as the worst mistake I ever made. And, remembering what happened, I just wanted you to have retribution in knowing that it at least bugged me every friggin' day

A. M. HATTER

since then." I chuckled nervously. "And even if you don't care, I just had to tell you…y'know?"

He scratched his chin. "I don't even know what to say. Um, thank you."

We stood there, speechless. I wanted him to hug me…punch me…*something*.

"Why didn't you say anything in high school?" he asked.

"Maaan! I don'know! I guess 'cause it was common sense," I laughed.

Some woman glided up to Duane, "Hey Al! You slow-poke, the party started!"

She seemed like a cheesy stunt double of me. Our skin tones were comparatively the same, height—the same, size—the same, we had the same general features, the same "cooler than thou" attitude with a sprinkle of *the last one in the pool is a rotten egg!!!* Hell, she even had my walk.

"Al??" I giggled.

"Yeah, she calls me that…she has this thing with first names," he explained.

"Hey, that's what was on his business card when we met, so that's what I call him," she explained.

"Oh, baby, this is Victoria. She's the girl that hung with our neighborhood group."

Her eyes burst open. "Ohhhhhh! Okayyyy! Wow! So *you're* the infamous Jelly!" she said, laughing as I managed to force a giggle.

I gave him a puzzled look. *How the fuck does this chick know me??*

"Vic, this is my fiancée, Sharon," he said.

LOOKIN' IN THE MIRROR

"Wooooooahhhhhh! Are you *serious*???" I looked on in disbelief and grabbed her hand.

As I looked at the ring she said, "You're welcome to come, if you can make it! I wanted you to be in the wedding, since you guys were so close back in the day, but we didn't know how to get in touch with you."

I looked up slowly, "Really? Wow, I'm honored that you even thought about me. Thanks." I glared at the ring again and let her hand go. "Man! All these people gettin' married... I feel old now."

"Noooo, you're not old! 'Cause if *you're* old, then *I'm* old...and *I* ain't old!" she joked. "So will you be able to come?" She perked up.

"When is it?" I asked.

"April twenty-seventh," she replied.

I started digging in my purse. "Well, I'll certainly try to come," I found a pen and some paper to jot my number and email, "Just call or email me and I'll give you my address so you can send the invitation."

She took the paper, "Okay," she said glancing over the info, "I'll be sure to get in touch with you."

Sensing that the visit was over, "Okay, well... I'm gonna get to the party. I think they're playin' my song. It sounds like somethin' by Michael Jackson, and that's my dawg!" I said. "It was nice meetin' you, Sharon...guess I'll see you guys at the wedding."

They waved goodbye together, like an old 'Nick-at-Nite' show and I turned my back to them, walking to the dance. *Vic, don't cry. Don't cry. DON'T CRY. You knew this was gonna happen*, I told myself.

A. M. HATTER

We're all grown ass people and life goes on. Shit happens. There are other fish in the sea. You will NOT succumb to the shortage propaganda. He is not the only one.

My roommate walked up, "Hey."

"Hey," I replied flatly.

"Did you do it?" she asked looking at me as if my puppy died.

I nodded, looking straight ahead. "Yeah."

"So what happened?"

"We talked about random stuff…I apologized…he was shocked…he's gettin' married," I said blandly.

"WHAT???" she exclaimed.

"Yeah."

Her mouth dropped to the floor. "He's gettin' *married*??? When???"

"Yup. April twenty-seventh."

She looked devastated. She was more shocked than I was.

"Are you gonna go?" she asked.

"If I can make it…yeah…I guess so."

"Man, I don't know if I could go my lost love's wedding. I know I wouldn't be selfless enough truly wish them a happy life. I'd be lyin'." She stared into my face. "Are you okay?"

I turned my eyes slowly in her direction, and then my head, and a tiny self-assured grin crept across my face, "She was *just like* me, man."

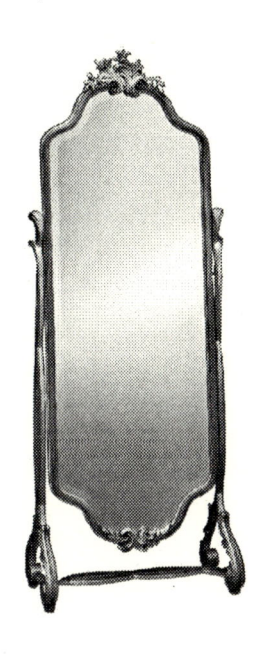

The Next Day

A. M. HATTER

    To admit the truth, would be to say that I was floored by Duane's news. I was JUST starting to get a lil cocky about maybe getting a look or two out of him. I know I was only being mildly realistic, though. (Damn Disney movies! YOUUU DID THIS TO MEEEE!) Forever the hopeless romantic, I am. I only put reality in my face just to be able to say that I considered the possibility. But I never really believe it.

    Dang, it seems like everyone is growing up around me. But what's the alternative? Get married??? HELL no. But then…I don't want to stay single all my life and feel like I missed out on something. Ha, isn't that interesting: I don't want to get married and shit for security, or "to bring love into the world." It's just to add it to my roster of accomplishments—to be able to say, "I even got married and had kids." I'm such an ego.

    I hate growing up, but eventually you have to face the music: after so long, it's just you. All your friends are married; you can't hang out anymore. Ya girls can't stay out late. Ya homeboys roll in *wagons*. Next thing you know, you're thirty-seven, forty-five, never married. All the single guys your age are bustas (most likely why they're not married, either). All the other single chicks your age are clingy and needy…desperate and shit. All they do is get together to watch sappy movies and get drunk, gripe about men and start crying. Ughhh. I *WILL NOT* be a 'Waiting to Exhale woman'. I *REFUSE* it!

    So now, I guess the question is am I okay? How do I really feel?

LOOKIN' IN THE MIRROR

It kinda hurts, I guess... But what was Duane to me, *really*? Because it feels more like an egotistical loss; not like the punch-in-the-gut that a "he was my one true love and he cheated on me" would give you, but more like a "*What*??? This ain't supposed to happen!" And kind of like a "Dammit, somebody took the last pair of brown leather boots on sale for $35 that I really wanted!"

Never had'm, but I really wanted'm.

He was the nostalgic artifact that you leave at your mom's house when you move out on your own, fully intending to return and claim it; only to find out that in your absence, your mom cleaned out your room and threw away something she didn't know you wanted. Now you're stuck with a missing memento—be it a pair of your favorite beat down shoes, an old necklace, or a letter from an old friend. And you wanna get mad, but you can't because you never said anything.

Duane was an option. That's what he was. And as long as I have options, I'm okay. But now I've lost one—and one I really wanted...if only *just to see*.

"So how do you feel?" Kenya asked. Apparently somebody (no doubt, my roommate) filled her in on the story.

"I don't know," I replied after pausing to assess my feelings. "I don't know."

"I understand. ...But you'll get through it," she said.

"Well, I have to... What else would I do? Run over the side of a bridge? It's not that serious. [Short pause.] There's nothing I *can* do but suck it up and move on."

"Well, yeah…that's true," she replied, "But your guy is out there. You'll find him."

Ever the fucking romantic, she is.

"Oh well…he better find me, 'cause I ain't lookin'."

"You were lookin' for Almer," she retorted.

I paused. *I know this half-information-havin' girl didn't just think she came back on me!* "Uhhh, *actually*, I wasn't. You can thank Candace and *my roommate* for that. I was perfectly fine before. But noooo, we're in the sports bar one night and she wants to get all *per*sonal! *Then* she told Candace the next day. Next thing I know, they're both comin' at me like [wimpy voice], 'You gotta tehhhll him. You neeed closure!' [regular voice] I knew I shouldn't have listened to them. Now I'm all damp-sponge and shit. I didn't even wanna come to this damn reunion. It's not like I really missed anyone here."

"That's for damn sure," Shawn interrupted as she entered the room, "Y'all ready? 'Cause I'm finished packin' now."

"I am," I answered.

"I got a couple more things to put in my hanging bag," Kenya replied and left to do so.

"What time is our flight?" Shawn asked.

"I don't know. Ask Candace," I replied, looking for my ticket.

Shawn poked her head out the door, "CANDACE! ……CAN-DACE!"

"YEAH!" she replied from the kitchen.

LOOKIN' IN THE MIRROR

"WHAT TIME IS OUR FLIGHT???"

Candace checked her ticket. "WE GOT THREE HOURS!"

Shawn looked back at us, "Well, we need to leave in about thirty minutes."

"Yeah," I agreed.

"'Cause it'll take us about thirty minutes to get there…we'll have enough time," Shawn poked her head back through the doorway, "ARE YOU FINISHED PACKING??" she yelled back to Candace.

"YEAH!" Candace answered.

Shawn and I sat there in silence, then she looked at me with a grin on her face. "Duane, huh?"

I looked up. "Dammit, not you, too."

"I ain't sayin' nothin'." Then she started giggling. "But *all* this *time*, man! …Really?"

"Not really… I mean, I thought about him every blue moon through college or what not, but I was fine with it 'til you-know-who started eggin' things on. You know how she is. I was gonna be realistic about the shit and leave it alone, ya know? I'm a grown ass woman."

"But she wouldn't leave you alone, huh?"

I rolled my eyes. "As I said, you know how *she* is. Hell, she's the reason Candace got in on it."

"So you were stuck with the cheerleader and the bulldog."

"Right!" I sat there for a second. "Man! News sure traveled fast. How did you and Kenya find out over the course of six hours???"

"We were talkin' about it last night when you and Candace went to get the pizza."

"Oh."

"So…are you mad…or sad…?"

"I was feelin' down earlier…but, you know…well, for one, I *gotta* get over it anyway 'cause life goes on. But, I realized the real feeling I had was just that I didn't get my turn first."

She laughed, "You are *such* a man!"

I laughed back. "But…it ain't really like I can get mad 'cause, he's marrying me anyway."

"HUH??"

I laughed. "See, I met his fiancée last night, right?"

"Yeah."

"And the girl acts *just like* me."

She shot me a skeptical expression.

"No, I'm serious! The girl walked up and I'm lookin' at her like, 'Who the fuck is this?' y'know?"

"Uh-huh"

"The girl looked like me, she acted like me, she even *walked* like me!"

"That girl that he was dancin' with? In the, uh…black and silver pantsuit?"

"Yeah."

"She didn't look like you!"

"No! I don't mean she look-looked like me… I mean she had similar features, like her nose and eyes and stuff."

"Oh." She thought about it. "…Well, yeah. I guess you got a point," she replied, rolling her eyes, looking at me strangely.

"And she talked like me, too… She didn't have my voice, but she acted like me."

LOOKIN' IN THE MIRROR

She shook her head, "You spent all of *two* minutes with this girl, but you know all about her personality?"

"Okay, I admit that all this is circumstantial, but I'm tellin' you…that girl was all—well, you know how excitable I am, right?"

"Yeah."

"And you know how I start actin' really happy about stuff when I'm taken off-guard?"

"Yeahhh."

"Anyway," I shook my head, "You know me, you know how loud I get. And last night, when they told me, I'm all 'Woooaaaah! You're engaged!' And she's like, 'Ohhhhhhhhh! The infamous Jelly!!' And—well, it just seemed like she responded a lot like the way I usually do."

"Hmmm. Well, if it'll help you sleep at night… Okay! Sure! She acts *just like* youuuuuu!" She winked and continued, using all the signature hand gestures from a musical. "All of this is *purely* out of the ordinary. And *man*! She suuure did look like you! I think he went and found your twin, Vicki!"

We started laughing.

"Man, forget you. I didn't make fun of you when you were whinin' about Donald wantin' to have a baby!"

Using the Gene Kelley romance movements, "He only wants to marry *you*, Vicki. But you dissed him in the third grade and now he has to marry your clone!"

"Man, whatever. You ain't funny."

A. M. HATTER

Man, Shawn made me feel straight-up, stupid. I knew I was on the loony bus for even considering (no, admitting to) the whole fiasco anyway, but she didn't have to bust me out like that. Then my phone rang. I was saved by the bell.

"Who's callin' *me*?"

"I bet it's Lamar!" she laughed.

"Nah. Lamar doesn't call me anymore, so ha." I looked at the phone screen. "Ah, it's Rob…"

"Oooooo! Rob the thick man!" she whispered, laughing.

"Hey sweetheart. When are you comin' back?" he asked.

"Actually, we're leavin' in a couple hours."

"Oh, okay," he said with a happy tone, "You comin' over tonight? I rented some movies."

"Man, I'll be sleep when we get back. We're takin' Metro straight to the house."

"Oh. So when can I see you again?"

Not that Rob isn't cool, but it annoys me when he puts me on the spot that way because I don't know when I'll feel like seeing anybody. I'm the type of person that doesn't make plans and I don't try to spend too much time with anyone. He, on the other hand, arranges dates ahead of time—all the time. Maybe other women like that, but it gets on my damn nerves. I like space!

"I don't know…I don't know, Rob," I felt so wack, giving an answer like that, "Just let me get back and sleep off the jetlag first. I'm hella tired already."

"Yeah. Alright."

I motioned to Shawn to say something.

"Hey! Vic! You ready?"

I put the phone to my chest, "Yeah! Be out in a sec!"

"Well, let me go. We're about to head down to the airport."

"Okay. Travel safe…"

"Thanks, talk to ya later. Bye-bye."

[End]

"I don't get it. Why do you still talk to him if he crowds you so much?" Shawn asked, looking at me as if I'd just said, "Hey look, I can bend my lip under my chin!"

"'Cause he's really a cool guy. He's just a little—"

"Possessive?"

"No. Nahhh…He's just angling."

"Didn't you give him the disclaimer?"

"Of course. We had a whole conversation about it. But he swears up and down that he's gonna be the one to snag me off the market," I laughed. "If he wasn't so cool, it'd bother me. But he keeps me occupied, so I'm okay. And I can always tell him 'no' so, it ain't really a problem."

I leaned over on the bed.

"But I don'know…I'm kinda tryin' to see if I can get used to the idea of being serious."

Her eyes opened wider, "Whaaaaaat? You mean… *Rob* has you thinkin' about bein' serious???" Her jaw dropped. "I can't be-*lieve* this shit!"

I just laid there, kind of smiling, kind of queasy.

A. M. HATTER

That was a surprise for me also. I'd always been firmly planted in protest of the 'learn to love' notion. With me, it's either you do or you don't. And it's not that I really couldn't get on the Rob party wagon, because he was contending pretty well…maybe a level four. He's a cool guy and we share a lot of the same interests. But unlike me, Rob isn't a very passionate person—nurturing, but not passionate. Plus, he's kind of square, straight-laced and… See, he's a "credible" personality. If you want someone to deliver the news, he's your man. But for me, I need more of a Rob-Vinny combo.

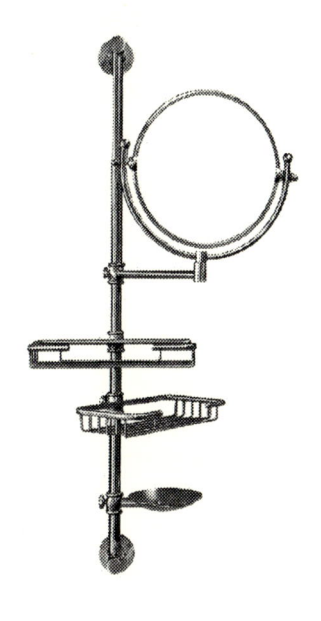

Saturday, October 26

A. M. HATTER

Antoine came into town. Every year we get together the weekend of October 24th to go to Will's brother's grave. It's hard to believe that it's been ten years. This is always a hard time 'cause they were in the car together when a drunk driver hit 'em. His brother died; he lived. But while we take the time to mourn his brother's absence, there's always this irrepressible vibe comin' from the rest of us that's thankful for Will's presence.

After all the sad stuff, we went to the bar for a couple of drinks. You know, the type of place where everybody and their uncle is there, with two beers facin' 'em and one mug three-quarters of the way down. It's a cool spot, but the only thing I don't like is that when I come out, I smell like a Phillip Morris factory. Carlos announced that his wife, Andréa, is pregnant, and Nouri broke the news to Ant that he popped the question to Tanya last month. So that lifted everyone's spirits; although, Nouri kinda makes a brutha feel sorry for himself 'cause he got a good-lookin' sista, while the rest of us just sit around complainin'. Ant was trippin' 'cause so much had changed since he'd last been home—a ten-pound gorilla sittin' on the table that nobody wanted to mention, 'cause the last time he was here was when Denise left.

Anyway, Will's eyes went roamin', as always, checkin' out the women walkin' by. *Good to see he's back to normal.* Ant sat there workin' on his longneck, lookin' pretty chilled, but like somethin' was on his mind. I leaned back in my seat. Carlos and Nouri were

LOOKIN' IN THE MIRROR

characteristically quiet; Carlos sat pickin' at his nails, and Nouri—on his fifth beer—was just mellowing out.

"So, uh, how're things workin' out with Denise?" Ant asked.

"So, Ant, is the A-T-L still treatin' ya right?" I replied.

He looked dead at me, then turned away with a smirk.

I grinned, "Actually...I'm through."

"Whaaaat? For good this time?" he replied.

"Yeah, man. I'm out, I'm done," I said.

Will muttered, "It's about damn time."

But I ignored him because he didn't know what it was really about.

"So, how is da A-T-L?" I asked.

"Man," he paused, eyeing his beer, "it's just...I don't know. I'm just tired of Atlanta now."

Will went off like a siren, "WHAT??? *Tired*??? How can you get tired of Chocolate City?"

"I know. Sounds crazy, man, but it really ain't all it's cracked up to be," Ant explained.

Will, still dumbfounded, "How can you say that??? All the *women*!"

"Hell, if you can find some that really are women," Ant laughed.

"Yeah, gay dudes *are* in effect over there," I added.

"Man, if you stay out late enough, you can just roll down Peachtree and all the transvestites are out...just right there in the open! And you know they're men, 'cause they got hard ass legs, you know, big hands and shit. Their faces are all big and mess."

I laughed at him.

"But *THE WOMEN*," Will lamented.

"Shit, the women be on each other," Ant took a drink off his beer as we laughed. "But really, the women ain't even all that, man."

Then Will, Carlos, *and* Nouri replied—in unison, "*What*?? You *crazy*!"

I just laughed.

They continued with the, "Shit, man," and the, "Whatever, dawg. You outcho damn mind," and other grumbling.

"Man, that's just the way I feel…I mean, when I first got there, it was straight, y'know. I was goin' to the club, feelin' like grade-A material, 'cause man, dudes out there are all lame—on that thug shit, y'know. Ain't no *real* bruthas in the A-T-L."

He continued, "But man…women out there are on some bullshit, for *real*. You go out, dressed nice, you think *you're* gonna be the one collecting numbers right and left. Nope. They're on that thug shit, too. One night, I was out with my boy. All these high-cappin' ass hoes out there, just passin' on by, kee-kee-in' at these dudes 'cause they were sittin' in a Yukon on spinners."

Will didn't see the problem, "That's 'cause they're *hoes*. That's what *hoes do*! If you hang with chickenheads, you're gonna find chickenheads… Quit hangin' with chickenheads, man!" he replied, laughing.

Ant nodded. "Right…so, you try to follow what your folks say and 'find the good girl in church'. Which is cool, 'cause, *man*, Atlanta churches got a *gang* of women! But then you feel guilty 'cause—and I don't care what anybody says—you're just workin' the church. Goin' up there to hook up and shit. What is that?"

We started laughin' at him. I felt one of his editorials creepin' in.

"But I tried it...I met this chick at New Birth. That's this big church out east. Sista was bangin'. Kinda tall, like...5'9, 5'10, 'bout one-seventy."

"Mmm!" Will responded.

I was like, "Damn, she built like Mustang, huh?"

"Hey-ll yeah. Smooth brown skin, hair to her shoulders—*real* nice. But, man...you know the first night I called her, she gon' start tellin' me about some money drama."

We all knew that routine. The broad that tries to talk all nice and sweet, like it never happens, but she just needs you to spot her a "lil" cash (of course "a little" always means a few hundred) just-this-one-time...

"That was the first time I'd *ever* talked to her, since we met, right? That broad asked me for some money 'cause she couldn't make her rent," Ant said.

"How much money did she need?" Carlos asked.

"Three-hundred dollars!"

"Three-hundred dollars!" we repeated in shock.

"Yeah, man," Ant continued, "So I'm sittin' there wonderin' how she *just happened* to fall three-hundred dollars into the hole like that, y'know? So I asked her what got her behind. You know what that girl told me?"

"What?" I asked.

"She gon' say, 'cause she wanted to go home to Philly for All Star Weekend."

"Awwwwwwwwwwwwwwwwwww," Carlos responded.

Nothin' but sighs and grumbles.

"Man, *triflin'* women. That's it. That's what's out there. If it ain't the chick with tats *all over* her body, it's the chick you think is fine as hell until she pulls out a black'n'mild. A bunch of grown ass women that still live with their parents. Or, or, the 'abstinent' women who wanna talk dirty on the phone…"

We laughed at his pisstivity.

"Or the good Christian girl that…*ain't*—"

I interrupted, in falsetto, "I go to church four days a week, and suck dick *seven!*"

We all laughed. But Ant was really in the mood to blow off some steam 'cause he just *kept goin'*. I figured this would probably make its way into one of his articles.

He ranted on, "I get so pissed off 'cause Black women always wanna talk about what *we* ain't doin'…they can't find a man or whatever…but here, we got three single, professional Black men and we got the same problems. But does anybody talk about that? No. They just wanna man-bash like bruthas just ain't doin' shit."

"Maaaan…that's the truth, bruh," I said, "Y'know, I used to think somethin' was wrong wit' me 'cause it seems like I always get the dumb ass broads. But now I know…shit, that's what's out there!" I laughed.

LOOKIN' IN THE MIRROR

Will laughed too, "But what makes it worse is if ya didn't get *them*, ya wouldn't get *no* play, 'cause the ones you *wanna* holla at just walk by. Try to be nice and just *speak*, they just roll their eyes."

"Man, I hate that shit. They swear they can't find a man, but they're forever dissin'," Ant leaned forward, gettin' into another story, "I met this girl at a networking group once. See, the group meets a couple of times a month and, you know, we just talk about societal issues or whatever...so anyway, this woman came to one of the sessions. And she was *fine*. She was like 5'2, short 'fro, round lips, bright eyes, I'm tellin' you...man...she was *gor*geous. And then she started talkin'. She was articulate. She had a good job—she had degrees from Duke *and* Yale! The girl was only twenty-seven! Man, I was sittin' there like," he dropped his jaw, "I couldn't believe that shit. I just *knew* I was gonna take her home to ma."

"Daaamn, maaan...that's what's up," Will responded in awe.

"So I went over to talk to her after the session, but the minute I told her I was a teacher, she looked at me like I just didn't have any business talkin' to her—breathin' her air," Ant said angrily.

"She did you like that?" Nouri looked on, in shock.

"*Hell* YEAH," Ant replied, "But there was this other chick in the group that I've been knowin' since the AUC. The stuck up chick saw me talk to my friend after she dissed me, and they got to chattin' a little later. I guess my friend told her that I went to NYU or that I'd written in a few mags, got a couple of books out, 'cause the next time I saw her, she gon' try to speak."

"That's messed up," Nouri replied.

"Man, I'm not hatin' on you when I say this, Nouri, 'cause you got your woman and I'm happy for you. But, you don't have to deal with all the jaded attitudes like they have towards us. They come at you with a fresh perspective, 'cause you don't have the media blastin' you every second. And I'm not sayin' that you don't have your own stereotypes to battle— especially with all that's goin' on in the Middle East, but at least you can move up. For us, we're just thuggin' ass, no-job-havin', make-a-baby-and-leave bastards, y'know? And our most famous representations in the media perpetuate those images 'cause the pinnacle of Black manhood today is to exemplify the most negative profile possible. So we got all these thuggin' ass rappers, talkin' about shootin' folks, and athletes that get in trouble with the law…"

"Don't for-get ath-letes that cheat on their wives, and make-babies-and-leave," Will added, soundin' kinda toasty. The funny thing about Will is, even though he'll get tipsy, he doesn't get stupid. He can carry on some of the most analytical conversations you'll have while he's under the influence. The only difference is that he just talks slower.

Antoine grinned, "Yeah. Those, too."

"Heere's my beef," Will started, "the broads that got this loong ass lawwndry list of what *they* want from a maan…but they don't bring anything to the table."

LOOKIN' IN THE MIRROR

"Aww, hell yeah. They're good for expecting too much," Ant replied.

Will got nothin' but nods on that one.

I joined the conversation adding to that point, "Yeah, it just gets me how broads think they can just marry into money. They wanna run up to these cats from TV, like they don't have a big ass neon chickenhead sign plastered across their head."

Will scowled, "Really tho'. But check this: what about the ones that tell you they're about to break up, but don't—even though she's cryin' to you every other night, about how dude beatin' on her, cheatin' on her...blahh, blahh, blahhh."

Old Serious, Ant, was poised to jump in again, but the rest of us laughed.

Ant rejoined the discussion, "Tell me this: have y'all ever been told that you need a help mate?"

We all looked puzzled.

"Nooo," I replied, wondering what the hell he was talkin' about.

"Con-sidering the conver-sa-tion, I assume by 'help mate', you mean a wo-man. But, what the hell is a help mate? And what, do they help you with?" Will asked.

"She can help me bust a nut," I mumbled under my breath. I thought they wouldn't hear me, but they laughed.

"You're sick, man," Antoine laughed, starting the story. "I went out with this woman. An older chick, like, late thirties, early forties."

"She was crazy, wasn't she?" I asked.

He laughed, "Naw, she wasn't crazy—at least, not like you mean, anyway. But, uh, we were eatin' dinner and talkin'. The whole experience was pretty mellow. She asked me why I'm still single, what kind of woman I'm lookin' for and all that. I forgot what it was I said that made her talk about the help mate thing, but all of a sudden she was just like, 'Oh, you need a help mate.' And I was like, 'What's a help mate?' Then she was like, 'A help mate is somebody who helps you at home, takes care of you…'"

We still looked puzzled.

"But I still didn't get it, so I asked for more detail and she goes, 'You know, someone to take your clothes to the cleaners, clean up the house, run your errands and stuff.' And, of course, I'm sittin' there lookin' at her crazy 'cause she's a cornball. I mean, if my girl messes up, she needs to clean up after herself, but I can run all my errands my-damn-self."

"Right?" I replied, when Carlos stepped in.

"Sooo, she's sayin' that you're supposed to marry, like, a personal assistant?"

"Yeah!" Antoine replied. "She had this whole argument, talkin' about how the bible says that the woman is a help mate for the man, and…I don't know, some stupid shit she was talkin' about…all that 'women stay at home' business."

Will pointed out, "I don't get why pee-ple won't just let that go. All that's not even ree-uh-listic to-day. With real estate, and cost-of-living expenses, ballooning the way they are, you can't support a two-parent house-hold and a cou-ple-uh-kids on one in-come. That's in-sane. What is she *smo*-kin'?"

LOOKIN' IN THE MIRROR

"I don't know, but a lot of women out there are hittin' that same pipe," Ant said.

"Wait a minute," Carlos said, "she expects you to get up in the morning, go deal with some stupid ass public school kids, and leave her tired ass at home all day? Fuck that! If *I* gotta go to work, you do, too! Getcho ass, up!" he yelled.

Will gave him pound, "Now, *that's* what I'm tal-kin' 'bout."

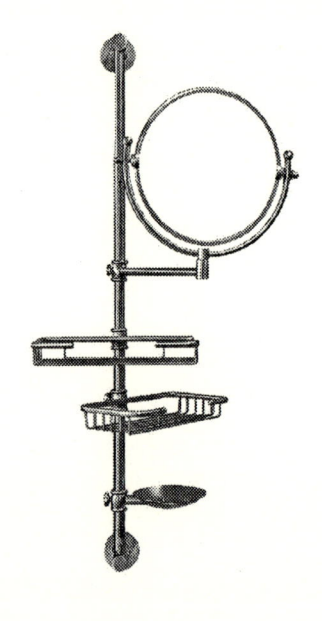

October 31

Thursday Night

LOOKIN' IN THE MIRROR

So we collected at my house before goin' to the Halloween party. Mia was upstairs adding the last touches to her outfit. All of us fellas sat downstairs in the meantime, laughin' at each other. We'd decided almost right after last year's party (where we emerged as the victors in Batman villain outfits—Mia was *SO* sexy as Catwoman), that this year we'd go as 80s singers. We wanted to go as U.S.-hated international figures, for which Nouri would pose as Moammar Gadhafi (he tossed around the idea of going as a hip-hopped out Osama bin Laden), and Carlos as the Panamanian President Noriega. But we couldn't think of entities for the rest of us. Besides, all the backwoods rednecks would probably drag Nouri off into the bush, thinking he really is Osama, considering he's Iranian. They don't know the difference.

But the theme we chose was pretty cool. I 'bout laughed my ass off when I saw Nouri. That dude rolled up in my driveway and got out the car lookin' like Al B. Sure! It was *over*! And he gon' walk his monkey ass up to the door singin', "I can tell you how I feel a-bout youuu, niiight and dayyyyyyy!" I was like, "Gon'...man, get away from me." Up there tryin' to serenade somebody with his glued-on eyebrow patch.

Will wanted to be Ice Cube, circa just-out-of-NWA, 'cause he just *had* to wear a jheri curl wig. That dude was too happy when he found the right wig...actin' all giddy and mess. For about two weeks, he went around answerin' his cell talkin' 'bout, "Who dis?" The funny thing was, he kinda looked like Cube for real when he put on all the clothes. Antoine & I went as Milli Vanilli. At first we wanted to be Full

Force, but we didn't have enough people. Plus, we wanted to wear some fruity outfits. So we figured, what's cornier than broad shouldered suit jackets and biker shorts? Then, we put on pointy athletic cups that we got from this novelty shop to make it worse. Madonna ain't the only one that can maximize her goods. Strike a pose!

(Vogue!)

And Carlos's ass...

"HA!!!" Ant blurted, as soon as he walked in.

But Will didn't recognize him, "Who the hell are *you*?"

Will's way of mocking people is to say whatever he's gonna say in the voice of Chief Wiggins' son, Ralph. So he looked at me, laughing and said in Ralph's voice, "Hi, I'm random Latin guy. I'm creative!"

We laughed at Will's joke, though he was the only one who didn't catch on.

Carlos stood there, lookin' annoyed 'cause it seemed so obvious.

He replied, "Punk, I'm sharp like the naps on the back-uh yo' neck. ...Wit'cho Soul Glow ass." Then he started dancin' like the dude in 'Partners In Crime'—the one where he took Keenan Ivory Wayans' activator. He was up there doin' the MC Hammer, talkin' 'bout, "Rock! [Squirt, squirt] Don't stop! [Squirt, squirt] ...Do the jheri curl!"

"Ohhh, I know who you are!" Nouri said, laughin' as I simultaneously recalled a particular pop one-hit wonder.

"Hey...wait. I know who you are! ...You're, uhhhhh...Rrrrreee-cohhhh! Swahhhh-vayyyyy!"

Who'da even thought about Gerardo, *but* him? I don't know why we didn't see it in the first place. What other 'Latin sensation' wore a leather jacket and a wife-beater, with a bandana on his head? (All of them?)

Carlos always has some Geed costumes. I remember one year, before we knew Nouri, we went to this Halloween party as crooners. Carlos came up lookin' like a Don damn Juan, wearin' this white suit. He even grew his hair a little and got some weave— you know, tracks, so his hair would reach his neck— talkin' about he's Julio Iglesias. How 'bout that dude took a *few* women home that night! Hell, *I* wanted to get with him. (That's a joke.) But that was before he married Andréa, of course. If he did that mess now, they'd have about five kids—at once.

But Will took it home that year. I mean, Carlos was smooth, but Will's stupid ass shaved his hairline back and went as Peabo Bryson. I couldn't've done it, but that was *the bomb*! It takes Will to do somethin' that damn stupid.

Then Mia came down...she had us tricked. She'd been tellin' us that she was gonna go as Tina Turner in 'Mad Max'. But she pulled a 360 and tripped us all out! We never saw it comin'. That girl came down the stairs with this big hair, stickin' straight up and all this make-up on...she was like, "What do you think?" We started crackin' up. It was good. Really creative. It was one of those things that you forget until

A. M. HATTER

you see it again: Patti LaBelle, in the "New Attitude" lampshade hair era.

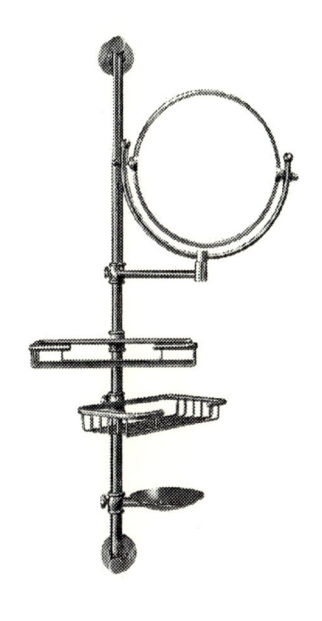

Sunday, November 15

2:30 p.m.

"You *sure* you can handle this?" Will asked Carlos.

"Yeah, man. It's cool. Andréa's down, too. We're gonna use him to help with the baby. It'll teach'm not to have his own before his time," Carlos laughed.

"That's a good concept," Will smirked, "I like that."

Carlos and Will and I met up to go to Millie's house to break the news of my possible transfer to her and Dante.

We got out of the car and walked to the door. "Hopefully I'll find out what's gonna happen before Christmas. If I do have to move, I'll probably take him with me when I drive everything up then send him on a flight back down here," I said.

Will knocked on the door. "Yeah, that's a good deal. I kinda like that."

We waited for someone to answer the door, but Millie can barely walk and Dante was probably locked up in his room.

"Man, lemme call this fool, tell'im to come get the door," Will griped, pullin' out his cell and dialing the number.

"Hey, Dante, it's Will…"

"Come get the door, we're standin' outside, man…"

"YEAH! OUT-*SIDE*…"

"Don't worry 'bout that…"

"Boy, just get the door!"

Dante came to the door laughing. "Sorry, I didn't hear y'all knock."

LOOKIN' IN THE MIRROR

We filed in. Will grabbed him and put him in a headlock. Carlos gave him a soft kick in the butt. I grinned and shook my head. When Will finally let him go, Millie was just makin' her way into the room, shakin' and movin' about an inch per hour on her cane.

"Heyyyyyy," she said, "How y'all doo-in'?"

She looked at Carlos. Will went over to her to help her sit down.

"We're doin' all right Miss Millie," I said.

"We wanted you to meet our friend Carlos Miss Millie," Will said.

Carlos stepped forward to shake her hand.

"Hel-lo, Car-los," she said breathing heavily, "So...how long...have you...known...Gerald and...and Will-yum?"

"Oh, we grew up together Miss Millie," Carlos answered.

"Ohhh! That's nice... You...say...you grew up to-ge-ther?"

"That's right," Will said.

"That's, *good*...it's good..." she nodded to Will, "to have friends...that...that you've known...for...a long, time..." she coughed harshly.

Will sat with her, holding her hand. "Yes. That's right Miss Millie."

"Doo...you...know, Car-los...Dante?"

"Yeah. I know'im. All Gerald's friends hang out at his house on Saturdays. Carlos is the one that taught me how to draw, grandma. I told you about him. He's the one teachin' me Spanish."

She smiled at Carlos. "Thank you...for...spendin'...time, with Dan-te."

Feeling unnecessary, Dante got up to leave the room.

"Dante, you need to stay in here," I said.

He did the teenager hard sigh thing. "Man, I was playin' Madden."

"Dante, what'd I say?"

He sat back down.

Will started the conversation, "Miss Millie…we have some news to break to you and Dante."

She looked at him. "Is," she coughed into her handkerchief, "any-thing…wrong?"

"No," Will said, "there's nothin' really *wrong*. But the news is kinda happy *and* sad." He glanced at me. "Gerald might get a promotion with his job," Will started.

She beamed. "That's, good! …That, is, very…good," she coughed again, "I…am…so, proud…of, you. It's…taken…so, long…for, us, to…to, be able, to…get jobs…like yours."

"Yes, that's right," I nodded.

"You…are, so…blessed," she coughed, "My…husband…Charles—I…told you…about…Charles, right?"

"Yeah, you told us," Will answered.

She nodded and continued. "Charles…worked…fifty-five, years…and we, never…got out…of Houston," she shrugged, "We couldn't…afford to go. …And when, we could…we weren't, allowed…in other, places…you know."

We sat there, lookin' contemplative.

LOOKIN' IN THE MIRROR

"Don't, let me…hold you, boys…finish…your, news," Millie instructed.

"Well," I continued, "like Will said, I may get a promotion…I just interviewed for it earlier this week and they're going to announce it in another week. They may stretch it out until right before Christmas…But, uhhh, if I get it, I'll have to move to Washington, D.C."

Dante perked up, then looked away. He seemed like he was tryin' not to cry.

Millie nodded. "Well…I hope, you will…keep," she grunted, "in…touch," and reached out for a hug.

I got up to walk over and hug her. "Oh, of course," I kneeled on one knee, "You *know* I will! I gotta keep these guys in line."

She smiled.

"But I wanted to take Dante with me when I move, and then fly him back down," I said.

Dante sat up. "Ooo. Can I go grandma?"

She looked at me sternly. "Will…he, be…back, in time…for…school?"

"Definitely. Definitely. And Will's gonna pick him up from the airport to bring him back here," I assured her.

She nodded. "You…can go, Dan-te. …But…you, better…mind, Mr. Gerald…"

"Oh, don't even worry about that. If he cuts up, *I'll* cut into *him*," I warned.

"I'm…gonna, miss…you," she said, reachin' to kiss me on the forhead.

I smiled.

A. M. HATTER

"Yeah," Carlos said, "We'll all miss him."

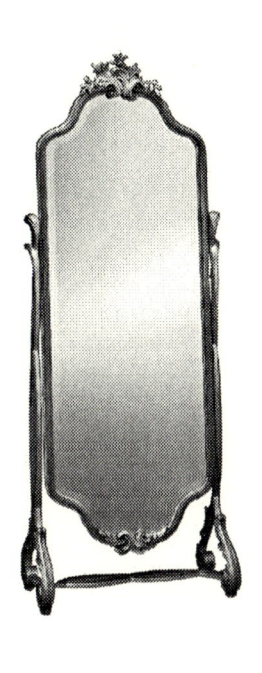

Monday, December 30

At Home After Work

A. M. HATTER

Today just wasn't my hottest day. It started with this old woman at work named Louvenia. She's the type that has a bible in her desk drawer (I'm not kidding)—the kind that has a zip-up flowery jacket with ruffles and strap handles—and preaches to you about what's in it whenever someone makes a random comment.

For instance, say I'm in thick conversation with someone sitting next to me. I profess to them that I hate when…I don't know—my mom tells me what to do. Then she'll chime in with, "You know, the bible says it's not good to hate." Whether it is or not wasn't the point of my story—and who was talking to her anyway? Did I ask for her to provide the lesson of the day? NO. And why is she telling me about what's in the bible? She doesn't know anything about my personal life. I could be Baha'i, Muslim, Buddhist, Wicca, or anything else for all she knows; in which case, her bible and the philosophies represented within wouldn't technically apply to me. Why won't she just shut the fuck up?

I can't stand people that preach at work.

At any rate, I was irritated again by her zealotry because she, I guess, wanted to stage an intervention or some shit? I don't know. For some reason, she invited me to lunch with her, which bewildered me because I'm sure she knows by my general body language that she annoys me to freaking insanity, and we keep our distance. I tried to get out of it, saying that I wanted to eat alone, but she insisted, noting that my normal lunch buddy (now, Anita, since Turk's been gone) wasn't in the office today. So I reluctantly agreed to have lunch

LOOKIN' IN THE MIRROR

with her, but I should've insisted on eating alone because when I sat at the table, I was greeted by two other old women who have reputations in their own departments for their "apparent theological degrees."

Man, these chicks were straight trippin'! They were out of their damn minds!

They came at me talking about, "So Louvenia tells us that you're an atheist. I've never met an atheist before." And then they started with, "Why don't you believe in marriage?"

What the fuck??? Since when do these chicks know anything about me *or* what I think?! And even if I was an atheist who didn't believe in marriage (among many other "charges"), what are they gonna do about it? Isn't it *my* business? And, what, are they gonna broker a marriage for me now? Have some suitor shell out a few camels for my hand in matrimony? Freakin' assholes! What the *hell*???

I can't stand that bitch. It was just like this one time (back when President Bush addressed the country, like, every day and relentlessly pursued Iraq as a world threat…back before that midterm election where all the Republicans snagged seats)—I still wonder if she started that shit with me on purpose, because she just strolled up to my desk and started talking, "Did you hear the president this morning?"

"No, I wasn't watching TV. What happened?" I replied.

"He addressed the nation…I kinda heard him, but I didn't wanna listen 'cause I know what he's tryin' to do. You know he's tryin' to get the U-N to side with him, right?"

A. M. HATTER

"Yeah, I know. He's been writin' letters and crap for a while now."

"I just hope they don't try to draft my sons," she said.

"Draft? They can't do that. Didn't they rule that unconstitutional?"

"Girl, that don't matter! You see they're tryin' to get 'In God We Trust' taken off our money."

To her dismay, I didn't respond with the passion she was looking for. I just kinda shrugged my shoulders, and flashed this blank look of indifference.

She continued with her rampage, "They're tryin' to take God out of everything now. That's why we're in this mess."

"Well...the country *was* founded on freedom of belief."

Why did I say anything??? Mental note: learn to shut the fuck up.

"So you agree with them takin' 'God' off the money?"

I shrugged my shoulders, "I really couldn't care less." (I personally don't understand what's so crucial about having 'God' on currency, anyway. There really shouldn't be anything on there but official markings and statements of its worth—but that's just me.)

"I don't see what the big deal is," she said, "Why can't they just leave it on there?"

I don't know why I kept talking...like I just *have* to break things down or some shit...

"Well, if you have anyone who doesn't call their supreme being 'God,' it makes them feel uncomfortable. If you have anyone who doesn't believe in a supreme being, they feel isolated. It's not just about what you feel or what John Doe feels. If the government followed the true precepts that the founders had in mind, there wouldn't be anything involving religion on government property."

(On the other hand, I don't see anyone getting "uncomfortable" about getting out of school and work for Christmas—"winter"—vacation…or Easter and stuff. I don't see anyone giving their money back to their employers, citing that they can't accept money with "God" on it because they don't believe in one.)

"Well they said it in the pledge!" she foolishly asserted, thinking she bested me.

"Actually, 'Under God' wasn't even in the original pledge. The government added that in the sixties or somethin' in protest of the Soviet Union's stance on religion… And excluding the blatant hypocrisy surrounding what the U.S. founders did to the Indians and African slaves, freedom is why Europeans fled Europe in the first place. The Catholic church just wouldn't stay out of people's business."

"So the whole country can't believe in God? We can't have God on *anything*?" she asked.

I struggled to remain cordial through her idiotic statements, though my expression (which always tells the truth) probably registered somewhere between *What the hell are you talking about?* and *That doesn't make any fucking sense.*

"Well, you can put God on your car 'cause that's personal property, or if you wanted to advertise God, then you can buy ad space somewhere and put whatever you want in it."

A. M. HATTER

"No faith in nothin'…that's what it is," Louvenia grumbled.

Soooooo, if someone doesn't paper mâche 'God' on all materials they come in contact with, then they have no faith??

THEN, another co-worker felt so inclined to chip in, "Not puttin' God first…not going to church…" (Who was talkin' to his monkey ass?)

It's intriguing to me how people levy so much weight on staying in church to be a good person, when some of the most crooked, backbiting people one could ever know are people in church. Why can't you just make a decision to be a good person and do good things, regardless of attending church or affiliating with a major religious sect? The two don't necessarily go hand-in-hand.

And still, the two continued preaching, "That's why they got kids shootin' up schools—"

"And having kids at thirteen…and watchin' sex on TV," the other assisted.

Are they tag-team evangelists or something?

And of course, I had to finish *(Lord, please teach me to shut up!)*, "No, *that's* because people don't wanna be parents and raise their kids responsibly!" *Duhhhh.*

But anyway, I had just gotten home, and as if I wasn't annoyed enough from The Lunchtime Religious Intervention Hour, I had to go home and deal with questions again. That man just won't get off this exclusivity kick. He's not a bad guy; in fact, he's contending pretty well, but he's making me claustrophobic! I can't breathe! Every week, his wannabe-Morpheus-ass is telling me I'm "the one" and shit. I can't take this! And I don't wanna fuck it up because our friendship is well balanced. (Hell, I might be crazy but I'm not stupid.)

So, I had just gotten home. I'm sitting on the couch, watching my soaps on tape. Erica Kane was a split second from telling this woman off and—

Ding-Dong!

Annoyance ran through my body like electricity. *Damn, it was just getting good*, I thought.

"Oh, hey. Come sit down. Erica Kane was about to tell this woman off."

"Oh, really? The ugly woman?"

"Ain't she ugly??" I replied.

"Hell yeah. And I don't know why they act like they don't know. All the characters talkin' 'bout, 'She's very beautiful.' Whatever! *That* broad looks like tree bark!"

We laughed.

"But listen—" I said as I got ready to press play, "Erica caught her in the Wild Wind chapel and gave her the smirk."

"Oooooooo! She means business now. You don't mess with Erica when she gives the smirk!"

"Right!" I concurred, laughing, and hit play.

I have to admit, it's cool having a man to watch the soaps with you. It's been a while since the last time we watched them together. We were straight clowning through the whole show. He's so good that he even knows what's going on in the boring parts that you fast-forward through. Man, I remember one time I fast-forwarded through damn near a whole episode of Y&R

because they kept showing Ashley and Cole talking about Victoria losing her baby.

They'd show one scene and go back to Ashley and Cole, then show another scene and go back to Ashley and Cole; commercial, Ashley and Cole, another scene, Ashley and Cole. It was so stupid! And every time they went to Ashley and Cole, all they'd do is paraphrase how bad it was that Victoria lost her baby!

 Cole: Man, that's gotta hurt, losing a baby.
 Ashley: I know. Losing a baby…that's so sad.
 Cole: It's terrible, ya know? To have that happen… I mean, losing a baby.
 Ashley: How do you feel?
 Cole: What do you mean, how do I feel? She lost her baby. I feel terrible!
 Ashley: Losing a baby! Gosh, I just can't fathom that kind of pain.
 Cole: I know, losing a baby. It's just horrible.

Anyway, just when I thought things were gonna go smoothly, he started up with the sappy crap.

"You know, every time I'm with you, I feel this… *connection*. It's like…we're *supposed* to be together, y'know?"

I shrugged. "I don't know. I don't really think about it."

"You don't think about me?" he asked, looking really lonely and partly shocked.

"Man, don't even try to push me into that corner. I just don't think about it. I let things flow. If good things happen, they happen. If not, see ya later."

"I guess you really are cold-hearted, like your friends say."

LOOKIN' IN THE MIRROR

*WHAT??? Now, how did we get to this?? Man, I swear he's just like a friggin' woman! What's wrong with letting things flow? I'm not angling to broker a deal. I just live life. Why am I crazy for not making it some kind of race? And I **am not** cold-hearted! And fuck my friends, if that's what they think. Apparently YOU don't know me either, jackass. Hell, you're just mad that I'm not eating out of your hand. Just like how really skinny guys get all sore when they find out that I'm not attracted to them.*

I usually find that people's opinions of me are quite slanted when they're at the other end of the stick.

"If I'm so cold-hearted, then you must be a real dumb ass for wantin' to be with me."

"Maybe I am."

"Well, if that's the way you feel, then you can leave."

"Wait, wait...this isn't what I was tryin' to say."

I chuckled sarcastically. "Well, I don't know where you thought you were headed by callin' me cold-hearted!"

"Vicki, just calm down a sec. I'm tryin' to pour my heart out to you."

I wanted to lean back so he wouldn't get any of it on me.

"You are the most intriguing woman I have ever met," he said.

Thaaaat's more like it! Ego food! Yaaayyyyyyy! [Head...getting...bigger...]

"Your taste in music, the things you do, the way you write—the ideas you express. You're just so different!"

[And bigger...]

"You are *so* cool to kick it with. You're fun, you're frugal, *and* you're pretty. When I look at you, I just wonder how someone so beautiful can be so cool."

[BIG-GER!!!]

"Usually cute women are stuck up, or stupid...really superficial. But you're smart... and *real*...I mean, you might not always say what I wanna listen to, but at least I know it's the truth. I just don't get that from anyone else."

AArrrrrrrrrrrrrrrrrr! [Head turning into animal.]

"It's all so in sync with the way I feel," he looked down for a sec, then back at me, "I've never felt this way before."

WARNING! WARNING!

He reached into his pant pocket and pulled out a black velvet box.

SOS! Mayday! Mayday! Tell him you have to take a dump or something!

My attitude was bad enough already without the panic scene from 'AIRPLANE!' in my head. I hoped that he really wasn't about to do what I thought he was going to do. But despite my fears and apparent cold-heartedness, this fool got down on one knee and said those words that I'd been dreading for at least six years now.

"I want you to be my wife."

LOOKIN' IN THE MIRROR

Fffff-T!
Sssssssssssssssssssssssssssssssssssssssssssssssssssssss sssssss.
   [Head deflating.]

ABOUT THE AUTHOR

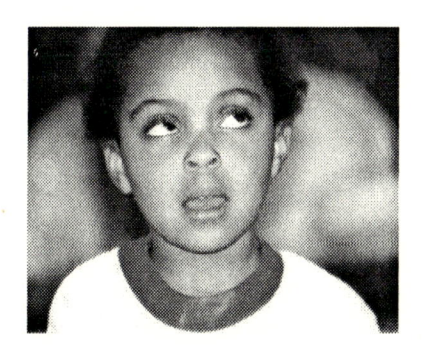

A.M. Hatter has been writing since she was very young. During her elementary years at Monte Casino in Tulsa, Oklahoma where she grew up, she displayed great aptitude for grammar, spelling and sentence structure, as well as fostering passions for drama and art. But it was the amount of television she watched as a child, she believes, that set the tone for her understanding of story structure and character development.

By the age of eleven, during the height of the Teenage Mutant Ninja Turtle craze, she wrote and sketched her first piece as an episode where Shredder created female counterparts for the turtle heroes in an attempt to take them down. She continued her literary development, winning ribbons in oratory contests during her preteen years, and went on to write other work while in high school at Booker T. Washington and in college; but, in the eight grade, started what she calls the most effective point of her development: an obsession with movie structure.

At the age of 18, she was starving for a new atmosphere and went to Mississippi to attend Jackson State University. With a keen understanding of standard composition, she chose to major in journalism to grasp a new insight to the art form and, during her matriculation, haphazardly rekindled her propensity for art with a minor in graphic design. She excelled in her major and became a bright star among her peers and faculty. In extracurricular activities, she participated in many organizations, from the marching band to student government. She won a campus-wide poetry contest, became the staff movie critic for the school newspaper, and developed a frame and first episode of a soap opera as a class assignment.

Now, at 26, Ms. Hatter has lived in the Atlanta, Georgia metro area for three years and maintains a very ambitious, yet fun-loving lifestyle. Her hobbies, like the book she says, are things that she aggressively delves into, so they become work as well, though she enjoys it all. In her spare time, she enjoys working in graphic art, writing, horseback riding, skydiving, sports, and movies. She also mentors a young girl through the Big Brothers, Big Sisters of Atlanta organization. Her goals include a sequel to this book, more novels, and lots of travel.

Printed in the United States
19888LVS00001B/31-204